SOLDIERS!

A Chronicle from the 31st century

Part Two

John Dalmas

Sky Warrior Book Publishing, LLC.

Published by Sky Warrior Book Publishing, LLC.
PO Box 99
Clinton, MT 59825
www.skywarriorbooks.com

Editor: David Lee Summers.
Cover art: William R. Warren Jr.
Publisher: M. H. Bonham.
Cover Layout: Mitchell Davidson Bentley
Printed in the United States of America
    0   9 8 7 6 5 4 3 2 1

Dedication

*This novel is dedicated to gamers, who
in the story universe, kept military science alive
and viable through nine centuries of blessed peace,
till their talents became needed and their foresight validated.
And in our world to my good friends: Sgt. Phil Yarborough,
Cory Rueb, the late Rod Martin, and the late Bill Cooper.*

*And finally
to the memory of the most distinguished warrior
I have personally known, Captain William C. Ashby,*
187th Airborne Regimental Combat Team,
Korean War, 1950–1953

Introduction to SOLDIERS!
the Story Behind the Story

SOLDIERS (at that time without the exclamation point) was published as a mass market paperback by Baen Books in May 2001. Jim Baen liked it well enough to make it a list leader for the month, with an expensive brushed metal cover illo. The sell-through of copies shipped was 79.2%, which was and is outstanding.

It had its season in the sun. Now it's out of print, the rights have reverted to me, and I'm releasing it as an e-book. Aiming it at new readers, including readers who don't often read science fiction. There may be, though, readers who read it before and would like to revisit it. They are more than welcome.

Of all my novels, SOLDIERS! is my favorite. I say this with some trepidation, but it's true. SOLDIERS! *is* my favorite, and the people dwelling within it are among my favorite fictional (creations? personalities? souls?): Jael, Esau, Qonits (the Wyzhñyñy scholar), Sergeant Arjan Hawkins Singh, Charley Gordon, Admiral Soong, Ophelia.... (From where did they come? How did I know them?)

Some gamers complained, even bitterly, at the book's dedication to gamers, **because it is not well suited to gaming.** They took me by surprise. It wasn't written to be adapted for gaming. Rather, among other things, *it is an appreciation* of the potential role of gamers in keeping military science alive through a long time of peace, despite social/cultural disapproval.

Several reviewers commented on its human aspects —

"One develops a real affection for many of the characters..." James K. Burk

"Dalmas focuses not on the experiences of an individual soldier or the whys and wherefores of strategy and tactics, but on the social pressures and changes that war causes." Carrie Barrera

"Slam-bang action...with a heart and a soul." William C. Dietz

"Too many military SF novels ignore the essential unevenness and tragedy of war. John Dalmas knows better. His *Soldiers* have both courage and heart." David Brin

SOLDIERS! is rooted in a supposition—that over time, humankind will evolve mentally, emotionally, and culturally. And explores what we might be like in 900 years, with a future history that includes "the Troubles" (pretty much the entire 22nd century)—94 harrowing years of terrorism and low-grade warfare tailored to avoid large scale disasters—including generations of martial law. I've actually assumed we're on our way to being more civilized, sane and just, an evolution driven by history, and by *memes* (the term *truisms* fits here) rather than *genes*.

Further, in my story universe, humanity has become driven less by a compulsion for novelty or self-aggrandizement than for humanity, ethics, tolerance, and environment. But we remain notably flawed, troubled, and sometimes self-righteous—for starters.

Meanwhile, the Troubles has made all things "military" anathema, and political and religious zealotry are looked at as almost obscene. For a time there were "return to the past" movements, in the form of ethnic and religious agrarian communities on Earth. But at about the same time, a hyperspace drive was developed that enabled deep-space exploration. More and more habitable worlds were discovered, and colonization inevitably followed, a sort of cultural safety valve helping us through early racial adulthood. Tentatively at first, then more confidently, this grew into "the Dispersion" of the 23rd and 24th centuries—mainly of groups avid for a self-sufficient world of their own, where they could live the way their version of God, or of good sense, would most approve.

And zeal satisfied tends to be zeal deflated. Depressurized.

Even with the more fervent dissident groups gone to the stars, Terra still has prejudices, differences of opinion, disputes, but they've become less angry, more civil. While on the colony worlds?—a sect with a planet of its own is less subject to wounds and abrasion; it experiences far fewer insults and resentments, and its assumptions are subject not to suppression but to testing.

In a word, humankind has become *peaceful!*

Meanwhile, space exploration has failed to turn up compelling evidence of non-human spacefarers. And as centuries pass, it seems more and more that we may actually prove to be the only high-tech life form in our galaxy. Thus while alien boogymen still lurk in the depths of human imagination, they lack substance, and there seems little point in maintaining a military that might conceivably turn and bite us.

That is the state of human affairs when our story begins— *with another space-faring life form showing up in the fringe of human expansion.* A life form with genocide fixedly in mind— and an armada of 16 thousand ships! And suddenly a military seems urgently important and effectively absent.

So: Come with me, and we'll visit a space ship very far away.

Chapter One
Harvesting Trouble

Captain (Lieutenant Commander) Christiaan Weygand's handling of the survey ship *Vitus_Bering* reflected several astrogational facts of life. Warpspace differs from hyperspace in many ways besides the number of dimensions. For Weygand's purposes, four of those differences were decisive. (1) Hyperspace drive is far "faster" than warpdrive (which in turn is far "faster" than gravdrive). (2) In hyperspace, astrogation is approximate, with vagaries whose effects accumulate over the duration of a jump, while in warpspace, astrogation is quite precise. (3) In warpspace, the F-space potentiality is far less distorted by nearby planetary masses. With sufficient skill and care, one can venture minutely near a planetary mass. In hyperspace, approaching as near as a million miles to a planet no larger than Pluto would destroy the ship. And (4), warpdrive is suitable for covert encroachment; particularly since warpspace does not produce emergence waves in the warp-space potentiality.

Thus Weygand had first brought the *Bering* out of hyperspace two weeks short of the Tagus System, after a forty-seven-week jump. It was time to locate himself in F-space—familiar space, "real" space—and take a new set of astrogational readings. It was common to think of it in golfing terms, as sizing up the "lie" before hitting the approach shot—the final hyperspace jump to the Tagus System.

Then he'd generated hyperspace again, to re-emerge in the system's remote fringe—far enough out that the *Bering*'s hyperspace emergence waves would be undetectable on Tagus.

Theoretically of course, the Wyzhñyñy could surround the system with alarm buoys or picket boats parked twelve or fifteen billion miles out, in the cometary cloud. But given the enormous spherical surface that went with such a radius, to provide and place the necessary number of sentries would be impractical at best.

Survey ships had some drawbacks for such missions, but

one decisive advantage: their superb instrumentation. Even from where she'd emerged, 29 billion miles from the primary, the *Bering* could plot the orbits of the system's planets and major satellites. And do it in a few hours, applying the mechanics of planetary systems to the tiny orbital segments observed. The info was necessary for the warpspace "chip shot" Weygand made next.

◇

That chip shot—that warpspace jump—took more than a day to bring the *Bering* near enough to Tagus's sole moon to detect it in the F-space potentiality. But once in F-space, and so near to Tagus, the ship's electromagnetic output could quickly be detected from the planet's surface, or by ships in the vicinity. And Drago Draveç's experience had been that the Wyzhñyñy left a space force at their colonies. Something one might assume without evidence.

Weygand had known all that since he'd been given his first mission briefing, a year earlier. It hadn't troubled him then, and it didn't now. He ordered key personnel wakened from stasis, and still in warpspace, maneuvered into the lee of the moon before emerging. Hidden from the planet, less than a mile from the lunar surface. Which just now was the bright side, for on Tagus, the moon was near the "new" phase.

After a brief sensor scan, he landed.

Now, he told himself, *now come the real challenges.* Find the Wyzhñyñy colony at the old pirate base. Put down a team to collect hornets and bring them back to the *Bering,* which was to remain behind the moon. Then send marines down to take some Wyzhñyñy prisoners and bring them up. After that he'd generate warpspace, the science team could start their examinations, and they'd all fly home.

Simple but not easy. The hornets alone sounded daunting; Weygand had had a lifelong aversion to stinging insects, and Morgan had said the Tagus hornets were as big as his thumb. But with decent luck they could capture their hornets and be gone without the Wyzhñyñy knowing they'd been there. Capturing Wyzhñyñy, on the other hand…that would bring them into physical contact with the enemy. He carried two squads of marine commandos in stasis, under a captain, with gunnery sergeants as squad leaders. Two squads! How many fighting personnel did the Wyzhñyñy have on Tagus? A division? Half a dozen divisions?

But War House wants those prisoners, he thought. *And what do I know? I'm a survey skipper, not a general.*

A lot depended on how slack the Wyzhñyñy had become here, after a standard year without anything resembling a threat. Because if any of them—the *Bering,* the scout, the collection boat—caught the Wyzhñyñy's attention, the prospect of getting away with prisoners would be nil.

"Captain, sir," said a man behind him, "the personnel you requested are being revived."

Weygand swiveled his command chair halfway around. "Thank you, Chief. And the steward?"

"The steward is preparing their meal."

"Good. Tell Captain Stoorvol I want to talk with him as soon as he's finished eating."

There was no rush, but the sooner done, the sooner gone.

<>

They'd drilled the procedure back in the Sol System. The *Bering* had emerged off Luna's farside (and been snooped by a police craft from nearby Yerikalin Dome). The Tagus rainforest had been represented by the Marañón Ecological Benchmark Preserve, in Terra's Peruvian Autonomy. And to make the drill complete, the hornet team had returned (illegally) with a bunch of outraged Terran hornets. None had been the size of a man's thumb, but they were big-time mean.

There too it had been Captain Paul Stoorvol who'd piloted the Short Range Scout, SRS 12/1. And beside him, as here, had been Alfhild Olavsdóttir, blond and perhaps forty years old, stocky and fit-looking. Now as then, Stoorvol guided the scout smoothly across the lunar gravitic field, veering around occasional topographic obstacles, then slowing as he approached the limb of the moon. He stopped when he'd cleared it, parking a bare hundred feet off the surface.

From there they got their first look at Tagus, a little less than 170,000 miles away. Alfhild Olavsdóttir inhaled sharply. "Holy Gaea!" she said. "It's gorgeous!"

Her oath annoyed Stoorvol; he disliked Gaeans. But the annoyance was remote; his feelings were often somewhat remote. Besides, lots of non-Gaeans used that oath, and somehow Alfhild Olavsdóttir didn't strike him as a Gaean. A deist maybe. Deism was supposed to be big among scientists.

At any rate she was right: Tagus *was* beautiful. Colonized worlds invariably were; it went with being Terra-like. At the moment, what dominated his view of Tagus was the world ocean—a vivid blue with white cyclonic swirls. The equatorial zone showed a modest continent whose predominant blue-green suggested heavy forest.

After perhaps ten seconds of planet gazing, Stoorvol called up his instrument display, checking for technical electronic activity. He found plenty, from a single south-coast locale. Two other sources appeared that the scout's shipsmind identified as surveillance buoys parked above the equator at an altitude of 4,600 miles. He marked their locations with icons, but just now his primary interest was the surface location. Centering it on his screen, he magnified the site. It was nearly rectangular, a six by eight-mile area cleared of forest—distinct enough to be measured by his scanner from 170,000 miles out. He marked it with another icon.

"That's probably the colony," he said. "Or one of them. We'll have to check the other hemisphere, but except for size, this one fits Morgan's site description. It's equatorial and on a south-coast headland—an open block with forest on two sides, the ocean on a third, and an inlet on the fourth."

Olavsdóttir nodded. "It's hard to imagine a natural opening looking like that."

Stoorvol held the scout where it was, and they kept alternate, one-hour watches. Whoever wasn't on watch used the main cabin to nap, snack, exercise, or otherwise break the monotony. The scout's shipsmind didn't experience time in the same way humans do, and it also had external tasks. It assigned an arbitrary meridian to Tagus, bisecting the visible Wyzhñyñy settlement. With that and the equator as references, it mapped the gravitic matrix and what could be seen of the surface—topographic and water features, broad vegetation types—along with much that didn't show on the surface, including gravitic and magnetic gradients and anomalies.

And recorded the frequency bands of Wyzhñyñy radio traffic.

The humans, on the other hand, had no duties except to watch the sensor display and the planet itself. It was an invitation to drowse, so an alarm had been provided. The watch wore a communications earpiece, and when anything broke the slow and regular unfolding of the sensor pickups, an alarm ruptured any doze or inattention.

To ease the monotony, Alfhild Olavsdóttir recited in a quiet voice, extensively from the Icelandic *sögur*—the sagas. More than any other Europeans, even the Finns, the Icelanders had retained their old language as the primary domestic, social, and cultural idiom. Terran was their language of science, business, and the world at large. As for daydreaming—Olavsdóttir could be an enthusiastic, even a formidable lover, but she seldom fantasized sex. Except occasionally to compose erotic poetry about some lover in her past. But she did not do that here.

On his watches, Stoorvol's thoughts included women, Alfhild Olavsdóttir for one. She was a lot older than he—ten or so years—but interesting. According to the skipper, she was a Ph.D. planetologist with a bachelor's in invertebrate zoology. The academic degrees had made her eligible for this mission, but no more eligible than many others. What had made the difference, Weygand said, was her temperament, and her record as a field leader. "Those, and being smart as they get."

Smart, Stoorvol thought, *meant different things to different people.* But she'd made a good impression on him when they'd boarded the scout and she'd seen him stash his rucker in a locker. "Why the rucksack?" she'd asked. He'd always resented gratuitous requests to explain himself, certainly from people he didn't know well. So he'd simply said it held things he might need, and with a nod she'd let it go at that.

Besides thinking about women, he revisited old conflicts—fierce rivalries as a kid growing up; fistfights at boot camp and on pass; and later, one at the academy, where fights were seriously frowned on. He'd almost always won, but the last had nearly gotten him expelled. He'd been young then, he told himself. He looked at things differently from the vantage of twenty-eight years.

And he thought about how the collection missions—the collection of hornets and the collection of prisoners. (He was to protect the first mission and lead the second.) If everything went according to drill... Things seldom did, of course. It wasn't wise to rely on scripts. They were fine as a starting place, and even as a guide, but they weren't likely to survive a complete mission. Major Asahara had stressed that in Military Planning 202. Because others, notably the enemy, had their own scripts, and typically the physical universe added serious unforeseens. Things happened, and necessity often demanded snap decisions, with different people commonly responding differently. And in case his cadets didn't believe him, Asahara, as game master in their electronic war game labs, would throw in unforeseeables that required unexpected and often drastic improvisations: new tactics, new strategies, even new objectives.

Stoorvol could still quote the major, or nearly enough to make no difference: "Say you have a battle plan that will win this major battle for you. And a seriously chancy departure from it that, if successful, could win the war. But if unsuccessful would be a disaster. Discuss the factors in choosing, and create examples."

For days the class had gone round and round on that. It had been the most valuable discussion they'd had. And among the factors had been alien mentalities. Because if they ever fought a war—a real war, a serious war—it would be against alien invaders. None of them doubted it. It was the truism behind every plan War House made, everything it did. It had been for centuries.

In Stoorvol's ruminations, any verbalization was silent and

in Terran. As with most Terrans, Terran was his only language. Olavsdóttir had commented that his surname looked Norwegian with an Americanized spelling, probably from the late 19th or early 20th century. That had been news to him. The Americas had been Terra's great ethnic melting pot; the rest of the world was only now catching up. He'd never wondered about his ancestry, which besides various European roots, included Dakotah, Ibo, Samoan and Kachin.

<>

Hour by hour, the Wyzhñyñy settlement site crept across the face of Tagus, toward the terminator near the east limb of the visible hemisphere. Before the continent disappeared, a larger edged into sight. On the same watch, a settlement appeared on the new continent, and later a third, both marked by electronic activity. One was at a northern latitude, in what appeared to be steppe. The other was in a large basin between two high, subtropical mountain ranges. Neither was at all like the tropical rain forest Morgan had described.

"So," Stoorvol said, "now the question is whether there's a fourth one down there somewhere."

Some hours later they were satisfied there wasn't. The first one was the right one. Meanwhile they'd learned the number of surveillance buoys parked off the planet—four of them, parked to provide coverage of the colonized continents.

Their next task was to scout Tagus's surface. Stoorvol was about to generate warpdrive when they learned there were indeed Wyzhñyñy warships in the system. Their sensors picked up one of them a scant few hundred miles from where they watched in SRS 12/1. It was departing Tagus's single moon, and crossing to the planet in gravdrive. Why the Wyzhñyñy had been on the moon, or very near it, and whether others still lurked there, neither Terran knew.

So instead of generating warpspace and crossing invisibly to Tagus, Stoorvol backed away in gravdrive, then returned to the *Bering* with a short warp jump, to let the captain know about the Wyzhñyñy ship.

<>

Captain Weygand promptly sent another two-man team out in SRS 12/2, to watch from the limb.

After listening to Stoorvol and Olavsdóttir, he decided to skip the surface scouting. With four Wyzhñyñy surveillance buoys, and possibly a space force on the moon's nearside, they might very well get only one chance before having to flee the system. So the first crossing would be for hornet collection—much the most feasible and least dangerous of their two missions.

The logic was inescapable, but it left Stoorvol ill at ease. In his heart of hearts, the most dangerous foray held priority, and at any rate, live Wyzhñyñy prisoners seemed more valuable than hornets to the war effort.

Some hours later, the hornet collection team boarded the 46-foot collection boat, the *Mei-Li,* sometimes termed "the nursing whale" because she was carried outboard. The hornet collection team consisted of Alfhild Olavsdóttir and two entomology techs, plus both squads of marine commandos for ground security. Paul Stoorvol would pilot the crossing, with PO1 Achmed Menges as copilot. Two weapons techs rode in the *Mei-Li*'s gun bubbles.

Slipping the magnetic tie that held the *Mei-Li* to the gangway lock, Stoorvol separated from the *Bering.* At 200 feet from the surface, he activated the strange-space generator for warpdrive. Then departed the vicinity of the *Bering* much faster than he would have in gravdrive, though not remotely approaching full warpspeed. Not this close to planetary bodies. Invisible from F-space, they quickly cleared the limb, and saw Tagus again on their screens. Not as a blue and white sphere against deep, starstrewn black, but a computer artifact—a featureless silver globe against utterly starless indigo blue. Shipsmind could mock up something very similar to the planet's F-space appearance, even dubbing in star images. But the Admiralty specified silver on indigo for simulations in warp space, to remind the watch it wasn't real.

At the Marine Academy, Captain Esteron had shown them a screen full of mathematics, telling them it best represented the warpspace view of a planet. He hadn't expected them to sort it out. He'd simply been making a point. He went on to discuss warpspace in non-mathematical terms. In a sense, you couldn't be *in* warpspace; warpspace has no material content. A ship "in warpspace" actually occupied an anomaly. Before generating warpspace, you're in F-space—familiar space—which is "permeated by the warpspace potentiality." The strange-space generator generates what can be thought of as a "bubble" of warpspace, which is free to move within the warpspace potentiality at "speeds" greater than light in F-space. And that "carrier bubble" of warpspace contains an inclusion—a bubble of F-space intimately surrounding the scout and its contents. A ship within a bubble within a bubble.

According to Captain Esteron, it could be *understood* only through the appropriate mathematics, and even that depended on what's meant by "understood." The bottom line was, you can leave Terra in warpdrive and arrive at Alpha Centauri in far less time than a photon could. And without inertia. In warpspace you're not only exempt from the light-speed limitation; your ship is stationary within its own little universe—its "carrier bubble."

Stoorvol had decided then not to worry about it. Accept it, yes. Get used to it, sure. Learn to control it, damn right! He'd quickly done all three, and become a competent warpspace pilot—not very difficult in routine circumstances.

Especially with the safekeeps built into shipsminds, to constrain warpspeeds in the vicinity of planetary bodies. For there, the "interfacing" of F-space and warpspace is more or less distorted, and pseudo-speeds must be moderate. Otherwise distortion could rupture your carrier bubble. Which could leave you abruptly in F-space, with momentum a function of your warpdrive pseudo-speed. If that happens at a pseudo-speed greater than c, ship and contents are converted instantly into energy. The resulting explosion is terrific.

Even at only a few-score miles per minute, a ruptured carrier bubble would convert a crew into strawberry jam.

Thus the crossing to Tagus took twenty-eight careful minutes. But they were also twenty-eight invisible minutes. The odds of a Wyzhñyñy ship passing in warpspace near enough to detect your carrier bubble by chance were extremely low. While the prospect of being detected in warpspace by a ship in F-space was essentially nil.

The danger lay not in the crossing to Tagus. It lay in the fine maneuvering very close in. There, complex interface distortions made travel vectors tricky, and carelessness or clumsiness could easily be fatal.

<>

So while the crossing took twenty-eight minutes, finding a suitable place to emerge required two hours of slow and careful sensor groping. Finally Stoorvol found what he wanted—a gorge. He recognized it by the nature of the grav-line distortions in the F-space potentiality, blurred though they were, and it was on the right part of the right continent. He groped his way almost to the bottom.

Emergence would cause a momentary surge of 80-kilocycle radio waves, a distinctive artifact that would hardly be misinterpreted. It was the primary reason he'd wanted to emerge deep in a gorge. A surge there would hardly be picked up by a ground installation, nor by any of the surveillance buoys, given their positions in space.

Once back in F-space, he keyed the gravitic matrix, and shipsmind gave him coordinates—0.65° east of the Wyzhñyñy settlement. The gorge was visible on the map the scout had generated during their surveillance from the lunar limb. It was one of the larger leading down from a broad basaltic plateau to the ocean, and the *Mei-Li* had emerged only thirty feet from the bottom.

He turned the helm over to PO-1 Menges, who raised the craft almost to the rim. Then two of the *Mei-Li*'s work scooters transferred the marines, plus Olavsdóttir and the two entomology techs, to the plateau top. Stoorvol flew one of the scooters.

He left most of the marines on the rim with Gunnery Sergeant Gabaldon, to set up an inconspicuous defense point. Then, with Olavsdóttir, two marines and a pair of hornet traps, Stoorvol left on one scooter. Three other marines and both entomology techs followed on the other, with four more traps.

The scouts' gravdrives were designed to have a minimal EM signature, though even that might be picked up if they rose much above the rainforest canopy.

"Just tell me where to go," Stoorvol said. Olavsdóttir scanned across the forest roof. "Take me higher," she said. "I can't see enough from here."

He glanced at the coordinate grid on his display, then raised the scooter straight up, while the planetologist looked around. At two hundred feet above the forest she spoke again, pointing. "There," she said. "There's a pretty good opening over there about half a mile."

He saw where she meant: a two-acre gap in the forest canopy, probably a blowdown patch. "Right," he said, and took the scooter down almost to the treetops before heading there, dodging the occasional emergent that loomed above its leafy neighbors.

The gap proved unsuitable, filled with a dense growth of young forest half as tall as the surrounding older stand. They traveled several miles and checked four more gaps before they crossed a long low ridge and saw what they needed. A mile ahead, on the far side of a smaller gorge, a sizeable area of forest had burned. As they drew near, Olavsdóttir said, "That's it. Set her down there."

They landed near the center, away from the gorge. Clearly the fire had been intense. It seemed to Stoorvol he knew the place from Morgan's reports. This lesser gorge was the approach to the old pirate base. And the fire? The Wyzhñyñy had razed the forest there after they'd traced Morgan to his bolt hole.

Olavsdóttir wasn't speculating on the burn's origin. She was soaking in its ecology. The forest regrowth was still patchy; much of the ground was covered with herbage and low shrubs. Flowers were rampant, and "berries" abundant. Insects in quantity visited both, probing blossoms or tapping fruit juices with their proboscises. There would be hornets, she was sure. And if they were nearly as large as Morgan had described, they'd be predators, preying on other "insects."

She turned to the field entomologists. "This is it, people," she said. "Let's do it." From her small day pack she took something that, unfolded, proved to be a hat with a net rolled on its brim. Putting it on, she secured the net around her collar, then donned tough gloves. The techs did the same.

Then she turned to the scooters where the marines stood watching with their captain. "Stay here," she told Stoorvol, "and leave your repellent fields off. They disorient insect behavior over an area a lot larger than the repellent radius."

Stoorvol watched the hooded collectors walk off in different directions across the burn, heads swiveling slowly as they searched. Sergeant Haynes grunted. "She didn't need to tell us that. We know the drill."

"She's not used to the Corps," Stoorvol said, "and civilians generally need reminding. Otherwise no telling what they'd do."

He'd hardly said it when his radio beeped. He took it from his belt. Its transmitter was directional, so he pointed it east. "Stoorvol," he answered. "This had better be good. If I can read your signal, they can pick it up at the Wyzhñyñy base."

"Captain, a bogie just passed over!" The voice was Menges'. "Crossed the gorge about two hundred yards north, headed west! If anyone on board was looking our way, he'd have seen us. Or if they had their sensors on... They shouldn't pick up our radio traffic though. Way different wavelengths."

Unless they're scanning. "What kind of bogey?"

"A smallish craft of some sort, sir."

A smallish craft. That could be different things, some armed, some not. "Thanks, Boats. Gabaldon, are you on?"

Sergeant Gabaldon answered from the rim. "Right, Captain."

"Okay. Listen up both of you. They *probably* didn't see you. Otherwise they wouldn't have gone right on like they did." *I hope,* he added silently. "Gabaldon, get your people back aboard the *Mei-Li,* now! Boats, as soon as they're on board, fly south down the gorge, a mile at least, and even with the rim. Find a place where you can fit that frigging barge back into the forest, between the trees. Far enough back that you can't be seen from the gorge. Or from the air." *And let's hope the Wyzhñyñy don't scan the forest with grav sensors.* "Another thing: when you're in your hiding place, register your coordinates to four decimals. But don't send them till I ask. Keep radio silence. Got that?"

"Yessir," Menges said. "Radio silence. Are you coming back now, sir?"

"Hell no! We've got hornets to catch! Now remember: don't send again till I tell you. Stoorvol out."

He looked toward Olavsdóttir moving slowly across the burn, and clicked his helmet mike. "Doctor, a bogey may have spotted the *Mei-Li.* I'm moving both scooters under the trees. Continue as you are. If I trigger my alarm, crouch down and make yourselves as small as possible. And *don't*—repeat *don't*—flatten yourself on the ground."

"Thank you, Captain," she answered.

Thank you, Captain? For what? Doing my job? Stoorvol powered up his grav drive. *Don't knock courtesy,* he chided himself. Sergeant Haynes started his scooter, too, and they headed for the burn's nearest edge. There, back beneath the trees, they set down about a hundred feet apart. From the burn came a pleased shout: an entomologist had found a hornet's nest. Stoorvol hoped to hell they'd get what they needed quickly. He wanted to get back to the *Mei-Li* and off the planet as soon as possible. The collection order called for six nests—for statistical reasons, he supposed. It could keep them out there till dark, which meant till morning. A disturbing possibility.

◇

Achmed Menges found a suitable location, unloaded his marines again, and had two of them guide him between the trees until he saw a glade ahead. He stopped sixty or eighty feet short of it, with a clear shot to scram if he needed to. By that time the gorge was a hundred yards behind him, and marine lookouts at the rim could no longer see the boat. Menges shut down all systems except shipsmind, to reduce detection risks, then waited while the *Mei-Li* grew slowly hot and stuffy.

◇

On being relieved, Tech 1 Gortha turned his log over to the

new watch officer. The Wyzhñyñy ensign glanced at it. "What is this?" he asked.

Gortha didn't need to look. He'd logged just one item that wasn't routine. "It's a call from the courier bringing Colonel Dorthût from Grasslands, sir. While crossing High Falls Gorge, the pilot spotted a wrecked alien craft in the bottom."

The ensign's hackles rose. "Wrecked alien craft? How did he know?"

"I suppose, sir, because none of ours is reported missing. And because there are no aliens left on the planet."

"You *suppose?*" The ensign's jaw muscles bulged like melon rinds along his cranial keel. The observation had been radioed in nearly five hours earlier. Such a lapse was intolerable. Reaching to the work station keyboard, he tapped three keys.

A voice issued from the desk speaker. "Dispatcher's station, Tech 1 Rrûnch."

"Rrûnch, this is the officer of the watch. The dispatcher you relieved—is he still there?"

"No sir. He just left, sir."

"Get him! Now!"

"Yessir!"

The ensign heard the quick soft thudding of feet, and waited scowling, fists clenching and unclenching. There were more footfalls, then a voice. "Tech 3 Agthok, sir. How can I help you?"

"Who piloted the courier from Grasslands?"

"Tech 2 Kroliss, sir."

"How can he be found? Promptly?"

"Sir, I saw him enter the messroom about…forty minutes ago."

"Thank you." The ensign bit the words out and disconnected, then with an angry finger stabbed more keys. "This is the officer of the watch. I must speak to Tech 2 Kroliss at once."

"He just left, sir, carrying a mug of something."

"Go and get him! Tell him the watch officer wants him at the watch office NOW! And call me when you've done it!"

"Yessir!"

An unpleasant rumble issued from the watch officer's throat as he disconnected. *A mug of something!* he thought. *As if I had any interest in that!*

Tech 1 Gorth was glad Ensign Rrishnex wasn't on *his* watch. But he didn't ask permission to leave. He'd slip away after Kroliss arrived. He wondered why the ensign didn't just order someone else out to investigate. Probably, he decided, because Kroliss could find the place more surely.

◇

Gosthodar Qishkûr, Governor of the Okaldei, lay on his AG couch with his torso upright. His eyes were obscured by their nictitating membranes, and his upper torso rocked back and forth like a dodderer's. Not a reassuring sight, thought General Gransatt.

"If it was mine to decide?" Gransatt asked. He was tempted to answer falsely, for it seemed to him the gosthodar would order the opposite of whatever he recommended. But he would not lie; not so blatantly.

"Lordship," he said, "I would order all scouts and all fighter craft to muster here. Then search the plateau between the Broken Hills and Long Inlet on the west, and the Green River on the east. Search it so that nothing living avoids detection. All attack squadrons to be on two-hour stepped alert, ready to destroy any aliens sighted. Until we find the alien and wipe him out, or are very very sure he does not exist."

The gosthodar's rocking increased, the sight transfixing his general. After a long moment the gosthodar spoke, his voice reflecting his age. "I thought we did all that a cycle ago," he said. "Was that not you in charge?"

Gransatt's hide heated; it required effort to avoid bristling. "That was not comparable. Then we needed to search the entire planet. A single region can be searched far more thoroughly."

The gosthodar ignored the general's omission of the honorific. "Mmmm. But that first scouring—did it not begin with an intensive search first of this very region, then that of Grasslands and Basin? And despite all that, was an alien not found reconnoitering this very settlement some weeks later?" Qishkûr had stopped rocking, and his eyes had cleared. "You say you would make very very sure he is wiped out. That he ceases to exist. But what does such certainty mean? You were very sure before, and I accepted that. Until suddenly, there came the alien who had hidden under the hill. Then he died, and you were very *very* sure. But I was no longer so sure anymore. Eh?"

The general's hide felt hot as fire. He did not reply.

"And now this. How can you have so much certainty about what you will accomplish this time, and so little in what you accomplished before?" Briefly his head swayed from side to side in rejection. "I, on the other hand, believe you did *well* before, you and your fliers. Not perfectly it seems, but well. This was an alien outpost world, nothing more. There were no towers. No ghats. Not even towns. There were never more than a few sophonts here, and your fighters killed most of them. The few survivors, those who did not succeed in fleeing the planet, scattered to different regions, where they have hidden. In caverns no doubt. It seems they have an affinity for caverns.

"But they cannot hide forever. They must surface, walk beneath the sky, bathe in the streams" —his words slowed for emphasis— "and grow food. And when they do, our surveillance buoys will find them. The aliens know this. They are not ignorant primitives. This appearance today—if it is real; if the report is not an aberration—this appearance is an act of desperation, perhaps to collect supplies from some old cache."

The gosthodar repeated himself, as if savoring the aptness of the phrase. "An act of desperation." He paused thoughtfully. "There may be caverns behind the cliffs of the High Falls Gorge, as there were behind the lesser. You must seek them, and destroy any you find."

He straightened, his old voice sounding fuller, less aged. "You will **not** gather the squadrons from Grasslands and Basin. You will do your searching with what you have here. If your fears reflect fact, and the aliens retain some little potency, to gather the other squadrons here would expose Grasslands and Basin to destructive raids."

The old head swayed again, side to side, side to side, and for a moment the eyes closed entirely. "Go," the old voice said, suddenly raspy again, "and heed what I have said."

The general backed away, arms spread, forelegs bent, belly low, trunk and head lowered in deference. "As you direct, your lordship, that shall I do. And as you enjoin, your lordship, that shall I not do."

The gosthodar was rocking again.

◇

Tech 2 Kroliss had marked his approximate crossing point on Lieutenant Zalkôsh's map. Zalkôsh, piloting the armed scout, reached High Falls Gorge about two linear miles north of the marked point, at 5,000 feet local reference. He saw no alien craft below, nor did Kroliss, who sat beside him.

If there was an alien craft down there, they would probably have seen it. Nonetheless, Zalkôsh began descending on a gravitic vector. The gorge meandered sufficiently that one just might be concealed down there by a rock wall. And at any rate, he wanted to examine the bottom.

Tech 2 Kroliss could imagine serious personal problems if they found no alien craft. It would strongly suggest there'd been one, and that it had escaped. The obvious alternative conclusion would be that he'd hallucinated. So far, the lieutenant hadn't seemed to judge.

Zalkôsh paused some twenty feet from the bottom, then started southward along the curving gorge. Both he and Kroliss watched intently for any sign that an alien craft had been there. It was the dry season, and the stream level was low, exposing the larger rocks that had fallen from the walls. If an enemy ship had made a forced landing, it should either still be there, or have left signs of having been there.

It occurred to Kroliss that the alien ship might have been hovering just above the bottom when he'd seen it, and left no trace. Left because he, Kroliss, had flown over. That's what a Board of Investigation would think, and a court martial.

Zalkôsh proceeded for more than a linear mile past the point where Kroliss reported crossing. Then he switched on his transmitter, accessing Security directly.

"Security, this is Lieutenant Jethka Zalkôsh, reporting on the alien sighting. I have examined more than three linear miles of gorge bottom, centered on Tech 2 Kroliss's reported crossing point, and have seen no sign of an alien craft. I suggest other scouts be sent to search this entire quadrangle, and that the surveillance buoys be instructed to intensify surveillance of this region. Unless otherwise instructed, I will continue south down the gorge to the ocean, or until I find an alien craft.

"Zalkôsh out."

Kroliss imagined himself assigned to the death platoon, making amends to the tribe.

◇

Hours had passed when one of the marine lookouts trotted up to the *Mei-Li,* to report that a small alien craft had snooped the gorge from the north, just above the bottom, and passed out of sight southward. *A scout,* Menges thought. He felt extremely nervous. Other Wyzhñyñy might be flying a search pattern above the plateau, sensors scanning.

He'd heard that the Wyzhñyñy didn't take prisoners, and wondered what might happen to him if they did. He decided he'd prefer a pounding from energy bolts. A quick death. Meanwhile he wondered how the hornet hunters were doing. He wasn't about to break radio silence to ask.

◇

While the entomologists and Olavsdóttir hunted for hornets' nests, and Captain Stoorvol's men napped, Stoorvol had scanned the known Wyzhñyñy radio frequencies. Hearing a lot of traffic but learning nothing, except what Wyzhñyñy sounded like on the radio. Finally, after five hours, Olavsdóttir collected her sixth colony of hornets. Stoorvol had seen no bogies, and had no idea what the situation was at the big gorge. When everyone and everything was loaded and secured, he took off, the second scooter close behind. He'd wait till he was nearer before radioing Menges and getting the new coordinates. Assuming the *Mei-Li* was still intact, and Menges alive and free.

◇

Before the additional Wyzhñyñy scouts lifted from Seaside Base, their pilots were briefed. Among other things, they were given Tech 2 Kroliss's description of the alien craft: green, and about the size of a corvette. Actually, at eighty-three feet in length, a Wyzhñyñy corvette was seriously longer than the forty-six-foot *Mei-Li*, and proportionately broader. A corvette could hardly be maneuvered into the rainforest.

<><

Stoorvol's two scooters had barely cleared the trees behind them when one of the marines shouted, "Bogies aft!" Both Stoorvol and Haynes accelerated, snapping heads back, then darted down into the pirate gorge, to careen south together below the rim. They were quickly past the burn, then slowing sharply, lifted again to rim level, curved into the rainforest and proceeded eastward among the great trunks and dangling lianas. The whole sequence took perhaps fifteen seconds.

"Captain," said Olavsdóttir, "that was exciting!"

"I'm glad you liked it," he answered drily. "Now let's hope they don't find us with their sensors." He switched on his transmitter. "Menges," he said, "this is Stoorvol. What are your coordinates?"

He got no answer. *The forest damps transmission at both ends,* he told himself. Ten minutes later, in a glade, he lifted above the trees and tried again, using more power. The reply was brief and faint, but readable. He fed Menges' coordinates into his scooter's navcomp, acknowledged Menges' reply, then ducked into the trunk space again and continued eastward.

"I didn't see the bogies," Olavsdóttir told him.

"Right. They probably continued east when they lost us. But they'd sure as hell have reported us, which must have stirred things up considerably." *And they haven't found the* Mei-Li *yet. That's the hopeful part.*

He pushed as fast as he dared. The sun had been low when they'd left the burn, and once it set, this near the equator, it would get dark quickly. He didn't lift above the trees for a peek around. Didn't see the Wyzhñyñy scouts ground support fighters and APCs posted above the big gorge, waiting for word from the surveillance buoys. He didn't need to. He assumed they'd be there, they and more.

"How's our cargo doing?" he asked.

"All right so far," Olavsdóttir answered. "But after a few more hours in those traps, they'll start dying."

Shit! "How much good will they be to us dead?"

"The composition of body fluids will begin to break down, probably including the venom. How much useful information we'd get then is impossible to tell. Some, possibly."

Stoorvol grunted. *So we'll push,* he thought. He stopped to rearrange personnel and transfer cargo, all the civilians and the hornets going to Haynes' sled. Stoorvol would haul the other four marines, in case a rearguard action was needed, or a fighting decoy, or someone to run interference. "If we run into trouble," he told Haynes, "don't hesitate to ditch the scooter and proceed on foot. Meanwhile load your belt nav from the navcomp right now, and be sure you take it if you ditch. And for godsake don't abandon the hornets!"

◇

The two scooters went on again, side by side now. If they were detected beneath the trees, hopefully they'd read as a single unit. In the trunk space—the forest gallery—the light grew dimmer, more dusky. They were half a mile from the *Mei-Li* when bolts from a trasher ripped into and through the forest canopy, exploding overhead and on the ground. Broken branches and wood thudded and pattered behind him. Stoorvol shouted as if he had no helmet transmitter. "Set her down and run!" Then he darted upward through a gap in the foliage, evading branches as if by magic. In the air above, his marines poured blaster fire at the nearest Wyzhñyñy gunboat, targeting its sensor arrays. Then he dove through another gap, and zigzagged erratically away from the hornet scooter. An APC was firing into the jungle as if tracking him.

He landed skidding, 300 yards short of the *Mei-Li*'s coordinates. "Off," he barked, then triggered the scooter's delayed destruction charge and sprinted sixty yards before it blew. For a few seconds he lay panting, then got to his feet. His commandos were unhurt. After orienting himself in the deep dusk, Stoorvol sent the others on to find the *Mei-Li*. Alone he paused, squatting by a fallen forest giant overgrown with lichens, moss, and toadstools. The firing had stopped when the scooter had blown. Now it began again, and he sprinted around the root disk to crouch behind the great log. More debris rained down.

Clicking his transmitter, he spoke. "Gunny, do you read me?"

"Loud and clear, sir."

"Boats, do you read me?"

"Loud and clear, sir."

"Good. Gunny, if you've got any men on board, get them off now, ready to fight.

"Boats, Haynes and the civilians should reach you with the hornets soon. On foot. As soon as they're secured, get the *Mei-Li* out of there, without lights if possible. Gunny's people will help you. Did you both hear that?"

"Loud and clear sir."

"Loud and clear sir."

"Good. And Boats, those hornets need to reach the *Bering* as fast as safely possible; otherwise they may die, and dead they won't be much good. Then we'll have come all this way for nothing. Do *not* wait for me; I'll be keeping the Wyzhñyñy distracted."

It seemed to him he'd already done a pretty good job of that. Otherwise they'd probably have found the *Mei-Li* and pounded hell out of her.

Meanwhile the trasher fire had stopped again. He suspected what that might mean, and getting to his knees peered over the log toward where the scooter had been. A minute later he saw Wyzhñyñy troopers lowering through the canopy in slings.

Crouching, he padded off into the gathering darkness.

◇

With the help of his helmet's active night vision, Stoorvol found his way readily. Even with his belt nav, and knowing his own and the *Mei-Li*'s coordinates to four decimals, it would be easy to miss the boat in the jungle. Abruptly, gunfire sounded from multiple locations overhead: the rapid thumping of trashers, and the sizzling cracks of trasher bolts burning vacuum trails through the air. But without the tearing crashes of detonations in the forest roof, or the dull earthy whumps as they exploded against the ground. This continued for perhaps five long seconds, then cut off. The sound and its cessation told him what the target had been: the Wyzhñyñy had been firing at the *Mei-Li* as she accelerated outward. But there'd been no explosion as of the collection boat blowing up or crashing. Menges had gotten away into warpspace.

Which meant that Haynes and his civilians had run all the way, carrying their hornet traps… Either that or Menges hadn't waited. His fists curled at the thought.

At any rate the situation had changed. He was here until he either died or was picked up by the *Mei-Li,* when and if she returned for Wyzhñyñy prisoners. Stoorvol had ridden from Terra in stasis, and barely knew Weygand. Some commanders might justify leaving the system with what they had—the hornets. But there were others who'd try for the jackpot, especially since it seemed not to endanger the *Bering* herself. Weygand, it seemed to him, might be one of them.

As for himself, Stoorvol intended to get at least one Wyzhñyñy prisoner. Stash him somewhere, properly stunned, safe from rescue or escape. When they'd left Gabrovo Base in the Balkan Autonomy, every one of his commando carried a stunner, a gag, and a fifteen-foot roll of tape in his rucker.

As if on cue, he heard faint voices in the direction he'd come from, and maxxed his sound sensor. Alien speech, and not via radio. It sent a chill through him. How many times, as a boy, he'd day-dreamed that!

In a perverse way it also irritated him. Their stealth discipline was lousy! They probably thought their quarry was out of reach in warpspace. They were also moving his way. Spotting a strategically situated liana, he tested it, then climbed thirty feet or so to the crotch of a tree.

Now the Wyzhñyñy angled off toward the gorge, perhaps to be picked up and returned to their base. Out of his reach. That would never do. Climbing back down, he trotted after them, blaster ready. Shortly he spotted a Wyzhñyñy soldier and shot him in the back, then dropped into a hole left by the uprooting of a mouldering, wind-thrown tree. Blaster pulses hissed, fired blindly into the darkness.

He stayed where he was for several long minutes, blaster ready. Probably they'd sent a squad back to look for him, and they'd missed his hole. Cautiously he raised his head, then screened by the log, crept toward another large tree a few yards away. A liana had rooted to its trunk, and he climbed it, to fit himself into a crotch forty feet up. It wasn't comfortable, but it mostly hid him. Minutes later a squad of Wyzhñyñy appeared—the searchers returning from hunting him. He shrunk behind one half of the fork, hoping the concept of an enemy who could climb trees hadn't occurred to them. As they passed, he got the closest look he'd had at one. *Centaurs? Not hardly,* he told himself. Leave off the neck-like torso with its arms, and it looked like an oversized mastiff.

But beyond a doubt, they could run a lot faster than he could.

◇

The warp jump from the gorge back to the *Bering* had been quick. Menges had reemerged in F-space above the lunar farside not far from the survey ship, then closed in gravdrive. Olavsdóttir and her techs had promptly disembarked with their winged captives.

Briefly Sergeant Gabaldon told the skipper what he wanted to do. The skipper never blinked. "Go for it," he said. So Gabaldon claimed the pilot's seat, and with Menges as his copilot, moved away from the *Bering,* generated warpspace, and headed back for Tagus.

This time he didn't need to grope for the gorge. As sensed from the F-space potentiality, the gravitic coordinate system was blurred, but he had a "sort of" fix on Menges' old hiding place.

His plan, such as it was, was based on two operational premises. (1) The Wyzhñyñy were already alerted; and (2) the mission now demanded quickness, not stealth; aggression, not caution. But not stupidity, either. The immediate challenge promised to be finding a place to pull into the forest. He couldn't expect to find Menges' old hiding place; his fix wasn't that good. But his warrior muse smiled on him: he emerged above the gorge at close to rim level, within recognition distance of the gap between trees that Menges had used before. Jockeying the *Mei-Li* fully into the forest, he set her down.

His marines were already gathered at the gangway; he keyed it open and they moved out, taking defensive positions nearby. The naval gunners sat tense and ready at their heavy weapons. Gabaldon opened his transmitter and spoke. "Stoorvol, this is Gavaldon. We're parked where Menges hid earlier, but close to the rim. Do you read me? Over."

◇

The message took Paul Stoorvol by surprise. "Gunny," he murmured, "there should be a platoon or so of aliens very near you. Maybe just north, if you're where you say. They seem to be waiting for a ride home, or maybe for orders. They've given up hunting for me. I'd about decided I needed to do something more to keep them around. Right now I'm in a tree, a couple of hundred feet from... From the rim."

He'd stumbled orally because the Wyzhñyñy on the ground had opened fire, at either the *Mei-Li* or the marines. He doubted that anything the Wyzhñyñy had on the ground was adequate to breach her hull metal, but if they concentrated on her sensor array... Or if a gunboat was still hanging around...

From his perch he could make out two Wyzhñyñy, eerie gold by night vision. He unslung his blaster and shot them both, not to draw attention—the firefight with the marines held that—but to help the odds. Then he climbed down the liana, unslung his blaster again, and clicked his helmet transmitter.

One of the *Mei-Li*'s guns began hammering heavy bolts at the Wyzhñyñy, bolts crackling and thudding. Stoorvol realized he could be killed by his own people.

"Gunny," he said, "I'm on the ground now. Their attention is on you. I've killed two more of them, and I'll take out as many more as I can. We need to settle this now. Their command is likely to pour support forces in quickly. Over."

"Received. Received. This is Miller in charge. Gunny's out of touch; left the ship. Miller out."

Out of touch? "Got that. Stoorvol out." *Gunny knows what he's doing,* Stoorvol told himself, and this was no time for discussions. He found himself a new spot, a large tree with a broadly buttressed base. He wished he had a bag of grenades, instead of just the two on his harness. Taking one off, he charged it, then peered around a buttress and chose his next target— three Wyzhñyñy thirty yards away, crouching together behind a fallen tree. He threw the grenade to land just behind the one in the middle, then ducked behind the buttress again, heard the explosion and peered out. All three seemed dead.

The firefight ahead of him went on as if he weren't there, so he darted forward in a low crouch to where his latest victims lay. There he raised up enough to peer over the log. Ahead as well as to the sides, he could see numerous Wyzhñyñy kneeling behind trees and the occasional fallen trunk. And casualties. The marines weren't laying down much fire now though, as if there weren't many of them left. The thought flashed: *How many? Four? Five?* But the *Mei-Li's* starboard gunner, in his armored bubble, was still pumping out the heavy stuff.

With bursts of rotten wood, bolts blew through the log within ten feet of Stoorvol. To his right, a Wyzhñyñy he'd thought was dead, stood as if to flee, then stopped as if in freeze frame, staring at the marine officer. Stoorvol shot him down, then turning, began to shoot at every Wyzhñyñy he could see.

It seemed the final straw. All along the Wyzhñyñy line, aliens rose to flee. Stoorvol crouched low again, and from his thigh pocket drew his stunner. To his left, a Wyzhñyñy cleared the log in a bound, so easily and gracefully it startled the marine. As it landed, Stoorvol thumbed the trigger. The Wyzhñyñy stumbled, pitched forward and lay still. Another followed, and it too fell.

The starboard gun hammered a dozen more trasher bolts after the fleeing Wyzhñyñy before it stopped. Then, heart in his mouth, Stoorvol stood and jumped onto the log, waving both arms overhead. The *Mei-Li*'s gangway slid open, its ramp extruding. Three marines rode out on an AG freight sled, followed closely by two crewmen riding another.

"Over here!" Stoorvol shouted, again as if he didn't have a radio. "I've got two prisoners stunned." The marines veered to the north as if they hadn't heard. It was the crewmen who responded to Stoorvol, quickly setting down where he indicated. He helped them load an unconscious Wyzhñyñy on the sled. "Your gunner did good work with that heavy weapon," he said. "He broke them with it."

'Wasn't that," the older crewman grunted, lifting the second Wyzhñyñy's hindquarters.

"What, then?" It seemed to Stoorvol the man was going to give him the credit, for taking them from behind.

"Wyzhñyñy aircraft are on their way, sir. They'll be laying heavy fire in here." They finished getting the second Wyzhñyñy aboard, and as if that was a signal, an alarm horn blared from the *Mei-Li*.

"Come aboard, Captain," said the older. "That's Mr. Menges' twenty-tick warning."

Menges? Where was Gabaldon? And the marines with the other sled? He realized then; it was casualties, not prisoners they were collecting. Instead of getting on the sled, Stoorvol started toward the marines, but the senior crewman drew his stunner and thumbed the trigger. Quickly the two crewmen dumped the inert marine officer onto the sled with the prisoners, then sped to the gangway and inside the *Mei-Li*.

The marines, on the other hand, hadn't even looked toward the ship when the gangway slid shut. The senior crewman activated the sled's restraint field, felt it snug around him. "Jesus, Buddha, and Rama!" said the younger. "What's the matter with those marines? They should've come!"

Another alarm clamored through the boat, warning of imminent takeoff.

"They wouldn't leave their buds behind," the elder said.

"They were probably all dead!"

"Apparently it doesn't make any difference to them."

They felt the *Mei-Li* lift, pull backward from the forest edge, then swing about. At once it took flight, for five seconds of acceleration before warpspace generated. After a long moment's stillness, the senior crewman released the restraint field. Two others appeared, and helped transfer the inert prisoners onto AG litters, to be taken to Holding.

When the two Wyzhñyñy had been taken away, the younger crewman gestured toward the unconscious Stoorvol, still lying on the sled. "He was going to help them, wasn't he?"

"Yep. Who knows? Maybe those hyenas eat enemy casualties."

He said it absently. His mind was on the *Mei-Li*'s last remaining scooter, with Gunnery Sergeant Gabaldon piloting. It had left shortly after the *Mei-Li* landed. The crewman had heard enough to know the strategy: the sergeant would drop into the depths of the gorge, speed north a couple of miles, then climb a couple, to watch for Wyzhñyñy aerial reinforcements. Finally he'd seen some coming: gunboats and APCs. A lot of them.

Chapter Two
Moribund

"They are both moribund."

The *Bering* had left Tagus's moon less than two hours earlier, and Christiaan Weygand felt comfortable now about questioning the expedition's scientists working on the alien captives. The two Wyzhñyñy lay strapped on examination tables, wires and tubes leading from them to a life support system and a bank of readouts. If everything above the withers had been covered, and you overlooked the feet, they might have passed for some Terran mammal in a large-animal clinic.

"What actually does 'moribund' mean?" Weygand asked.

Dr. Maria Kalosgouros was a formidable, humorless woman, a vertebrate exobiologist of major professional status. "Captain Stoorvol's stunner had been set to render a 250-pound human unconscious for a period of one to three hours," she answered wryly. "Unfortunately its effect on Wyzhñyñy of similar mass is far more profound. They are dying, and there is nothing I can do to prevent it. I doubt their own physicians could, working with their own life support system."

Weygand regarded the two Wyzhñyñy glumly. *And we paid eighteen marines for them, good men. Valiant.* Not many, by the standards of war, but they'd been his, in a manner of speaking. "I presume you can still salvage information from them."

"Valuable information. Subcutaneous injection of minute quantities of African bee venom has resulted in encouraging tissue responses. But unfortunately their capillary circulation is virtually nil." She gestured at the bank of small monitor screens, where thin lines of colored light jittered microscopically, or sparsely, or flowed smooth as oil. Esoteric numbers showed occasional small changes. "I have injected the brain of one," she continued, "but that is not analogous to venom reaching the brain systemically. I could learn far more with studies on specimens functioning at something approaching normal.

"Still, we are learning far more than we knew before. And through Mädchen," she added, referring to the *Bering*'s savant, "I am sharing our results with Dr. Minda Shiue, at the University of Baguio."

Weygand had heard of Dr. Shiue. The Nobel Committee might meet in Buenos Aires now, instead of Oslo, but its awards continued to shine. "Just now," Kalosgouros went on, "she is at War House, to help interpret our results. I believe they are sufficient that the African Bee Project will be continued."

"Thank you, Dr. Kalosgouros," Weygand said, bowing slightly. *We do what we can,* he added silently, recalling the cost.

Back on the bridge, he buzzed Dr. Clement and asked how the hornet venom chromatography was going. Her answer was gratifying. In important and surprising respects, Tagus hornet venom resembled that of *Apis mellifera scutella.* She was proceeding optimistically.

Chapter Three
Portal to Justice

The Peace Front's Kunming headquarters occupied the sixth and seventh floors of a building no longer stylish. Paddy Davies' corner office was not large, given his position, but it easily accommodated the five guest chairs with keypad arms and monitors. Like the rest of the furnishings, they were not new, but in recent centuries, equipment had obsolesced slowly.

Two of the guest chairs were occupied, while Paddy sat at his modest desk. He and Jaromir Horvath were already familiar with the text on the wall screen. The third person, Perfeta Stolz, was reading it, "flipping pages" with her keypad. Rapidly. She had a quick and practiced eye and mind. Occasionally she triggered a hypertext link for details.

The pages bore a header: "Summary of Charges and Evidence Against Joseph Steven Switzer."

Davies watched Stolz, not the screen. To him, her strongly-built body and broad face suggested Native American lineage. (Actually she was half Igorot on her mother's side, and a quarter Buryat on her father's.) When she'd finished the last page, she looked across at him.

"He doesn't stand a chance of acquittal," she said. "The best anyone can do for Switzer is enter a guilty plea and ask for the mercy of the court. The government has generally handled Peace Front cases quite moderately." She paused, aware of what these men really wanted. They didn't like what she'd just said, and they'd reject what she'd say next, but it was necessary to say it. "A court-appointed attorney can do that as well as I, at no cost to you."

It was Horvath who answered, his voice dry and sour. "Leniency is not the objective," he said. "We want maximum mileage from the media."

"Mr. Horvath, I can guarantee lots of press, but it won't help the defendant, and it won't turn public opinion."

Paddy answered this time. "We know it won't turn the

verdict. As for the public? It will be worthwhile if we can simply touch them. Touch their souls. Keep the shame of this war before their eyes."

He thinks in clichés, Stolz told herself. *They both do.* "What you want me to do will aggravate the court," she pointed out, knowing that wouldn't impress them either. "It could even result in a sentence more severe than it might otherwise be."

Horvath answered again, surlier than before. "There are other legal firms we can hire."

She locked eyes with him, his challenging, hers steady and unyielding. "And what of Switzer?"

Paddy stepped into the breach. "An appropriate question, Counselor. But I've talked with Joseph, and he agrees. He wants us to make the most of this. For the Front and for peace. Before we pass the point of no return."

Stolz examined her broad brown hands, their nails neat and strong but not pampered, then looked back up at Davies. "You realize that it's Mr. Switzer who must ask for the change of attorneys. I can propose it to him, but it is he who must request it of the court."

"Of course. Of course. And quite as it should be. I cleared it with him before calling you."

Once more Horvath broke in, drawing a grimace from Davies. "We don't pay your firm a retainer for arguments about what we want."

"Nor have I given you one," Stolz answered calmly. "You pay a retainer for our prompt attention and our professional opinion. I have given you both." Abruptly she stood. "I will talk with Mr. Switzer. If he agrees, I will represent him, but I will also inform him honestly of the prospects." She returned her gaze to Davies. "You will be paying the fees, and I will get you what you pay for: public attention. *With* Mr. Switzer's agreement." Davies got to his feet and stepped from behind his desk, hand extended for hers. "That's exactly as we want it, Counselor. I have a copy of the cube for you…"

◇

Stolz reviewed the cube in her office, looking for cracks

in the case and finding none. *Hmh!* she thought. *He dreamed up the mission, knew the risks, and volunteered to carry it out. But knowing the risks, and having them crash down on you, are two different things,* she reminded herself. *He's lucky this isn't a vengeful, reactive government.*

◇

The next morning, a slump-shouldered Joseph Switzer stepped into a small concrete room. He wore blue prison clothing, faded by many trips through the prison laundry. A guard gripped his arm. In the middle of the room, two chairs were bolted to the floor, facing each other five feet apart. His court-appointed defender stood by one of them. Switzer's gaze dropped to the floor again.

"Shall I leave now, Counselor?" the guard asked.

"Yes, thank you," the defender said. Without a word, the guard let go of Switzer's arm and left the room, closing the door behind him. Then stood looking in through its thick glass window.

Switzer simply stood unmoving. The attorney was notably taller than he was. Her kinky brown hair was cut close as a cap. Her professional black pant suit emphasized her slimness, and made her caramel complexion seem light by contrast.

"Shall we sit down, Joseph?" she asked gesturing. He nodded, stepped to a chair, and they sat down facing each other.

"I'm told you've asked that I be replaced by another attorney, one hired by the Peace Front. If that's what you wish, I'm required to step aside."

His voice was low and husky. "That's how I want it."

"The Peace Front is less interested in minimizing your sentence than in making the Front look good. Do you realize that?"

He nodded, barely.

"Are you aware of how strong the evidence is against you?"

Again his nod was slight.

"Perfeta Stolz is an excellent attorney. But it is entirely possible that I can get you a lighter sentence than she can.

Because leniency would be the entire thrust of my effort, while hers will be on getting the Front as much publicity as possible. Do you understand that also?"

"That's how I want it," he repeated.

She searched his face for some sign of defiance or stoicism, or perhaps nobility—the noble martyr. She found none of them. He looked defeated, his eyes avoiding hers. Not a promising hero for the front. But Stolz had a reputation as a courtroom psychologist, and for skill in preparing her clients.

"Well then," she said, getting to her feet, "my best wishes for a successful trial." *However you define success.*

Her blessing didn't sound entirely genuine. She was a competitor, a young soul, and didn't think much of surrender.

<>

Arraignment took place in a small closed chamber. Journalists were not allowed, though the attorneys might well find the media waiting in the Justice Building courtyard.

Besides the panel of three judges, the chamber held Joseph Switzer, his counsel, the prosecutor, a bailiff, and two deputies flanking the accused. Switzer looked much better than he had three days past. He wore a business suit, stood straight, and looked not at the floor now, but at the chief justice. Though avoiding eye contact.

Chief Justice Gil Hafiz spoke mildly to him. "For the record," he said, "are you Joseph Steven Switzer?"

"Yes sir."

"Have you been given a copy of the indictment?"

"Yes sir."

"Have you read it?"

"Yes sir."

"Do you understand the charges?"

"Yes sir."

"Good. Do you wish to speak for yourself, or do you want your defender to speak for you?"

"I want my defender to speak for me."

All three judges turned their eyes to Perfeta Stolz. "Counselor," Hafiz said, "how does the accused plead?"

"Your honor, as Mr. Switzer's counsel, I move that the indictment be set aside. The shooting took place on Lüneburger's World, not on Terra. My client was born on Lüneburger's World, grew up there, and has Lüneburgian citizenship. Also the military reservation was not Commonwealth property. And per Commonwealth versus Patel, CE 2781/05/17...." She completed the citation, along with the Supreme Court decision. "Therefore, the accused should be remanded to Lüneburger's world, and tried there by the appropriate authorities."

The chief justice glanced at the other judges, who sat attentive and impassive, then he leafed through his notes before looking back at Stolz. "As you know, Counselor, the legal term is 'full rights of residency,' not citizenship. And your client had applied for and been granted full rights of Terran residency, with the accountability that accompanies it."

Hafiz cocked an eyebrow at Stolz; she knew her plea had no grounds. She was preparing to play to the public, and within minutes of leaving would be speaking to the cameras. In his view it degraded the law, but within broad limits it was her right. If her client agreed, and if he understood what he'd agreed to. Hafiz was tempted to query the accused, but held his peace. He'd do nothing that could be used as a basis for appeal.

Instead he continued to address Stolz. "Furthermore, at the moment of his injury and death, the victim was an employee of the Commonwealth government engaged in his governmental duties. The person who actually shot the victim was also an employee of the Commonwealth government, who at the time of the shooting was engaged in *his* governmental duties. Thus per Article 12, Section 3, of the Commonwealth Criminal Code, the crime unquestionably comes under Commonwealth jurisdiction. The murderer, a soldier, pleaded guilty as charged, before a court martial. His plea was accepted, and he has begun his sentence. Thus it is now appropriate for this court to try your client for the crime of contributing to murder."

Stolz stood for a long moment as if disappointed—as if the court's decision was unexpected. Then she spoke again. "In that case, your honor, I must request a jury trial for my client."

The judges had expected that, too. Jury trials were infrequent on Terra—three-judge panels were the norm—but in certain classes of crimes they could be granted. The chief justice turned to the prosecutor. "What say you to that, Mr. Prosecutor?"

Hafiz knew the answer to that as well. The Office of the President had sent down a policy that if requested, jury trials would be granted members of the Front for alleged crimes of the First Category. Basically Hafiz disliked the policy. As a rule, juries came to the same conclusions as a panel of judges would have, while requiring much more time, expense, and turmoil. But he appreciated the government's situation.

The prosecutor grimaced slightly; such a trial would turn into a Peace Front circus. "If the defense wants it so," he grumped, "we will not object."

"Very well, Counselor," Hafiz said. "Your client shall have a jury trial." She had, he knew, a reputation for being very good in jury trials.

She bobbed an almost bow in acknowledgement. "Thank you, Your Honor. Meanwhile my client will not come to trial for a week or more. Therefore I respectfully request his release on bond."

The prosecutor's exhalation was more hiss than sigh. Obviously she intended to fight over every proposed juror, eating up all the time possible, and providing a magnet for public attention. A Peace Front circus indeed.

The chief justice smiled slightly. "Counselor, your request is denied."

"On what grounds, Your Honor?"

"On the grounds that whatever the outcome of his trial for contributing to the crime of murder, he will still face charges of inciting to mutiny."

Stolz frowned. "Your Honor, I do not see what that has to do with my request. My client has complied with every order, responded to every request, without resistance." She appeared to grope for words, settling for "He is not a violent man. He decries violence, by persons as well as by governments."

"The trial should cast light on that," Hafiz answered wryly.

"It is, of course, possible to contribute to the crime of murder without intending that it go that far. We'll see. Meanwhile your client stands before this court accused of two Crimes of the First Category. In such cases, the court has full discretion with regard to bail. Mr. Switzer has much reason to fear the outcomes of his trials, and there is an entire social class who would willingly undertake to conceal him or help him flee."

Stolz's features had stiffened. "What social class, if you please, Your Honor?"

"Let me answer it this way, Counselor. Who is paying your fees?"

She answered indignantly. "The Peace Front, Your Honor. The party which more than any other decries this war and all violence."

"Exactly." *She plays her role well,* he thought, *for someone who belongs to the Center Party instead of the Front.* He'd respect her more, he told himself, if her first allegiance was to the accused. But there was little she could do for him at any rate, and if the Front wanted to use Switzer for propaganda... He hoped, though, that Switzer really understood what was going on.

She wasn't done yet. "Your Honor, I have one more request. A number of journalists have asked to interview my client." She took a small flat case from her pocket and held it out to him. "I told them to put their requests in writing, and that they might have to agree on one or two doing the interviews for all."

The chief justice declined to receive the data chips; they were irrelevant. *She took you by surprise on that one, Gil,* he told himself. *You're slowing down.* "Denied again, Counselor," he replied. "If the court granted such privileges to accused felons, activists would commit crimes simply for the pulpit they provided."

"Your Honor," Stolz said unhappily, "except for the jury trial, you have denied every request I've made for my client."

"True. In fact, it seems to me you made those requests anticipating their denial. And I have no doubt you'll make good use of them after you leave this chamber."

◇

He was right, of course. She spent half an hour standing before cameras on the plaza outside, speaking carefully, but airing all her complaints. The court would provide the media with recordings and transcripts of the proceedings, but meanwhile she'd put her own spin on them.

Chapter Four
Battle Master

The CWS *Altai,* flagship of the 1st Sol Provisional Battle Force, was in hyperspace just seven days short of the Paraíso System. Its admiral, Alvaro Soong, lay propped on a pillow in his stateroom, hands cupped behind his head, reviewing. He was not a notable worrier. His usual style was to treat things matter-of-factly. But he'd made a decision—made and implemented it—that could wipe out whatever chance humanity had for survival. At least civilized survival.

His rationale was that the chance being risked was thin. And if his decision worked out, it could substantially improve.

If it worked out. He'd approached it on a gradient: "Just how good *are* you at battle games, Charley? Let me write a set of opening circumstances, and see what you can do with it."

Both men—the one who occupied 210 pounds of primate body, and the one who weighed only 58 pounds, most of it a "bottle" of metal and synthetics—both knew what lay in the back of the admiral's mind. *Are you good enough to direct a real battle with real warships? Are you really? Because the odds are heavily against us. I may be better at directing a space battle than any other officer in this battle force. At the Academy, my cumulative battle game score set a record. But if you can beat me decisively enough...*

Basically he was praying for a true genius in war gaming. And Charley had passed the test with ease, even flair. And a second, and a third...

Soong himself was the default choice, but after extensive testing, he'd chosen Charley. For a while the choice had been reversible. Now it wasn't. Not if they were to engage the armada in the Paraíso System. They'd programmed too many changes into the *Altai*'s battlecomp, trying to take maximum advantage of Charley's talents.

Briefly the admiral turned his attention to his stateroom "window"—a large wall panel that in F-space usually gave a real-time view of the stars more clearly than an actual window could. But in hyperspace, the default view was of the F-space potentiality, as interpreted by shipsmind, and it was neither esthetic nor ordinarily interesting. Usually it showed nothing at all. So he'd requested views of Terra. Terra, which he might never see again. Just now it showed the Swedish taiga—its trees sparse and stunted in the ever worsening climate. In the background was the great icesheet of the Kjölen Range, intensely, painfully white in spring sunshine. It covered the fjells as far north and south as the view permitted, and oozed slow white tongues of ice down the valleys toward the sea. A magnificent view, it also provided perspective. Many townsites and historical sites had been buried by the ice in this and many other valleys, leaving the region virtually abandoned. A few—a very few Sami had stayed, long since genetically more Swedish and Norwegian than Sami. They had relearned to herd reindeer, a valid lifestyle, given the climatic shift.

A thought surfaced: if the Wyzhñyñy prevailed, would they undertake to root out such tiny, harmless enclaves? That was what some of the colonies had been: small harmless enclaves in planetary wilderness. And seemingly the Wyzhñyñy had rooted them out. From the alien point of view, he supposed it made sense.

He pulled his attention away from the screen. In a week he'd emerge in the Paraíso System—the first inhabited system at which he could intercept the invader. How terrible, how overwhelming was that alien armada? How good were his Provos—his 1st Sol Provisional Battle Force? What chance did humanity have?

You'll be the first to know, Alvaro, he told himself.

He was not expected to win this battle, in the usual sense. Thank the Tao. He was to attack the enemy, cause as much damage as possible, then disappear into hyperspace before the invader could destroy him. And in the process learn as much as possible about enemy weaponry and tactics. Those were his orders. Engage, flee, and report.

The decisive part—the most dangerous moment—would

be just before escape into strange-space. That moment after the shield generators had shut down, but before the shields had sufficiently decayed to allow generation of a carrier bubble.

War House deemed those waited-for reports so vital, they'd invested five of a seriously limited resource to make sure of them. In each battle group, the point battleship carried a savant communicator, and through that savant, a liaison officer was to give War House a running account of the fight. Then, when the fleet had escaped into hyperspace, the surviving commanders would debrief, again via savant.

Though War House didn't know it in advance, the *Altai* was the exception. Her savant would be far too busy directing battle actions to give a running account. And afterward he'd rest, as long as needed, before channeling Soong's debrief.

Soong hadn't told Kunming about his new battle master; War House might forbid following through on it. It seemed to him he would himself, if he were admiralty chief. Because War House hadn't personally tested Charley Gordon. And the battle would involve most of the battle-ready human warships and crews.

And if somehow Kunming found out before the fact, and forbade it? Probably he'd ignore them. He'd spent weeks as Charley's assistant, developing strategies and tactics, modifying and remodifying procedures. But in simulation tests, he'd been a spectator, while Charley interacted with the *Altai* and the rest of the battle force in ways no one had thought of before.

Early on, the admiral had been visited by anxiety, but the weeks of development and tests had left him quietly confident. Not of victory, but of Charley's genius and skills, and the wisdom of his own decision. The limitations of ships and weapons remained, along with the unknown abilities and resources of the Wyzhñyñy.

And that two-edged sword known as Murphy's Law, which threatened both fleets. Soong wondered if the Wyzhñyñy recognized Murphy's Law. It seemed to him they must. It was inaccurate, of course. Murphy's Law— "whatever can go wrong will go wrong" —had been predicated as humor. It was irony, not science. But by changing one word, you expressed a truth: "Whatever can go wrong *may* go wrong."

In any case you did what you could, and Charley could outdo anyone. In normal gaming, a battle master gives the battlecomp a general strategy and a set of candidate tactics, via brief code words or phrases, very explicit. The battlecomp takes it from there, until that instruction is overridden by a new code word or phrase.

Some gamers sometimes give a single such order. The secret to whatever success they have lies in accurately evaluating the initial situation, and selecting or creating an effective strategy. The exercise itself is run entirely by the computer.

Charley, however, had come to the job with very major advantages. He knew the *entire* catalog of standard command codes, and had added numerous others of his own to make use of his special talents. And no one, to Soong's knowledge, was nearly so nimble with them. Charley could rattle off a sequence of appropriate commands, for a number of units, almost at the speed of thought. "Appropriate" involving the necessary allowances for unit momenta, signal time, equipment response times, and of course his own delivery rate in a command sequence.

The battlecomp could, of course, handle the command function by default. But it could not know what Charley usually knows: the event vectors *of the moment*. His central genius.

Meanwhile, in simulation, every warship in the fleet was carrying out battle actions bizarre and unimagined, even by the centuries of tactical wizards who'd labored anonymously at War House desks, programming, testing and gaming.

Because creative and imaginative though they'd been, none of them had envisioned a resource like Charley Gordon.

◇

Estimated conservatively, the Provos would arrive in the fringe of the system twelve days before the Wyzhñyñy's projected date of arrival. With the short closing jump, and a force no larger than Soong's, hours would be enough to form opening battle formations. So far, Charley's fleet drills had been in the virtual reality of the *Altai*'s shipsmind. The rest of the fleet didn't know there was a new battle master. In the Paraíso System, the entire fleet would participate, its ships coordinated under Charley Gordon's direction, mediated by the *Altai*'s shipsmind.

<>

Soong was on the bridge four hours before scheduled arrival. Already isogravs showed the system's primary, an F9 star without a name of its own, unless you consider catalog numbers. As soon as shipsmind had computed the optimum emergence solution, the admiral ordered an approach course and emergence tick, informing his battle force via that awkward set of phenomena called hyperspace radio.

When that order had been acknowledged, he sent another: all hands were to be out of stasis before emergence, and ready to receive a live, all-hands briefing from the admiral and his battle master. Because the battle plan, tactics and protocols had changed greatly. The fleet's officers and crews needed to be set up for that; informed of what had happened, and how. Reassured, and given confidence in the new command situation.

<>

On naval spacecraft, the signal for hyperspace emergence is a gong, mellow and golden, repeated over five seconds.

Then the Provos popped into F-space scattered over a significant period—more than a millisecond—to occupy a million-cubic-mile volume of F-space shaped like a watermelon seed. Against a scintillant backdrop of stars, cold in aspect but hot, hot. The brightest, most vivid, being the molten-yellow primary only four billion miles away.

The admiral gave his people thirty seconds to appreciate the sight. Then he began his all-hands address.

"Officers and crew of the First Provos. We are in the fringe of the Paraíso System, and in a few minutes we'll begin to form battle units. Not the formations we've formed before, but something new. Something better. Something that will enable us to truly raise hell with the enemy when he appears.

"Eight weeks ago I made a discovery. I discovered that one of us is a genius above all geniuses in battle gaming. As a graduating midshipman, I set the Academy's official all-time cumulative scoring record for space-battle games. So I tested and retested this newly discovered genius, then tested him some more. In every test he humbled me, and as a result I've made him battle master. Given him the duty I love best of all, because this will be no game. It will be for real, for the future of humankind."

He paused, letting them absorb it.

"He improves our odds of victory by a factor of ten. "So I want to introduce this man to you, this supreme battle master. You need to know him and hear him. He is a gift from the Tao, and one of the finest human beings I have ever known."

Up to this point, the camera had given the viewers a close shot of their admiral, showing him from the waist up. Now the viewpoint backed off, showing him standing beside a wheeled, motorized stand.

"Our new battle master's name is Charley Gordon. Not Admiral Gordon. Not Captain Gordon or Commander Gordon. *Charley* Gordon, a civilian. He is also our flagship savant."

The admiral's calm features seemed to gaze through the screen at them, as they sat or stood, surprised or puzzled, in messroom, wardroom, engine room, bridge, on battleship, cruiser, corvette.... He continued.

"A savant. 'Savant' is short for 'idiot savant,' because most of them aren't able to function mentally as we do. But all have talents that the rest of us do not.

"Charley Gordon is different. He has savant talents, *and* he reasons...superbly. He was born in the Brazilian Autonomy, in Rio de Janeiro. As a child he dwelt constantly at death's door, till at age twelve he was bottled, to save his life. Now..."

Their admiral waited again, then gestured at the cart, and the module on its top. "This is Charley Gordon," he said, then indicated the small sensor set that topped it. "He sees and hears his immediate surroundings with these. But through his connections with shipsmind, he sees much more. At will.

"And now I'll let him tell you more about what he does and how he does it."

Almost no one spoke, anywhere in the fleet. Inwardly Soong fidgeted. Because Charley had told him almost nothing about what he'd say. "One of my differences," he'd explained, "is that I function best when playing by ear."

Now Charley broke the silence, in a voice that was not in the least robotic. One might almost have called it merry. "I am Charley Gordon. I am thirty-three years old, and for most of those years I've been war gaming. It's as if I was born for it.

"My response to almost anything is an action. An action! Me, who lives in a box! I act electronically, via whatever mechanisms I'm connected with. Including my vocator, with which I'm speaking to you now, and by whatever artificial intelligence or other server I'm connected with. In this case shipsmind, especially its battlecomp function.

"As battle master I have certain innate and very important advantages. For example, I absorb books and other data sources like a sponge absorbs water. And none of it leaks out or evaporates. Instead it integrates, unifies, forms a coherent system. Where it harmonizes according to natural laws I can only sense, but use intuitively. Use in ways analogous to the ways I communicate with War House in real time, even though Kunming is hyperspace months away."

Soong had gotten used to talking with Charley Gordon; now he was listening to him with different ears, crew ears. *Great Tao!* he thought. *He's charismatic! How did I miss that? He positively radiates intelligence and assurance! This will work better than I'd hoped.*

"Some of what I tell you may sound strange," Charley went on. "But most of you have had technical training and games experience, so you will understand. If not at once, then when you've seen it in action.

"Equally important..." He paused. "Let me put it this way. Things happen in sequences. A cause results in an effect, which causes another effect. Et cetera. The causes may include a human decision, a weather incident, an argument, leaky plumbing...almost anything. Such cause/effect sequences I call vectors, and vectors often intersect, and interact.

"For example: Some geophysical incident—say a tidal wave resulting from a volcanic eruption—destroys a village in the Sulu Archipelago. As one result, a surviving villager migrates to Zamboanga, where he meets a stranger at a mosque. They talk, and decide to become robbers together. Ambushing a well-dressed man, they steal a message plaque he'd carried in a body wallet. The message is in a Tamil dialect which neither knows, but..." He paused. "One thing leads to another, and before long, one robber is dead at the hands of Han smugglers, and our ex-villager is hiding among pilgrims enroute to Mecca."

His listeners could hear the calm and smiling competence in Charley's voice. "A vector in progress, you see. Now we Provos are on a vector which will soon intersect the vector of the Wyzhñyñy armada. And when those vectors intersect, they will result in a spray of new vectors.

"My greatest advantage as battle master is, I am able to sense the relevant vectors—*and their probabilistic futures.* Some vectors remain fixed over long periods of time: a planet in its orbit, a comet in its orbit. Eventually they may intersect, but very probably they will not. It would be useful to know in advance.

"Many other vectors are very erratic, like a spoiled child unrestrained in a toy store. Even those I can often foresee with some confidence. And while I do these things intuitively, I know them consciously."

The admiral listened intently. Charley had never brought up these things to him, though by hindsight they'd been apparent in his gaming.

"Mostly," Charley continued, "I can't project them very far. Many intersect with too many other effective vectors. Human and alien choices, and of course chaos functions, can cause vectors to change, and give rise to new vectors. But I am generally a few steps ahead of events, and that is a very important advantage.

"Beyond that, I coordinate factors and data very very well. Not as precisely as a shipsmind, but on a higher level. For what is termed 'intuition' in an artificial intelligence, is simply the use of stochastic processes to extrapolate beyond or around areas of weak or ambiguous data. Human intuition can go well beyond that."

◇

Soong listened while Charley wrapped up his talk. Among other things, the savant knew when to stop. When he was done, the admiral added a few closing comments, then ended the session. It seemed to him they'd pulled it off. Or Charley had. Over the next day or so he'd know absolutely, one way or the other, by fleet performance.

Meanwhile *Altai's* shipsmind had uploaded the contents of its upgraded battlecomp to the rest of the fleet. And when the all-hands session was over, the admiral called for a command conference on the closed command frequency. A few hours later, the force was ready to begin simulation drills.

◇

The simdrills went so well that three days later the force began "steel drills." In these the battle groups moved physically in space while *Altai's* battlecomp threw sequences of enemy responses at them. From his battle command station on the bridge, Charley rattled off rapid shorthand instructions to shipsmind, instructions forwarded by radio to the rest of the force. Which fought as separate but coordinated battle groups.

In F-space, maneuvers were as limited as ever; one thing Charley couldn't do was cancel inertia. But by anticipating "enemy responses," he permitted individual battle groups to transit from F-space to warpspace with minimal losses. And his control and coordination of beam fire and torpedo attacks against enemy movements was deadly.

It was all pretend, of course, but the Provo crews had gained a large degree of optimism, and an enthusiasm that made the whole venture exciting. Even the "losses" of Provo warships did not greatly cool them. They were, they told each other, going to teach the Wyzhñyñy the cost of bringing war to human space.

Alvaro Soong was not as optimistic. The drills had been as realistic as possible, short of shooting at each other. But it was still a limited reality, because Wyzhñyñy weaponry, tactics, nerve—even the number of their fighting ships—was unknown. Which was, he reminded himself, the main reason he'd been sent there, he and his Provos. At the least, he needed to maintain engagement long enough to forward a definitive picture of Wyzhñyñy battle capacities to War House. To inflict substantive damage would be a bonus.

Chapter Five
A Time of Truth

The armada had emerged from hyperspace so often in this galaxy, it had become routine, and no longer drew Quanshûk to the bridge or to his feet. He watched from the AG couch in his quarters.

"...five, four, three, two, one..."

Stars exploded onto the screen, but their beauty no longer lifted him. Even the question, would one of its planets be habitable?, had long since become routine. The armada emerged every shipsday or two—at every star whose isogravs suggested any possibility of a habitable planet. Usually staying only long enough to discover there wasn't one. Sometimes five minutes was enough. Sometimes they sent a survey ship for a closer look. When one seemed clearly habitable, they stayed several days, and left with a sense of accomplishment. But after so many, even that was routine now.

This emergence came during shipsnight, and Quanshûk closed his eyes again. The bridge would call him if...

His comm yammered, and he jerked wide awake. "This is the admiral," he answered.

"Your lordship, there is something you need to see. Perhaps on the bridge?"

The voice was that of Captain Krûts, the Meadowlands' master. "I'll be there momentarily," Quanshûk answered.

"Shall I notify Lord Qonits and Admiral Tualurog, your lordship?"

"At your discretion."

The admiral jabbed a key, then got stiffly to his feet, his arthritic joints complaining. He was medicated, always, but not so strongly as to banish pain. He was grand admiral, and would not risk dulling his mind.

At first, after getting up, he didn't walk well. He carried himself well—torso erect, long head high—but his steps were short and painful. Qonits caught up with him at the entry to the bridge, and they went in together.

Krûts was waiting for them, and pointed at the large screen centered in the monitor array on the bridge's forward bulkhead. It showed a compressed representation of the system, with the conventional armada icon, and other icons marking planets. Two others—flashing orange lights—marked detected sources of technical electronics.

Two sources. One was the second planet. The other was in the near fringe, it's system azimuth 134° from the armada's. Quanshûk stepped quickly to his admiral's station, and called for an enlarged view of the fringe source. Or cluster of sources, for that's how the monitor showed them. At nearly nine light-hours distance, there was no visual resolution. A side-bar numbered them, however—230 individual sources; 230 ships.

Quanshûk frowned. Two hundred thirty. Why were they here? They were far too few to do battle with him.

Then it struck him. Turning, he scanned the bridge crew. "An evacuation fleet," he said, then elaborated. "On most of the human worlds we've come to, much of the population had clearly been evacuated. Very probably we're looking at an evacuation fleet." He turned to his chief scholar. "Wouldn't you say, Qonits?"

"Indeed, my lord, that would explain them."

The chief scholar looked less than sure of it. But then, being skeptical was part of a scholar's job.

◇

In the Provo force, an electronic bosun's pipe shrilled through the corridors and compartments of the *Altai* and every other manned ship. Followed by shipsvoice: "Now hear this! Now hear this! All hands report to mustering stations by 1022 hours. All hands to mustering stations by 1022 hours." Then the sequence repeated. Every hand knew; this was it: the time of truth. "All hands" calls were infrequent. To repeat it like this…

Ten-twenty-two; in ten minutes.

To top it off, after a few seconds music began to issue from the ships' speakers. Music! That was different. The admiralty had established "instant tradition" for its new fleet, including an "unofficial" fleet theme, dubbed "Spacing Off to Dilly Doo." Dilly Doo being a planet in a very old, off-color space tale—a sort of Valhalla where spacers supposedly went when they died, to binge and bawd. The recording—by the pipes and drums of the Caledonian Regimental Band—dated from before space flight. Its name then had been "Scotland the Brave," something few spacers were aware of.

By any name it was stirring. And when they'd finished Dilly Doo, the Caledonians continued without a break, playing other martial music.

Meanwhile men in bunks swung their legs out, put feet on the deck, and went to the head to relieve themselves and splash cold water on their faces. Men in rec rooms shut off books and games, officers in wardrooms finished their coffee and rolls or set them aside. Something major was up, and no one on board had any doubt what it was.

Most mustering stations were messrooms. Personnel on duty could watch on their duty monitor. By 1022, every man and woman aboard every ship was in front of a screen; in sickbay perhaps a screen above the bed.

It was not shipsvoice that spoke to them. They'd have been surprised if it was. It was "the old man" himself, the admiral. A close shot of him—chest, shoulders, head. Dark eyes dominating, jaw firm. "Men of the 1st Provos," he began. The thirty-one percent who were women took no offense. The term "men" as a neuter collective had been accepted for a long time.

"We have found the enemy. The Wyzhñyñy armada arrived in this system at 1010 hours, only nine light hours away."

The admiral's face was replaced by a representation of the Paraíso System, showing the relative positions of the two fleets, as icons.

"By now they have surely read our electronic signature, and are wondering what in the Tao this small fleet is doing here. Knowing that we will have read their emergence waves, they will expect us to flee. They will expect that nine hours hence, our electronics will disappear from their sensors."

The admiral's face replaced the schematic. "At 1030 hours we will generate warpspace—and at 1230 hours emerge within the fringe of their armada." He paused, then spoke more loudly and sharply. "And show them what humans can do in a fight! Especially with *our* battle master."

His voice resumed its usual even delivery. "Each of you knows your role in this. Your duty; what you are to do. I expect your best. We will shock the invader; we will bleed him; we will make him wish he'd never left home."

Then he raised his arms in closing, and "Dilly Doo"—"Scotland the Brave"—returned to the corridors and compartments of the 1st Provos.

Except on the "maces." Maces had no crews. They had the dimensions of cruisers, but beam guns as powerful as those on battleships. Built to stand accelerations up to 100 gees, they could accelerate and decelerate at rates that humans, and presumably Wyzhñyñy, could not remotely match. And they could fly high speed evasion courses. Not extreme evasion courses, but courses that beam guns would have trouble getting locks on. At least beam guns on human warships.

"Flying guns" they'd been called. It would have been as accurate to call them flying generators, for those guns required great power. And more: the newer squadrons generated two-layered shields. Their interior design had been modified to accommodate not only larger power generators but larger shield generators.

As for their battle judgements and responses—the shipsminds aboard maces were second to none. And like every other Provo shipsmind, they'd been reprogrammed to respond to Charley Gordon's unique style of command.

<>

Rear Admiral Tualurog had taken over the grand admiral's station on the bridge, allowing Quanshûk to return to bed. It was easy duty. Shipsmind could manage the reforming of battle wings, and the even more numerous transport and supply ships. Cleansing the humans from the habitable world was the colonizing tribe's responsibility. The Grand Fleet remained briefly on standby, to lend support as necessary.

The tribe was already inbound in warpdrive, with its regiments of shock warriors, its divisions of non-warrior reservists, its integral ground support wing, and its own insystem defense force: a flotilla of cruisers and corvettes. The ground forces were supported by two bombards—massive ships designed solely for ground bombardment—assigned to the planetary guard flotilla. These would destroy defense installations and troop concentrations, if any. And all technical facilities and population centers. After that, ground-support "hunters" helped "beat the bushes," guided by surveillance buoys parked in near-space.

If the planet's defense forces turned out to be troublesome enough, the fleet could send down marines and additional ground support squadrons. But that was undesirable. It meant either delaying the armada's departure.

As for possible human incursions from space—the departing armada would leave a pentagonal battle group in the fringe: five battleships with a screen of cruisers and corvettes, ready to move against any threat. While a planetary guard flotilla was left insystem, to guard against landings.

◇

Like hideous trumpets, alarm horns blared through the *Meadowlands,* jerking everyone awake. A single, eight-second, ruff-raising discord that cut sharply to a voice, strident but concise: "Battle stations! Battle stations! Battle stations!"

Quanshûk was on his feet and into the executive corridor more quickly than he'd moved for months. The ship was already fighting, its ever-present fine vibration amplified by the demands of heavy beam guns and the generation of her force shield. She jarred as a salvo of torpedos exploded against her newly generated shield, throwing the admiral against a bulkhead. The corridor lights flickered, then held.

On the bridge, the only sound was quiet words spoken to closed-channel mikes. Quanshûk's practiced eyes took in the monitor array—diagrams; animations; live tracking shots, some foreshortened, others natural; enemy ships identified by pulsing red darts. Words flashed on the systems-status display. Beams of white light, war beams, crisscrossed screens, and not all ships were marked by the haloes indicating shields. Where war beams had locked on first, the shield generation process aborted.

Quanshûk's mind elaborated what his eyes could not: glowing red hull-metal puddling where a beam was locked, flowing and spattering away from the contact. Breached hulls, exploding, imploding. Torpedo salvos bursting on shields, disrupting some, blowing their generators. Where this happened, beams might find the hull for a coup de grâce. Then he was at his command station, jabbing keys, eyes snatching data from the thirty-inch station monitor. A diagram popped on, summarizing the firefight as it proceeded. Seemingly the attackers had not been picked up at once, for even as the sequence began, they'd reached substantial speeds from the standstill of warpspace emergence, and already had shields up.

The grand fleet's shipsminds were entirely in charge, coordinated so far as possible by the command shipsmind aboard *Meadowlands.* Once alerted, its response had been instantaneous, a reflex. The bridge watch could only try to catch up. Quanshûk's fingers stabbed keys, slid magnification tabs, his mind clearer and sharper than it had been for years, free of fear, anxiety and blame, watching patterns unfold in the action. Enemy fire control and coordination was superb. Almost solely they targeted fighting ships, the beams from several converging not only on one, but on the same part of its shield. Each battle group moved and fought as a vee through and out of its own sector of armada space, leaving a corridor of destruction.

A few of the ships destroyed or left derelict were attackers, but his battle formations were too incomplete for successful fire coordination. At twenty-eight seconds a few enemy shields thinned, then more in quick succession, to disappear before their ships blinked out of sight into warpspace. And somehow in their moment of vulnerability, few were found by beams. Then there was peace, marked by glowing broken hulls.

Quanshûk's brief battle high dissolved into shock. With an almost insolent dispassion, shipsmind informed him that the encounter had lasted thirty-four seconds, and presented him with a fleet losses report. Four battleships and eleven cruisers.... Enemy losses, one battleship and three cruisers.... The admiral stared blankly.

Then the next wave hit, as unexpectedly as the first. Alarm horns squalled. The *Meadowlands* was jarred by another salvo of torpedos. Again the lights flickered, and for a moment the bridge was lit only by the monitors, before the lights came back at half strength. This new wave accelerated impossibly, in randomized zigzags despite their momentum, while their bright war beams reached far forward. The admiral and bridge crew could do little but watch the monitors. Again the attackers' fire coordination was excellent. And far ahead, what seemed to be the first wave had emerged again from warpspace, sweeping through the still-mustering Fourth Battle Wing.

The second wave disappeared more quickly than the first. Then the reemerged first wave winked out again. Quanshûk sat dazed but upright, waiting for shipsmind to report losses. Even as the numbers appeared, shipsvoice reported new incursions, elsewhere within the armada. The admiral hardly reacted, leaving the battle to shipsmind.

<>

Ophelia Kennah guided Charley Gordon off the bridge and into the corridor, Alvaro Soong following. With F-space and the Wyzhñyñy left behind, shipsmind, along with Soong's operations officer and the ship's captain, could tend shop very nicely. Soong would stay with Charley until the savant had settled down. Then, if Charley was in shape to channel, he'd report to War House.

In the corridor, Charley couldn't restrain himself. "Oh, Admiral!" he said, "it was...marvelous! I am absolutely *wired! Wired!*" He paused just a second. "You do know the term, sir? It dates from the first drug era, before the Troubles, and means intensely exhilarated. I have *never* felt like this before!" He laughed. "Did you hear that, Admiral? Laughter from a bottle! I'm like Ebenezer Scrooge, after awakening on Christmas morning! Like a drunken man! Isn't that remarkable? Even though I was just instrumental in destroying the biological housings of thousands of souls, sending them back to central casting, so to speak. And feel no guilt! No guilt at all! Isn't that remarkable? Oh! I'm even repeating myself! I don't usually do that. Do I, dear Ophelia? I don't think I do.

"And Admiral, do you know why I feel no guilt? Because it is part of the great dance. Part of the great learning. And because... *We may have just saved the human species!* The vectors are distinctly encouraging now!" His voice lowered conspiratorially. "They are. We have not won yet, but we have crossed a watershed, believe me."

Charley fell silent then, and it seemed to Soong he should reply, at least acknowledge Charley's words. "I believe you, Charley," he found himself saying. "You did marvelously well."

They were at Charley's door before the savant spoke again. He was no longer wired. "How many enemy ships did we destroy, Admiral?" he asked.

"I don't recall. A lot more than we lost." Soong opened the door for Kennah, who wheeled Charley into their suite.

"Admiral, I am suddenly very tired," Charley said. "I'm not sure I can channel just now."

"That's fine, Charley. Take a nap. As long as you'd like. War House knows in general how the fighting went. I'll have one of the point ships let them know that you were the battle master, and that you need to rest now. I'll debrief to them later."

"Thank you, sir." Charley almost slurred the words. "Ophelia, dear, I think two hours will do. Two hours."

"Fine, Charley. Two hours."

Charley's sensor lights dimmed out.

"He's asleep now, Admiral," she said quietly. "I'll call you. Or if there is a need, you call me."

She paused, tipping her head to one side, then added: "I would not worry, Admiral, about Charley's stamina. I have never seen him unable to continue channeling. It is after he finishes that he—sometimes sags. I believe he could have conducted the battle as long as necessary, but once he disconnects, he must rest."

Soong nodded. "Thank you, Kennah," he said, then left. She'd looked and sounded tired herself. *I wonder,* he thought, *if she doesn't somehow lend energy to Charley when he needs it.*

◇

Afterward, Alvaro Soong himself felt emotionally drained, and lay down intending to nap. But found himself reviewing, instead, sorting material for his debrief. His Provo's losses had been heaviest during the brief moments of shield decay, before strange-space could be generated. All told he'd lost five battleships out of twenty-five; twelve cruisers out of seventy-five; nine corvettes out of fifty. And only eleven maces out of sixty, despite high-risk assignments; they were hard to hit, and those with layered shields, hard to kill. War House would make something of that.

He also had good figures on Wyzhñyñy losses, give or take a very few. Fourteen battleships, forty-two ships seemingly equivalent to cruisers, and thirty-seven others he'd lumped in his mind as miscellaneous. Proportionately his own losses had been far heavier than the Wyzhñyñy's. But by the time he reached rendezvous, in the fringe of the Dinébikeyah System, the new battle units waiting to join him would more than make up his losses. Much more.

The Wyzhñyñy, by contrast, would get no replacements. Well, in a sense they would, because most of their warfleet hadn't actually been engaged in this fight. Call them on-site reserves; not potential future reinforcements like his own.

At any rate, his Provos, including Charley, had carried out their mission: they'd learned a lot about the Wyzhñyñy and done "substantive damage." The flip side of that being, the Wyzhñyñy had learned a lot about his Provos. He'd hardly catch them so unprepared again.

Tomorrow he and Charley would start work on how Charley might control a fleet several times as large as he'd managed today. With a sigh, Soong sat up. He really should nap on the battle experience, before debriefing to War House. Which meant stilling the thoughts that swirled in his consciousness. Buzzing sickbay, he arranged for a potent sleeping pill, then buzzed

Ophelia Kennah. Let Charley sleep as long as he needed, he told her. A few extra hours shouldn't seriously dislocate War House.

Chapter Six
Wyzhñyñy Addendum

Grand Admiral Quanshûk had gathered himself sufficiently to lead Rear Admiral Tualurog and Chief Scholar Qonits to his quarters. As always, his orderly had made the bed, cleared and washed the counter, put things away... Only his desk was as it had been, the orderly being forbidden to touch it.

The three high-ranking Wyzhñyñy stepped inside. Quanshûk closed the door behind them, then went to his desk and triggered the recording system, before stepping to his small bar. "Admiral Tualurog, what is your pleasure?"

The rear admiral named it, a product unadorned with flavorings. A fighting man's taste. Quanshûk poured two of them, the second for himself, then looked at Qonits. "The usual?"

"If you please, Grand Admiral."

Quanshûk poured him a non-alcoholic beverage. "We have finally met resistance," he said, "and I did not much care for it. They stung us sorely. But we have learned from it." He drummed clawed fingertips on the bartop.

Tualurog grunted. "The humans are cowards, afraid to stand and fight."

"It served them well," Qonits said off-handedly. "In ancient times our ancestors used hit and run attacks. It enabled them to survive, and eventually prevail."

Tualurog scowled. In his opinion, Quanshûk greatly overrated his chief scholar. _Qonits is high aristocracy, he told himself, and Quanshûk, being a snob, gives his words too much weight. Back in the empire, scholars were listened to for their knowledge, not their advice. But here the empire was beyond reach, and they were in the process of establishing a new empire. Which needed to maintain the integrity and honor that had made the old one great. In time it might prove necessary to take steps.

Quanshûk sipped, then sipped again. "What have we learned today, Tualurog?" he asked.

"One, that we must take nothing for granted. The enemy may strike when least expected. Two, in the future we must emerge and muster well out in the cometary cloud. At a distance from which our emergence waves will be too attenuated to read from the planets. Allowing us to form battle formations without disturbance. And three, we must take and hold the initiative whenever we detect the enemy."

Quanshûk nodded. "The first is self-evident. The second will slow our progress severely, but I will keep it in mind. As for the third—prepare a list of specific measures to be taken. In doing so, assume we will continue to reform in the inner fringe. And let me know of any troublesome aspects that arise."

He turned to Qonits. "What do you have to say, Chief Scholar?"

Qonits bowed, bending forelegs and torso. "Grand Admiral, we need to review and revise our tactics in general. In past wars, fleets have tended to meet in close combat, sometimes no more than a mile apart, to pour war beams and torpedos at each other until one breaks. But it seems the humans do not fight that way."

Quanshûk's lids half closed, hooding his yellow eyes. "That is not necessarily so," he said. "This time we met only a small force. Their version of skirmishers perhaps, sent to test us. When we meet their main force, its situation and tactics may be different."

He paused, sipping again, not voicing the rest of his thought: that when they met next, the humans might have the advantage of numbers. So vast an empire! Then it would be to the humans' advantage to stand and slug.

"Nonetheless," he continued, "you are right. We must review our tactics, and be prepared to counter such hit-and-run attacks. Or use them if we are ever at a numerical disadvantage."

He looked at Tualurog. "Admiral, I leave it to you, to you and shipsmind, to review our tactics and recommend changes. I also want procedures for reorganizing formations more quickly after emergence. We need to provide a better-coordinated response." He turned back to Qonits then. "Chief Scholar, I want you to rethink everything we do. And have shipsmind make a complete analysis of human psychology, in the light of their language, and of their tactics to date."

A sigh hissed from the grand admiral's lipless mouth. "And now," he said, "you are both dismissed."

<>

The two Wyzhñyñy nobles ignored each other as they left. *Analyze human psychology!* Tualurog thought. *What idiocy! We need to kill them, not analyze them.*

Analyze them, thought Qonits. *I should have done that earlier.* In fact, he realized, he had analyzed them to a degree, in conjunction with improving the translation program. But today had made it much more urgent.

<>

David and Yukiko had been anticipating Qonits' arrival; his or someone's. Earlier they'd jumped half out of their skins at the battle alarm, and twice swallowed their hearts when the Wyzhñyñy flagship had been jarred by torpedo strikes. Meanwhile the apparent firefight might have changed their situation. They might not be as well treated after this.

But Qonits knocked and identified himself as usual. "Come in!" they called, almost in unison.

Had Qonits been better able to read the nuances in human voices, he might have recognized relief. He entered, his bodyguards with blasters at port arms. *So far, so good,* David thought. To his eyes, Qonits seemed normal.

"Good day, humans," said the chief scholar. It had become his usual greeting. "I am sure you noticed the—uproar? The uproar earlier."

"It would have been impossible not to," David answered. "What happened?"

"Can you not guess?"

"There must have been a fight. Between your fleet and some of our warships. It was to be expected." Actually, only when it happened had he and Yukiko realized how little they'd expected it.

"What do you know about your people's warships?"

Qonits asked.

This time Yukiko answered. "Very little. We are not of the soldier or spacer classes. Perhaps captives from one of them could tell you something."

"But you know about ships."

"Not warships," David said. "Not weapon systems."

Probably, Qonits told himself, *they actually* are_*poorly informed on warfare.* They'd have some general knowledge of it, but clearly they were not of the warrior gender. Or "class" as they called it. He could not imagine people like these carrying out so daring and fierce an attack. *I may know more about their warships and tactics than they do.*

"You didn't tell us whether we were right," Yukiko put in. "Was it a small fight? It didn't seem long enough to be a full-scale battle."

"Quite small. Your people fought well, but there were far too few of them."

"Ah." David nodded thoughtfully. "A scout group, feeling you out."

"Feeling out? What is feeling out?" Qonits thought he understood, but preferred not to make assumptions.

"To feel out is to test. See how you respond; how easy you'll be, or how difficult."

Yukiko nodded. "If they learned enough this time, maybe next time they'll launch a fleet attack."

David looked around nervously. "Maybe it will come soon. Maybe the main fleet is nearby."

"Or perhaps..." Yukiko began, then stopped.

"Continue."

"Perhaps they plan to contest your conquest of this system. I suppose you were in F-space during the fight. So you must have been in some star system."

"Yes, we were, we are, in F-space. But your ships have fled away. Those not destroyed."

"Perhaps the next system then," David suggested absently.

Qonits frowned. "Your rulers—" he said thoughtfully. "Are they elected by all the nobles? Or only by the high nobles?"

Yukiko actually laughed. "Neither," she said. "They're elected by all adults."

Loosely speaking, it was true.

◇

Qonits didn't stay long, and left thoughtfully.

Chapter Seven
Battlefield Proxies

Paddy Davies' corner office was too small for a quorum meeting of the Peace Council. So the utility room, used for coffee breaks, all-hands briefings etc., had been cleaned up. Thermal coffee mugs had been set at twelve places, while cookies and assorted raw veggies occupied trays and bowls.

The council members were from several continents, and usually convened via the Ether. But not this time. Günther Genovesi, the Peace Front's attorney, treasury secretary, and sometime emergency financier, had called for this meeting, insisting it be live. And the entire suite boasted effective anti-snooping equipment. So the complete council was there except for Francesca Yoshinori, currently being held without bond on weapons charges, in Concepción, in the Chilean Autonomy. Her proxy on the council was Yolanda Guzman.

Jaromir Horvath rapped the gavel plate. "Günther asked for this meeting," Horvath said, "so I'll turn it over to him." He paused, then added drily, "He didn't confide in me, beyond telling me it has to do with membership and finances." Laying the gavel down, he turned to the heavy, Levantine-looking man to his left, the one council member who was truly wealthy. "The chair is yours, Günther."

Genovesi stood, and got down to business without acknowledging Horvath's comments. "I asked for this meeting for three reasons. First, you're aware that over the past eleven months, our membership has declined by eighteen percent. The reduction in income is troublesome, but even more troublesome is the weakening of leverage caused by our decline. Not that we've publicized it, but none of you is naive enough to suppose the government doesn't know.

"Second, and much more important, we've had no significant effect on the war plans of this government. We need to discuss changes in strategy. New ideas.

"And third—" Finally he looked at Horvath. "Third, we

need a change of leadership. Yaro, you are the chairman and cofounder of the Peace Front, and more to the point, you've been our chief theorist and strategist. But when an organization needs to grow—in size, influence and results—and instead shrinks..." Genovesi shrugged. "It's time to change leaders."

He scanned the men and women sitting around the long table. No one shook their head, not even Horvath, who hadn't changed expression. "I will not," Genovesi continued, "propose someone for the chairmanship yet. But keep the matter in mind while we discuss this lamentable decline. This failure."

He turned to a stocky, militant-looking woman. "Kuei-Fei, give us your thoughts on the matter."

Kuei-Fei the complainer, Horvath told himself. He'd never gotten along with her. She wanted his chairmanship, and no doubt Moneybags would see that she got it. As for himself— he'd be better off rid of it.

He could taste the bile rising in his gorge.

She got to her feet and began. "The basic strategy has been wrong," she said, "based almost entirely on demonstrations that only a small fraction of the population could get to, take part in. Seen on the telly or holo, they draw attention. And sometimes new members, too many of whom later leave because there is no active role for them. No role most of them could afford."

Or because, Horvath thought, *between the media and the government, they end up convinced by stories of more and more human worlds conquered by murdering aliens.*

It was Paddy Davies who interrupted the woman. "And what would *you* have us do?" he asked. "Mind you, I'm not challenging what you say. I'm asking for examples."

She scowled, not trusting his disclaimer. "An example? We publicized the African bee project, and staged demonstrations against it in over forty cities. But few attended except for the demonstrators and the media. Those who watched, watched at home, safe from involvement. Most of them thought the bees were a good idea. Even most mainstream Gaians approved."

Horvath scowled. *What do you expect when a movement goes mainstream?* he thought. But beneath the thought lay a realization—that without the mainstream, their job was impossible. They needed to capture the mainstream, turn it against its government masters.

"But suppose..." Kuei-Fei went on, "suppose we'd arranged to have African bees collected? Whole colonies. And had them released in major cities here on Terra? Then people would have looked differently at the bee project."

When she paused, Horvath had his chance. "They'd have looked differently at *us,*" he growled. "We'd have multiplied our enemies ten-fold, to no good purpose."

Coloring, she went grimly on. "Our demonstrations over capturing and murdering Wyzhñyñy colonists backfired; another poorly chosen issue. People considered the dead marines heroes, and resented our calling them murderous kidnappers who'd endangered any possible negotiations. And even though the dead Wyzhñyñy won't be seen on Terra for months, word that they're being brought here for display and study has weakened those of our allies who claim the invasion is a hoax. Meanwhile, Paddy's public proposal to negotiate—invite the Wyzhñyñy to settle on worlds not already colonized—was lost sight of in the bombast and furor of the demonstrations."

She turned to Paddy. "The media prefer a show to ideas, but without the show, it's the ideas they'd feature."

"And what would you think," Paddy said, "of printing fliers with our main arguments? Given in simple statements, catchy aphorisms. And passing them out to the demonstrators, with instructions to use them if questioned by the media. They always question demonstrators."

She nodded. Her face remained severe, but when she spoke again, her tone was milder. "That might be useful, if the ideas in the fliers are clearly tied to the matter being protested."

Horvath interrupted again, getting to his feet. His tone was domineering, but short of scornful. "You tell us our basic strategy is wrong, then you veer off into talking about tactics. What *strategy* should we follow?"

She locked eyes with him. "A strategy that grows out of one basic fact: We have nothing to lose, Horvath. Nothing except possibly our lives and liberty. If our goals are worthwhile—if *peace* is worthwhile!—we've got to go all out. Take risks! Considering the time factor, and the direction things are going, BIG risks!" Her words had been growing louder, more combative. Now they slowed, softened. "You've been a fighter all your life, Yaro. You led student rebels against university administrators before you were twenty, and got expelled. Four years later you led blue collar technicians against ISUTA schedule controls, and your people lost jobs. Then you learned to work within the system, learned to compromise without ever giving up. Learned to keep the pressure on, educating, politicking, building inside and outside support, but always pushing. Going for the best compromise possible, and more often than not getting more than anyone thought you could."

Horvath watched her narrowly. *What's your point, woman?* he wondered.

Her eyes had never given way as she spoke. Now she examined the nails on her right hand, fingers curled and palm up, like a man. Her voice became reflective. "You developed an operating style that worked for you." She paused. "And you brought it with you when you started the Front."

Again she met his eyes. "But this is not a labor dispute, or a political dispute, or an environmental or economic dispute." Her voice intensified. "It is a war against war, Yaro, and we need to fight it differently. Find the enemy's greatest weakness, and attack it. Regardless of risk, because the stakes are *so* great, and time is against us."

She looked around the table. "Many voices have urged the government to declare martial law, but Chang and Peixoto have refused. Because they're smarter and more far-sighted than those who've pressed them for it. They appreciate that the people *hate* martial law. For more than ninety years our ancestors lived under it! Generations never knew anything else! Meanwhile they watched their technical infrastructure erode, saw their physical-biological environment degraded to a point where it seemed almost beyond recovery. After all these centuries it's still not completely recovered."

She stopped, standing silent, clenched jaw jutting, eyes hard, and let them wait till it seemed someone would surely burst out, demanding she finish. Then she spoke again. "We need to create a campaign that will force them to declare martial law. A campaign of acts by individuals and small groups. Of violence. Of destruction." She paused for emphasis. "And of assassinations. Aimed at the most egregious, or most heinous, or most corrupt government war action we can find. At the same time risking a backlash against us. And there *will* be one."

Then she sat down. No one applauded. No one even said "hear hear!" For another dozen seconds the room was silent. Finally Genovesi spoke. "Well. That's said. Now we need to look at what issue or issues to use as a focus, a target, for that serious violence. Which is what it will take to bring about martial law."

◇

Guzman suggested accusing the government of planning to use neutron bombs. The nuclear strikes in the Hitler War; the brief and suicidal, nuclear religious war of the 21st century; and finally the cynical neutron bombings of the Troubles, had made nuclear weapons—nuclear technology of any sort—anathema in the Commonwealth. It was the deadliest accusation possible.

Paddy Davies was adamant against it. "If we make such a claim," he said, "we'll need plausible evidence. *Plausible* evidence! Considering the seriousness of the charge, the public will demand it. *I'd* demand it. And in all our gathering and winnowing of information and gossip, we've found no whiff of that or any other nuclear plans." Then Horvath stood, guaranteeing it would backfire, and Kuei-Fei pointed out that there wasn't even an infrastructure to provide the means for such a program. When Genovesi called the question, not even Guzman voted for it.

Afterward, discussion became listless, the proposals feeble and unpromising. Then Genovesi suggested that if crimes against Wyzhñyñy didn't seem to resonate with the public, crimes against humans might.

We've already plowed that ground," Horvath said.

"Not all of it," Kuei-Fei countered. "We can attack the newly leaked loosening in military bot agreements! Loosening designed to shanghai the wounded out of their bodies!" They were, she felt, nothing short of outrageous: Reduced eligibility standards for the wounded. Battlefield proxies authorized to "speak for the unconscious wounded." The use of a stasis drug to prolong the survival of the mortally wounded till they could be bottled. Bottled and thrown back into the shame of battle, instead of peacefully joining with the All Soul. And as an issue, it came with built-in support: some mainstream media had already criticized these changes as designed to allow abuses.

The discussion wasn't enthusiastic, but before lunch they'd approved the issue without dissent.

After lunch they discussed and voted on a change of leadership: previously, the chairman had worn the policy and planning hats, and the vice-chairman the operations hat. That was now changed. Günther Genovesi was elected chief executive officer, which included chairing meetings. Kuei-Fei Wu became planning officer. Jaromir Horvath accepted the post of whip; he would make sure people did what they'd agreed to. And Paddy Davies would be public relations director.

Of the old "big three," only Fritjof Ignatiev continued in his previous post—the Voice of the Front. Its orator.

Fritjof Ignatiev, a dedicated soldier of peace, who bore no management responsibilities and wanted none. He was not very intelligent, and remarkably enough realized the fact.

Chapter Eight
New Jerusalem:
Encounter in Space

Vice Admiral Carmen Apraxin-DaCosta had been born with more than her share of intellectual and leadership potential, and grew up in a family tradition of service in the fleet. Even as the fleet shrank to become a simulated fleet, existing in the real world as no more than light squadrons sent to hunt pirates. A remote ancestor had been Fleet Admiral Gavril Apraxin, who'd served during the Troubles. Hero of the Lesser Congeries, and post-mortem scapegoat of the *President Akiro* disaster.

In childhood she'd pretended—believed?—she was that remote progenitor, reincarnated—the sort of thing children often play at mentally—but she never thought of it anymore. She was Carmen Apraxin-DaCosta, with her own life to live and her own career to fashion. Things she'd done conspicuously well.

On her flagship the *Uinta,* her attention was on something much more urgent. She'd just emerged from her closing jump to the New Jerusalem System, and shipsmind had promptly reported an alien pentagonal battle group—the Wyzhñyñy system defense force—also in the inner fringe, only 189 million miles away. At the same time, shipsmind tagged each enemy spacecraft by its complex electronic signature, each a composite of several system signatures. It wasn't as definitive as fingerprints, but between overhauls it was reliable.

Shipsmind had also registered the Wyzhñyñy's small planetary guard flotilla, parked only 90,000 miles off New Jerusalem. It was large enough to be seriously dangerous to a planetary assault, but far too small to threaten her task force. She'd ignore it till she'd dealt with the more potent system defense force.

Meanwhile she ordered the planetary assault force to generate warpspace and head insystem, getting it out of what she hoped would prove the primary danger zone. Sending one of her three battle groups as escort. She hardly considered moving against the system defense force. Almost surely it wasn't where it seemed to be, or wouldn't be for long. Because shipsmind hadn't registered it in realtime; the finite speed of light got in the way. Given the distance, her current read showed it as it had been seventeen minutes earlier. So she would wait.

She was right; ten minutes later the aliens disappeared from her screens. They were nearly seven minutes underway, almost surely headed for either her main force or New Jerusalem, presumably the first.

She presumed correctly. In just six minutes they appeared abruptly in F-space, but not all in one place. Their commander realized he was seriously outnumbered, so his battle group emerged as five subgroups, in five locations around the human perimeter. Each subgroup consisted of a battleship, with a screen of what Apraxin thought of as cruisers and corvettes.

It was a far more favorable tactical situation than Spanish Soong had faced, and Apraxin was ready with more than shields. Six weeks earlier, via savant, Soong had sent Charley Gordon's detailed suggestions and instructions. Afterward she'd spent several days with her AI chief, programing and installing it all in *Uinta*'s shipsmind. That had been followed by weeks of simdrills, as she rode hyperspace toward the New Jerusalem system. They'd emerged in F-space 280 billion miles from New Jerusalem, for an astrogational read and to re-form formations. While there she'd uploaded Charley's "export" system to her fighting ships; it was designed for use without Charley at the helm. Then they'd done simdrills together.

Everyone was enthused with the new battle system, with the admiral less expectant than most. Simulation was simulation. Reality was reality.

<>

Almost at the instant they emerged from warpspace, the Wyzhñyñy launched an all-out attack. But except for selecting their opening gambit, they left their actions entirely to their battlecomps, coordinated by their flagship's battlecomp. Even against Apraxin's superior force, that opening gambit provided an initial advantage. But the twists and turns of battle required better extrapolations and coordination than the Wyzhñyñy flagship provided. Apraxin's Liberation Task Force won decisively. Of the ten battleships she'd committed, seven survived, along with twenty-three of thirty cruisers and thirteen of twenty corvettes. During the battle, several Wyzhñyñy ships had ducked back into warpspace, and not all had returned to resume action. When it was over, *Uinta*'s shipsmind "accounted" for them all, based on their signatures. When last seen, those not definitely accounted for had already been rated seriously damaged, and were probably no longer functional, lost irretrievably in hyperspace.

It appeared to be a wipeout, but Apraxin accepted her success guardedly. The purpose of the Wyzhñyñy's system defense force had surely been to protect their colony from incursions. And given that purpose, if she'd been the Wyzhñyñy admiral, she'd have broken off contact as soon as it became apparent her force would otherwise be wiped out. She'd have disappeared into warpspace with what she had left, to begin a guerrilla campaign, harassing and bleeding the human invaders. In fact, that kind of warfare had been her greatest worry—hers and War House's.

That the Wyzhñyñy admiral had pressed his attack till his force had been destroyed was suspicious. What had she missed? What ace had he hidden under the table? Or did he simply lack flexibility? She'd keep her force alert.

Meanwhile her principle concern had to be a successful planetary assault. Commodore Kereenyaga, in charge of the assault flotilla, had been a classmate of hers at the Academy, and graduated with honors. While Vice Admiral Ver Hoeven, in charge of the escort, was an excellent officer. Each knew his job. She knew next to nothing about the Sikh general in charge of the ground forces, but she had confidence in War House's personnel judgements. He'd at least be competent.

She turned her attention to the real-time view on the bridge's central screen: myriads of stars against bottomless black. *Serenely beautiful and utterly deadly,* she told herself, *a sort of Uma and Kali dichotomy.* But the dangers of the universe tended to be passive: vacuum, stellar temperatures, abrupt gravitational gradients…and to varying degrees were predictable and avoidable. Sophonts like *Homo sapiens,* using observation and imagination, developed systems of avoidances and protections within which they could live, grow, and explore quite nicely. Most of the time.

But within those safeguards, the powers of imagination and knowledge that provided them could also spring all sorts of deadly surprises on competing or disliked sophonts—of one's own life form or others.

◇

Jilchûk shu-Tosk was both gosthodar and commanding general on what had been New Jerusalem. Just now he was peering intently at his wall screen, which showed a representation of the local solar system. Orbits were indicated by fine lines. The primary was near the bottom, and several planets were shown at various removes. All out of scale, the separations greatly reduced. "Jiluursôk"—the name the Wyzhñyñy had given New Jerusalem—was centered near the bottom.

"There, my lord," said his aide. Near the top, where the captain's light arrow pointed, a redness pulsed. *It looks like a small red cloud,* thought the gosthodar, *a spray of blood.*

The aide thumbed a projection, and a small window framed the redness, then expanded to occupy the entire screen. The spray of blood became a ragged formation of ships; 127 of them according to the read-out. Reducing the separations further showed each ship marked by the icon of a Wyzhñyñy warship class appropriate to its mass.

The gosthodar did not for a moment doubt what he was looking at: an alien task force, outnumbering and presumably outgunning the system defense force. *Humans* they called themselves, according to the grand admiral's chief scholar. It was satisfying to have a name for them.

"When did they emerge?" he asked.

The pointer indicated a digital event-time posted unchangingly in a lower corner. "There, sir: 023.61."

The gosthodar looked, then moved his gaze to the familiar

real-time read in an upper corner. "Hmm. Less than five minutes ago. Well done, Captain." He pressed a key, and his amplified voice boomed unexpectedly from every speaker in every office, barracks, barn, work place, vehicle, infirmary, armory…on the planet. "An unidentified fleet has arrived in the near fringe," he announced. "It is presumed hostile. All personnel will carry out their Procedure One duties immediately."

In his mind he imagined the groans. Most would think it a needless drill. "Supervisors will ensure full compliance," he continued. "Anyone who fails to properly complete their checklist on schedule will be assigned to a penal platoon." *There,* he thought. *Now they'll take it seriously.*

He'd visited the great limestone caves right after they'd been discovered, and had seen their potential at once. As soon as their refugees had been rooted out, he'd assigned the necessary resources to make them accessible and habitable. "Captain," he said, "see to the transfer of my personal goods. I will stay here till my emergency headquarters has been activated."

The captain saluted sharply. "Yes, General!" he said, and left. *This,* thought Jilchûk, *will be interesting.*

Like all his tribe, he'd never fought in a battle. Now he would command one. The cleansing of this world had been quick and easy, and his warriors had been disappointed. Not that they'd complained; that would be inappropriate. But he knew his genders and their psychology, the warriors especially. Now they'd get their wish.

The gosthodar didn't worry about the enemy war fleet 900 million miles away. That was Admiral Zhokdos's responsibility. His immediate concern was the enemy's bombards that even now must be moving insystem in warpdrive. When they emerged, of course, they'd have to deal with Commodore Xarsku's planetary defense group, but even so, the humans might have a bombard overhead by nightfall. His defense forces needed to be underground or widely dispersed by then.

To prepare for a possible counter-invasion was standard procedure, and he'd begun while his warriors were still mopping up the scattered surviving natives. With the swarm still in the planning stage, he'd requested a full division of warriors. They'd given him a brigade; in times of swarming, warriors of fighting age were always in short supply. If he'd asked for a brigade, they'd have given him two battalions. Three at most, and reminded him he'd have some 65,000 colonists of other genders, all of military age, all well-trained for war.

But they were not warriors.

On the other hand he doubted the humans even had a warrior gender. If they did, there'd have been some sign of them. And while the sophonts here had been enduring and elusive, they'd also been primitive, and definitely not warriors.

<>

Major General Pyong Pak Singh, and his operations aide, Major Etienne Stuart Singh, watched the action from sixteen miles up. The command compartment of the HQC-1—his armored command floater—had split-screen monitors showing the New Jerusalem surface. One window displayed a real view, magnified to show the details he wanted. The other showed a military map, generated by his shipsmind from real-time sensor data, with a window locating the real-view scene on the map.

So far his own people were not involved. His troops—even his aerial units—were still aboard their transports, parked some four hundred miles out. Apraxin's main force had destroyed the Wyzhñyñy system defense force in the near fringe, and one of her battle groups provided cover against a small planetary defense flotilla hiding in warpspace.

The planetary assault force had already begun pounding the Wyzhñyñy on the ground. Pak could see where a "Dragon"—a heavy bombardment ship—had stomped what once had been major Wyzhñyñy installations. Leaving fine rubble and bare ground, churned in places, seared in others. That phase was over now. Two marine "wolf packs"—squadrons of heavy, "Dire Wolf" ground-support floaters—were down there raising hell with Wyzhñyñy armor hiding in the woods, plus whatever Wyzhñyñy aircraft they could find.

He'd locked the real-view scene on one of the wolf packs, following it. It was guided by two newly placed surveillance buoys 360 miles out, protected from ordinary target locks by electronic gnomes, and from ground-launched rockets by riding constantly changing, randomly generated coordinates. (The Wyzhñyñy buoys had been clinkered, to sink, then free-fall as they lost their residual AG.)

He'd seen one Dire Wolf destroyed by ground fire. Radio traffic reported two others downed. The marines' good services came at a price.

His waiting troops, he supposed, were getting restless. Some no doubt eager to experience action, use their hard-earned skills. They *were* young. Others just wanting to get the waiting over with. He was in no hurry to land them. Let the wolf packs finish off all the Wyzhñyñy armor and air units they could find. Apparently the Wyzhñyñy didn't have concealment screens. His own concealment-screen generator had been delivered barely before he'd left Lüneburger's World.

It had occurred to him that military technology was restricted by more than the limits of science. Culture and history entered in—what your philosophies allowed, especially religious philosophies; to what degree creative imagination and innovation were given play; who you'd fought, and when, and under what circumstances.

If there's a technological mismatch down there, he thought, *I hope it's in our favor.* He especially hoped the aliens didn't have nuclear weapons. He was reasonably sure Admiral Apraxin didn't. That even the Commonwealth didn't.

Chapter Nine
The Ground War Begins

"We'll let them come to us, and show us what they've got." That's what General Pak was supposed to have said, or words to that effect.

1st Battalion had moved into position in the middle of the night, and the Jerries, with their trenching tools, had dug like badgers. (What Jerries knew as "badgers" weighed upwards of forty pounds, and dug out any whelping dens they found, whatever lived there.) In the forest edge, the top two feet of soil was thick with tree roots that had to be cut first, but once through that, Esau and Jael had really made the dirt fly. Made a foxhole to be proud of! Eight feet long and six deep, with the required firing step. Then he'd built a little roof over one end— sections of young trees, overlaid with bark he'd stripped from a large tree, covering it all with dirt from the hole. At the other end were three dirt steps they could use to get out in a hurry. He'd driven long stakes into the bottom, to keep the steps from breaking down.

Now they stood on the firing step, waiting. Behind him, wilderness stretched all the way to the Ice Sea. He'd seen it on a monitor, while riding down in the shuttles; a view he'd never imagined when he'd lived on this world. In front of him was a broad field, way bigger than any he'd seen before on New Jerusalem. Green with some crop he didn't recognize— something the Wyzhñyñy had brought with them. About knee high just now.

The Wyzhñyñy didn't farm the way his people had, who needed lots of woods for each farm. In the older settled districts the rule was, at least one acre of woods for every three or four acres of field and pasture, depending on fertility. Enough to grow back, each year, all the wood you cut that year. Trees needed for building-logs, and for splitting out planks, roof shakes, and everything else needed. But especially for firewood, to take you through the long winters—a pile the size of the house. And logs and poles for fence rails. His dad had said about 8,000 rails for forty acres, plus replacements.

Esau didn't doubt the number. He'd sawed and chopped and split enough just in his own few years. But the Wyzhñyñy had cleared away the farm woodlots. Didn't need them, apparently. Seemed they liked open ground best.

Ordinarily, Esau preferred to meet trouble at least halfway, but it was a mile or so across to the next good cover. It was hilly over there—maybe sinkhole country—not suited for farming. They'd been told it was where the Wyzhñyñy would attack from. He sure as heck wouldn't want to cross a half mile of open ground with people shooting at him.

What he and his folks were waiting for was a whole new level of trouble. And a chance to learn what they were up against before they went charging into something. Even after Pastor Lüneburger's World, where they'd trained and trained, supposedly doing everything they'd do here. Done it by day and by night, in heat and in cold, hungry, wet, and sleepless.

But two main things were different: on Lüneburger's they hadn't killed anyone, and nobody'd tried to kill them.

Excepting Moses Wheeler, who'd murdered poor Spieler—shot him from behind—and the miserable dog turds back on Terra that'd sabotaged batches of stuff. Grenade detonators, power slugs...and parasails, particularly Isaiah Vernon's. "Sabotage." It'd been a new word to Esau. Sergeant Hawkins said it was supposed to be done with now. Things got inspected in the making, the packing, and the shipping, and the "saboteurs"—the people to blame—got caught and put in jail.

Now the getting ready was over. Somewhere off across that field was a whole army of Wyzhñyñy, wanting to kill all the human beings they could. Including himself. They'd already disappeared the seventy percent of the human beings that chose to stay. They'd included just about all the older folks, and most of the younger with families of children.

And not satisfied with killing everyone, they'd knocked down and burnt every building, their foundation stones cracked and scattered. Or so the army said.

When he'd been a child, Speaker Motley had taught them the Testaments. And one thing he'd stressed was that the Lord God claimed all vengeance for himself alone. *Which doesn't leave much for us,* Esau told himself. But it seemed to him the Lord wouldn't hold it against him for feeling satisfaction whenever his blaster cut down a Wyzhñyñy. And he intended to cut down a lot of them.

<>

Standing beside her husband, Jael Wesley thought not of killing but of dying. Not morbidly or fearfully though. In his *Book of Contemplations,* Elder Hofer had described Heaven as a place of perfect justice and grace and love. In the lowest realm of Heaven—what some called Purgatory—angels helped the newly dead confront the wrongs they'd done, and those done to them. Helped them learn to truly forgive, themselves as well as others, with complete responsibility and love, till they became angels themselves. Then they moved higher, learning from more experienced angels of the splendors of Heaven's higher realms, growing in godliness, readying themselves to join the archangels.

She'd never been able to envision what it would be like, but it seemed fitting, and she had no doubt it was true. Some did doubt. She'd had it in strictest confidence from a girlhood friend who'd doubted. Miriam had stayed behind during the evacuation, and was almost surely long-since murdered. Doubt had been a burden to Miriam, but Jael was sure her friend was in Heaven. Knew it without question. Miriam had always treated people with love, except sometimes her wretched brother, who bedemoned her whenever the notion took him. He'd be dead now too, unless he left in one of the evacuation ships.

It'll be interesting to die, Jael thought. But she was in no hurry. A person was born to live their life as best they could. Live it through, and die when it came time. She smiled. Her time was not yet. She and Esau were supposed to have children, bring them up in love, send them on their way with joy, and see her grandchildren through their childhood. Being a man, Esau had the advantage there. On New Jerusalem, pregnancy and childbirth taxed a woman sorely, and not many lived to see their grandchildren grow up. She would though; loving and spoiling them. She felt sure of it.

◇

Isaiah Vernon waited in the forest shade. The day was warm, and the breeze that rustled the leaves overhead didn't visit down among the trunks. Sitting in the shade meant his cooling system didn't have to work hard.

They'd arrived near the end of the season known as "greening," when the new growth was burgeoning, and thunder showers were most frequent. *We're lucky the weather was good when the marine squadrons were doing their work,* he told himself. The rumor was, today would be the day the Wyzhñyñy would attack. Then he'd learn what war was really like, and whether they—organics, bots, the army—were as good as they needed to be.

Probably more than anyone in the division, it seemed to him, he had a perspective on being killed. Been tested, proved, and come through cleanly, to be reprieved almost after the fact.

He looked back to their first months in training. The prospect of killing had begun troubling him sorely. He'd known the stories of Joshua, David, Judas Maccabeus and others who'd won victories for the Lord. Fighting, killing, being killed. Without them, the worship of Jehovah probably would have died out, and the Hebrews as a people might easily have disappeared, ceased to exist. Then there'd have been no Jesus. But at least *some* of those Hebrew heroes had been harsh ruthless men, lacking the love that Jesus came to teach. Strange men to serve the Lord. And what of the sixth commandment? "Thou shalt not kill!"

Some said that didn't apply to the Wyzhñyñy; that they had no souls. Isaiah didn't believe that for a minute. Except for the number of limbs, they were too much like human beings. Like the Assyrians and Romans—human beings who didn't know Jesus.

He could have asked his questions of Speaker Spieler, but it had seemed to him the speaker would only tell him what he already knew, resolving nothing.

One hazy autumn evening at Camp Stenders, he'd taken his misgivings to Sergeant Hawkins, who'd told them to let him know if they had problems. The Sikh would have a non-Christian perspective, but Isaiah couldn't doubt his Christian compassion. And it seemed to him that what Hawkins had to say might fit with the teaching of the Lamb of God.

He could remember that evening clearly and in detail. It wasn't so far back, if you didn't count the time in stasis on the way to New Jerusalem, but it seemed longer than it was. That was before his body'd been killed—before he'd wakened in a bot body. There'd been a knee-high railing protecting the little patch of lawn in front of the orderly room. He and Sergeant Hawkins had sat down on it in the thickening dusk, and he'd described his problem.

After he'd finished, he'd waited. Sergeant Hawkins had sat gazing northwestward, where the dark gray sky was smudged with the last dusky red of sunset. Had sat there for perhaps a minute without talking. When finally he spoke, it was quietly. "Yeah, I can see how that might trouble you. Try this out for fit. The human species has all kinds of people, right?"

"Yessir."

"Some of them are pretty good people, but don't have much tolerance for those who openly disagree with them. They might be good friends—even fiercely loyal friends—but they're intolerant. Do you know people like that?"

Isaiah had smiled. "It sounds like my older brother. Father was at wit's end sometimes, when Peter got in fights. Started fights! All in the service of what he thought of as right. Peter must have averaged a fight a week. I don't think father had ever been in a fight in his life."

He hadn't been in one himself, he realized. Not even close. He'd never thought about that before.

"So your father was more—Christ-like than your brother?"

Isaiah chuckled ruefully. "I'd say so. Yes."

"So if the Lord was going to choose one of them to fight a battle…"

"But the Lord doesn't *need* someone to fight for him! He's God! He can do whatever he pleases." Even as he said it though, Isaiah realized how many Bible stories—Old Testament stories—told of God sending men to fight his battles.

"True, as far as it goes," Hawkins replied. "But I'm thirty-one years old, and I haven't seen much evidence of God taking direct personal action in human conflicts. Looking back at history, I can name a number of powerful rulers—let alone other people—who did terrible things over many years. In the twentieth century alone there were two rulers each of whom executed millions of people, or starved them to death. And caused the deaths of millions more in what came to be called the Hitler War. If God was inclined to act personally, surely he'd have stopped them. Sent down a bolt of lightning to fry them, or just not let them choose to do such things.

"Instead, one of them, named Hitler, decided he wanted to conquer the other one, named Stalin. So he invaded Stalin's country, the biggest country on Terra. And Stalin gradually wore him down. It was a world-wide war, with most nations involved on one side or the other, but Hitler couldn't have been stopped if it hadn't been for Stalin, who was probably as evil as he was."

Hawkins paused, pursing his lips thoughtfully. It seemed to Isaiah his sergeant wasn't really sorting his thoughts. More like he was figuring how to put them.

"So I don't think God acts directly," the sergeant said at last. "I think he lets humans of good will work things out the best they can. At least that's what Gopal Singh taught. In the case of Hitler and Stalin, there were two other powerful rulers, named Churchill and Roosevelt, who helped Stalin when he most needed it. Even though they both knew and feared Stalin, too. But stopping Hitler seemed more urgent."

The names had meant nothing to Isaiah. Terran history hadn't been taught on New Jerusalem, only some of the lessons learned from it. He wondered if Elder Hofer had learned some of them from the Hitler War. He must have known about it; he'd lived back in the 21st and 22nd centuries. Back before ever his people emigrated.

Sergeant Hawkins had grinned at him then. "I got carried away talking," he said. "What was your question again?"

"Uh… About killing. It feels like a sin to me, war or not, and I'm supposed to do a lot of it when we get back to New Jerusalem." He'd paused. "And I'm not sure I can do it."

"Umm. As a child, did you ever do anything wrong?"

"Yes I did, but mostly in my mind. I got angry more often than anyone suspected. A time or two I even cursed. Within the privacy of my mind, I even did acts of violence and lust. But never in physical action, except the sin of Onan, and even in my mind probably not as much as lots of folks. I believe I was born with a softness of spirit."

Again the sergeant had chuckled. "In Sikh schools we're taught that Jesus of Nazareth said 'you must be born again' to see the kingdom of God. In the Gopal Singh Dispensation, we believe that people really are born again. Again and again, mostly not recalling our earlier lives. Born again to live in all kinds of circumstances, good and bad. Male and female. Sometimes doing really cruel things, and gradually developing a sense of responsibility for them. Until in time we learn not to do them anymore. Except in extreme situations, like some wars." He grinned at Isaiah. "It's my impression that you're an old experienced soul, who just now happens to be wearing a young body."

Isaiah's thoughts returned to the now, and he looked down at his new body. His bot body: large, hard, and fearfully strong. If he were inclined to violence, it would be a terrible body. But maybe violence *was* all right, in the service of God.

That wasn't what Sergeant Hawkins had been leading up to though, because he'd gone on speaking. "There are souls of all ages," he'd said. "All a part of the One, some call it the Tao, others the All Soul. You say God. And mostly, I suspect— mostly it's younger souls who take up the sword, for good or bad. During the Hitler War, I suspect the generals on both sides were mostly souls who'd lived enough lives to feel sure of themselves, but not enough to be seriously troubled by killing. Bad men and good men, but none of them Christlike."

Isaiah had frowned thoughtfully. "Jesus got mad once," he said. "Violent. He shouted at the money changers in the temple, tipped their tables over and ran them out."

"Well then," the sergeant had said, "you've answered your question yourself, haven't you?"

He'd nodded, but not very confidently. It had seemed—still seemed—there was more to it than that. "I guess I pretty much have," he'd answered.

Hawkins had laughed, a friendly, sympathetic sound. "We're human beings. Strictly speaking, there's not too much we *can* be entirely sure of. Not even those of us who feel absolutely sure. But the One doesn't hate us or punish us for making mistakes. We do what seems right to us, make our mistakes as many times as necessary, and learn from them."

The sergeant had gotten up then. "I guess we've looked at your question about as well as we can right now," he'd said. "Sooner or later we'll get it solved, maybe on New Jerusalem, or maybe between lives."

They'd separated then, Isaiah going to the hut. He'd told Sergeant Hawkins things he'd couldn't have dreamed of telling anyone before. When he'd been eleven New Jerusalem years old, his father had taken him aside and spoke to him about the sin of Onan, and told him that in God's eyes it was a very small transgression, when done privately. As if to set his mind at ease. But he'd never expected to tell anyone about it; surely not till he had a son of his own.

Maybe the sergeant didn't know what the sin of Onan was; probably he didn't. But even if he did, it had seemed to Isaiah the sergeant wouldn't think ill of him for it.

He remained a little uncomfortable with what his sergeant had said about living a whole string of lives though. It seemed—heretical. But Jesus *had* said "you must be born again." It seemed there was more than one way of taking that. And in a way, it kind of fitted with some of the things Elder Hofer had taught. Though he didn't think Elder Hofer would much like the idea.

During the months since then, it seemed to Isaiah that

somehow or other that conversation had defanged the issue of killing Wyzhñyñy, because it no longer really troubled him. He still wondered now and then—maybe feeling a little discomfort—but it didn't *plague* him now.

A sudden booming snagged his attention. Artillery fire. The surveillance buoys had reported that the Wyzhñyñy had quite a bit of artillery left, here and there. Probably hidden from the Dragons. The army didn't much use artillery, unless you counted field mortars and tanks. Mostly it depended on aerial attack to deliver destruction behind hills and the like. He wondered if War House was going to regret that.

Then his lieutenant's voice spoke in his sensorium. "Load up, men. Time to get your feet wet."

To Isaiah, the command produced a sensation like he'd felt when they'd loaded on the floater for their first parachute jump: a sinking feeling in the belly, even though he didn't have a belly any longer. As his long metallic legs strode up the ramp of an APF, he heard the artillery's followup sound: the crashing of shells much nearer than the guns that fired them.

Lord God, he prayed silently, *let me do what is right in your eyes.*

<>

When the booming reached Esau Wesley, he knew what to expect. Actually he knew and he didn't. Live fire exercises, with the rush of rounds passing overhead, and buried explosives simulating shell bursts, had given them a notion of it, but they weren't the same thing. He realized that before the first rounds struck. Stepping down from the firing step, he crouched in the bottom of the foxhole, Jael beside him. *This is it!* he thought. *The games are over!* The thunder of howitzers told him; that and Jael's wide eyes, and Captain Mulvaney's calm voice in his ears.

Then the shells arrived, the noise indescribable. Many exploded in the treetops. Wood and shell fragments whirred and whistled, thudded and slapped. Dirt flew, hissing. The couple ducked under their little roof. The ground shook, and now Esau was glad for all the tough woody roots; they helped keep their foxhole from caving in on them. Jael's eyes were no longer wide. They squinted, perhaps against flying dirt, perhaps in response to the noise, the violence.

He read her lips. "Blessed Jesus," she murmured, then said nothing more. The shells kept arriving, roaring. After the first salvo, they arrived more irregularly. Along the line, the sound was a steady roar, but the nearer explosions were sometimes overlapping, sometimes single. Esau spit dirt. Heard a scream. A tree crashed down. "Medic!" someone cried. Captain Mulvaney's voice spoke in his ear, in his skull: "Listen up, B Company. They're sending out armor—tanks and APCs. Stay down, ready on my command. Blastermen, fix bayonets."

As squad leader, Esau was no longer its slammerman. He slipped his bayonet over the studs of his blaster barrel and clamped it firmly. Then, unable to resist, he stepped out and popped a peek over the berm. What he saw riveted his attention. The tanks, those still coming, were already halfway across, riding their AG cushions, their antipersonnel slammer pulses invisible in the sunlight. Other tanks had stopped, more or less askew. He saw one take a heavy trasher pulse and hit the ground skidding, plowing dirt. No one emerged from it. Close behind came the APCs. He became aware of Jael tugging at him, and ducked down again, staring at her. "Good lord!" he said. "What a sight!"

She did not rise up to see, simply looked anxious. Captain Mulvaney's voice spoke in their ears again. "B Company on your firing steps!" Esau stepped onto the firing step again, hardly able to restrain himself, wishing he still carried a slammer instead of just a blaster. The line of tanks, much thinned, was about a hundred yards short of the forest. An angled file of killer craft swept across the field, armored belly turrets laying trasher fire on the tanks. Which kept coming, those that could. Another file of aircraft followed. Not many tanks were left, and a number of APCs sat smoking.

"B Company, fire!" Mulvaney almost shouted it, excitement in his voice. "Give 'em hell! Wipe 'em out!"

Esau rested his blaster on the berm and sought targets. The

artillery had stopped, but Wyzhñyñy tanks continued to pump heavy trasher bolts into the forest. Wood still flew; branches and treetops still crashed down. The APCs had also thinned, and as if on signal, stopped sixty to eighty yards away. Wyzhñyñy poured from them—real Wyzhñyñy! Others, from crippled APCs, were already coming on foot, running at speeds a human couldn't hope to match, firing their blasters with a sweeping motion from what might be thought of as their waists. Esau had set his for semi-automatic. He fired aimed fire, almost every shot a mortal hit. When he paused to insert a fresh power slug, he saw Jael firing aimed fire too. She'd become skilled with the blaster—not as good as he was, but good.

All along the line, Wyzhñyñy kept coming. A running Wyzhñyñy launched himself to clear the Wesleys' foxhole, his blaster muzzle swinging toward them. It had no bayonet. Esau squeezed off a bolt that tore the Wyzhñyñy open, spraying them with fluids and tissue. The alien landed behind them in a heap. Another lay on its belly—blood flowed from its neck, red blood!—its torso upright, swinging its blaster toward them. Too high; Esau fired back as pulses passed barely overhead.

They kept coming, coming. Another flight of friendly aircraft swept the field, and another, and another, killing, but the attackers did not pause. Esau half heard fighting behind him. Those who'd broken through had been engaged by reserves.

"Trasher crews! Trasher crews!" This in a voice new to Esau. "Our own armor is moving in from the north, with camouflage fields and red pennants. Don't shoot the good guys! More Wyzhñyñy armor is coming, all of it tan."

That was nothing Esau needed to worry about. He kept firing, glad he'd started with a full bandoleer of power slugs. This wasn't likely to stop for a while.

◇

The bot APF had settled through a hole in the canopy about three hundred yards back from the forest edge, and unloaded its five-bot squad. They were somewhat back from where the shells were landing, except for the occasional long round. Their built-in radios told them the first wave of Wyzhñyñy was halfway across the field. The bots didn't immediately run to engage them. No foxholes waited to shelter them—bot tactics centered on high mobility—and they were too few to waste.

Instead they waited till the barrage stopped, then started toward the fighting at a lope. Their camouflage fields hid them better than any fabric could. Again they paused, near the end of 1st Battalion's battle line, but still back within the woods. The line was anchored by a battery of anti-armor trashers, themselves well armored. They'd waited to fire till the barrage lifted, to avoid the special attention they'd otherwise have drawn. Now they were firing trasher pulses at Wyzhñyñy tanks and APCs.

The bots stayed where they were. Sergeant Ali Al-Daiyeen was in touch with the battery CO, and with Division's G-2B, which monitored constantly the input from the surveillance buoys. The order to move would come from them.

And come it did. The battery had been flanked, with Wyzhñyñy in the woods behind it. Now the bots moved, running smoothly. A dozen or more Wyzhñyñy had sheltered behind standing and fallen trees, and were shooting at the battery, suppressing protective fire from its dug-in blastermen. Another twenty or more had begun moving along behind the Jerrie defense line, attacking foxholes with blasters and grenades.

"We'll handle them," Al-Daiyeen radioed back. "Tell your people to keep firing. We'll be fine." Then, to his squad, "Podelsky, you and I'll take the skirmish line. Vernon, you three take out the Wyz moving west. Go!"

Isaiah and his two loped off, eyes seeking. Seconds later they saw the other Wyzhñyñy, kneeling behind trees, firing at the foxholes, forcing their occupants to keep their heads down while grenadiers moved in, crawling on their bellies like dogs.

"Get 'em!" Isaiah said. They moved in, firing both clamp-ons: the right-arm blaster, and the left-arm, short-barreled slammer. The Wyzhñyñy who survived that first burst of fire, responded sharply and violently. Isaiah felt pulses strike his armored body, and ignored them, striding along the line, pumping short bursts, unaimed but accurate. Shortly the Wyzhñyñy were all dead or dying.

"Anyone damaged?" he called. None were. "Ali," he said, "we're done here. Where next?"

"Back where we were before. I'll let G-3 know we're available."

Running to rendezvous, Isaiah felt a sense of accomplishment. He'd killed half a dozen at least, and it felt right.

◇

General Pak's HQC-1 had lifted to thirty miles. He'd asked Tech how high he'd need to be to keep from being spotted by Wyzhñyñy on the ground. Assuming their fixed flak installations had been taken out by the Dragons. Fifteen miles ought to do it, Tech had answered, depending on how good Wyzhñyñy field equipment was, and how much they had on their minds. It turned out that fifteen miles wasn't enough, but given the power of his viewing equipment, Pak could see well enough from thirty.

Watching had taught him a lot. The Wyzhñyñy had impressed him with their relentlessness in the teeth of heavy fire, heavy casualties. The amount of armor they'd used also surprised him. He hadn't thought so much of it would escape the Dragons and wolf packs.

In the ground fighting, his own air squadrons, armor, and anti-armor batteries, had reduced it seriously, though at greater cost than he liked to see. But War House had established the opening strategy: draw the Wyzhñyñy into battle—the Wyzhñyñy had taken care of that for them—and destroy their capacity to make an air and armor war of it. Turn the campaign into an infantry war, and keep War House informed in detail.

The Wyzhñyñy had been on-world long enough to make major inroads in the supplies they'd brought with them. Reports from Tagus had indicated they'd begun growing crops there almost at once. That fitted his observations here. They were concentrating on self-sufficiency.

One of the Dragons had destroyed two Wyzhñyñy cargo ships parked above a range of forested hills, lightering down cargo. Thick smoke had risen from the wreckage, as if they'd held something like grain, and it was burning. Where were their cargos being stashed? He'd seen no buildings. Caves perhaps? He'd look into that. And surely there'd been more than two cargo ships. Perhaps the others were hiding in warp space.

How much supplies had been stored in the buildings the Dragons had destroyed? Hopefully the Wyzhñyñy were in poor shape to fight a long ground war. At any rate they were a lot of parsecs away from their supply source, the Armada, presumably with no way to communicate with it. As for his own supply ships—hopefully they were safe.

If not… He'd handle his assignments, and hope that others handled theirs. But there were no promises.

<>

It seemed to Esau he was a different person than he'd been when he and Jael had finished their foxhole that morning. Since then they'd fought off four attacks, each one lasting what seemed like hours. The last had come at dusk, and it was different from the earlier attacks. This time the Wyzhñyñy hadn't used tanks and APCs. It was as if they'd run out. But they obviously had plenty of howitzers. Shells had come raining down on the forest's mangled edge, tons and tons of them, and everyone stayed hunkered down. Captain Mulvaney would tell them what was happening.

Mulvaney got updates from his platoon officers, and from Battalion. Battalion was in constant touch with HQC-1's all-seeing, automated command surveillance system. Which had separate channels to all regimental, battalion, and wing commands on the ground.

Esau knew none of that. He knew only what Captain Mulvaney said in his ear. Wyzhñyñy infantry were coming, lots of them, on foot. No tanks, no APCs, just troops at a trot. "Six hundred yards…" Mulvaney had said. "Five hundred… Four hundred… Their artillery's quit firing! Be ready!" The roar of shells arriving cut off just after Mulvaney said two hundred. Then Esau and Jael stepped onto the firing step, spare power slugs held in their teeth for quick reloading. He barely had time to think *my God!* The Wyzhñyñy were coming at a hard run, a solid rank of them, unthinned by aerial attack. Neither Wesley used aimed fire now, just shifted their shoulders from side to side, pouring out deadly streams of pulsed energy in the dusk.

The Wyzhñyñy had fallen like grain before a scythe. But behind that first wave was another, and even with spare power slugs in their teeth, it took a moment to seat one.

The Wyzhñyñy broke through, really broke through, because even having had replacements, quite a few foxholes were down to one man, or none at all. There were enemies on all sides, and 1st Battalion clambered out of their holes to fight. When a power slug burned out, they fought with bayonets. But not *that* many Wyzhñyñy got through, and reserves had come up. Then some of the oncoming Wyzhñyñy turned and ran, and in minutes only humans were left.

Then the reserve battalion took over the foxholes. 1st Battalion pulled back and mustered, then marched an hour northward through the forest, to where their sleeping bags and shelter tents had been stacked. The company cooks had a hot meal ready. The survivors ate, set up their shelter tents, crawled exhausted into their sacks and went to sleep.

Esau stayed awake long enough to wonder how many in B Company had died and how many were wounded. 2nd Platoon hadn't come off too badly, and he'd lost only three of ten in his squad.

Only! Give us another couple days like this, he told himself, *and there won't be any 1st Battalion.*

He looked at Jael, curled up already asleep. She always looked so pretty, sleeping—pretty face, sweet lips—but in the dark he could only remember them.

For the first time since childhood Esau Wesley prayed. "Oh blessed Lord," he murmured, "don't let her get killed. If it's got to be one of us, take me. She's twice as good a person as I am, and if I lose her, I'm afraid I won't be worth shit."

Then he slept.

Chapter Ten
Aftershocks and Second Thoughts

The tribe of Jilan was one of the more traditional. Among them, when some momentous event turned out poorly, the gosthodar would consult with his ranking advisors or officers, then take a strong sedative and sleep on what he'd learned. When he awoke, he'd eat a light breakfast, including a mild brain stimulant, then go alone to a place beneath the sky, to ponder. Preferably some high place, and always by day rather than by night. At night, Wyzhñyñy were susceptible to dark moods. And at any rate it was necessary to sleep on the debrief, allowing the mind and spirit to sort things out, often in dreams.

Gosthodar Jilchûk left his new field headquarters in the limestone caves, and climbed to the ridgetop. The ridge was not particularly high—some two hundred feet local elevation— nor especially steep, but he arrived sweating, breathing hard, his haunches severely fatigued. His original home was not a heavyworld, and he was middle-aged, and disinclined to keep himself fit. At the top, he walked along the crest till he came to a promontory overlooking the countryside. A place where he could sit beneath the sky while the forest behind him kept the sun off his back. There his orderly inflated the gosthodar's field mattress—high ranking persons were not expected to sit or lie on the hard ground—and arranged it in the shade. Then watched dutifully while his ruler adjusted it slightly.

"Can I be of further service, your lordship?" he asked.

"No, Ethkars. Depart. I'll call if I need you."

◇

Ethkars left, picking his joyless way down through the forest, paying no heed to the esthetics around him. He had an infant in the nursery, and while parents were less given to worry than the nanny gender, it was his first-born. And given the gravity on this world, the pregnancy had been difficult. He was glad his mate would carry the next one. Meanwhile the tribe was isolated on this world, and yesterday's slaughter had depressed morale.

◇

On his promontory, Jilchûk gazed across a landscape of broad fields—croplands and domesticated pastures. Still surrounded by forest, but his people were making progress. Or had been before the enemy bombards visited.

Until his people had applied their civilizing touch, the settled districts had consisted of small fields and primitive dwellings, mingled with woodlands. What kind of history, what kind of culture must these humans have had to prefer such an arrangement? Clearly they were socially fragmented. Until the day before, he would not have expected such unity of action from them in battle, nor such hard-bitten dedication. Apparently this *was* a warrior gender he faced. His previous evaluation had been in error.

It was not a painful conclusion. Jilchûk's stoic, practical personality was well-suited to military command. And mistakes were easily made when dealing with unfamiliar life forms. The point was not to repeat them. It had been an error—natural but an error—to depend so heavily on his warrior brigade. The first attack should have told him that. But it had so nearly succeeded! Surely the next charge…

Until he'd lost more than half his warriors: killed, missing, and disabled.

I should have used my reserves in the first attacks—let the humans expend their air and armor on them—and then sent my warriors. The humans could never have withstood them then. We'd have chewed them up. Like most two-leggers, the humans had mobility problems. Break them—make them run—and they were doomed. They simply couldn't run fast enough.

Fortunately, they too had lost more of their aircraft and armor than they could afford. They'd fought off that last attack with infantry. *Best not to take too much for granted though,* he told himself. *They had plenty of air strength earlier. It's a good thing you moved most of your armor into caves before their bombards arrived.*

In the second phase, the human's heavy ground support

fighters had almost surely been aerospace craft. While those used later appeared to have been simply aircraft. Had the human space force pulled out already, leaving their ground forces on their own? It seemed unlikely, but... He thumbed the mike on his harness. Intelligence would know if the space force was still in the system.

<>

Vice Admiral Carmen Apraxin-DaCosta didn't have a hilltop, nor at the moment the luxury of solitude. She sat on a chair beside her bottled savant, Melody Boo'tsa, who lay in trance. According to the records, Melody was fifteen years old, with a "mental age" of four. Just now she was in receiving mode, channeling the deputy chief of space operations, Admiral Kaidu Ghazan. Her vocator provided an excellent copy of Ghazan's strong baritone, his delivery, and the modest accent Apraxin had always supposed came from a childhood in a traditional community.

"Carmen," he was saying, "I appreciate your concern. But you need to leave the Jerrie system no later than Terran 15.08.15, at 2400 hours. That gives you approximately twenty-nine hours. You need to rendezvous with Soong in the fringe of Dinébikeyah at system coordinates 2700/1700/00, no later than Terran 15.11.28. He'll need you."

Apraxin considered. "The Wyzhñyñy planetary defense flotilla here still hasn't poked its head out of warp space to show us what it has in the way of firepower. And it may include remnants of the system defense force. I'd like to leave Ver Hoeven's battle group, just in case."

"What evidence do you have that it's actually needed there? That it would be more than just a source of comfort?" Before she could respond, he went on. "Judging from your brief observations of their original planetary guard force, it looks as if Kereenyaga can handle it without Ver Hoeven's help. So. How many functional remnants of their system defense force do you think might show up?"

She hesitated. "The maximum and the minimum," he added.

"The maximum would be all five of them: two cruisers and three corvettes. The minimum would be none; zero."

It took him four seconds to respond. "You may leave three cruisers and four corvettes of Admiral Ver Hoeven's group."

"Thank you, sir." She pushed on quickly. "What about the marine mother ship? In case the Jerries on the ground need the squadrons. They're short squadrons now, and anyway they'd be of no use to Soong."

This time there was a long pause. When finally Ghazan spoke again, he sounded like someone who'd about reached his limit. "Admiral," he said, "I have checked with Marshal Kulikov. He says you can leave the mother ship on one condition: her squadrons are to be used only if the troops on the ground are faced with extermination. The Jerrie's primary purpose is to find out for us how the Wyzhñyñy fight on the ground: weapons, tactics, psychology...all of it. And the force size Pak was given is the baseline in the study. It's not to be fooled with. If he scrubs the Wyzhñyñy, great. The government may even name a Day for him. But..."

"But his people are expendable," Apraxin said matter-of-factly. "I understand."

Ghazan didn't reply immediately. *You needn't have put it so bluntly,* she chided herself. Finally he spoke. "That's right, Carmen. That's how it is. That's how it will be at Shakti, too. And at Terra, if it comes to that. Resources can't be wasted. Invested but not wasted."

Old Hard Head Kaidu. But he called you Carmen to soften the message. "Right, Admiral," she said. "I understand."

"Fine. Anything else, Admiral?"

"No sir. I'll be at Dinébikeyah on time and ready."

"Very well. And I repeat—everyone here is pleased with your results. Yours and Pak's both. Ghazan out."

"Apraxin out."

She nodded at the savant's attendant, then watched while the young woman spoke the brief formula that brought the savant out of her trance. A matted photo, presumably of Melody Boo'tsa, had been neatly taped to her module. The eyes were pink, the broad white face faintly so. *An albino,* Apraxin thought. Albinism had become avoidable, and extremely rare. Now Melody Boo'tsa no longer had a face of any color. Just a bottled CNS, a soul, and a unique sort of mind. With the unknown energies, and access to strange dimensions, that enabled two human beings to communicate across scores of parsecs, instantaneously.

"Thank you, Melody," she said quietly, then to the savant's attendant: "and thank you, Sofi. You may not fully appreciate it, but without teams like you two, humankind would have no hope in this war. None at all."

She paused. "I have a personal question for you. I presume your briefing on Melody was much more thorough than my own, and there's something in her file that sparked my curiosity. Either she has a long compound middle name, or several middle names. Can you clarify that for me?"

Even as she asked, it seemed to her a pointless question.

"Yes, Admiral, I do know. I'm her cousin."

The comment startled Apraxin. Sofi's complexion was a rich brown. *Hmh. And why not? Any racial stock can have albinos.*

Sofi had paused, as if waiting for Apraxin's attention again. When she had it, she continued. "She was named Melody when she was born. But our community is quite traditional. It retains many of the old customs, including giving another name later on. One that tells something about the person."

Sofi's gaze had slid aside and downward. After a moment though, it met the admiral's again, briefly.

"It is not customary to tell it outside the community, but I will tell you. You may find it—significant to our needs."

Apraxin's eyebrows rose slightly.

"Melody didn't speak sentences until she was four. Some of her first clear sentences were about things that hadn't happened yet. But later they would. Most of the family thought they were coincidences, but her aunt—my mother—and also her father, thought they were prophecies. Because when she said them, she spoke better than usual. So Melody was given another name:

Naan' voh ti' ta ka. Because she has knowledge of the future.

"It is how she came to be here. She has an uncle who teaches mineralogy at the University of Northern Arizona, and he told the chairman of the parapsychology faculty about her. So she was sent there for study, and I was sent to be with her. To take care of her. And then the war started."

Apraxin exhaled through pursed lips, and nodded slowly. "I *am* glad you told me, Sofi. If you ask her questions about the future, does she tell you things?"

"I have tried a few times. She never answered. When she predicted in the past, it was always—whatever it was. Not something asked about."

The admiral frowned thoughtfully. "Will you work on it with her, Sofi?"

"Yes, Admiral. You know, sir, most people think of Melody as something empty, with very little mind. But she is—in there, sir. She listens. Hears. She hears what we hear, and she hears things we don't hear. I don't think of her as mentally deficient. I think of her as *Naan' voh ti' ta ka.*"

The admiral stepped back. "Thank you Sofi. This could be quite important." She started to turn away.

"Admiral?"

"Yes?"

"You said that teams like Melody and myself are all that give humankind hope in this war. But without people like you, there could be no hope at all. It is the people like yourself—the fighting people—who are primary in this time."

◇

When Apraxin left the savant's suite, she headed for the wardroom, and a snack. While thinking about Melody's supposed talent for predictions, and whether they grew out of something like Charley Gordon's vectors.

She'd wait a bit, she decided, let Melody rest, then visit her again. Meanwhile saying nothing about it to War House. Let Sofi work with her, and define the possibilities.

◇

Smoke from Kunming's many fires hung in the air. Stinking

smoke, of half-burned, retardant-soaked fabrics, charred wood, melted synthetics. And perhaps burned bodies, though that could have been the product of their poisoned moods.

An hour earlier, when it was still dark, fires could still be seen from the prime minister's balcony. Chang and Peixoto had watched together. They'd been watching, on the telly or from the balcony, since the previous day, when the first fires were reported. Had seen them grow, while the over-extended fire department did its best. Sirens had ululated in every part of the city. There had even been fires within the government complex—one in the Palace of Worlds itself—despite the surrounding force shield.

The word was, most had been set in warehouses and retail stores, at least some by small teams of arsonists protected by gunmen, all masked.

Just now the two leaders were closer to arguing than they'd ever been. "We have no choice!" Chang said. "Tirades on the talk channels, demonstrations in the squares, slander and libel of ourselves and others—those could be borne. But arson and murder? They have gone too far now! Martial law is the only answer we have, for the short term!"

Peixoto's bleak eyes scanned the half of the city visible from his balcony. He thought what such a campaign of destruction could have done a thousand years earlier, when so much more was flammable. When every vehicle carried within itself a large quantity of explosively flammable liquid.

And at last report, what had happened here had happened in 137 other cities, to some degree or other. And worse, 183 assassinations and a number of assaults had been reported, mostly on military personnel.

A leak had triggered it, and when he discovered who... Peixoto shook his head. *You'd have released it yourself, if the victory had been greater. Big enough to blunt the Wyzhñyñy advance.*

He'd never imagined the Peace Front would do something like this. What was left of the Peace Front. Probably not more than one percent of the population remained members. But of

Kunming's 2.7 million, that came to 27,000. Of which perhaps a thousand had been actively involved in this night of shame.

He looked down at the much shorter president. He'd almost forgotten Chang's demand. Now he shook his head again. "I cannot agree to it. Not yet."

He sensed the almost voiced response: *Then I will resign.* Unvoiced because Chang Lung-Chi would never abandon him in a dilemma. Never. Instead what the president said was, "When, then?"

"I'm not sure, good friend. But it's what their council wants us to do. We both know that. And we both know why."

<>

A rumor passed through the city later that morning: a counter demonstration would be held that evening at Wellesley Square, to defend humanity's right to defend itself. By noon the story was on the newscasts, the talk shows; and everywhere in the city you could *feel* the energy growing, swelling.

It shook the Peace Front's ruling council. They'd expected a public backlash, but this… Paddy Davies made a call, and Günther Genovesi's luxurious limo picked them up from the roof of their building.

By nightfall, demonstrators were packed into Wellesley Square and the streets feeding into it, far outnumbering anything the Peace Front had mustered. Among them, carrying a child on his shoulders, was a very tall, strongly built man with the lantern jaw and strong cheekbones common among the Goloks of Tibet. Carrying the child had not been entirely a good idea. The boy's short legs had rubbed off some of the Golok brownness from the man's jaw and ears. But it was night, a man carrying a child was surely benign, and as long as the child remained on his shoulders, the break in his camouflage was unlikely to be noticed. Besides, the crowd's attention was on the top of Martyr's Hill, where a large bonfire lit the night. It would damage the concrete slab on top, but that could be repaired.

There was no orator, nor any martyr. Instead, at the brow of the hill stood a cheer leader, capering like a court jester. It was no longer possible to hear him, even with his hand-held bullhorn. Once he'd begun shouting, the crowd—more than half a million—had picked up his chant and drowned him out: "MAR-TIAL LAW! MAR-TIAL LAW! MAR-TIAL LAW!"

A mile away, Foster Peixoto stood on his balcony, watching and listening. From so far away it was simply an immense roar, but he knew the words. A minute earlier, before the crowded joined in, he'd been watching on the telly, on a closed police channel, and had heard the chant begin.

Rumor and security reports had prepared the president and himself, and they'd perceived both opportunity and danger. But now, facing the reality alone, Peixoto feared, truly feared, a mob psychosis. He'd never imagined this volcanic potential in the people. What might happen next? An explosion of violence? A stampede, killing scores? Hundreds?... Lynchings? The beating to death of anyone pointed out as a Fronter, whether accurately or not? And however moderate?

As usual, the response was to be Chang's. A response prepared late and hurriedly, and based on faulty assumptions. They'd expected self-appointed spokesmen to make speeches or pep talks, not this primal chant. *Chang will have to rethink his speech as he gives it,* Peixoto told himself. Otherwise the crowd might start to move, to act. Fists clenched he gestured. "Now!" He spoke his urgency aloud. "Now!"

◇

The Golok wasn't aware he'd joined in the chant. Also he'd forgotten the child on his shoulders. His body knew it was there, and subliminally allowed for its presence, but his conscious awareness had been swallowed by the flames, the man cavorting so near them, the crowd consciousness, and above all, "MAR-TIAL LAW! MAR-TIAL LAW! MAR-TIAL LAW!"

The spell had no power of its own. It was a manifestation of the half million human beings in the crowd. Overhead, police floaters kept the hovering news floaters outside the "eighty-up, eighty-out limit." But one floater moved inside the limits unmolested, and began to circle the mound not greatly above it, at about the diameter of its base. On a spar projecting beneath it, a powerful light now strobed. Not painfully, but the chant began to unravel, weakening, as more and more eyes follow the light. Then the cheerleader stopped; the chant staggered and died; and a great stillness spread through the crowd.

As if suddenly aware of the heat, the cheerleader moved partway down the grassy slope, farther from the flames. And from the floater, a voice issued. Boomed! After the great chant, it did not seem so loud, but in fact it was very loud. The entire crowd could hear it. The voice was one they all knew, from numerous public addresses over the years, by Chang Lung-Chi as candidate, senator, cabinet minister, and eventually president. The most trusted and admired public figure of recent decades, at least.

With the death of their chant, the crowd's minds focused on the president's words.

"Citizens and friends," he said. "We have come together here to rescue our species and our commonwealth from a dual threat. A *dual* threat! A powerful, ruthless invader…and our own hard-won hatred of war and violence."

For several seconds the voice stopped, but the floater continued circling, the light still strobing.

"A hatred of war, a hatred that turned into a war against ourselves. A war by the Peace Front against its own species.

"But I have not come to you to declare war against the Peace Front. My hands—all our hands—are fully occupied with saving the human species from the invader. We will capture and prosecute the criminals who set the fires and committed the murders, also those who helped them, and those who directed them. But we must not—we *must not* kill the spirit of peace, the spirit of pacifism within us! If it were not for human pacifism, we'd have destroyed our civilization centuries ago, with nuclear war, or biological war, or some other depravity. Centuries ago! With the survivors, if any, driven back to the caves and hovels, to the fear, and ignorance, and superstition, and famine, and brutality!—from which our ancestors struggled."

The circling continued, but the strobing had stopped.

"The prime minister and I have not been open with you. There are matters we've kept from you, hoping to avoid the kind of violence that happened yesterday. But tonight you have opened our eyes and our minds to your awareness. Your readiness.

"A few weeks ago our new warfleet, under Admiral Soong, fought its first real battle with the Wyzhñyñy armada. The Front was correct about that, though they got the details all wrong. Our fleet was greatly outnumbered, and the fight was brief and costly—a test of ships, weapons and tactics. But the Wyzhñyñy losses were much greater than ours. And our losses have been more than made up in the weeks since the battle.

"And just days ago, a small fleet under Admiral Apraxin-DaCosta arrived in the New Jerusalem System. There it destroyed a smaller Wyzhñyñy fleet." Again the president paused. "Then the New Jerusalem Liberation Corps was landed on its home world, and fought—*and won!*—the first human ground battle against the Wyzhñyñy invaders.

"These victories were far from decisive. Overall our forces are still severely outnumbered. But they are growing, and we can now say that things look hopeful. Not favorable yet, but hopeful."

Another pause. "You came here this evening and demanded martial law. Something our species—for good reason!—came to hate and fear centuries ago. But now you've decided it's necessary for the survival of humankind. So under the extraordinary powers granted by parliament for the pursuit of this war, and with the agreement—the pained, grieved agreement—of Prime Minister Foster Peixoto, I herewith proclaim—martial law!"

Remarkably there were no cheers.

"We avoided it as long as we could, and will continue it no longer than we must. If we should continue it too long, we'll depend on you to let us know. But I do not imagine it will come to that."

Again a pause. Loosely the spell still held the crowd, the spell that had grown out of their mutual, deeply felt need, but quiet now.

"And now I have a request to make of you. I want you

to do something further, for yourselves, your government, and your species. Do it as honestly as you know how." Again he paused, and when he repeated, it was slowly, deliberately, and less loudly. "As honestly as you know how. If you believe you know someone who may have been involved in the terrorism of yesterday and last night, do not undertake to punish them. Instead, notify CLUES/TERRORISM on the Ether. Someone will investigate as soon as possible.

"Now I am going home to bed. You may want to do the same."

<>

Most of the crowd left quietly. Others hung around talking, also quietly. The tall "Golok" left with the child, who slept now, draped over one broad shoulder. The man said nothing to anyone, but his long face looked thoughtful.

Chapter Eleven
Killing and Dying

Four days had passed, three of them on patrol, since the Battle of the First Days. APFs took platoons to designated map coordinates, and picked them up six or eight hours later, somewhere else. The patrols were to watch for any sign of Wyzhñyñy activities, but mainly they were keeping sharp, and getting a better sense of the wilderness fringe that was their stronghold. Meanwhile their platoon leaders checked out uncertainties on the detailed, large-scale maps Division had brought from Terra. Maps from high altitude photographs, made years earlier by Terra's foreign ministry. Which on worlds like New Jerusalem had little to do, and cooked up unobtrusive, hopefully useful projects to pass the time.

Patrolling also served to integrate the replacements. There could be no replacements from off-world, of course. So the platoons with the heaviest losses had been deactivated, and their remaining personnel distributed to others to fill the holes. 2nd Platoon's replacements had come from 3rd Platoon A Company, which had also been airborne qualified.

They were all Jerries, of course, had been trained alike, and their limited combat experience had been similar. But their unit folklores had different characters and stories. Still, a couple of days was all it took to become brothers. The many casualties had made them more conscious of their mortality and brotherhood.

After breakfast on the morning of the fifth day, Ensign Berg mustered 2nd Platoon in a light rain. "Men," he said, "today we're going to do something different. The surveillance buoys report what seem to be four small groups of fugitives hiding out from the Wyzhñyñy. You may possibly know some of them. The general's sending us out in four armored personnel floaters, each with a squad, to pick up the fugitives and bring them in." He looked at his men expectantly. "How does that sound?"

Their response was not the enthusiasm he'd anticipated. It

was Esau who finally answered. "Sounds fine to me, sir." This brought a circle of nods. "But we may hear some things that won't exactly warm our hearts. A lot of folks that stayed weren't kindly disposed to those of us that decided to leave. Called us deserters; said we lacked faith in God. It turned out they spurned God's offer of escape, instead. Some of them'll hate us for that, too. Hate us for being right."

Berg nodded slowly. "I expect some may at that," he said, then briefed them on policies and procedures.

<>

By the time they took off, the rain had stopped and the sun had come out; steam rose from the forest roof. Esau knelt beside the copilot. He'd called up the regional orientation map in his map book. An X marked the reported location of the group he was to pick up, while the floater's location was a tiny moving icon. But mostly it was the ground he watched, the Milk River Hills. The only good orientation feature was the Milk River, named for its milky tinge. These hills were not rich in streams. Except for the Milk, they tended to be short, appeared from springs as full-grown creeks, then disappearing into the ground. All of them were a milky green.

The forest was heavy. Some of the species he could recognize from the air. Scattered whitewood, with large pale leaves, its wood light in weight, favored for sawing or splitting out boards; dense groves of "cedar," narrow-crowned and with lanceolate leaves, the best of all for building logs; here and there steelwood, some of them towering, its hard and heavy wood slow to decay; and "redwood," with roseate wood and red-tinged leaves, a favorite for cabinets and other dressy things. Jael had had a redwood hutch, crafted by her grampa as a wedding gift.

Esau pulled his mind away from that, and back to the hills they flew over. Hills not fit for farms, he told himself. *Best left for God's livestock, not man's.*

They were getting close now. The floater icon almost touched the X. Down there were folks who'd stayed behind. He wondered how they'd fared the past year, and how they felt now about those who'd left. *Not that it matters greatly,* he told himself. *Leastways it shouldn't.* As Speaker Crosby had said: "God made diversity amongst his people for a reason. They *will* disagree, but He loves them all. Speaker Crosby had stayed, but he'd wished them well. "I'm too old to go flying off to the stars," he'd said. "And my flock needs me."

Some of that flock had already condemned him for "encouraging desertions."

Esau called up a quadrangle page, its much larger scale showing considerable detail. Including a second, smaller X. He guessed the larger was a camp, and the smaller a hunting party, now about a mile west of it. The smaller X moved slightly while he watched, still westward toward a meadow. "Go to the smaller X first," he told the pilot. "Before they get any more separated than they are."

"Right," the pilot said. Esau went aft to the open hatch, hooked his safety line, then knelt, leaning out. He'd already keyed the speech output of his helmet comm to the floater's bullhorn. Below, all he could see was treetops.

"Helloo!" he called. "You down there! An army's come to clean out the Wyzhñyñy—the aliens. If you hear me, fire a gun. We can pick you up at that meadow off west."

He heard no gunshot, and the APF's grav drive produced only a low hum; if there'd been a shot, he'd have heard it. *Maybe,* he thought, *they've run out of powder.* There'd always been folks, a few, who preferred a crossbow or longbow for hunting. They'd have an advantage now.

"Fine," he called. "We'll go to your camp and wait there."

The pilot heard, and swinging the floater in an easy curve, headed for the larger X, where the map showed a creek along the foot of a ridge. Trees overhung it, but in places the water was visible from overhead, milky green like the river. Probably, Esau thought, there was a cave there.

He tried the bullhorn again. "Helloo! You down there! An army's come to clean out the aliens. I'm coming down to talk with you. If you want, we can take you to camp with us. Feed you up proper. Fix you up with shoes, and new clothes."

He could imagine what they looked like after hiding out in

the wilderness all that time. They'd hardly have a shoe between the lot of them. Maybe moccasins. He disconnected from the bullhorn and spoke to his squad.

"Talbott, I'm leaving you in charge. "Turner, you'll come down with me."

Turner nodded, and Esau turned to the pilot. "Sergeant Pindal," he said to the Indi flyer, "find a place close by, where we can let down."

The pilot glanced back, nodding. "Right, Sergeant," he answered, and in a few seconds had parked his aircraft over a small blowdown gap. "Will that do?"

The two Jerries were snapping on letdown harnesses as Esau looked down. "Yup. Good enough." There wasn't much visibility through the gap; branch growth was filling it. But it would do. Two letdown spars had emerged from their housings, one on each side of the floater, above the door. Esau stepped out backward and began his descent, controlling it by voice while signaling with his arms to refine the centering. It was something they'd all done before at Camp Nafziger. Then he was through the gap and into the trunk space. No one was waiting. When his feet touched the ground, he pulled the safety clip and slapped the release. "All clear," he said.

His harness disappeared upward on its cable; meanwhile Turner had landed beside him. They were about a hundred feet upslope of the stream, and seventy or eighty yards downstream from the X. "We'd better take our helmets off," Esau said. "Otherwise no telling what these folks will think we are."

Both men tipped their helmets back, letting them rest on their light field packs. Then they went downslope to the creek. From there they could see a young boy waiting a couple hundred feet upstream on the far bank. Esau started toward him, waving. "Howdy!" he called. "I'm Esau Wesley, from Sycamore Parish. This here's Malachi Turner, from Tanner's Run."

The boy didn't answer, just watched their approach, his eyes feral in a thin face. He wore only a loin cloth; his wide frame all sinew and bone. Too much bone. *About ten years old,* Esau decided, thinking in New Jerusalem years. Perhaps thirteen in Terran years. *Hasn't been eating any too good. Looks like a string of eels hung on a rack.*

Esau stopped. "Malachi," he muttered, "get me a couple rations out of my pack." Turner gave them to him, and they went on. When they reached the boy, they could see he was frightened. Esau reached a hand to him. "My name's Esau," he said. "What's yours?"

"Zekial. Zekial Butters."

"That hunting party off west—I talked to them from the, uh, the airboat that brought us. Told them I was coming here. They should be along directly. You're not here alone, are you?"

A quick headshake.

"Is your mamma here? Or your grampa?"

He began to tremble! "My mamma—and my sisters."

Esau frowned. "What's the matter, Zekial?"

"We don't have no hunting party out. Some men came here yesterday. They..." He choked, his face writhing like a nest of snakes. "They..." Abruptly, unexpectedly, he burst into tears and fled up the slope, disappearing behind a laurel brake. Esau had backed off a step, glanced thunderstruck at Turner, then looked around. A footpath angled upslope from the stream toward a bluff, and the two troopers strode up it. Soon Esau saw a wide opening in the rock face. Without slowing he called.

"Helloo! No need to worry! Help's a-coming!" From behind him, Malachi could hear what else he said, half under his breath. "This better not be what I'm afraid it is."

The cave began as a sort of open-sided gallery that narrowed inward. A small mound of embers glowed beneath the overhanging rock shelf. There were sleeping furs, and on the ground, a patch of dried blood three feet across. Esau swore again, and gestured toward the narrow gap that led deeper into the limestone. "They must have gone farther back in, scared spitless." *If they're still alive.* "Go back in there a little ways and see if you can talk them out. I'm going to call Sergeant Pindal, and find out where those others are."

He seated his helmet again. He didn't need it to radio the floater—his throat mike would serve—but he wanted its HUD.

"Sergeant Pindal," he said, "this is Sergeant Wesley. We've got a situation here, but I'm not entirely sure what it is. Where's that party I talked to first? What way are they going now? Over.""They're about a quarter mile west-northwest of where they were before. They're bypassing the meadow, as if they didn't want to be picked up. Over."

"So they're still headed away from here. All right. Jael, do you read? Over."

"I read. Over."

"I may need a woman's help here. I'm not sure, but I'm afraid I do. I want Sergeant Pindal to let you down by the creek, just below the big X. I'll be there to meet you. Pindal, are you still reading? Over."

"Still reading. Over."

"After you put Corporal Wesley down, I want you to follow those sons of bitches that took off. Corporal Talbott, do you read? Over."

"I read. Over."

"When Sergeant Pindal catches up to them that ran off, talk to them with the bullhorn. Tell them if they don't stop and give themselves up, you're going to blow them to bits from the air. Got that?"

"Got it, Sarge." He paused. "Do you really want us to kill them?"

Esau hadn't thought it through. Now he hesitated. "No, but don't let them get away. Tell them twice, and if they keep going, I want Sergeant Pindal to shoot ahead of them. Close as he dares. You still reading, Pindal? Over."

"I read. But I don't like what you're telling me. Over."

"Just shoot ahead of them. And if they veer off, do it again. I'm afraid they may be murderers, and worse. Worse than the Wyzhñyñy, because they're doing it to their own people. Over."

"I still don't like it. There's nothing in our orders that covers shooting at locals. Look. I'm just about over the creek. You down there yet? Over."

"I'm on my way. Ten seconds will do it. Turner, keep trying to talk them out of the cave. I'm going after Jael."

◇

It was Jael—her woman's voice—that talked the mother and her two daughters out of the darkness. They pointed out where the renegades had dragged off her husband's body, and her oldest son's. While she talked, the younger son showed up again. He too had seen his father killed, and had fled back into the cave, where his baby sister had gone. The two had spent the night hidden well back in the darkness, but they'd heard the screams and crying. When the renegades had left, their mother and older sister crept back in with them, to huddle there without speaking. But Zekial had heard their attackers say they'd be back when they had meat. Finally he'd crept out, intending to find some other people, and ask for help. He'd barely emerged when Esau had called down on the bullhorn.

Esau radioed the floater again. Yes, they were still following the hunting party. No, Talbott hadn't hailed them. He'd been afraid it might make them scatter. Esau told him that was good thinking. "Pindal, stay after them, but not close. They'll stop somewhere. When they do, I want the squad to let down a ways off, and move in. Surround them if you can, then use your stunners if you can get close enough. I'm going to radio Division about this. I suspect General Pak will want them alive."

The floater dropped back a few hundred yards, following the X on the pilot's HUD. Esau called Division and was referred to the senior sergeant major, who was perturbed by a squad leader bypassing the whole divisional chain of command. But when Esau explained the situation, the sergeant major patched him through to General Pak. Who ordered out a platoon, to make sure the renegades didn't escape.

They succeeded in capturing only two. The other two suicided before they could be stunned.

◇

That wasn't the only ugly situation that 2nd Platoon B Company ran into that day. The other three fugitive groups were all extremely glad to be found, and all three reported seeing or hearing about Wyzhñyñy soldiers eating humans. One group had found the remains of a feast by a Wyzhñyñy patrol. The victims had been neatly dismembered, and some of the bones were charred. The crania had been opened and the brains removed, maybe as a delicacy. Along with the human remains were plastic packages, apparently from Wyzhñyñy ration cases.

Word spread like a grassfire not only through the Jerrie division, but through the Indi armored regiment and air squadrons, and the Burger engineers.

Pak was concerned that his troops might commit atrocities of their own, as retribution, which would harm morale and discipline. So on his closed command channel, he ordered his company commanders to speak to their troops about it.

<><

In camp the troops ate standing up, in company mess tents with high tables. It was in B Company's mess tent that Captain Michael Mulvaney Singh spoke to his four platoons. The rumor was, he was going to brief them on their next action, so there was considerable tension in the mess tent. More than before the battle they'd already fought, because now they knew what to expect. Or thought they did.

The rumor was wrong. "I suppose you've all heard about the Wyzhñyñy having eaten people here," Mulvaney said.

The reply wasn't loud, but it was ugly.

"Obviously they're meat eaters, and we look enough different, they may have considered humans to be nothing more than animals. Meat for the larder. I suspect we cured them of that notion the other day, when we killed so many of them."

His soldiers muttered agreement, sounding not quite as ugly as they had.

"In combat," he went on, "a soldier—human or Wyzhñyñy—is apt to be too busy, or at too much risk, to eat or mutilate dead enemies. Even if he was inclined to, which you and I aren't. His attention is on destroying live enemies and staying alive himself. But at other times some people might be tempted to mutilate an enemy.

"I can't imagine any of you doing something like that; it's as contrary to your religion as it is to mine." He scanned them again. "So that makes it between you and God. But in this world it's also between you and the army. Because mutilation is strictly against regulations, and the penalties are severe.

"Any questions?"

No hand raised. No one spoke.

"Good. Enough said then. And speaking of eating, Sergeant Ferraro is serving apple pie with brown sugar for dessert at supper. Make sure you save room for it."

<>

Returning to his office, Mulvaney looked back at the event. He could understand Pak's concern. But at the same time, he felt that in bringing the matter up, he'd insulted his Jerries, just a little.

<>

Jael, on the other hand, wondered about the difference between mutilation with a knife, and mutilation with, say, a grenade in combat. Probably, she decided, it was the difference between meanness of spirit and necessity.

<>

Gosthodar Jilchûk scowled at his staff. They'd told him all they knew, and given him their opinions on everything he'd asked about, but he still knew too little for effective planning. There was no real border, no defined front, and he could choose his area of operation. The enemy, on the other hand, knew everything he did above ground as soon as he did it, and responded. They no doubt had reconnaissance buoys, an intelligence staff, and a high-powered AI working up contingency plans twenty-four hours a day.

Abruptly he slammed a fist on his work table, making his staff flinch. It was that or shoot the map on his wall screen. The cursed thing was dead as a stone. No movement. No life. It didn't even flinch at his temper the way his staff had. It showed things as they'd been when his surveillance buoys had been destroyed, except for changes made by Intelligence, none of them in real time.

Most numerous were the approximate locations where he'd lost reconn floaters and their escorts to enemy action.

The humans responded quickly to invasion of their airspace. Obviously their buoys picked up and monitored his own aircraft as soon as they emerged, and had interceptors up promptly. As if their duty crews waited in their aircraft.

They seemed willing to lose aircraft, certainly over their own territory, as long as they shot down his. And his scouts were at a disadvantage; their missions required more or less predictable flight behavior. He couldn't continue losing aircraft at the rate he had been, and he had no way of knowing what the enemy had left.

His Intelligence chief had pointed out that the humans seemed more interested in shooting down the escorting fighters than they did the scouts—in bleeding his fighting strength than in denying him information. Though they were doing a good job of that too.

Seemingly the human commander was leaving the initiative to him. But they were planning something. They hadn't invaded just to lie around.

He scowled, big jaws chewing on nothing. Back in the forest, his expensive aerial scouting showed a poorly defined "blind area" of something between twelve and twenty square miles. Probably circular. His Tech chief believed the humans had some kind of concealment screen, unlikely as it seemed. At any rate the "blind area" showed nothing at all in the way of humans, or of any mobile life forms large enough—or in large enough groups—to register. But they were there. Something had to be. Large mobile objects could be detected outside of it, some of it wildlife, some clearly military. And the humans were thinning areas of forest, possibly preparing defensive positions of some sort.

Jilchûk shook his head. He'd have to settle for a ground reconnaissance in force. Meanwhile one thing seemed definite: the humans had landed in inferior numbers. Perhaps to be supplied from space, for a war of harassment and attrition.

Attrition. He could play that game, he told himself, information or not.

<>

B Company, 2nd Regiment, had set out on foot through the forest. B Company plus a platoon from C Company, because the mission required five platoons. One augmented infantry company to take out a tank battalion. Sergeant Esau Wesley felt proud that B Company had been chosen. He thought of it as the best in the division.

His wife looked at it differently: someone had to get the mission, and B Company was it.

To carry out their mission, they needed to penetrate twelve miles into what the Jerries were calling Wyz Country. Twelve miles through open country with nearly flat terrain. Twelve *straight-line* miles from the wilderness edge, but by the meandering Mickle's River, it was more like twenty.

The tank battalion was parked in the narrow band of floodplain woods that stretched along the Mickle's banks. Actually at a place where the woods were wider than anywhere else for miles. There, according to the buoys, they'd find not only the battalion's tanks, but its headquarters, trucks, repair and overhaul facilities…all of it.

At each corner of the encampment stood a newly-erected flak tower. The Indi assault pilots knew all they wanted to about those. Enough to guess the specifics: a swivel-based, multi-barreled, look-and-fire trasher on each tower, powerful enough to bring down an armored attack floater with a single burst. Or one pulse suitably placed.

Though B Company didn't know it, surveillance buoys had observed the tower construction in progress, but hadn't reported it. Region-wide, the buoys saw far more than humans could hope to deal with, so back on Terra, programmers had designed perception sets to notify Intelligence of opportunities and dangers. But inevitably the programs overlooked some things.

Thus when four thick concrete slabs were poured in a nondescript stand of trees on a minor river, no relevance was perceived. Then four assembly floaters began assembling four tripod towers on the slabs. The buoys registered and tagged this internally, while awaiting further observations. Then some unrecognizable equipment was installed on the towers, and a pseudo-organic data processor, 360 miles out, notified Division that something was going on.

But it was an Indi scout pilot who said "Huh! Those are weapons! Gotta be." So he reported it, then left his planned flight path for a closer look. But the Wyzhñyñy didn't respond, there was nothing else peculiar about the place, and whatever might be perched atop the towers was concealed in a cab.

And there was nothing else on the site but trees. And only hours later, Intelligence had their attention on something else: a Wyzhñyñy tank battalion, with its attendant ground transport and aerial escort, had appeared beside a limestone ridge deep within Wyz Country. Almost certainly it had been concealed in a cave. And they were promptly joined by a floater escort, which along with the antiaircraft armament of the tanks demanded caution.

So Operations decided to let be for the moment. They'd wait and see where the tanks were going. In less than two hours they knew. As for why... For one thing they were a lot closer to prospective battle sites.

General Pak wondered if they were simply bait, because by then he suspected what those towers were. Though he'd never heard of flak towers.

Then he learned how good the Wyzhñyñy ordnance was. He sent two flights of armored attack floaters to rip up the tank park—and lost six of the eight aircraft! Next he sent a flight of rocket-armed stand-off floaters, and discovered the potency of Wyzhñyñy electronic countermeasures.

So he turned to infantry and inflatable boats.

<>

B Company reached the Mickle River by twilight, in the forest three miles outside Wyz Country. The Mickle was not very large there: forty to fifty feet wide and four to eight feet deep in the main channel. What made the mission feasible was, even in Wyz Country the Mickle's floodplain was wooded. That was one similarity between Jerrie and Wyzhñyñy land-use practices: neither culture farmed floodplains, even along rivers that didn't often flood during the growing season. Here and there the buoys showed a break in the woods, where convergence between some meander and the bordering terrace pinched out the floodplain on one side or the other. But except for those infrequent breaks, the buoys showed woods along both banks for all twenty meandering miles through Wyz Country.

The troops unloaded their boats, demolitions etc., on the river bank, then Captain Mulvaney ordered the grav sleds back to Division with their Burger crews. He watched the squads inflate their boats and put them in the water. Then troopers held them by the handlines while their gear was loaded. The current would carry them along, and the eight paddles with each boat would speed them. They'd had two training sessions with rubber boats back at Camp Stenders. Not much. But the three wilderness miles before they reached Wyz country would give them the feel of boats, oars and river.

The number one boat was smaller, the scout, with only five paddlers and a bow lookout. Mulvaney strode to the number two boat, where seven staff noncoms, including the medics, sat waiting with paddles. Corporal Jensen stood in water over his knees, steadying the boat. Crouching, Mulvaney boarded, settled on his seat in the bow, and looked back while his troopers boarded the other boats. Lieutenant Bremer had settled in the stern, holding the steering oar. Mulvaney raised an arm and gestured. "Let's go, men!" he called. With that, Jensen clambered aboard, took the eighth paddle, and they were on their way.

They suspected what this night might hold for them, but they didn't dwell on it. It wasn't real to them yet.

◇

Isaiah's Vernon's camo field was not only black at night, it also obscured his electronic image. Nonetheless, he waited quietly behind a tree trunk. They'd been told to use cover when they could.

He didn't wait alone. The entire regimental bot platoon was there: 22 bots against a Wyzhñyñy incursion thought to be of company strength. The Wyzhñyñy were getting close. On Isaiah's HUD, their linear icon had almost reached his platoon icon. Even from his east-end position he couldn't see them yet, but he could hear them. He'd maxxed his sonic sensitivity. They're trotting, he thought. "Lieutenant," he whispered, "this is Sergeant Vernon. I hear them now."

Koshi answered from the other end of the ambush line. "On my command," he murmured. "Not before. Unless they see us and open fire first."

The Wyzhñyñy were skirting a tangled patch of old tornado blowdown, thick with fallen trees, brush and saplings. The platoon waited along its edge, Koshi at the west end. By the time the Wyzhñyñy reached him, they should all be exposed, or almost all. There was no cleared field of fire, but by opening fire together, they should be able to take out much of the enemy force in the first seconds. Then they'd rush the rest; take them out while they were shocked and confused. Those that fled, they'd let go; even bots couldn't catch them. Let them tell what had happened to them as best they knew. See what that did for morale back in Wyz Country.

The first Wyzhñyñy who trotted into view was the point man, followed by two other scouts. The nearest passed perhaps six feet in front of Isaiah, who'd have held his breath if he'd had lungs. The rest of the Wyzhñyñy followed in single file, Isaiah counting them.

He'd gotten to 143 when Koshi said "NOW!" Then the entire platoon opened fire with both arms—blaster and slammer. There were screams and roars as Wyzhñyñy fell, kicking, thrashing, or simply falling. The first return fire was almost immediate, homing on muzzle pulses. Isaiah took a hit; his camouflage field flashing from the energy received. They'd all been shot with hard pulses before, deliberately in training, to prepare them. So he ignored it, looking for more targets. Knocked down another, and another... The Wyzhñyñy didn't go prone to fire, but stayed on their feet. After a few seconds, those still standing paused to reload. Isaiah had exhausted the power slugs in his clamp-ons, and jacked in replacements.

"TAKE THEM!" Koshi ordered, and the bots charged, juiced by an electronic analog of adrenalin. The Wyzhñyñy hadn't expected this. Those who'd reloaded fired. The others ran. Two slammer pulses jarred Isaiah, his camouflage field flaring strongly, reflecting from the visor of the Wyzhñyñy who'd fired them. Isaiah grabbed him by the head, jerked, twisted, and threw the Wyzhñyñy violently to the side, off his feet, before shooting him.

He paused, and saw no Wyzhñyñy standing. The order was to kill the conscious wounded; a safety measure that was also a merciful act, with no Wyzhñyñy medics on hand. Unconscious enemy wounded were to be taken prisoner, but no one had told them how to distinguish the unconscious wounded from one playing possum. And at any rate, slammer and blaster wounds were typically fatal.

A few minutes later, when the platoon gathered around Lieutenant Koshi, there were no prisoners. Only a Wyzhñyñy body tally: 119. There'd probably be more scattered along the path to Wyz Country, dead of wounds. Courtesy of a buoy, Isaiah's HUD showed icons moving rapidly east-southeastward.

The platoon started back to camp at an easy lope, Isaiah feeling embarrassment along with exhilaration. It had been almost too easy, killing so many with so little injury to themselves. Then he wondered if the Wyzhñyñy had felt that way when they'd wiped out the local humans who'd declined evacuation. The thought didn't entirely erase his discomfort, but it allowed him to dismiss it.

<>

It had been Esau who'd suggested it, when Ensign Berg gave the platoon its first briefing on the mission. "We ought to paddle along close to the edge," he'd said. "Trees hang over the water there. Cover, in case some Wyz scout flies over. And generally, the outside of a meander is better than the inside. The current cuts deeper, so we can stay close to the bank, under the trees, and be harder to see. The inside of a meander is likely to be shallow, so we'd have to keep farther to the middle."

Afterward, Ensign Berg ran it past Captain Mulvaney, who mentioned it to General Pak at a planning review. "What's the young man's name again?" the general asked.

"Esau Wesley, sir."

Pak remembered the name now; that was the young sergeant who'd unearthed the renegade fugitives. "Keep an eye on that young man, Captain. He sounds like promotion material: smart, and takes responsibility."

Mulvaney had grinned. "We've made a project out of him, General, since early on. Especially his platoon sergeant."

Back at B Company, Berg told Hawkins what Pak had said, but the sergeant didn't tell Esau. It seemed to him it might make the Jerrie self-conscious; make him try too hard. What he did tell him was that Mulvaney had told the general, giving <u>him,</u> Esau, the credit.

From the time they started downstream, noise discipline was absolute. The buoys had been ordered to give special attention to the Mickle and its vicinity, but you couldn't know for sure. There was Wyzhñyñy livestock here and there; and probably Wyzhñyñy herdsmen, indistinguishable by buoy imagery.

Esau's advice was heeded: they stayed mostly near the river bank, and on the curves favored the outside. Once Captain Mulvaney's HUD showed a Wyzhñyñy floater pass over, more or less in line with the river where they were, but it didn't react.

They moved rather briskly, without seeing or hearing anything threatening. The major moon— "Elder Hofer's Lamp" —rose at about 2330 hours, so during the last hour of their river trip, the visibility was better than earlier. That increased the tension level, but not drastically except during one interval when there was no woods along the east bank, and direct moonlight reached the water.

For several minutes, Captain Mulvaney had been paying more attention to his HUD than to the river. The icon of his sole scout was nearing the tank park. "Almost there men," he murmured. "Easy now. Quietly. Quietly." He rounded a bend. Ahead lay a straightaway about a hundred and fifty yards long. "It's just before the next bend," he whispered. Then added "kill your HUDs." The lines on the HUDs were hair-thin, but even so, they were a needless risk now.

This was far the most dangerous stage of the operation yet. Mulvaney felt a focus and acuity of senses greater than anything he'd experienced before in his thirty-three years.

◇

As squad leader, Esau rode in the bow of his boat, watching the river banks, the woods, and the boats ahead, his senses as focused and acute as his captain's. The inside of the last bend had been on their left, the side they wanted, and they could have run right up on the mudbank there. It would have made for easier unloading. But then they'd have had to approach through the woods, and riding the current was quieter.

He'd glimpsed one of the flak towers, its platform and cab—turret actually—not much above the treetops. He ignored it; he had more immediate things to pay attention to. On the straightaway he saw no good place to land. The east bank was a natural levee about five feet high, about the highest he'd seen. And abrupt; almost impossible to pull the boats up. This hadn't been apparent in the images from the buoys. They'd either have to leave men behind to hold the boats, or struggle them up onto the levee, making a certain amount of noise. Or let them float on unoccupied, which would leave the company stranded.

But it didn't come to that. Just before the next curve, the high bank had been dozed—sloped and smoothed for easy access to the water. As boat by boat they reached the bend, the bow man slipped into the water close to shore, water waist to chest deep, and guided his boat to the sloped-down bank. Their gear on their backs, shoulders, and harness, the rest also slipped over the side, and transferred demolitions and other gear to shore. Then quickly but quietly they raised the boats from the water, carried them ashore, and very quietly stacked them four high. As soon as a squad had landed their boat, they moved up the bank, weapons in hand, and formed a defense line at the brow while others landed behind them.

Captain Mulvaney had been the first. Wet to the hips, he crawled to the brow of the bank, and with night-vision examined the Wyzhñyñy encampment. From time to time he raised his visor and used his night binoculars to pick up details. Trees obscured the view, but he saw enough to put the scene together.

The buoys had given him the basic layout, subject to uncertainties. There were definitely no tanks on the side toward the river. They were lined up along the other three sides, well-spaced, forming a box several acres in size. Inside the box lay almost everything else—mainly shed-like prefab buildings that no doubt served as battalion and company headquarters, mess halls, machine shops, and probably officers' quarters. And mounds that had to be bunkers; probably concrete, covered with earth. They couldn't be deep, Mulvaney thought; the water table couldn't be more than six feet below the surface. By each tank was a tent large enough for its crew to live in. Outside the "tank box," at least on the far side, were more tents. Probably squad tents for the battalion's infantry company or companies. Except for them and the flak towers, everything seemed to be inside the box.

The only activity Mulvaney saw was one Wyzhñyñy soldier walking to what had to be a latrine. When the Wyzhñyñy opened the door, subdued light shown out until it closed again. He saw no sentry, not one, though there had to be some. Even here, miles and miles from known human forces, and no indigenous population that might snoop or steal. Inwardly Mulvaney shook his head. It was hard to conceive of a military installation with no sentries out, especially at night.

Only after several minutes of careful scanning and listening did he give up on spotting the sentries. Keying one of his command switches, he whispered to his platoon leaders, confirming sectors and objectives, and giving orders.

<><

Ensign Berg had led 2nd Platoon through the woods as quietly he could, keeping well outside the three-sided tank box. He'd sent scouts ahead and off his right flank, and they'd reported two sentries. They'd reached the edge of the woods on the east side, the side farthest from the river. Now they lay in pasture grass, facing the woods, waiting for Captain Mulvaney's command.

Not far inside the woods, but outside the tank box, two flak towers rose above the trees, marking the southeast and northeast corners. If the towers opened fire on them, the platoon's orders were to run for the woods as hard as they could, firing as they went, regardless of what awaited them there. Though hopefully the flak gunners couldn't depress their guns enough to target them. Nearby, livestock grazed, mostly "calves." Remarkably placid, they hardly reacted to the strange bipeds. The long row of squad tents—almost surely the battalion's infantry bivouac—lay just within the edge of the trees.

The platoon lay in a line, ten or fifteen feet apart. Behind it, Elder Hofer's Lamp rode the sky. *Hopefully,* Esau thought, *if some Wyzhñyñy infantryman left his tent to take a leak, and looked to the east, his eyes would lift skyward, rather than studying the pasture.*

2nd Platoon had had much the farthest to move, and it seemed to Esau that everyone else should already have been in position. But Berg had radioed their readiness three minutes earlier, and nothing had happened yet. When the captain was ready, he'd let them know. Then 2nd Platoon was to pour heavy fire into the tents, drawing Wyzhñyñy attention for a critical half minute or so, hopefully starting an eastward reaction.

Apparently things were hung up somewhere.

Esau didn't fidget, physically or mentally. Back on Lüneburger's World, he'd become good at waiting, despite his sometimes impatient disposition. Especially during the maneuvers at Camp Nafziger, he'd developed an absolute focus in ambush situations, like a tiger waiting to rush a heifer. For him, time became little more than sequence, its durations known but muted. Now his implacable gaze was on his personal sector of fire. Irrelevant thoughts did not visit his mind.

Finally Berg whispered in their helmets. "Fire on my command. Five. Four…" From somewhere in the woods came a premature burst of blaster fire. "Fire!" Berg snapped.

Each 2nd Platoon trooper began spraying long bursts through the tents in his sector of fire. The Wyzhñyñy response was prompt, survivors spilling out, blasters in hand, running for the nearest sizeable tree. *No foxholes or breastworks,* Esau realized, offended by the lack. Danged Wyz took too much for granted.

2nd Platoon's muzzle pulses and visible trajectories guided the Wyzhñyñy return fire. But they weren't used to the low target profile of prone humans, and the platoon's lack of cover wasn't as costly as it might have been. The firefight settled to a more measured exchange, the Jerries firing short bursts now, rolling sideways for target disruption, seating fresh slugs as needed.

Their job was not to suppress the Wyzhñyñy infantry—they lacked the necessary firepower—but to inflict maximum casualties, while distracting it from the defense of the tanks and flak towers. Meanwhile the whole base was in uproar. Firing seemed everywhere. Magnesium charges flashed brilliantly, and armor petards roared, as 3rd Platoon's Jerries worked and fought, destroying and dying along the rows of tanks.

It was Sergeant Hawkins' voice that spoke next in 2nd Platoon's helmets. "1st and 4th Squads, move into the woods and support 3rd Platoon. 2nd and 3rd Squads spread out and continue firing."

"Let's go, 4th Squad!" Esau said, and springing to his feet, darted to his left in a series of sprints and dives, his people following. They'd already been at the south end of 2nd Platoon's skirmish line, and despite Wyzhñyñy night vision, they quickly ceased drawing fire. Wyzhñyñy attention seemed focused on those humans still shooting at them.

So Esau shifted from sprint-and-dive to a crouching run, swerving more and more westward, guiding on firefights in the woods. At the same time he clicked his helmet comm to the command channel. 4th Squad was to suppress Wyzhñyñy tankers protecting their vehicles from 3rd Platoon demolitionists.

As he ran, he glanced back at his squad. Their spacing discipline was good, and remarkably, most of them seemed to be there. "Work with your fire team," he warned. "Teamwork!" Then they were in the woods. In the eruptive, roaring flashing chaos, teamwork tended to dissolve, troopers responding to the moment, firing, taking cover, throwing grenades, even bayoneting. The blaster racket was punctuated by the sharper sounds of gunfire. The Wyzhñyñy tankers carried only projectile weapons—pistols and carbines. Tankers who climbed into still intact tanks, initiated their AG engines. Demolitionists darted up to tanks and clambered onto them: slammed petards against access panels, or magnesium charges into shaper muzzles or air intakes, triggered charges and time fuses, then moved on if they could.

Esau and Jael kept aware of one another, less by conscious intent than by something deeper. Captain Mulvaney's voice spoke on the command channel. "4th Squad, 2nd Platoon, are you near the southeast tower?"

Esau crouched beside a tree. His answer was a rush of words. "Sir, this is Esau. I'm not far from it, and Jael's with me. The rest of the squad's close by, but I don't know how many's left. There's fighting all around, like things were stirred with a spoon."

"The southeast tower demolition team can't get up the tower," Mulvaney said. "They're under heavy fire. Take your squad and suppress it. We *must* take out that tower!"

Yessir." Esau changed channels. "4th Squad, 2nd Platoon, move to the southeast tower. We need to take out enemy fire that's holding down the demolition team there. Otherwise we may not have a ride home. And give me your names while you're on your way, so I know how many of us there are."

Then he started, his stocky body darting from tree to tree. Behind one he stumbled on a trooper with his head blown half off. Behind another stood a wounded Wyzhñyñy, guts dangling, looking the other way and firing a carbine. *They're tough!* Esau thought. With superb night accuracy, he snapped off a single pulse that blew out the Wyzhñyñy's brain. He could die himself in the next second, but his warrior muse wasn't entertaining thoughts like that.

Now he saw the tower, a thick-legged tripod in a clearing some eighty or ninety feet across. Jerries lay on its slab, at least two still alive, returning fire from behind tripod legs. He could see several sources of the Wyzhñyñy fire that kept them on the ground. Pointing he growled. "Jael, that one's yours." Then he moved toward another, whose attention was on its target. Someone else loosed a short burst, putting that one down. Esau found a third, almost hidden from view, threw a grenade behind the Wyzhñyñy and dropped to the ground.

After it blew, he took stock, then opened the command channel again. "Captain," he said, "this is Esau, 2nd Platoon, 4th Squad. We seem to have cleaned out the folks shooting at the southeast tower team, but no one's going up the tower. I don't think they know it's cleared yet."

"Good work, Esau. I'll tell them. They're hung up at the southwest tower, too. Go help."

Esau ordered 4th Squad, then started himself, glancing at the southeast tower as he left. They'd gotten lines up earlier. Now two people were climbing them.

Intense fighting continued around the parked tanks. Bolts passed within feet of him, and he dove for the ground behind a tree. Jael's voice spoke in his helmet. "I got him!" she said, and Esau was back on his feet, running again for the southwest tower. He approached the Wyzhñyñy harassers from behind, shot one, then came under fire from another. Hit the dirt behind a tree, legs protruding on one side, head on the other. Fragments of bark and wood flew, and he scrabbled on his belly to better conceal himself. No further pulses struck, and cautiously he looked around the base. Saw a Jerrie kneeling behind a fallen Wyzhñyñy, peering toward the southwest tower, blaster ready.

Gathering himself, Esau darted to the man and knelt beside him. One of 4th Squad; a replacement, Tom Clark. "You know if any of the others are around?" Esau asked.

"I've seen Joash Steele and a couple others. That's all. I've been keeping track of you, best I could, you and Jael. Helps she's so small."

Jael trotted toward them, then something heavy, a slammer, cut loose at them, and she scrambled for shelter while Clark and Esau hit the dirt in opposite directions. Esau belly flopped, and kicked around into a prone firing position. The enemy weapon fired another burst, and Esau fired back. The enemy fire stopped, and they saw a large powerful body thrashing on the ground.

"Clark," Esau said, "I'm going to see if anyone's still alive over there." He thumbed toward the tower. "You folks keep anyone from plugging me."

"Right, Sarge."

Esau got to his feet and ran to the tower, briskly but not sprinting. Five Jerries lay dead there. Now Jael sprinted across to him and flopped prone. "I wish you'd get down," she said. "You're too good a target, standing like that."

He knelt. "And I wish you'd have stayed over there," he answered.

Ignoring the comment, she pointed toward the trees. "Someone over there's firing at the top of the tower," she said. "I think he's one of ours."

Esau peered where she'd pointed. At the moment there wasn't much blaster fire close by, though someone was banging away with a pistol. Slowly and deliberately, probably short on ammunition. "You stay here and cover me," Esau said. "I'll check it out."

Part of a large tree lay on the ground, cut to make room for the tower, and not cleaned up. He ran over to it, and finding two Jerries kneeling in a large fork, joined them.

"What are you men doing here?"

The one who answered never took his gaze from the top of the tower. "We were sent to give covering fire to the tower team, but they all got shot. Now he's covering me, and I'm covering the grapples."

"Grapples?"

"The team fired two grapples at the tower platform, and they both caught on the railing. Then two guys tried to climb it, on those little seats that ratchet up when you pull on the rope. They both got shot. They're hanging up there in their harness.

Esau hadn't noticed them before, one almost to the top, the other some ten feet lower. The blasterman raised his weapon and fired another burst at the top of the tower. "One of the Wyz just came out," the man said. "The way he dropped, I think I got him. They can crawl along the platform without us seeing, but they have to get up to free the grapple. I'm hoping I can kill enough of them, they can't man their guns."

They're probably worried about that themselves, Esau thought.

"The team had three grapple throwers," the blasterman said, looking at Esau for the first time; a quick glance. "There should be another one out there among the bodies. With a climbing seat," he added suggestively.

Esau squinted, then decided, and ran back to the tower in a crouch. Among the bodies, he saw what he needed: a satchel charge with shoulder straps, and a sort of drum with handles. On top of the drum lay something resembling a grenade launcher. A three-hooked grapple was seated in it, and from a slot below the muzzle, rope led to a hole in the top of the drum. Beside it lay a harness, with a little seat, and an attachment. He knew how it worked; 2nd Platoon had been introduced to them, though they hadn't tried them out.

The heaviest fighting was near the center of the woods now, as if the demolitions teams had finished their work or been killed. No one seemed to be shooting at him for the moment, but that couldn't last. And there was more gunfire than blaster fire now—a bad sign. He dismissed it; he still had work to do. The satchel charge had a detonator in place, with a short length of fuse taped on the side, and an igniter. Taking off his combat pack, he removed a phosphorus grenade and hooked it on his harness next to his remaining fragmentation grenades. Finally he lay his blaster by his pack and slipped his arms through the straps on the satchel charge.

Picking up the grapple gun, he handed it to Jael. "Bring this," he said. Then he carried the drum to the edge of the slab, took the grapple gun from Jael, and eyed the platform atop the tower. "Well," he muttered, "here goes nothing." Raising the gun, he pulled the trigger. The recoil almost separated his shoulder, and the blast hurt his right ear like a knife thrust. The grapple flew upward while the launch shank flew free. Rope sped from the drum; the grapple struck the turret, then clattered to the platform.

Jerking on the rope, he felt no resistance. The grapple

popped from the platform and caught on the pipe atop the bulwark.

He turned to Jael. "This is an order," he said, pointing. "Go back there and shoot at any movement on top that's not me. I don't want some sonofabitch unhooking this, or shooting down at me. Then, if our folks start getting pushed out of the woods, I want you with them. I'll get out all right."

She nodded soberly and ran toward the trees. As she did, Esau saw the blasterman in the fallen tree fire another burst at the top of the tower. The clatter of the third grapple had stirred them up overhead.

Carrying the now-depleted drum, he went to where the seat lay, and attached the ratchet to the rope. Then he buckled himself into the harness-like seat, located himself beneath the grapple, and after a deep breath began to climb hand over hand, the ratchet securing every gain. He got the rhythm of it at once, climbing as rapidly as his short arms allowed. Thinking that if an energy pulse hit the satchel charge on his back, there'd be nothing left of him for a Wyzhñyñy to eat.

Just below the platform he paused, removed a fragmentation grenade, pulled the safety clip, thumbed the plunger, then lobbed the grenade over the railing. It roared. With quick strong movements he reached the railing and bellied over it, releasing his seat harness almost before hitting the platform. A Wyzhñyñy body lay there. Rising to a crouch, he moved to his right, came to the open gunport, and removed the phosphorous grenade from his harness. As he activated it, he realized the gunport shield was sliding shut, but he had only one phosphorous grenade, so he tossed it anyway. If it had struck the shield, he'd have died horribly.

Ignoring the screams from inside, he scuttled to the door, shrugged out of the satchel charge, then tried the latch. Unlocked! Bullets smacked the turret near him. He depressed the igniter, stepped behind the edge of the armorsteel door, and opened it. Someone inside fired blindly, bullets spanging on the bulwark behind him. He slung the thirty-pound charge in by a shoulder strap, slammed the door and fled in a crouch, around the curve of the turret to the grapple and over the railing, not bothering with the seat. He started down hand over hand. *I should have thrown a fragmentation grenade in ahead of the charge,* he thought. *Someone in there's still alive and fighting. If he brings the charge out and throws it over the railing, I'm a goner.*

He heard the roar, and knew he'd pulled it off, but had no time to exult. Still thirty feet up, a burst of blaster fire passed too near. He slid—would have let go and freefallen if it weren't for the concrete slab beneath him. Almost at the bottom, he gripped the rope hard again, braking, felt searing pain in his palms, and hit the slab hard enough his knees buckled, aware that another burst of blaster fire had missed him as he'd dropped. He sprinted for the trees.

"Here!" Jael almost screamed it as she stepped into sight, and he veered toward her. "Folks are pulling back!" He realized he'd heard that on his helmet comm, and ignored it. Together they ran, Jael leading. Not northward toward where the company had landed, but westward, toward the curving river. Northward would take them into a no-man's land.

<>

Ensign Kemau Zenawi Singh arrived in a staggering run, carrying a man who weighed more than he did. Wyzhñyñy weapons racketed behind him. Crossing the break of the bulldozed bank, Zenawi hit the sandy slope on his butt, sliding feet first. Company medics were working on wounded. He rolled the body off his shoulder. "It's Captain Mulvaney!" he gasped, then lay back heaving for breath. "Somebody get Lieutenant Bremer!"

He'd passed Bremer and hadn't noticed. Now the lieutenant appeared beside him. "What? Captain Mulvaney?"

"Yessir. Hit by a bullet. It exited through his face; his mouth. We were heading back here and suddenly he went down. I think he was hit again, while I was carrying him."

"Blessed Gopal!"

"You're in charge now, sir."

Bremer turned to look at Mulvaney, but a kneeling medic

was in the way. "Sir," the medic said without looking back, "the captain is dead. Bullet through the brain."

Bremer sounded unbelieving. "Don't just..." He groped for an appropriate word. "Just *kneel* there! Give him something!"

"I have, sir. Stasis 1. But it's too late, believe me." He rose to a crouch and started back to the wounded.

Bremer turned again to Zenawi. "Kemau," he said, "what do I *do?*" His eyes looked large, desperate.

"Sir, you know the situation better than I do. But I presume we have a defense perimeter covering the beach."

Bremer's head bobbed rapidly. "Yes. Of course. Of course."

"I'd hole up here on the beach and give the rest of the men time to get here. Then take to the boats and go downstream."

"*Downstream?* Good lord, man! Downstream is the wrong direction." Bremer sounded close to panic.

"Downstream," Zenawi repeated calmly. "It's in the plan. That's where they're supposed to pick us up. Unload on the other side, far enough away that hopefully the evacuation floaters can get in safely and land. The last I knew, the enemy still held the southwest tower."

Bremer was breathing hard now, hyperventilating. "We have men in the park here. We can't leave them. We'll simply have to charge! Clear the Wyzhñyñy from the park and bring out the casualties."

Zenawi's hand gripped his wrist. "Don't order it, sir. Every man in your company will die. You'll carry the weight of it on your soul forever."

Forever was how long Bremer's stricken expression would stay with Zenawi; the XO was over the edge. "Let me take care of it for you, sir," Zenawi said, and clicked his all-personnel channel. "B Company, this is Zenawi for the company commander. Perimeter hold fast. The rest of you retreat to the beach in an orderly manner!" He repeated it. "In three minutes we begin evacuation. In three minutes we begin evacuation. Perimeter, don't shoot anything on two legs!"

◇

Jael and Esau reached the river downstream from where the Wyzhñyñy had bulldozed the riverbank. Going over the levee top, they picked their way along the steep sideslope, gripping brush on the levee brow to keep from sliding into the water. Esau wasn't even aware now of his torn palms. In two or three minutes they were within the Jerrie perimeter undetected. Overhead, bullets popped, ricochets sang, blaster pulses hissed. It was then they heard Zenawi's order. Ahead they saw men kneeling on the smoothed-down beach. A moment later they reached it, and crouching, trotted to the officers they could see.

"I need to report to Captain Mulvaney," Esau said.

Lieutenant Bremer, the tallest man in the company, rose abruptly, as if there were no hostile fire. His face twisted. "Wesley!" he snapped, "where's your rifle? And your pack?"

"Sir, they're back under the southwest tower. I…"

"GO GET IT, SOLDIER! RIGHT NOW!" His face swelled with sudden rage. "GET THAT SONOFABITCH OR I'LL SHOOT YOU FOR COWARDICE!"

Esau stepped backward as if slapped.

A black hand gripped Bremer by a sleeve, pulling him down, and the XO went suddenly slack. "Sir," Zenawi said, "Captain Mulvaney *ordered* Wesley to the southwest tower. Let's hear what he has to report." Zenawi's black face turned to Esau. "Captain Mulvaney is dead, soldier. Is the southwest tower disabled?"

Esau was still in shock at Bremer's outburst. It was Jael who answered. "Yessir. Esau disabled it, sir. That's why he doesn't have his blaster. The tower team was all dead, but there was a grapple gun laying there, and a satchel charge, so he went up alone, all that way. Threw a phosporous grenade in the window where the guns shoot out; I could hear them screaming up there, clear from where I was. Then he threw the satchel charge in and came back over the railing, and slid down the rope. And the turret blew up! The steel door flew off the hinges, off into the trees, and Wyz on the ground were shooting at Esau, so's he fell the last ways. And lit on his feet! Then we ran!" She paused. "And now here we are."

Zenawi peered at her, then looked at Esau again. "Good work, Wesley!" he said. "Now you better get your head down. Be a shame to get killed before you even get your medal." Still stunned, Esau squatted, and Zenawi reached out. They shook hands. The officer felt the wet stickiness, different than the feel of blood, and retrieving his own hand, glanced at it before turning to Bremer again. "What Wesley did was worth a medal, wouldn't you say so, sir?"

Bremer's nods were like twitches, the sight penetrating Esau's shock. The XO had lost his mind!

While they'd talked, the Wyzhñyñy fire had slackened. Now it stopped entirely. The silence was eerie. The only voice Esau could hear was Lieutenant Zenawi reporting to Division: The flak towers had been taken out. Send medivacs, APFs and fighter cover.

The group on the beach looked at each other, then at the woods. Along the Jerrie perimeter, men lay or knelt, holding their breath. Those who hadn't already fixed bayonets, did so. Surely the enemy was about to charge. It seemed to Esau that if they tried to evacuate, they'd be overrun while loading the wounded on the boats.

An interminable minute passed. Two. Abruptly the woods in front of them erupted with crashes of exploding antipersonnel rockets, and the formless roar of multi-barreled slammers sounding from the sky. Zenawi reacted at once, his words broadcast wideband. "Everyone to the boats! Head downstream! That's *down*stream. Fighter command, we're under air attack. APFs, pick us up at rendezvous, half a mile downstream, on the west bank where the woods pinch out!"

Torn palms still ignored, Esau had already run to the nearest pile of boats, Jael with him. Alone they manhandled a top boat into the water, where he stood holding it. Others grabbed a second. Soldiers were spilling onto the beach, a small flood. More boats were launched, and wounded were manhandled into them. For some reason the Wyzhñyñy air attack was focused on the woods instead of the beach. Zenawi helped Bremer into a boat, the XO like a doddering old man, then jumped in with him.

<>

The escape hardly used half the boats, and some of them weren't full. Some had still not gotten underway when Indi fighters hit the Wyzhñyñy attack floaters.

The rendezvous beach had no place to land, so the troops went over the side, towing or carrying casualties, then boosting and pulling them and each other up the bank. Floaters were waiting, with medics, who helped first at the cutbank, then at the floaters.

By that time a group of anti-armor floaters hovered over the tank park. These too were Indis, and their fire was not antipersonnel. They wanted to make sure no tanks remained fit for renovation.

Chapter Twelve
Afterward

Seven large APFs had landed in the Wyzhñyñy pasture, only twenty to fifty yards from the cutbank—an APF for each platoon, and two medivac versions for casualties. The unwounded had already pretty much sorted themselves by squads and platoons—their "families and extended families." Crew chiefs called out the names of the platoons they'd come for, and the surviving officers and senior sergeants began loading their people, recording who was there.

Blood had darkened Jael's right sleeve when Sergeant Hawkins stopped her. "You're hurt," he said. "Go get on a medivac."

"Yessir," she answered. As she left, Esau started after her, but Hawkins put a restraining hand on his arm. "The medivacs are just for the wounded," he said. "You'll go back with us."

Jael called back without stopping. "Show him your hands, Esau."

Esau held them out; Hawkins looked. "Go with her," he ordered.

"Yessir," Esau said, and left, moving sluggishly, the adrenalin worn off.

Hawkins continued loading what remained of his platoon. *Jerries!* he thought. *They're not used to having medical treatment available. They don't expect it, don't seek it. Add that to the warrior trait of ignoring illness and pain, and you get people like those two.*

He'd long ago decided that Jael was as much a warrior as Esau, simply less aggressive.

<>

The platoon APFs were ready, but the two medivac APFs were still being loaded. They'd leave together as a convoy, escorted by fighters waiting protectively overhead.

Jael and Esau were examined briefly, injected with painkiller, directed to seats, and strapped in. Except for painkiller, only Jael received treatment. A medic had cut off her right sleeve at the shoulder seam, exposing a ragged laceration of the right deltoid, apparently by a rocket fragment. She'd felt it when it hit, but they'd been busy launching boats. The medic cleaned her wound, then bandaged it. It was hard to tell how much blood she'd lost. A significant amount, he decided, but not dangerous. The water had been deep at the cutbank, and most of the blood had washed away in the current.

Esau's hands were ignored. They threatened no blood loss, and the medics gave priority to cases that might be serious. Most were. There'd been screams when casualties were manhandled off the boats and up the steep bank, but aboard the medivac, the sounds were muted groans, mutterings, and occasional cries.

A warning sounded, and the medics grabbed stanchions while the medivac first lifted, then accelerated. Then they continued treating wounded. Plasma injections were begun. Stasis 1 was injected where the wounds seemed mortal, and the dog tags had been stamped to indicate a bot agreement. Or where there was no stamp, but death was imminent, or limbs were ruined beyond repair. It wasn't all according to regs, but the surgeons could decide what to follow up on.

Tom Clark, one of 4th Squad's replacements, was aboard with a bullet wound through the belly. He'd been doped for the pain, but not too doped to accost a medic. "How about some of that stuff you give the bot cases?" he said. He fumbled for his dog tags. "I signed the agreement."

"Sorry, soldier," the Terran medic said, "but you're going to live and be good as new in the body you've got."

"Don't matter. With so many worlds to run the Wyzhñyñy off, this war's going to last a long time. So I'm bound to get killed sooner or later. I might better get my iron suit now. The more bots we have, the sooner we'll get it over with. And that way, who knows: I just might come through it all alive." His chuckle was a weak, dry sound. "Spend my old age rusting in the sun."

"Take it up with the doc," the medic told him, then patted his shoulder and went on.

Esau had watched, listening. The painkiller had taken hold; things seemed a bit remote and disjointed. But one thing was clear: there was a lot of hurting going on. All of it because some Wyzhñyñy decided to take away other folks' worlds. He'd known that much all along. He just hadn't realized everything that went with it.

Speaker Farnham had it right, he thought, *or the book did.* A lot of the time Esau hadn't been sure when a speaker was speaking his own words, and when they were the Lord's, or some prophet's, or Elder Hofer's. But what it amounted to was, when we have a task, we need to carry it through the best we can, and trust in the Lord. And it seemed to Esau that was the situation the army was in.

Shortly he felt the medivac settling downward. A minute later they were on the ground, and the rear doors opened. More medics came aboard, and within a few minutes, all the wounded had been unloaded. Esau and Jael were among the last—the least wounded—and walked to reception.

◇

Brigadier Consuela Hagopian clicked her video control, and the wall screen went blank. Despite her salt-and-pepper hair and the lines in her face, to Chang Lung-Chi she looked more than smart and confident. She looked combat-trained and fit.

"As you see," she said, "it was an informative night. We are *very* pleased with the performance of our Jerrie troops, their auxiliaries, corps command…all of them. Less happily, we're also impressed with the toughness of the Wyzhñyñy troops. But General Pak suspects our experience has been very largely with the Wyzhñyñy main force, their regulars, and he's probably right. I hope so, because they have lots of soldiers. Most of them second string, we think. Call them reserves. We suspect their entire adult population is armed and trained."

What she says matches what Olausson says, Chang thought. And Kulikov had spoken well of her. But what impressed Chang as much as anything was the way she pointed out errors and uncertainties without being slippery.

"After the Battle of the First Days," she went on, "both

sides have used their armor and air squadrons cautiously. We seem to have an advantage in the air, so we've been a little bolder with our air units. The Wyzhñyñy have been bolder with their tanks, but with the destruction of the battalion in the tank park, that may change."

"Meanwhile they have a large advantage in troop numbers. And a lot of artillery, while we...had to make difficult resource decisions in preparing for the ground war. And decided to rely on airpower as our main bombardment force. We intended our initial softening-up phase to largely destroy the Wyzhñyñy armor and air units, but we'd overlooked something. Our principal colonized region on New Jerusalem, now the Wyzhñyñy colonized region, has areas of karst terrain. With caves—something we'd overlooked. Wyzhñyñy command was foresighted; they modified some of them to shelter armor, and air squadrons, and for backup base installations."

She gestured a shrug, a graceful movement. "One might wonder that they felt the need to, but unfortunately they did."

"So," said Foster Peixoto, "what is the upshot of all this?"

"I'm getting to that, sir. But first I want to point out our advantages there. Our surveillance buoys above all—no pun intended. And our concealment screen seems to be quite effective against Wyzhñyñy aerial observation. Thus we know a lot about what they're doing, and they know rather less about what we're doing. In fact, in our own domain, our troops have the forest to cover their movements, while Wyzhñyñy aerial reconnaissance is harassed, hurried, and costly.

"The Wyzhñyñy have penetrated our concealment area with what appear to have been two-man ground reconn teams, that in the forest tend to be missed by our buoys. But that hasn't seriously compromised our concealment.

"Another long-term Wyzhñyñy disadvantage is supplies. They've been depending on supplies they brought with them, of course, and seemingly had been using the supply ships for storage. Though we don't know how much they may have transferred into cave storage. The two supply ships we caught on or near the ground, we destroyed. Others escaped into warpspace."

"Are you suggesting we can starve them out?"

"I doubt it will come to that. We believe the Wyzhñyñy will take desperate measures to avoid it."

"Suicide attacks?"

"In time perhaps. But we expect the Wyzhñyñy force in warpspace to make efforts to supply their people on the ground. Though the odds of their succeeding aren't good. Our off-planet flotilla is alert to possible emergences by Wyzhñyñy ships. Also we have Dragons and a marine mother ship standing by in near-space, for critical on-world emergencies."

She stopped expectantly. For long seconds the prime minister gazed thoughtfully at her before speaking. "I take it, then, that we need feel no concern about events on New Jerusalem, at least for the time being."

"I wouldn't go that far. The Wyzhñyñy remain a potent force there, but our successes so far are encouraging."

Now the president spoke. "Brigadier, you said nothing about Wyzhñyñy prisoners."

"Marshal Kulikov brought that up with General Pak this morning, when they discussed Pak's report. Pak had hoped to capture some live Wyzhñyñy prisoners in conjunction with other missions, but Wyzhñyñy do not surrender. Threatened with capture, their wounded suicide, preferably with a grenade, taking some of our people with them. Seemingly unconscious Wyzhñyñy are apt to be shamming, hoping to entice someone close enough. These things were learned in the first days of fighting. General Pak is now preparing a mission tailored specifically to capture and transport prisoners."

The prime minister sighed audibly. "Tell General Kulikov that both the president and I put a high priority on this."

They ended their meeting then, and the brigadier left. *Pak's capture mission!* she thought. *God to be young again!* She'd have bucked for airborne training and an assignment on New Jerusalem. *Ah well,* she mused, *I'm lucky just to be in the military at a time like this. Interesting that I chose the military in this life, instead of business or music or child rearing. This life, when the military has meaning.*

<>

Some personnel didn't like living and working underground, but Gosthodar Jilchûk was comfortable with it. He'd grown up in a cool damp region, and was not claustrophobic. And his quarters were comfortable; luxurious even. His walls, where not occupied with video windows, were hung with expensive tapestries from his old home world, and luxurious furs from the subpolar regions of this new home world.

Just now though, none of that impinged on him. He was busy digesting and assimilating what had happened the night before. He'd absorbed the available information and opinions, then dismissed his staff. Now he lay at a low writing table, torso upright, jotting and doodling as he thought, using a stylus on a jotting glass. Sometimes he used them to make notes. Tonight he used them mainly to bleed off pressure.

The bottom line was, he'd lost an entire tank battalion. Of fifty-four tanks, just six were repairable; ten at most. The day before, he'd been confident that despite the Battle of the First Days, he'd retained clear superiority in armor. *Getting so much of my armor underground before the human bombards attacked was the smartest thing I've done. No, the only smart thing I've done. I've been trading armor, aircraft and warriors for knowledge, and I've come out sadly short on the exchange.*

(Scribble scribble!)

When the bombards had left, he'd sent out his aircraft to challenge the enemy aerospace attack craft. Which unfortunately had proven more heavily armed and armored, and very well crewed. Now the question was: *why haven't the humans used them since? What are they saving them for? Or is there a rivalry between the humans' space commander and their ground commander? Perhaps even between the services themselves?*

He shook off the question. There was no way to know. He only knew he was overdue for some good luck.

(Scribble scribble! Jot jot!)

His latest rude surprise was that the humans had battle robots! Robots with responses more intelligent and nuanced than anyone could have imagined. They'd been reported on the Battle of the First Days—radioed reports from the confusion of close combat. But there'd been no verification, and no one had taken it seriously. The assumption had been that some of the humans, perhaps their master gender, wore full body armor. But the descriptions they now had seemed to repudiate that.

(His stylus had nearly stopped moving.)

So. Battle robots. That meant that humans had much more advanced artificial intelligence technology. But they couldn't have many robots. If they did, they'd have used them more extensively. Perhaps these were prototypes, or test models.

Don't talk yourself into any assumptions, he chided. Go about your business. Plan. Execute. Adjust. Exterminate. In the imperial dialect, the initials had long since become an acronym meaning victory.

Meanwhile he'd reduced one area of uncertainty. Seventeen two-man recon teams had penetrated the blind area at various points, and radioed when they'd done it. Eleven radioed additional observations from inside, and five had returned and been debriefed. None of what they'd seen had seemed noteworthy, but even that was worth knowing, and he knew now that the concealment field was not also a force shield. That had been predicted, but having it verified was vitally important.

(His stylus had speeded up. Now it moved furiously, in a sort of automatic writing.)

Especially in conjunction with something even more important: from the penetration points, Intelligence had mapped a decent approximation of the overall perimeter. It was circular! Which suggested a single, centrally located field generator. Laying heavy artillery fire on the center might very well knock it out, depriving the humans of their concealment. It might also cut off the head of their command structure.

But before I do that, I'll plan the ground attack to overrun them. With their concealment broken, I can commit aircraft for effective reconnaissance, and air support for the ground forces.

He looked at his jotting glass, where his stylus had been so busy while he cogitated. In the middle he'd scrawled undisciplined spirals and swirls, with scattered small ritual sunbursts. Taken together they formed a circular mass. And into the heart of it were arrows, as if into the center of a target.

A shiver rucked his fur from scalp to sacrum. It seemed to him this was going to work. He began to decipher the tightly scrawled notes he'd written.

<>

On the second day after the raid, Arjan Hawkins Singh walked into a patients' dayroom—a squad tent, with board floors on timber foundations. Courtesy of the Burger engineering regiment and its small but efficient sawmill. Only Esau and Jael were there; few of the wounded were well enough to use a dayroom. They sat watching a documentary on defense industries of the core worlds. It was a year out of date, of course, but interesting. Enlightening. Gave an out-worlder a notion of how things were done on the core worlds, and how all this *stuff*—ships, weapons, equipment—came to be.

Jael clicked off the player as Hawkins sat down beside them. "Hello, Sergeant..." she began, then stopped. What caught her attention was the dark place on each sleeve, where chevrons had been removed. Then she saw his collar tabs. "You're wearing an ensign's bar!" she said. "You've gotten promoted! Congratulations!"

There's an interesting change, Hawkins thought. *When I first knew them, she wouldn't have spoken first like that. Not with Esau present. She'd have waited for him to talk.*

"Does that mean Ensign Berg is dead?" Esau asked.

"I'm afraid so. Killed in the first minutes."

Jael blushed. She'd overlooked how promotions came about in battle. Suddenly congratulations didn't seem proper.

"And you're replacing him," Esau said. "I figured he might be dead when I heard you giving orders he'd usually give." He paused. "Does this mean B Company's not getting shut down? Even after all the casualties?"

"Yep. We're still in business. We've been reorganized, of course. We're down to three platoons of three squads each, with most of the squads down to eight men for now. But we'll get first call on replacements, as the wounded recover and do rehab."

That'll be awhile, Esau thought. From what he'd seen and heard, most wounds were a lot worse than his and Jael's.

"I could fight right now if I had too," Jael said. "I don't hurt much, and I didn't lose that much blood. Esau's hampered a lot worse with his hands than I am with my shoulder."

Esau held up his bandaged hands and looked at them wryly. Only fingertips projected. "At least Jael doesn't have to tell me not to pick my nose now," he said.

Hawkins laughed. He'd never heard Esau say anything remotely humorous before. "There you are!" he answered. "Every cloud has a silver lining."

"Captain Fong tells me I'll be back on duty in a week."

"That's what I heard, too. Good thing. I need you." He held out a pair of sleeve patches. "Ensign Zenawi is Lieutenant Zenawi now, our new company commander. He told me to give you these; you're 2nd Platoon's new sergeant. If you're nice, maybe you can get Corporal Wesley to sew them on for you."

Jael laughed. "Might be she would." She took the patches from the ensign. They were a staff sergeant's stripes: three chevrons and a rocker. *There ought to be two rockers,* she told herself. *The other platoon sergeants have two.* Probably, she decided, the army didn't like to jump someone two grades.

"And while you're sewing on chevrons," Hawkins added, "these are yours." He handed her a pair of buck sergeant's chevrons. "You're in charge of 3rd Squad now. There isn't any 4th Squad yet. Maybe later."

She took them without hesitating. "Thank you, Ensign Hawkins," she answered. "I'll do the best I can."

Hawkins went on to tell them that 2nd Platoon's fit-for-action were on R&R, with Jonas Timmins as acting platoon sergeant. They'd ridden AG sleds to the upper reaches of their old friend the Mickle, for a day's fishing. General Pak had foreseen the desirability of such days, and requisitioned abundant fishing equipment before they'd left Terra. Nothing fancy—gear you could use without instruction.

Esau had gone grim. "How's Lieutenant Bremer?" he asked.

"He's under—medical treatment. Had you heard something?"

"On the beach he said he was going to shoot me for a coward if I didn't go back and get my blaster."

Jael took command then, telling what had happened, and how Zenawi had stepped in. The story took Hawkins by surprise. He turned to Esau. "How did you feel when he said those things?"

"I couldn't believe I was hearing them. I felt...betrayed. Killed. Stabbed in the heart. Then Jael..." He described what she'd said, and what Lieutenant Zenawi had said. "And Lieutenant Bremer just sort of...caved in. Then I realized he'd lost his mind, and that he knew it. But I still felt...dirty, from what he'd said."

Hawkins nodded soberly. "Lieutenant Bremer's body wasn't wounded. His soul was, by all the killing. It was more than he could deal with. That's how some people are. He's in convalescence now. Major Ranavati is his doctor—a psychiatrist and Gopal Singh healer. The rumor is, when the lieutenant returns to duty, he'll be assigned to General Pak's staff, as assistant to Major Pelletier. Where he won't have responsibility for men in combat."

He grinned then, taking both Jerries by surprise. "As for you two—you did very well out there. Lieutenant Zenawi said in his debrief that you saved a lot of lives. If that tower had been in operation when our floaters came, it would have cost us dearly."

Esau nodded. "We could see that, Jael and me. No ride home probably."

Hawkins got casually to his feet, as if nothing heavier had been talked about than 2nd Platoon's fishing trip. "Well, I've got more wounded to visit. You two get well quick. Especially you, Esau, because a platoon leader's nothing without a good platoon sergeant to pass all the hard work to."

Then he was gone. Jael got from her inflatable chair, knelt

beside her husband and kissed him. "I'm proud of you, Esau," she said. Then she too grinned. "We've got to get well quick, so's we can slip off together behind a thicket."

He half grinned back at her. "You sure know what to say to a man. That'll about cut my healing time in half."

◇

Before supper, Isaiah Vernon stopped to visit. He was wearing a new servo. The old one's cooling system had needed work, and they'd decided to install his bottle in an improved model.

"Division got hundreds of them before we left Lüneburger's," he said. "In case enough people signed agreements and were injured badly enough to qualify. And for replacements like mine.

"From the beginning my old one hadn't worked as well as it should," he went on. "The robotics tech said I should have complained then, but I didn't know. I thought that's just the way they were. Then, when we ambushed the Wyzhñyñy patrol, I took some slammer hits, and coming back in, I started to heat up pretty badly. Sergeant Okinwobu told me to lie down, and radioed for an AG sled to come get me. Me and two others with damage.

"It made it more real to us—to me, anyway—that bot or not, you can get hurt or killed in those fights. But none of us did. We killed 119 Wyzhñyñy, by count, but none of us died. These servos are really good."

Briefly then they talked of other things, mainly things that had happened on Lüneburger's World. They said nothing at all about their families or where they'd grown up. Maybe later. Meanwhile those places, those people, didn't exist anymore.

◇

In adjacent cots after lights out, Esau whispered to his wife. "I've been thinking."

"What about?" she murmured sleepily.

"About Isaiah, and what Tom Clark said to the medic on the medivac. I think maybe I *will* sign a bot agreement. If it's all right with you."

She didn't answer at once. Then, "That's up to you, not me," she said.

But she didn't sound as if she really meant it. More as if she thought it was what she should say. And at any rate, in the morning he had other things on his mind.

Chapter Thirteen
Petition to Kulikov

It was late afternoon. General Pak was reading staff reports when his Intelligence chief rang. "General, the buoys have something you need to see. Corporal Chen has it framed for you."

Frowning, Pak looked at his screen and touched a key. He recognized at once what he was looking at: a column of tanks, or perhaps artillery, moving out of a forested, hilly area. Limestone hills. Magnification was set low, allowing him to see the column's full length. He zoomed in to examine a single vehicle—an armored, self-propelled howitzer—then backed off a bit. A whole unit of howitzers. Judged against Wyzhñyñy standing in open hatches, they were heavy stuff—perhaps eight-inchers.

Zooming back, he counted. A battalion of three batteries, each battery with sixteen howitzers, three squad APCs, an armored battery command wagon, a heavy salvage vehicle, and two ugly-looking flakwagons. He whistled silently. Forty-eight heavy howitzers in all! There was also a battalion command and support company with, among other vehicles, six flakwagons, and four of what could only be large, heavily armored caissons to replenish the ammunition carried by the howitzers themselves.

All of it loaded with bad intentions.

A total of twelve flakwagons! To send attack squadrons... He shook his head, thinking of the floaters lost against the flak towers.

He also thought of the Dragon parked 300 miles overhead, unavailable to him.

"Thank you, Captain," Pak said, and disconnected.

Request the Dragon, he told himself. *The worst they can do is say no.* He touched another switch, and in a second had Commodore Kereenyaga's yeoman on the radio, some hundred thousand miles out. "This is General Pak. I need to speak with the commodore at once."

In twenty seconds the commodore was on.

"Commodore, I'm afraid you have all the heavy ground bombardment capacity in the system. Except for the heavy artillery the Wyzhñyñy commander down here is moving against us. I need a visit from a friendly Dragon."

He listened to the commodore's reply, then answered "I'm aware of that. I was on the planning group. But our assumption was that forces like I face now would be destroyed before we landed....

"I understand. But the planning group didn't allow for the caves. If we had, your rules of engagement would read differently....

"Thank you. Tell them to call me if they have questions. And keep in mind that the clock is running on us down here."

He disconnected, glowering. War House wasn't going to like this, and they'd probably say no. But damned if he'd let the possibility pass without trying.

The artillery that had shelled his line in the Battle of the First Days had been organic to the Wyzhñyñy infantry units. This appeared to be additional. It was hard to imagine the Wyzhñyñy leaving so much artillery on a world whose land surface was 99.9 percent wilderness and had no military at all, or any weapons beyond single-shot hunting arms.

He called the column's speed onto the screen. If it kept on that road, it could deploy for firing in under three hours. And surely they'd have tanks and infantry on hand to protect it, more than his forces could deal with in the open.

He touched a key that would boom his voice into every headquarters and orderly room in the base. "Urgent! Urgent! All units," he said. "This is your general. Evacuate base on Plan C. Evacuate base on Plan C. Beginning *now!*" Then he keyed Air Ops. "You're aware of the Wyzhñyñy artillery on the road?... Good. I don't want any enemy in our airspace for the rest of the day. None! We're going to have a lot of people and equipment moving outside the concealment field soon, with only the trees to hide them. Questions?... Good."

He disconnected and allowed himself a gusty "whew!"

The order was given. If this was a false alarm, he'd look like a complete and utter ass. He grunted. *Better that than destruction, heavy casualties and regret.* At best his force couldn't all be moved out in time. But Plan C's priorities were set partly in order of replaceability, and partly for movement to a backup area that had only first-order infrastructure in place—little more than wells and unactivated biosumps.

Only then did he call in his general staff, and begin to sort things out. How would Wyzhñyñy command determine targets? Presumably they couldn't see through the concealment screen, and even that much artillery, firing blind into an area of twenty square miles... Ah. The Wyzhñyñy scouting parties. They'd been reported from a number of locations inside the perimeter. Their radioed reports would have allowed a decent map of the circumference, and Wyzhñyñy command would target the center.

Plan C allowed for that too. Headquarters Battalion would be moved first. All but his command center—a modified, platoon-sized APF that held his office and briefing room, along with emergency quarters for himself, his aide, his savant team, the corps sergeant major and two clerks.

The staff meeting was interrupted by the savant's attendant. "General," she said, "Genevieve has a call for you, from Marshal Kulikov at War House."

"Excuse me, gentlemen," Pak said, and walked to a room near the aft of the floater. Genevieve, who like Charley Gordon was bottled, was already in trance. When Pak had seated himself, the attendant nodded, and he began dictating. "This is Pak," he said.

The reply was immediate and to the point. "Explain to me, General Pak, why I should change the rules of engagement," the savant said. Very nearly in Kulikov's voice.

"General Pak" instead of Pyong. Not promising. Pak repeated the brief argument he'd made to Commodore Kereenyaga. He was operating more on intuition than analysis, and it seemed best to avoid specifics, except when answering questions that required them.

"So," Kulikov said, "you are not currently threatened with

destruction."

Pak was not intimidated. "Not at present. If I was, the commodore would have acted without referring my request to you. But the farther my base is from open country, the less I'll be able to react to Wyzhñyñy encroachment. They'll establish bases within the forest, where my fields of fire will be much more restricted, and my new base will be subject to attacks from any point the Wyzhñyñy choose. I'll have to move my Operations Command and air units deep in-country, disperse my combat units to fight a guerrilla war, then try to supply them by air. And direct and coordinate them based almost entirely on data from the buoys. If that's what you want, we'll do our best, and keep you informed."

There was a pause of some seconds. "That's a remarkably pessimistic view," said Kulikov. Even via Genevieve, the words carried a sense less of accusation than contemplation.

"Not pessimistic. Realistic. It all comes down to your purpose for sending us here. We were to provide the missing data base on Wyzhñyñy on-world tactics, potentials, and psychology. And we've already provided major data on all three.

"Whatever decision you make on this, we'll learn more for you. But data on fighting the Wyzhñyñy from something like an equal footing should be more useful than fighting a guerrilla war. And guerrilla wars are seldom successful without the covert support of a civilian population. Here there is none, and if you don't destroy this artillery threat, you'll have to bail us out later."

Another thought struck him. "Or maybe we've gotten all the information you need from here. Maybe it's time to stomp the Wyzhñyñy and let us mop up the remains. With all the—what? Terabits? Petabits?—of data from buoys, windscreens, helmet visors, the electronic communications of men and aircraft, all beamed live to Kereenyaga's shipsmind for sorting, selecting, sequencing—whatever it does with it..." His shrug was lost on Kulikov. "Eventually you'll get it by pod, though maybe not in time to be useful."

I wonder, Kulikov thought, *what he'd say if I told him Ari*

Geltman's been on Kereenyaga's flagship all along, sending us summaries via savant. Best let him learn about that later. "No chance, General," he said. "We've invested a lot in your Jerrie force. You're there for the long haul."

"It was a thought," Pak said, and got back on track. "As guerrillas we can give the Wyzhñyñy a bloody game. But if you send down a Dragon, we stand a very good chance of winning down here, and the data should be more useful."

Kulikov was seldom slow to decide; this was no exception. "I'll do this much," he said. "I'll have Kereenyaga send the marine wolf packs. They won't exterminate the howitzer battalion, but they'll club hell out of it: destroy a lot of equipment, and probably prevent the barrage.

"But I will not authorize a Dragon. Not now. A visit by a Dragon is like an act of the old Hebrew deity, Yahweh: a force beyond human will—or Wyzhñyñy will—to resist. Early on, the Wyzhñyñy probably wondered what had happened to the Dragons that hit them initially, but by now they've more or less convinced themselves they'll never see them again.

"If I send it now, and it leaves after simply destroying an artillery battalion, it will seem to the Wyzhñyñy we're toying with them. It would break their will, and what we learned after that wouldn't be worth much.

"The wolf packs are a much lower order of deity. The flakwagons will bring down some of them, and some of the artillery will escape. A trade-off that will favor us, but still a trade-off. And they'll assume we don't use them more than we do because we don't like the losses. Which we don't.

"Any questions or comments?"

"One comment, sir. The sun is low here now: about 30° above the horizon. If the wolf packs get here soon enough, and attack from the northwest, the flak gunners will have the sun in their eyes."

"I'll tell them. And Pyong, this request hasn't hurt your reputation here. You've been doing a fine job, and we respect your opinions." Kulikov paused. "Just don't overdraw your account. Now I've got to end this session and get those squadrons on their way. Kulikov out."

Pak stared at the box on a cart. "Thank you, Marshal. Pak out."

He looked at the clock readout on the screen. The marines, it seemed to him, would make it in time.

◇

Pak put the evacuation on hold as soon as the wolf packs entered the atmosphere. Then he watched the attack. It was he who'd brought the marine crews into harm's way; the least he could do was watch and root for them.

The Wyzhñyñy hadn't anticipated them, and the marines took full advantage of the sun, and surprise. Their first sweep focused on the flakwagons, and they destroyed about half of them. But given the volume of fire, a number of howitzers were also hit, some with hatches open. There were some splendid explosions. The second sweep followed closely, benefiting from the confusion. They killed three of the remaining flakwagons.

Before the third sweep hit, the remaining howitzers were fleeing for the refuge of the forest a mile away, drawing the Dire Wolves like magnets draw ball bearings. The howitzers' AA slammers were too light to mean much. Only ten howitzers made it to the trees. Not one was undamaged, and there were no operational flakwagons left at all. Three of the armored AG caissons were disabled. The fourth, despite the very heavy armor, had blown sky high, taking the battalion command wagon with it.

The field looked like an armor cemetery.

Briefly the marines hung around, dumping HE on the howitzers their sensors found beneath the forest roof. By then Wyzhñyñy fighters were arriving, and per mission orders, the marines left. Six of the large-bore behemoths never left the forest. The remaining four limped for home.

◇

A traumatized Jilchûk took heart from two facts. The first was hard to understand: He'd had a complete heavy infantry division only a few miles away, ready to move into the forest during the shelling, and attack the human base soon afterward.

The human attack craft had ignored it, as if they'd failed to see it.

And five of the attack craft had been destroyed. Five of the twenty-four; he'd made the humans pay. Perhaps the remaining nineteen were all there were. He wasn't about to take it for granted, but he could hope.

<>

Pak, on the other hand, knew. He also knew that three other Dire Wolves had been damaged, though they remained spaceworthy. Everything considered, that was a bargain, but it wasn't one he rejoiced over.

Briefly he considered sending a squadron of his own fighters to harass the withdrawing infantry, but thought better of it. After the marine heavyweights, his craft would be a weak anti-climax. Not the right note to close on.

The evacuated units en route to the backup base location were ordered to return. News of the marine raid and the destruction of the howitzer battalion, more than made up for the rush and hard work of packing and unpacking gear.

Chapter Fourteen
The Pecan Orchard

Pak stood in his somewhat crowded briefing room, speaking. In a dual role: as Liberation Corps commander, and chief of airborne planning. His listeners were his general staff; several officers of B Company, 2nd Regiment; and the leaders of three platoons belonging to other companies. The wall screen showed a map, and Pak held a pointer in his hand, moving an arrow on the screen.

"The buoys gave us several candidate targets," he was saying. "The one I've chosen is a harvest camp, in a cultivated lacustrine plain fifty-six miles east-southeast of here. The crop resembles grain, and since most of their harvest machinery was destroyed, they have a large crew harvesting with hand tools. It's one of a number of such operations scattered around the colony."

The window changed from a map, to a live view from 360 miles up, greatly enlarged. It showed a large field centered on an orchard. Lines of minute figures could be discerned, advancing slowly. The arrow pointed, and magnification jumped, showing a segment of one line, with Wyzhñyñy swinging harvest implements. In front of them, the crop stood higher than their withers. Behind them lay swaths of cut grain, with another line of Wyzhñyñy wielding what had to be large, long-tined rakes. "A count shows 220 workers, almost surely soldiers," Pak said.

Again the picture changed. Now the orchard occupied most of the screen. "Notice the three openings where trees have been removed. The object in the center opening is a rather small floater, parked, and almost certainly serves as the command center. The other two hold what seem to be mess tents." Again the magnification jumped, and the arrow pointed. "If you look carefully, you can discern what appear to be smaller tents beneath the trees, probably squad tents and latrines."

The focus and magnification changed. Around the orchard was a band of stubble field where the grain had been cut. The arrow pointed again, and again. "These are two flakwagons, 200 feet from the orchard, one at each of two diagonally opposite corners. They can target any air attack—or ground attack—from any side. But you will notice—" the focus moved to one of the flakwagons and enlarged it— "that they are not presently manned. Presumably their crews have duties within the orchard, perhaps in the kitchen—somewhere from which they can run to their guns quickly.

"Presumably the work crew has weapons, but they do not carry them in the field. Probably they're kept in their tents. But you've seen Wyzhñyñy run. Even in New Jerusalem's gravity, they can be armed and fighting within a minute or so.

"They muster each morning at 0911 hours to begin cutting." He gestured at his science officer. "Major Pelletier suggests the lateness is to let the sun dry the dew off the grain before they start cutting it. At 1308 they take a fifty-minute meal break, then return to the field and work until 1722. After another meal, most of them work until 2107."

Pak looked his people over. "That's a long day, and the work is clearly hard labor. They should sleep heavily."

He paused. "You're all aware that there are three different Wyzhñyñy physical types, one larger, with blue fur, another reddish-brown and not so large, and a smaller, dun-colored type." The blues were few, and apparently high-ranking, while the reds seemed to be elite troops. Though experience showed reds in formations of the duns, perhaps as officers.

He went on. "Major Naguib says he hasn't spotted any blues with the harvest crews, but he can distinguish both reds and duns down there. They're on separate work crews. There are somewhat fewer reds, and they don't work after supper. It's been asked why elite troops would be assigned to a harvest crew. They don't appear to be a punishment detail; their hours are shorter, and their work supervisors go unarmed. They may simply be undergoing reconditioning, after wounds or other injuries, or illness.

"I told War House about this last night, and this morning they told me they want six prisoners of each type. That may complicate collection, but there are plenty of both kinds available, so it shouldn't be a serious problem."

Actually Pak didn't like it; his audience read it in his face. The mission didn't need added complications. "Any questions so far?" he asked. "Comments?... All right, let's look at the action plan...."

<>

Jerrie troops were excellent squatters, as Jerrie farmers had been, when there were Jerrie farmers. Their legs were thick and strong, the knees and muscles limber and enduring. And at Forest Base there were no benches, so 2nd Platoon squatted a lot. Squatted during occasional field lectures and while yakking on breaks. Just now they squatted for a talk from their ensign.

With replacements drawn from other companies, 2nd Platoon was back at full strength, the only full-strength platoon in B Company. Nearly half of them were unfamiliar to Esau Wesley, who stood, not squatted, in front to one side, facing them. His hands were no longer bandaged. The new skin on his palms was bright pink.

"You may wonder why 2nd Platoon has been brought to full strength," said now-Ensign Hawkins, "when the rest of B Company is so short-handed. And you new men may wonder why you were pulled out of your old companies. Last evening, Division gave us their reasons, to share with you.

"But first I want to introduce someone to the new people." He gestured at Esau. "Staff Sergeant Esau Wesley has replaced me as your platoon sergeant."

Esau colored visibly. It occurred to him he didn't look like a platoon sergeant. B Company's senior noncoms were of every human pigmentation, but all of them, the survivors and the dead—were or had been tall. At least taller than his own five-eight. He nodded acknowledgement of the introduction, telling himself the Sikhs had chosen him for the job. That should be enough for anyone. And it was a job he'd wanted from the beginning, though he hadn't envisioned someone dying to make it available.

"Esau's here to meet you, and to hear what I'm about to

say," Hawkins went on. "Then he's going back to rehab. He'll be with us for good in two or three days. For you newcomers, Sergeant Esau got his job the hard way. He excelled throughout training, was my senior squad leader...*and*...at the tank park he took out the southwest flak tower single-handed. With covering fire from Corporal Jael Wesley and an unidentified trooper from another platoon. He climbed a rope ninety feet under fire, threw a phosphorous grenade in the firing port to suppress defense, and then, to make sure the guns would be out of service when our floaters arrived, he opened the turret door and threw in a thirty-pound satchel charge he'd carried up the rope on his back. Then he came back down." Hawkins grinned. "Fast, because he was being shot at. Left the skin from his palms and fingers on the rope, when he gripped it to keep from splattering on the concrete ground slab. It's hard to imagine anyone tough enough to do that on purpose. Great job, Sergeant."

Hawkins paused. He'd learned delivery by watching and listening to Captain Mulvaney, unconsciously adding a dash of theatrics. "Now," he said, "down to business. 2nd Platoon has a new mission; that's why it was brought to full strength. You'll get a complete briefing on it after lunch, from the Division briefing officer. I'm just giving you an introduction."

He looked his troops over. "Back at Stenders, airborne platoons were trained for a special mission, one we've had in the back of our minds ever since. General Pak has chosen 2nd Platoon B Company to *lead* a company-strength jump force to take Wyzhñyñy prisoners. The other platoons will be from C, D, and E Companies."

Hawkins didn't tell them the general's staff had had misgivings. B Company, it was pointed out, was by far the most shot-up in the division, and if brought to strength, 2nd Platoon would be half replacements. It would "lack unit cohesion." But he did tell them the general's reasons. It was the only airborne-qualified platoon with experience in raiding deep inside Wyz Country. The only platoon with combat experience in the desperate, helter-skelter situations that historically too often developed in airborne operations. Murphy's Law in action.

Every replacement assigned to Hawkins' platoon was airborne qualified, while its veterans had distinguished themselves in the chaos, and extreme and immediate danger, of the Tank Park Raid.

"It's not that other platoons couldn't lead," Hawkins went on. "They could. But the entire force can feel more confident because of B Company's performance at the tank park.

"And there's a third reason. The general wants B Company's CO, Captain Zenawi, to command the raid, even though he's the newest company commander in the division.

"So you see the confidence the general has in him and in us."

B Company's veterans already knew, via the rumor line, how Zenawi, as Bremer's subordinate, had prevented B Company's extermination. And been awarded captain's bars to go with his new mission. Captain Mulvaney would never be replaced in their minds and hearts, but the troops liked what they knew of Zenawi, and his platoon swore by him.

"And that's it for now," Hawkins finished. "You'll learn the rest of it later, from Division's briefing officer."

He converted then from Hawkins the seasoned older brother, to Hawkins their commanding officer. "2nd Platoon!" he barked, "fall in!"

2nd Platoon got to its feet and formed ranks. There was no opportunity now to talk about it, but the excitement they felt as they trotted to the log yard had a definite mixture of nervous tension.

The general had had an additional reason for deciding on Zenawi as mission commander. He'd been impressed by reports, but before deciding, had called him in and asked how he'd prepare his diverse platoons, if he was in command. Zenawi's off-the-cuff reply had clinched the job.

<>

Their real briefing came after lunch, from Major Naguib, Division's intelligence chief who often doubled as briefing officer. He showed them shots of the orchard. One of the Jerries commented that it looked like a "pecan" orchard, referring to a native species of nut trees. Afterward, all four platoons moved their gear from their own company areas to a new, temporary area with its own mess tent. For the two weeks of mission training, they'd live together, eat together, and train together. And play flag together in mixed teams.

◇

For six days they trained on "sand tables"—squares laid out on the ground and covered with sand. Each platoon had its own table, each with a simulated orchard. Woody fruit stalks, from what the Jerries called "cedars," served as trees. Among the trees, numerous plastic cutouts simulated squad tents and latrines. Two larger cutouts were mess tents. In the center of the orchard was a small plastic box representing the command center, and at a little distance, off two diagonal corners, smaller boxes simulated flakwagons. Wooden pegs represented Jerrie troopers; each trooper was given his own peg, and wrote his service number on it. Everyone and every squad drilled their own roles.

Each platoon was labeled with its company designation: B, C, D or E.

When they'd drilled the mission to the satisfaction of their platoon leaders and squad leaders, Captain Zenawi threw in complications. Troopers not reaching the drop zone, or the premature discovery of one squad or another. Or Esau being unable to fly the unfamiliar Wyzhñyñy floater.

On the very first day, Esau had asked three very basic questions: "How will we know how to fly their floater, and drive their flakwagons, and fire their flak guns?"

Grinning, Zenawi explained. "Indi ordnance specialists flew to the howitzer cemetery almost before the hulls cooled. With salvage vehicles, and orders to bring in a howitzer and a flakwagon in the best shape they could find. They brought in three flakwagons, and cannibalized them to cobble together one that works. So you'll all get a chance to start it, and drive it a bit." The faces he looked at were very interested. "They also brought in two power drums that were only partly expended, so those who need to will get to fire a trasher."

Back on Lüneburger's they'd been quickied on driving light AG ground vehicles, and had loved it. Now the idea of driving a flakwagon, perhaps even firing its heavy weapons, really brightened their eyes. Most of them, he reminded himself, were in their late teens and early twenties. "As for the floater," he went on… "Sergeant Esau, you'll have to settle for learning to fly one of ours, you and your squad. An instructor will talk to you about some of the possible control differences you may encounter in a Wyzhñyñy machine. Then it will be up to you to fly it if you can."

For despite his promotion to platoon sergeant, in this raid Esau would wear another hat. He was regarded as the best stealth man in B Company, so he'd been assigned the most critical single job on the raid: to *steal* the Wyzhñyñy command center.

And as 4th Squad's sergeant—they had a 4th Squad again—Jael had one of the next two most critical jobs.

<><

The next week they went over it all again, this time on a full-scale mockup, with themselves in the action roles. Themselves and F Company, which played the Wyzhñyñy much more effectively than calves had. In the struggles, lips were inevitably split, eyes blackened, noses bloodied. But when wrists and ankles had been securely taped, the captives were dragged from the orchard no more roughly than necessary, to be loaded onto genuine cargo floaters. The injuries were minor, and gave the medics something real to do. They also "treated," and transferred to medivacs, jumpers designated as casualties by umpires from Division. After the second day they ran their drills at night, for realism, and slept late in the morning.

When each drill was over, the casualties were declared whole and sound again, the enemy ordained human, and they all attended a critique of the exercise by the Division referee and Captain Zenawi.

The mock-up had been prepared in advance by a company of Burger engineers, on a prairie area 380 miles from base. To serve as the orchard, they'd planted rows of stout, ten-foot posts at appropriate intervals. Among the posts they pitched actual squad tents in which the troops would live that week, along with two mess tents and canopied latrine pits. They also installed the two inoperable, partly stripped Wyzhñyñy flakwagons.

By the end of the second week, everyone had familiarized themselves with the operational third flakwagon, and dry-fired its light, four-barrelled trasher. Each member of 4th Squad had maneuvered it around and live-fired the trasher.

Esau and his team had each flown a floater, with a certified pilot beside him. And more, on each subsequent day a new floater was brought, each with the control system differently rigged, for them to figure out if they could. Only once did the Indi floater tech have to solve a problem for them.

And every raider became proficient with the short bola—a tough, slender, thirty-nine-inch cord with weights on both ends. Properly thrown, they tangled the legs of rustled Wyzhñyñy livestock. Coupled with a quick and aggressive, three-man follow-up, and tough plastic tape, the bola would hopefully serve in lieu of stunners.

◇

On the last night at the prairie bivouac, Esau and Jael walked out of camp beneath a richness of stars that both beggared and lifted the soul. The Candle had set, and the Lamp wouldn't rise till near dawn. Esau had carried a poncho and an insect repellent field generator, and they'd gone to a cedar grove, to make love in the privacy of its deeper darkness.

Afterward they walked slowly back to camp, holding hands. "Do you recall," Esau said, "what I asked you after the Tank Park Raid?"

She didn't answer at once. Not as if she didn't remember, but as if she was thinking about it. "I remember," she murmured at last.

"What do you think?"

Again her answer lagged, then finally she told him. "I'm still against it, for me. But if you want to, I won't complain or say you shouldn't, because in most ways, to sign up is a good thing."

His only reply was a nod, and after a moment she spoke

again. "I read something when I was a child, in Elder Hofer's *Commentaries on the Testaments.* Even then it struck me as right, and I've reread it since. 'Beware what you set your mind on, lest you thereby create it in the world of phenomena.' He was writing about wishing ill on people you don't like, and the debt it might create for you in the eyes of God. But it seemed to me the meaning went beyond that.

"And I'm afraid if I sign a bot agreement, I might bring harm on myself, and maybe those around me, in order to fulfill it."

Esau frowned. He didn't find it convincing, but again said nothing. After a minute they made out the darkness of tents beneath the stars. "But if *you* want to," Jael repeated softly, "I won't say you shouldn't. Because... Because I may be worrying about nothing."

He turned, gripped her shoulders. "I'll let be," he said, "for now at least. And if I change my mind, I'll tell you before I sign."

"Thank you, Esau," she said, and reaching up, pulled his face down and kissed him. "You're a good husband, a good person, and I love you dearly."

◇

Two nights later, at 2350 hours, the Candle was well down, and high thin clouds screened the stars. Esau was planing in from the north, navigating by his HUDs. Now, by night vision, he could see the orchard itself.

What he didn't see were the sparks and vivid flashes far above.

As he drew nearer, he watched for the edge of the uncut grain. It wouldn't do to overshoot it. His night vision showed the standing crop darker than the stubble field. Ensign Hawkins had explained it—something about dew and 'evaporative cooling'—but it hadn't meant anything to Esau. He could also make out the broad path a crew had trod through the stubble, and steered so he'd land near it, but in the uncut crop. He could see two others who'd landed ahead of him. They were stuffing gear.

His encased blaster and stuffbag dangled on a line below

his feet. The ground leaped upward, the 1.42 gees of gravity jarring him even as he rolled. Then he knelt and looked around. He was, he decided, about three hundred yards from the orchard. Looking back he saw two more jumpers incoming. Their chutes and thermal coveralls were black, but by night vision the coveralls shone faintly golden, barely perceptible.

After pulling in his blaster, stuffbag and chute, he shucked out of his coverall, removed his musette bag and gear, and stuffed chute and blaster case into the stuffbag. It took seconds. By then two more troopers were on the ground. Another was coming in fast, and still another was in sight.

He called up a time readout; keeping on schedule was more important than having the full team. "Bag your gear," he murmured into his helmet mike, "and be ready to move. And keep low." The ripe grain was pale. Their black night-fatigues would be conspicuous against it. Dismissing the no-show from his mind, he murmured "I'm moving out. Keep twenty-yard intervals crossing the stubble." After two weeks of rehearsal they knew what to do, but reminders were standard.

He straightened just enough to locate the path through the stubble field again, then moved through the crop on all fours. Thirty yards brought him to the stubble's edge, where he paused, prone. The footpath didn't reach the uncut crop. He had twenty yards to go through pale stubble eight to ten inches high. There was no way to avoid it. Leaving his bulky stuff bag just within the crop, he began creeping, pulling with his elbows, pushing with his feet, blaster cradled on his forearms. Then he reached the footpath, where Wyzhñyñy feet had scuffed and trod the stubble down, baring dark earth.

Once more he paused, scanning for a sentry along the orchard's edge, a sentry on four legs, with a muscular torso rising from the shoulders like a short-furred neck with arms. When he'd finished his scan, his night vision had found just one. The Wyzhñyñy stood unmoving, perhaps forty yards left of where the path led.

The sonofabitch could be looking at me right now, Esau thought. *If I was him, I'd let me crawl closer, wait till I was almost there.* Meanwhile all he could do was keep crawling and watching, and if the Wyz raised his blaster, pot him first.

That was the first serious complication the captain had thrown into the drills: premature firing. If it happened, he'd have to change his team mission, and speed things up as much as possible. Until then, slow and easy were the key words.

Before he reached the orchard, he could see the sentry's head hanging. The sonofabitch was dozing on his feet! That was bound to be a bigger problem with four-legged sentries than with two.

Within the orchard's edge, Esau rose, moved ten yards to his right, then knelt waiting by a tree while Morris and Avery crossed, and spaced themselves. Only then did he start slowly through the orchard, threading his way among tents, avoiding tent ropes. He heard no sound, not even a Wyzhñyñy snore.

The control center, if that's what it actually was, sat in the middle of the orchard. Timbers had been set as a foundation, keeping the chassis twenty inches or so above the ground. No tents stood within ten yards. Its door was closed, but light shone weakly through the windscreen. There was no sentry. When Morris and Avery had reached the small opening and stopped, Esau lowered himself and crept slowly to the floater, belly to the ground. The floater was light-enough green, he didn't want his two-legged form outlined against it. When he reached the door, he looked around, then rose to one knee, slung his blaster, drew his stunner, and tried the external latch. It seemed to work like those on Terran floaters. Within the orchard there was no discernible breeze. Very slowly, very carefully, he opened the door half an inch. Dull light emerged. Quickly he stood, pulled it wide and stepped in.

The Wyzhñyñy charge of quarters had heard something. His torso turned, their eyes met, and Esau pressed the firing stud. The stunner's almost inaudible condenser hummed, the upright torso folded slowly, and the seated body fell sideways, toppling the low, padded chair.

Esau closed the door, and after a moment's fumbling, locked it. Less than ten seconds had elapsed since he'd entered.

Judging from marine experience on Tagus, the stunned CQ would never waken. There'd been no alarm, and the control screen was serenely featureless. *So far, so good,* he thought. *Let's just hope no Wyzhñyñy radios in now.*

Using his helmet mike, he reported his progress on the command frequency. The others knew what to do next.

◇

Jael's squad had landed east of the orchard. Its mission was to capture and hold the flakwagon that lay off the southeast corner, and with it, defend the raid from outside air or ground interference. Within four minutes of landing, she and her squad lay in the edge of the uncut crop, fifteen yards from the flakwagon. She could see no Wyzhñyñy on or inside the machine, but nonetheless they waited. They were not to move until either Esau had captured the control center, or there was shooting, or the tiny numerals of her HUD clock read 0030 hours—whichever came first.

They would not leave their stuff bags in the crop. The flakwagon controls were too far from the seat, even for a long-legged Sikh, let alone one of her people. So stuffbags would be used for seats.

She wasn't thinking about that, though. She was scanning the east edge of the orchard, and what she could see of the south edge. She'd found the eastside sentry, even laid her blaster sight on him. Southside was someone else's responsibility.

A voice in her helmet startled her. Esau's. "Raider command, I've taken the Wyz command center. Stunned the CQ. He's either dead or dying, and I've locked the door. So far as I know, no one knows we're here. Over."

"Acknowledged, Esau. Teams proceed with the mission."

◇

Jael looked around. She couldn't see any of her squad, but they'd all checked in. She crept across the intervening stubble to the flakwagon, Steven Tyler to her right, mirroring her move. Standing slowly, she peered into the cab, and saw only Tyler peering in on the other side. Her squad, she knew, was crouching in the standing grain, blasters ready. Stepping to the weapon platform, she pulled herself up to peer into the back. No one there, either. Smoothly she bellied over the armored side. A moment later, Tyler joined her. This flakwagon was a lighter-weight version of the one they'd practiced on. The armored sides were high enough to protect a Wyzhñyñy if he kept his head down, and the four-barreled heavy slammer had a gunner's shield.

She heard the cab doors open, a soft sound—Ambler and Hoke, as drilled. So far, so good. She felt calm as wash water. Stepping onto the gunner's platform, she activated the firing system. On the sighting screen, tiny lights showed traversing, elevation, and the power drum all engaged. The hum was louder than she'd expected, but according to the buoys, the wagon was 214 feet from the orchard. The gun swiveled, quick but smooth.

A Wyzhñyñy voice called, jerking her attention from the sighting screen. The east-side sentry was trotting toward her. Carefully she drew her stunner and knelt low, waiting. "Don't fire," she murmured into her mike. She wanted to avoid noise if possible. *Stun him as soon as his head appears,* she told herself, *and he'll never trigger his blaster.*

In her helmet, Jael heard one of C Company's people report the Wyzhñyñy's approach, body low, torso and head forward instead of upright. She expected its head to rise slowly. Instead it *reared,* blaster raised and ready. As she thumbed her stunner, she felt a monstrous pain in her belly, and lost consciousness.

◇

In the control center, the first blaster fire was followed almost at once by a fusillade, some of it sounding like a flakwagon. Esau swore—something almost unthinkable before he'd left home. He'd pretty much figured out the controls while he'd waited. Now he tried powering up, hoping nothing heavy hit the floater, especially the windscreen in front of him. Windscreens were supposed to be blast resistant, but he didn't trust something he could see through.

The gravdrive growled softly, and a HUD came to life on the windscreen—concentric hair-thin rings of blue light with a pale yellow spot in the center. Quickly the spot turned blue. The joystick knob was obviously made to turn on the shaft, so he turned it. A new HUD appeared, and the floater rose. In seconds he was above the trees.

"Raider command!" he said, "raider command! This is Esau! She flies! I'm above the trees now! Don't shoot me down!"

He turned the knob further, swiveled the stick and shoved it forward, sending the floater toward where Captain Zenawi's command post should be. In this contingency, his next job was to stand by as courier, bus driver, or whatever.

◇

Almost at once, Steven Tyler had shouted "Medic!" Then he saw the blood welling from Jael's lower abdomen. "God help us, it's Jael! And it's BAD!" Then the awakening blaster fire reminded him, and he mounted the gunner's seat, seeking targets.

Because the flakwagon teams would be outside the main action, an Indi medic had parachuted with each of them. At Tyler's cry, 4th Squad's medic had dashed to the flakwagon and clambered over the side. Now he crouched beside Jael. "Gentle Jesus!" he muttered. Blood flowed across the deck, spreading. In four seconds, with the fastest "scissors" on New Jerusalem, he'd cut away the ripped tatters of uniform; in two more seconds held a canister from which he sprayed a pressurized liquid into her abdomen, his other hand shifting her ruined intestines for better coverage.

In military jargon, the fluid was simply X-1. It would close the torn blood vessels within seconds, ending hemorrhage. After which surgical repair would be impossible in the division's field hospital. But without it…

Within a minute or so she'd be clinically dead, and soon afterward beyond CNS salvage. He checked a dog tag. Bot agreements were common these days, but her dog tag didn't show one. "Tyler," he asked, "do you know if she's said anything about a bot agreement?"

"I don't know of any."

The medic switched his com to the platoon frequency.

"Ensign Hawkins, this is Med Tech-1 Shinassi. I have a potential bot case here, Jael Wesley, but her tags don't show a bot agreement. Has she said anything orally? Over."

◇

Esau stared at the radio, shocked. He broke in at once. "Shinassi, this is Esau. Just before we loaded out, she said she'd decided to do it. Shall I pick her up? Over."

He was shaking all over.

"Thanks, Esau, but she'll keep. I've given her X-1; now I'll give her Stasis 1. Med Tech Amud Shinassi out."

In time! In time! Esau stopped shaking, but now a different specter hung over him. What would Jael say when she awoke?

◇

Though intense, the fighting in and about the orchard was brief and one-sided. The raiders were superbly prepared, attained total surprise, faced non-combat formations, removed the enemy's sole means of calling for help, and captured their heavy weapons before the Wyzhñyñy even knew they were there. Almost a textbook mission. When Wyzhñyñy APFs were sent, it was too late, and en route were attacked by strong Indi air units.

The bolas worked as hoped. In the confusion on the ground, the Jerries hadn't even tried to distinguish the larger, reddish-brown Wyzhñyñy—"the reds"—from the duns. They simply taped and loaded all they could before the order was given to pull out. And left with four more than War House had ordered—six reds and ten duns, as it turned out.

Early in the fighting, numerous duns fled the orchard, a major surprise. The flakwagons took a heavy toll of them. Except for a few who reached the standing crop and hid, all who weren't captured were killed.

By comparison, Jerrie casualties were moderate: seven died on the ground, and five more on the medivac or in the hospital. Only eight wounded survived, five of them bot cases. The high ratio of killed to wounded was normal for energy weapons, and in this fight, projectile weapons were not involved.

Two Jerries were injured when struck on the head by bolas

being twirled or thrown by others.

Captain Zenawi made sure that all the stuffbags were evacuated with the troops. Hopefully the Wyzhñyñy would never know how this incursion was made.

Chapter Fifteen
Wyzhñyñy Offensive

Before the Jerries had even arrived at Terra, War House had pretty much decided on the basic features of the New Jerusalem liberation campaign. It assumed that the Wyzhñyñy occupation force would be larger than any liberation force they could afford to send. If not, all the better, but the assumption was appropriate. They also assumed that the Wyzhñyñy would make an all-out effort to crush the newly-arrived Jerries.

So with work underway on the Wilderness Base, Pak had sent his fortifications chief, with two officers from the Lüneburger engineers, to plan quick but effective defenses in the forest. The Battle of the First Days had just begun when the three set out on grav scooters, armed with packets of photos provided by the surveillance buoys, and large scale, pre-war topographic/vegetation maps.

Construction began two days later. There wasn't time to plan in detail. Half the Lüneburger engineering regiment was committed to the work. No forts were built, not even bunkers. Instead they adapted modern tools to 16th and 17th century Scandinavian strategies. They should do nicely, if the Wyzhñyñy air support units were adequately suppressed.

<>

The Battle of the First Days had taught the gosthodar that attacking the humans across open fields was unpromising and terribly costly. The Tank Park Raid established that the humans were aggressive and daring. The human surveillance buoys made stealth operations impractical, and the destruction of his heavy howitzer battalion limited the punishment he could inflict on the humans without closing with them.

Then had come the night of the Pecan Orchard Raid, and everything changed. Not because of the raid itself; though insulting and mystifying, it had not been very damaging. But because of what else happened that night.

Commodore Xarsku had sent scouts into F-space to

exchange radio messages with the gosthodar, who used the opportunity to describe his problems. He wanted—according to him he needed—the destruction of the human's wilderness base. And given the base's concealment screen, and the human surveillance buoys, he insisted that this required powerful intervention from space.

Xarsku didn't know as much as he'd have liked about the human space force remaining in the system, but he did know it was substantially more powerful than his own. Nonetheless, his function was to support the colony, so he'd scripted an attack. A bombard would approach the planet in warpdrive, and emerge in F-space some twenty miles out. Using triangulation, and data from Jilchûk, it would then pound the entire blind area—an action that would take about half an hour. At the same time, two marine hunter craft would take out the surveillance buoys. Meanwhile two supply ships were to emerge as near to Jilchûk's main underground supply base as they dared, unload cargo as rapidly as possible, and leave.

Xarsku had no illusions; the supply ships would probably be destroyed before they finished unloading. But even so, they could easily make the difference between survival and starvation.

To cover these actions, Xarsku's planetary guard was to engage its alien opponent, holding its collective attention.

◇

Jilchûk knew little about space warfare, so he'd awaited the action optimistically. His intelligence section monitored Xarsku's radio communications throughout the action, and Jilchûk had followed it play-by-play.

Xarsku's plan was simple, and there was something to be said for simple plans. But this one had been predicted, so Kereenyaga was prepared. Even so, setting the place and time of engagement gave Xarsku an initial advantage, which cost the humans a cruiser and two corvettes. The gosthodar felt a swell of exultation. But the human's greater numbers and firepower soon drove Xarsku back into warpspace.

Meanwhile, near the planetary surface, Xarsku's hunters had destroyed the two human surveillance buoys. His bombard, on the other hand, lay broken and smoking on a forest ridge. It had never gotten into position. Designed for punishing, not fighting, it had been attacked by four of Kereenyaga's corvettes, whose simultaneous torpedo salvos had disrupted its force shield, destroying generator and drives.

As if in retribution, the hunters that had destroyed the buoys then scorched two swaths across the blind area before Kereenyaga's corvettes could engage them. One escaped into warp space. The other, crippled, careened into the forest miles away, and blew up.

The corvettes then caught the cargo ships in the act of unloading, and slammed torpedos into each of them before heading back into near-space.

When it was over, Jilchûk found solace in the destruction of the buoys. Also, substantial supplies had been transferred before the supply ships were attacked, and more after their fires had been controlled.

But the enemy on the ground had not been destroyed. Damaged, wounded, but not destroyed. Their destruction remained up to him. *Move quickly!* he thought. *Quickly and powerfully!* He'd told himself that before, he realized, but this time nothing would turn him. There'd be no hesitation, and no backing off. And with the buoys gone, the enemy couldn't know or predict his actions as they had before.

◇

General Pak watched Wyzhñyñy infantry—a very long column of fours—trotting easily down the road toward the forest. The bulk of their equipment and supplies were carried by AG trucks, and their speed of foot was sobering. He'd realized before he'd left Terra that this life-form would run faster than humans, but actually watching them... They and their guardian flakwagons, of which the Wyzhñyñy seemed to have an endless supply.

At least he could watch them. Presumably the Wyzhñyñy didn't know that Kereenyaga had replaced the lost buoys with another. The Jerries had promptly nicknamed it "Lonesome Moses," which surprised the general when he heard about it. It seemed irreverent for troops with their background.

Lonesome Moses provided less detail, less perspective, and had far less versatility than the buoys the Wyzhñyñy had destroyed, but it was infinitely better than no buoy at all. Immediately after the fighting on the First Day, Xarsku had sent a single daring Hunter to shoot down the first two. Kereenyaga had quickly deployed his reserve pair, and ordered his engineering section to cobble together a backup. Shipsmind had provided the basic information, and his engineers and technicians had provided parts and ingenuity. And with it now in place, they'd begun on still another, just in case.

Equally important was Colonel Schrager's Burger engineers, building defenses in the wilderness. The engineers and the Jerries. The colonel had suggested that progress would be faster with help, and that a battalion of resourceful backwoods infantry would be just the ticket. Pak had complied. A Jerrie battalion had pitched in with beam saws, AG sleds, and strong backs, felling trees and throwing up breastworks. Pak had visited the work in progress, and been impressed by the strength, energy and cheerfulness of the Jerries at work. They treated it like a holiday, hard though it was.

And urgent now, because Wyzhñyñy command was moving troops into the forest at two points, one division eighteen miles west of the howitzer cemetery, another thirty miles east of it. And strong reserves had been moved to several locations, with APFs. Obviously the Wyzhñyñy commander intended to attack at unpredictable points simultaneously. As soon as he'd made a breakthrough, his reserves would exploit it.

What Pak didn't know was, the key reserves were "reds"— what was left of the Wyzhñyñy warrior brigade.

Meanwhile Wyzhñyñy batteries were also on the roads, apparently detached from their infantry brigades. He wasn't sure what plans Wyzhñyñy command had for them, but he was sure he wouldn't like them. Lonesome Moses couldn't identify the caliber, but they seemed smaller than those destroyed by the marines. Five or six-inch bores, he guessed. They should have enough range to lay fire on the Wilderness Base, and on much of the defenses the Burgers had been building. It wouldn't be remotely comparable to what the Wyzhñyñy bombard would have done, but he was glad he'd moved his hospital and "bot shop" to the backup site, thirty-five miles north.

And the artillery were accompanied by tanks and flakwagons. Perhaps all the tanks the Wyzhñyñy had left. A simple count showed more of them than he had. What was building here, he did not doubt, was a decisive showdown.

We'll see, Pak thought, *what Major Phayakapong accomplishes with our own modest project.*

<>

Despite more than seven centuries of Commonwealth peace, the lineage of Major Patrick Feliks Phayakapong had kept and nourished a long military tradition. Privately for the most part. Eleven centuries earlier, an ancestor named McClintock had fought in the North American War of Secession. He'd been a private in J.E.B. Stuart's cavalry at the First Battle of Manassas, a sergeant at South Mountain, a lieutenant at Chancellorsville and Gettysburg, and finally a captain at Yellow Tavern. Where he lost his general to a Yankee bullet, and his shattered left leg to a surgeon's saw.

His experiences, pride, and storytelling began the tradition. Almost as far back, in various tributaries of the family line, others fought in the Crimean War, the Franco-Prussian War, the Boer War, the Moro Resistance, the European Great War…but either they were not storytellers, or their stories were lost. Members of the family had compiled histories of their ancestors' units and campaigns, but those weren't the same as personal accounts.

Then a McClintock great grandson fought in the Hitler War, serving as an armor officer under the fabled George Patton. A decade later he served as a senior officer under Walton Walker and Matthew Ridgeway in the Korean War. And described it all in his published memoirs, giving the tradition new life. Another forebear served as a sergeant in the U.S. Marine Corps in the Southeast Asian War, and another as an airborne ranger. The marine said he'd never have told his story if his grandfather hadn't passed his along. The ranger kept his memories to himself, but a buddy in his squad, in *his* memoirs, often referred to "Sergeant Walking Coyote," calling him a warrior's warrior.

All of this built and enriched the tradition. In yet another branch of the family, a British special forces officer had served throughout the difficult years of the guerrilla war in Malaysia. He'd shared none of it with his children, but a daughter assembled the basics from official sources, and interviewed aging veterans of her grandfather's unit. Another forebear fought, survived and escaped as a Shan guerrilla in the ill-fated Myanmar Revolution. His children recorded his reminiscences, which written down and translated, added fundamentally different material to the family lore.

Shortly before the Troubles, the core of the family went as colonists to Indi Prime, the first deep-space colony—one of only two sponsored by the government. During the Troubles, the deep space colonies were lost track of. But after reconnection, in every generation some family member returned to Terra to join the fleet (such as it was), or its marines, or the Terran Planetary Defense Force, and kept the tradition alive. Despite the long centuries of low public esteem, little opportunity for advancement, and limited meaningful function beyond study, brainstorming, virtual warfare, and weapons design. They kept the faith. And when they retired, it was usually to Indi Prime, often bringing with them a wife and child, or children. Twice from families with a military tradition of their own.

But Major Phayakapong was the first in a very long time to ride a battle tank. Occasionally, mainly in the moments before sleep, he took time to savor what he thought of as the privilege, wondering now and then if he'd been a tanker in an earlier life.

Just now however, his attention was on his mission, which so far had been uneventful. But that would soon change. His battalion had taken heavy losses during the Battle of the First Days, but in the reorganization that followed, it had been brought back nearly to full strength. On this mission, his infantry companies and their APCs had been left behind to help defend the base. His job was to strike deep within Wyz Country, and all he had with him were his forty-one battle tanks and eight flakwagons.

It was near midnight, and he rode in the turret of his command tank, its hatch open. The night smelled of damp soil and vegetation, for it had rained the day just past, then cleared, and now dew had formed. It occurred to him that the ancestor who'd ridden with Stuart would have smelled horse manure and urine instead, particularly near the rear of the column. Sometimes there'd have been the stink of black powder explosions. While the tanker who'd followed Patton and Walker would have smelled pungent fumes from internal combustion engines. And during combat? Probably the oxidation products of nitrocellulose. *Different times, different experiences,* he told himself. Tonight he'd smell ozone generated by heavy trasher pulses.

Via his visor HUDs, the jury-rigged Lonesome Moses kept him aware of where the Wyzhñyñy infantry columns were, where his target was, and where he was relative to both. The columns were coming together from various locations, merging on a few major routes. Several times he'd detoured to avoid discovery, for he was going south while the enemy was going north. And human tanks, like other human ground-proximity vehicles, looked different from Wyzhñyñy vehicles having the same function.

Just now the road ahead was clear. He stopped in a riverine woods, to let his men get out of their armored boxes, move around a bit, and relieve themselves. It was undesirable to enter action with a full bladder or colon.

According to his HUD he had just 1800 yards to go. Quietly he radioed orders. The column slowed, then deployed just behind the brow of a low rise, and a new HUD replaced the others all along the line. Just across the brow the ground dipped mildly, then rose again, becoming a steep ridge 1200 yards ahead. Less than 300 yards from where the tanks sat, forest began.

His tankers knew what to do. "On my count," the major said, then paused. "Ten, nine, eight…."

At zero the night flared. Penetration pulses slammed

deeply into rock, and for the first few salvos it felt really good. Then the rug was pulled from beneath the major's feet. Prior to the arrival of the Liberation Corps, the Wyzhñyñy had cut gun emplacements into the bluff. And after a very brief delay—the crews had been sleeping—they'd returned fire. Lots of heavy fire. He lost thirteen of his forty-one tanks and four of his flakwagons before he reached the riverine woods again. In their cover he stopped, to throw off the enemy gunners' timing, and reorganize. And open his turret hatch again. His HUDs suggested it was safe for the moment, and he didn't like the stink of sweaty fear.

Pat, he told himself, *you really kicked the hornets' nest that time.* Still, his heavy trashers had sent tons of rock crashing down on the road—and presumably onto the entry to the Wyzhñyñy cavern complex. Pak, from surveillance information, had concluded it was the Wyzhñyñy headquarters base. Actually it wasn't. It was a major Wyzhñyñy supply base.

<>

From the riverine woods, Major Phayakapong traveled mostly westward, targeted from time to time by Wyzhñyñy attack floaters, but unmolested by ground forces. The floater attacks were hit and run, directed mainly at his flakwagons, which gave as good as they got. And vice versa. He lost another tank, had two more with problems, and was down to two flakwagons. Then a flight of good guys arrived, and chased the bogies off. Shortly afterward his battered battalion reached the Mickle, and turning north, crossed on the first bridge they came to. They continued mainly west then, jogging north from time to time at crossroads.

Shortly before dawn they reached the relative safety of the forest, well away from any Wyzhñyñy. There the tankers paused to heat and eat field rations. Then they lay down on their fart sacks and slept in the open air. They could hear distant fighting, back in the forest, but it didn't keep them awake.

<>

The woods were thick with the devil's music: the rapid popping of blasters and slammers, the crackling of pulses creating miniature vacuums through the air, the hard sound of pulses striking trees.

Ensign Rrokiç spotted a source—humans behind a breastwork of logs. "Up there!" he shouted, then sheltered as well as he could behind a thick trunk. He hated to gesture; it attracted enemy fire. "Don't just lie there!" he snapped into his helmet mike. "Shoot, damn it! And don't bunch up!"

Ensign Rrokiç was a nanny—as large as some warriors, almost as strong—and protective. Genetically, protection meant care and protection of the young, but the master and warrior genders massaged the nanny protective instinct and extended it to cover defense of the species. The purpose being to turn nannies into surrogate warriors when necessary. In fact, the nanny gender provided many reserve unit noncoms.

Gender manipulation and noncom training worked about as well with Rrokiç as it did with any nanny. He yelled well, and could manhandle his troops when necessary. But the hard authority of the warrior gender was never really duplicated.

What was compelling was his rank, and the sense his orders made. His platoon took cover as best it could, behind tree trunks, or in the visual cover provided by the tops of trees the humans had felled. From there they fought back.

All day they'd been moving slowly through the damnedest mess Rrokiç had ever seen. The humans had felled thousands on thousands of trees, in unpatterned bands through the forest. Usually with the upper parts in your face. They weren't everywhere; that wouldn't have been practical. They'd been located to extend or connect natural terrain features, crowding the advancing Wyzhñyñy into whatever situations the humans wanted them. Or simply pinched them off, turning them back to find a way around. Typically they led into cleared fields of fire, and there was little anyone could do about it. *Little by little we advance,* Rrokiç told himself, *yet it seems we're always on the defensive.*

Now as before, when his platoon had taken what cover they could, the fight turned into a grenade exchange, delivered mostly by launchers. And his people were more exposed.

So he called for a flamethrower again.

◇

Near one flank of C Company's position, Captain Freddie Bibesco Singh crouched in his command post, scanning with his small camouflaged periscope. His blastermen, slammermen and grenadiers were reaping well. As before, the Wyzhñyñy had moved into the visual cover of the abatis. Now they'd no doubt call in a flamethrower. Meanwhile the Wyzhñyñy grenadiers and mortarmen were using timed fuses to produce airbursts, exploding above his troopers' improvised shelters.

It was time to deliver his new surprise. Setting his mike, he voiced the ignition command. Barely hidden by old leaves, ground vegetation, and the outermost foliage of the abatis, explosions erupted like a string of giant ladyfingers, as camouflaged shot-mines blew along a line of detcord. Debris rose, and cries of pain. Meanwhile his people kept firing.

From where he crouched, he couldn't see the Wyzhñyñy flamethrower being brought up, but from treetops a little distance off, his camouflaged snipers could. They'd already been making things hot for Wyzhñyñy mortar crews. Though they paid; the Wyzhñyñy had learned that this enemy climbed.

A sniper spotted the flamethrower and felled the Wyzhñyñy carrying it, but another picked it up. Then some Wyzhñyñy threw smoke grenades, concealing both flamethrower and mortars. "B Company pull out!" Bibesco ordered. His own smoke bombs popped and billowed, his blastermen and grenadiers got to their feet, his snipers lowered themselves on ropes, and they all pulled back. Concealed a short distance to the rear, out of sight of the Wyzhñyñy, were their squad-size APCs. These would take them to their next ambush position much more quickly than they could manage on foot, and they needed to set up before the Wyzhñyñy arrived.

Not all of C Company would ride with their squad. The medics loaded some of them out to the hospital, or to the "bot shop," or simply to Graves Registration.

◇

It was noon before Major Phayakapong ordered his crews

back into their tanks. General Pak had given him his next assignment. Three battalions of Wyzhñyñy armored howitzers were on the move, four batteries in each. With tank escorts. It looked as if they planned to establish fire bases—probably three of them. It was unlikely they knew about Lonesome Moses, and Pak didn't want them to, so he hadn't started molesting them yet. Phayakapong was to continue westward, and be ready to hit them after nightfall.

The major decided to pick his way through the forest for a while. It would keep him out of sight. He hadn't mentioned that he now had only twenty-five battle worthy tanks and two flakwagons. The general would already know that, or close enough, from Lonesome Moses, and anyway there was nothing to be done about it.

<>

Normally, in the evening, Esau heard all the sounds of the forest. Fell asleep listening to the chirping of crickets, the peeping of tree lizards, the occasional grunting basso of a bull owl, or the warbling alto of a mouse owl. Even, barely audible, woodborers chewing tunnels inside a nearby fallen tree. And best of all, from above the trees, the thin piercing whistle of night hawks catching insects.

But this evening none of it registered.

Most of the division had been fighting all day, in the forest off both east and west. Far enough away, he hadn't heard any of it. And it seemed to Esau that tonight the war—their war, on New Jerusalem—would be won or lost. Not over, but won or lost. Weren't hardly any fighting units left on base, except the strategic reserve.

Which included the airborne qualified platoons, and now they were being sent out, trotting northward through the evening forest. There'd been no time to drill the mission—it was that urgent—but their briefing had been thorough, with a demo on the screen.

Probably it would work out all right. They were all veterans, and drilled or not, they had a clear sharp picture of what needed to be done.

He glanced at the man he trotted beside. He'd known Ensign Hawkins for—about a year he guessed. Esau wasn't someone who kept a mental calendar. But he had little idea of what the ensign thought about in the privacy of his mind. Didn't know all that much about him. He'd grown up in a Sikh neighborhood in a Terran town called Padstow, where it rained a lot; had a wife and children; and before the war they'd lived by a lake somewhere. But what counted was, he was honest, and able, and treated people right. His platoon liked him and could depend on him.

Somewhere ahead were APFs: four of them, for four airborne platoons again. Tonight they were being called "A Company Airborne (temporary)," and 2nd Platoon simply "Hawkins' Platoon." But all four had jumped and fought together at the Pecan Orchard, and felt confident about each other.

Esau really didn't want to die yet, because he hadn't seen Jael since before her body had been killed. He needed to go visit her, so she could give him Tophet for lying to the medic, and maybe tell him she never wanted to see him again. He owed her that much, at least. When he'd got back from the Pecan Orchard, he'd gone off alone in the woods and wept hard bitter tears, with choking sobs that like to have torn him apart. But he'd have lied again if need be, because he couldn't just let her die, he loved her so.

Every day, floaters flew off north to the bot shop and the hospital, and he'd asked Captain Zenawi for a half-day off. But the captain reminded him that after someone got bottled, they spent a few days in a kind of sleep. For what they called "neurological detraumatization," that helped them heal.

Remembering had started silent tears. Bottled. He hoped it wasn't too bad. She could have been in the loving arms of God, if it hadn't been for him.

Now, courtesy of night vision, their APFs were visible among the trees, and his attention returned to real time. Above the forest roof there was probably a little twilight left, but down where they were it was dark night. The armored floaters were lined up in two ranks along a sizeable creek. From there they could lift through the slender break it made in the forest roof.

Major Chou was already there from Division, overseeing. He'd land afterward with E Company, to lead the demolitions follow-through.

They broke ranks to pick up their gear, which had been hauled there by AG cargo sleds. They wouldn't be jumping from high enough to require thermal coveralls. Gloves and winter underwear would do. They simply buckled on their chutes, snapped on their gear, checked each other out, then boarded their floaters and belted themselves onto their seats. Then the APFs rose carefully through the trees and into the young night sky.

<>

Sergeant Isaiah Vernon sat on another APF, on a short hop east. As part of Pak's tactical reserve, all six bot platoons were going out together as a combat team—132 warbots plus 12 salvage bots and a command staff of 4.

Their mission commander was Major Einer Arslanian Singh. The story was, Arslanian had been taking airborne training on Masada, got caught in a squall, and came down in a rock pile, tearing up his knees. Afterward, back on Terra, he'd specialized in bot tactics, even though there were no bots. That was before anyone had heard of the Wyzhñyñy.

Then had come the message from Tagus, and suddenly bots were dearer than diamonds. But at that time, having lost one's legs wasn't enough to qualify. Then Arslanian had another accident. Except the rumor was he'd set it up—had sacrificed his eyesight in order to be bottled. Isaiah didn't know if the story was true or not, but Arslanian ended up a major, commanding the 1st Jerrie bot contingent. He'd planned and led two different platoon actions. Now he'd lead a long company.

Isaiah, whose nature it was to like and accept people, was happy to have the major in command. Because this would be the most dangerous mission they'd been on. They'd be set down in the midst of a Wyzhñyñy operations headquarters, if they got that far.

<>

The evening breeze was cool and clean, but Major Patrick

Feliks Phayakapong's T-shirt was wet with sweat. They'd traveled buttoned up for a while, because after they'd left the forest they'd been shadowed by Wyzhñyñy floaters. Whether scouts or fighters he didn't know; Moses wasn't up to such distinctions. Then word came that a flight of Indi fighters were on the way, and he'd opened his turret hatch to watch. He didn't see much; most of it was out of his view. The Indi flight commander radioed that they'd shot down two of three, and the third had fled. The major appreciated that someone was looking out for him.

Meanwhile he was running low on time. His orders had been updated, and his HUD showed a Moses-eye view of the Wyzhñyñy force he was supposed to attack. Four batteries of howitzers—forty-eight guns in all—escorted by a company of tanks. Apparently they planned to set up a fire base to shell the Jerrie regiment manning the eastern forest defenses.

But the tanks had changed direction, apparently to attack his own battered force.

Eight additional batteries and another tank company were headed farther west on a different road, apparently to set up another, or other fire bases. Probably to shell Headquarters Base.

According to Moses, the Wyzhñyñy no longer had scouts up, or out on the ground for that matter. Hard to believe, but if true, then neither enemy force knew what he was doing in real time. "Well crap," the major muttered, "it's now or forget about it." He keyed his mike and ordered twelve tanks, two groups of six, to diverge from his line of advance. Each group was to hit the Wyz tank force from the flank. To maximize surprise, he'd tell them when to fire, unless of course the Wyz fired first.

Then, if it looked doable, he'd take the rest of his force through or around the Wyz tanks, and attack the east base howitzers. It looked like the best move he had available.

Calling Division command, he told them what he planned. "Fine. Do it," Pak said. "And Pat, you need to know I've got airborne raiders scheduled to take out the central fire base. That's why I let the Wyzhñyñy scouts shadow you as long as I did. It fixed their attention on you.

"The jumpers will be in mortal jeopardy if the tanks from the east base show up there. So the more hell you raise, the better chance the airborne will have. They've got a very tough and dangerous job. Like yours."

◇

The first salvo of 5.6-inch shells—forty-eight of them—was fired while the APFs were en route. To Arjan Hawkins it sounded like a distant thunderstorm. And the guns continued in unison, which struck him as peculiar.

If we'd gotten off half an hour sooner, he thought, *we might have prevented it.* But there hadn't been time, and at any rate, a half-hour earlier it hadn't been dark enough.

For weeks the Burger engineers had worked their butts off day and night, building the base, abatises, and breastworks. And the backup base. Now they were working furiously, without Jerrie help, to move the more sensitive Headquarters Base installations there.

The flight was short, even though they bypassed the fire base and jumped six miles to the south—a subterfuge to avoid Wyzhñyñy suspicions. Now the troopers of Airborne A temp were planing back northward beneath their parasails. Even with night vision, Hawkins couldn't see most of his people. But they had their HUDs.

The salvos paled the darkness with great flashes of light, and as Hawkins planed nearer, the booming became less like thunder. It just sounded like artillery. His central HUD showed the fire base. Its layout seemed idiotic, though obviously the Wyzhñyñy didn't think so. The HUD was too small for detail, but Lonesome Moses had provided the essentials during the briefing, and Hawkins had imprinted them mentally. Six ranks of howitzers, eight in a rank, formed a compact square. Their spacing provided aisles, adequate for firing safety, and for howitzers to jockey in and out if necessary. Grav sleds would no doubt use the aisles to distribute ammo from the two massive caissons on the south edge. The border of dot-like icons along the east, south and west sides indicated squad APCs: twelve on the east and west, and eight on the south, where the center of the rank was occupied by the caissons and a heavy, armor-recovery vehicle. About twenty yards off each corner were two flakwagons, eight in all.

If a wolf pack were available, that compactness would make a marvelous target, but an airborne attack would have to suffice. His platoon's primary job was to take out the flakwagons at the two south corners, and the APCs along the south side. Dreiser's Platoon would take out the west-side APCs, along with the two northwest flakwagons. Castro's would handle the east side. Hussain's was the reserve, ready to defend the landers when they came in with Division's demolitions company.

The overall mission was etched clearly in Hawkins' mind. But if even two or three flakwagons escaped destruction, or most of the APCs survived, there'd be serious problems in carrying it out. Especially since it wasn't enough just to disrupt the barrage for the time being. The howitzers, or most of them, had to be destroyed. Which meant Demolitions' floaters needed to land safely.

He didn't consciously review all that. It was part of his mental data base, not looked at. Just now, Hawkins was manipulating his black, night-jump parasail to set him down in his platoon's designated drop zone. When he reached 100 feet local altitude, he let his gear drop, felt it jerk the dangle line, felt its air-drag, sensed the ground reaching for him. The strong gravity slammed him hard. He felt agonizing pain, and almost cried out. His left leg had broken below the knee. Broken badly. He knew it at once.

Fortunately the breeze was light, and his chute had collapsed. He released his harness, and hand over hand pulled in his combat pack, rocket gear, and blaster scabbard. Then he drew his combat knife, cut away his left pant leg, and stared. He'd already felt the blood. Now he could see a sharp end of broken bone protruding through skin and underwear, and shivered at the sight. Suppressing the reaction, he activated his casualty signal. *Get it tended to before the Wyz find out we're here,* he told himself. *The medics will have plenty to do then.*

He spoke to his helmet mike. "Hawkins' Platoon, this is

Ensign Hawkins. I've broken a leg. Esau, you're in full charge of the platoon now. Proceed with the mission. The medics will pick me up." He was surprised at how normal he sounded. Taking his blaster out of its scabbard, he loaded it, then lay back to wait for a medic. And defend himself if necessary.

<>

Esau was on the ground when he got Hawkins' order. *Foop!* he thought, then dismissed his chagrin. He'd already retrieved his gear. Now he slung his pack and blaster. At least to start with, his primary weapon would be his short-barreled, anti-armor rocket launcher. One of its three light-weight rockets was already seated. The other two he'd snapped on his harness.

Esau had been the cleanup, the last jumper out, so he was pretty sure the others were all down. "Hawkins' Platoon," he said, "you heard the ensign. Squad leaders assemble your squads." Almost at once he saw their light wands signaling, visible via a wave-length window in their visors. Each squad leader had his own signal. He gave them half a minute, then called: "1st Squad report... 2nd Squad report..." One after another they responded, all alike: "All present and accounted for, Sergeant."

Only one man hurt or missing. I hope the other platoons are that lucky, he thought. Though to lose your leader...

He looked toward the artillery. All that noise—the Wyzhñyñy sentries should be numb by now. *We'll know soon enough,* he told himself. He saw no sign of their infantry. *Maybe they're all in their APCs. We can hope.* The nearest were less than 300 yards away, but hitting them needed to be synchronized with the attack on the flakwagons all around the square. And Hawkins' Platoon was the key. The others were to start firing when it did.

"Hawkin's Platoon, any questions?... Form up to attack." They did, counting off by pairs, one man with his launcher in hand, the other with his blaster to provide covering fire. When the launcher-man had expended his rockets, they'd switch. Esau changed to Captain Zenawi's command channel. "Captain," he said, "Hawkin's Platoon is ready to move."

"Fine, Wesley. I'll tell you when."

Esau waited. *Any time now,* he thought.

Suddenly, midway between salvos came a premature burst of blaster fire from the Wyzhñyñy square, followed quickly by more. *"Hit 'em, Airborne A!"* Zenawi almost shouted it into his mike.

"Let's go, Hawkins' Platoon!" Esau said, and they started toward their targets at a lope. "Fire when you think you can hit your target!" Their rocket launchers were cheap and light, aimed simply by pointing. The briefing had specified not firing them at ranges beyond 50 yards on this mission, but that assumed they'd be able to approach that close before being discovered. So his troopers began firing at twice that range—when the first APC turret blaster began hammering slammer pulses in their direction. They took out both southwest flakwagons before either could fire, and rocket hits flashed at one, two, three, four APCs. One of the southeast flakwagons began firing at them before its guns were sufficiently depressed, the pulses angling skyward. But its controls were nimble. Its platform swiveled sharply, as the trajectory of its fire adjusted. In the instant before streams of trasher pulses swept toward them, troopers hit the dirt. If Esau had been able to squeeze between the grains of soil, he would have. He rolled his head to the side, to see without raising it. Pulses swept over him about knee-high, then he rolled to a knee and fired. The range exceeded 150 yards, but a second later his rocket struck the flakwagon, almost simultaneous with two others.

The remaining southeast flakwagon had busied itself with Castro's Platoon. "Hawkins up and at 'em!" Esau called, and the survivors were on their feet again, charging the south-edge APCs. A turret slammer didn't put out nearly the volume of fire a flakwagon did, but at least some had located their targets and were firing aimed bursts. Rockets impacted APCs, even as more APCs got their guns into action. And now the platoon was receiving blaster fire, as Wyzhñyñy emptied from troop compartments.

The surviving APCs were pulling out of line to evade

trooper attacks, and to disperse themselves as targets. One came almost toward Esau, its turret slammer riveting the darkness with bright pulses, and he punched a rocket into its front armor panel, unsure if it could penetrate there. The vehicle swerved, careened, then lost its AG cushion and stopped, plowing a short broad furrow in the ground. Wyzhñyñy emerged from the rear, and firing, began to back toward the base's perimeter.

Esau sprinted to take cover against the front of the derelict APC, his partner staying behind, delivering covering fire. In the shelter of the APC, Esau paused for a second, receiving Zenawi's radio traffic along with his own platoon's. There was more of Zenawi's; Hawkins' Platoon was busy at a different level, fighting. The battle had become a melee.

The APC didn't have rungs to the top, like the human version did. He climbed to the roof via a front cowling and the top of the driver's compartment, then lay there. Saw an APC pass, separating itself from the chaos, fired his last rocket and saw it hit the troop compartment. The vehicle continued. He threw away his now useless launcher, and with blaster in hand, scanned for opportunities. He was some thirty yards outside the original row of APCs, now marked by wreckage. There was shooting everywhere. Soldiers were running around on two feet and four. "Hawkins' Platoon," he said, "when you unlimber your blasters, fix your bayonets!"

He fixed his own by feel, his eyes busy elsewhere. A flakwagon appeared around the southeast corner, a little distance outside the square, its multiple barrels hammering bursts of trasher fire in the direction of anything it saw on two legs. It would pass within ten feet. He rolled onto his side, his right hand freeing a fragmentation grenade from his harness, setting it to "impact" by feel, tossed it as the wagon passed, then jumped. The grenade roared and Esau sprinted, gripped the rim of the armored side with one hand and tossed his blaster over, running hard. He lost stride, and almost his hold, then pulled himself up and over, coming down on a Wyzhñyñy body. Another Wyzhñyñy hung slack in the gunner's harness, bleeding, eyes wide, jaws gaping as if for breath. Esau recovered his blaster and put him to rest.

In the cab, they'd felt and heard the explosion, suspected what had happened, and querying the gun crew, got no answer. The vehicle stopped, a door opened, and a Wyzhñyñy head peered over the side. Esau shot it, then vaulted out, losing his feet as he landed, recovered quickly and fired through the open door.

"4th Squad! 4th Squad! This is Esau! I've captured a flakwagon! About...thirty yards west of the west caisson. I need a driver or two, and a gunner! Respond!" As he said it, it occurred to him he didn't know whether anyone in 4th Squad was alive. "This is Tyler, on my way!" "This is Hoke. I'm a-coming." "This is Felspar, on my way!" The answers came almost simultaneously. Esau waited tensely.

Hoke was the first to arrive. He and Esau shifted the Wyzhñyñy body to serve as driver's seat for Tyler. Tyler sat on it, and Esau climbed in back. Felspar had freed the Wyzhñyñy gunner from his gun harness, and with a little ingenuity had adjusted it for himself.

For a moment Esau hesitated. "Felspar, do you need me?" he asked.

"Be good to have someone to set a new power drum when I need it."

"Okay. I'm your man. Airborne A, Hawkins' Platoon now owns a flakwagon on the south side. For God's sake don't hole us. If anyone knows of a live Wyzhñyñy flakwagon, let us know. We'll see about taking it out."

He stepped onto the gunner's platform to see better.

"Wesley," Zenawi called, "there's one on the west side about a hundred yards out, stalled; I think her driver's hit. But the gunner's raising hell with Dreiser's Platoon, and it's got a couple of blastermen in back."

"I copy, Captain. We're on our way. Tyler, let's go. Felspar, don't fire at APCs now. I don't want to get tied up with fighting till we take out that other flakwagon."

"Wesley —" It was Zenawi again— "That other flakwagon has a driver again. It's moving erratically toward the southwest corner, firing heavily.

"Copy, sir."

The reported flakwagon rounded the southwest corner and came toward them. "I see it, Esau!" Tyler shouted. Felspar said nothing. He swung his gun on target and at once fired a long burst. Like the APC, the Wyzhñyñy-manned flakwagon swerved and stopped, but it still directed its fire elsewhere. Apparently its gunner didn't know they'd been hit by one of their own.

"Pull past it, Tyler. Felspar, wait till you've got a clear shot at the rear end, then pump her again."

Felspar liked this machine. It was a heavy flakwagon, like the one they'd trained on. They passed the other on the outside, at ten yards, and he fired a long burst into the rear. There was a surprisingly powerful explosion. A trasher bolt must have hit the enemy's power drum.

"Tyler," Esau said, "stop a minute. I want to make sure the sonofabitch is totally out of action." Then he slung his blaster on a thick shoulder and turned his back on the gunner. "Get me a P grenade out of my pack," he said. Leaning, Felspar got it for him. Esau hooked it on his harness, vaulted over the side, ran the twenty yards back to the other vehicle, tossed the frag grenade into the rear for insurance, heard it roar, and peered over the side. It looked like a slaughterhouse. The power drum that had blown had already been seated, and torn the trasher's firing mechanism apart.

Esau opened the cab door then. Inside were two Wyzhñyñy almost certainly dead. He tossed in the phosphorus grenade anyway, and slammed the door. He never heard the phosphorous grenade pop. Felspar, watching from the back of the captured flakwagon, saw Esau fall, and called Tyler, who called for a medic while Hoke jumped from the cab and ran to Esau.

"Steve," Hoke called, "he's breathing, but there's lots of blood running from under his helmet."

"A medic's on his way," Tyler answered. "Now get your butt back here! In back, to help Felspar. The captain wants us to knock out APCs before the floaters get here."

"Right. I'm a-coming."

Hoke wouldn't have believed the fighting was less than ten minutes old.

◇

Throughout it all, the howitzers continued to thunder. General Pak could hardly have been more pleased, despite the explosives raining down on his base, because it meant the howitzers were not pulling out. And he very much wanted them to be there when the demolitions company arrived.

They no longer fired in synch; it was as if the chaos around their borders had spread inward. But the volume of shells they threw across the miles remained as great.

Airborne A temp had done their job despite the fight's premature beginning. When the APFs disembarked the demolitions platoons with their petards and heavy rockets, the fire they faced was light. Briefly it lay low, while Hussain's Platoon moved in ahead of them to help finish off the Wyzhñyñy infantry. The other three jumper platoons had been seriously reduced.

More than the demolitions platoons had landed. There were two medivacs, and an APF with field medics and AG sleds to bring in the wounded. Esau was one of the first loaded. He was already on his way in, wobbly and on foot. A medic sprayed his scalp to inhibit further bleeding. Aboard the medivac, he'd refused to be installed on an evac litter. Refused to be bandaged, because he wouldn't be able to get his helmet back on. Refused to be injected, and shoved an insistent medic hard enough, the man fell on his butt. Tight-lipped, the Terran medical officer in charge let Esau be. He had better things to do than coerce some stubborn Jerrie. But when they got to the hospital, he'd see him charged and disciplined.

Meanwhile Esau posted himself out of the way, just inside the ramp, watching till it was nearly full. When the last of the wounded was being brought up the ramp, the doctor in charge again insisted to Esau that he lie down. Instead he got off.

Because Ensign Hawkins hadn't been brought aboard.

He then went to the other medivac. It was loading the dead while waiting for additional wounded. No, he was told, they'd seen no Ensign Hawkins.

"Well you got to go get him. I know where he's at. I'll take you. Not over there." He gestured toward the chaos of the fire base 300 yards west. "Over there, in our drop zone. He broke his leg."

"How do you know that?"

"He radioed and told us. And turned his hat over to me."

"You people have casualty signals, right?"

"Maybe his didn't work."

This Terran major too was getting exasperated. He needed to finish loading and get his wounded to the hospital. But at the same time… "All right." Turning he called. "Corporal Fong, go with the sergeant here and pick up an Ensign Hawkins. The sergeant will show you where. And make it quick!"

Esau could have ridden on the AG sled, but he walked instead, leading off. He wasn't wobbling now. Not striding, but trudging purposefully. Having something to do had given him new strength. He didn't know exactly where the ensign was, but he'd be somewhere in the drop zone. *Ensign Hawkins,* he thought, *if you'll help me to find you, I'll surely appreciate it.* Then he repeated his appeal, this time to God.

Three hundred yards north of the drop zone, the thunder of howitzers had stopped. With the guns themselves under serious attack, the base commander had ordered them to cease fire and evacuate. But the evacuation wasn't happening. These howitzers were not only of lighter caliber, they were less heavily armored than those the wolf packs had savaged, and Demolitions was having their way with them. The initial spacing made orderly evacuation awkward, and the first howitzers destroyed were on the edges, where they were most in the way.

Esau paid all that no heed. He was busy. He spotted Hawkins from thirty yards away, lying in thigh-deep grass. The medic couldn't imagine how he saw him. The ensign's casualty signal was indeed not working. With the pant leg cut away, his wound was obvious, but more serious, he was in shock, and unconscious. With Esau's help the medic loaded Hawkins onto the AG sled and piloted it to the medivac.

They were the last loaded, and the medivac took off hastily. Esau gave up his damaged helmet and allowed himself to be treated, then lay down willingly, and quickly slept.

He had no idea—none of them did—of what was about to happen at the fire base.

Chapter Sixteen
The Hospital

Casualties from the Fire Base Raid were only a small part of those received by the hospital over a forty-eight-hour span. The less seriously wounded were sedated, put in hastily set-up squad tents without floors, then largely ignored.

It was morning when Esau awoke, with a bad headache, and found himself on a folding cot with mattress. A mosquito bar was draped over it. Getting up he went outside, barefoot and in a hospital night-shirt, to find and use the latrine. He'd just settled down when another B Company trooper sat down next to him, a sergeant named Ferris, from 3rd Platoon. He had an arm in a sling.

"Morning, Esau," Ferris said. "What happened to your head? Jael hit you with a skillet?"

Esau might have scowled, but didn't. "Jael's in the bot shop," he said. "From the Pecan Orchard Raid. The Wyzhñyñy killed her body; she took a blaster pulse in the guts."

"Oh... Gentle Jesus, Esau, I'm surely sorry. I shouldn't have said that. War's no good place for jokes I guess. I was just wondering about your head being all bandaged up."

Esau nodded. Carefully. "The doctor says I took a fragment through my helmet, and it cut a groove across my skull. And scalps bleed pretty good; it looked worse than it was. I'll be back with the platoon in a day or two, if there's any of it left. We jumped the Wyzhñyñy fire base that was shelling headquarters base. I don't know how it finally worked out."

Before they left the latrine, Ferris told Esau there wasn't a whole lot left of the rest of B Company. They'd been in the breastworks, fighting all of yesterday and the night before, and even before that. The good part was, most of the casualties were wounded or bot cases. A lot of the fighting had been with grenades and mortars. People got hit with fragments, or lost arms or legs or hands. Or got burned; the Wyzhñyñy'd used flamethrowers.

Then in early evening, the Wyz had pulled back. Division figured that meant a heavy Wyzhñyñy barrage, so Colonel Leclerc pulled 2nd Regiment back, too. Then, with dusk thickening, the shells started roaring in. Sounded terrible, even from a ways off, and chewed up the forest pretty badly, but didn't really harm the abatises that much. Even most of the breastworks more or less survived.

The shelling stopped just when it had started creeping westward. The rumor was, a bunch of Indi tanks had hit the artillery base and shot it up pretty bad. Leclerc had sent 2nd Regiment back in, but the Wyz didn't come back. "What happened to me is," Ferris added wryly, "a broken limb fell out of a shot-up tree. Broke my collarbone. Heh heh heh. A tree taking revenge! I guess trees don't distinguish people from Wyzhñyñy."

Esau nodded without smiling. It seemed like in war, there were all sorts of ways to get hurt or killed. He wiped his butt and left. Feeling hungry, a sign, he guessed, that he was getting back toward normal. When he got back to the tent, a clean uniform lay folded on the cot. He put it on; it didn't fit too badly.

At noon, the mess line buzzed with stories and rumors. A guy from Dreiser's Platoon, Mellon, was there with a bandaged face. He'd lost an ear to a grenade fragment, and another had gashed his cheek and jaw to the bone. Best he could do was mumble; Esau had to concentrate to understand him. Mellon had gotten out later than he had, when two more medivacs arrived at the fire base. One left loaded. The other left only partly loaded; it had gotten too dangerous to stay. A lot of Wyzhñyñy reds had arrived in APCs—a battalion, he'd heard—and attacked what was left of Airborne A and the demolitions company. Then a dozen Indi tanks had arrived and pounded the Wyzhñyñy. Right after that, an Indi air squadron had swooped in and shot them up some more, but by then, Airborne A and Demolitions were pretty much used up. When the medivacs went back again for casualties, about all they found were dead.

But the Artillery Base Raid wasn't the major topic. Mostly Esau heard about the fighting in the forest. That's where most of the casualties came from. It sounded pretty bad.

◇

After lunch, Esau went back to his tent and lay down, but before he could get to sleep, a doctor came in, looking worn out. He told Esau he'd have to stay a few more days. Esau was glad to hear it. He felt used up.

Esau told him about Jael. The doctor gave him a note, saying he could go to the "Cyborg Processing Center" to see his wife, if she was allowed to have visitors. So after the doctor left, Esau did too.

He had no idea what to expect. The bot shop turned out to be somewhat like the hospital but smaller—a long low prefab building with several similar buildings attached along the sides like hover-fly wings. It was as clean as you could hope for; smelled like turpentine. Terrans in white coats moved through the halls, and went in and out of rooms.

He was directed to a desk, where he showed his note to a woman and said he'd like to visit his wife, Jael Wesley. Another woman, taller than he was, took him down a hall to one of the wings, to a room, and went inside with him.

On a cart was a sort of cylinder, maybe two and a half feet long, and eight inches across except at one end where it was bigger. There were wires and tubes and dials, with a couple of boxes attached. His heart sank.

"Jael," the woman said, "Esau is here to see you."

"Hello, Esau. I knew you'd come see me if you could. What happened to your head?"

The words came from one of the boxes. Esau's eyes welled up and ran over till they dripped on his clean shirt. It was almost like that night in the woods—the night he'd come back from the Pecan Orchard—except this time he didn't sob, just moaned. Because the voice wasn't Jael's. The plastic cylinder wasn't Jael. Jael was dead, and he hadn't let her finish dying. "I'm sorry," he choked out. "I'm sorry. I just didn't want you to be dead."

"Oh Esau, don't be sorry. I'm not." If the voice wasn't hers, the tone was. It reminded him of when she felt fond and

~ 200 ~

loving. "And I'll have my new body pretty soon. Sergeant Boucher took me to see it. You'll be impressed."

He pulled himself together. "I…will." It began as a question and ended as affirmation. "Yes, I surely will… That *is* you in there, isn't it. The voice isn't yours, but it's you. I recognize…I recognize the soul."

Jael laughed quietly. It didn't exactly sound like a laugh, but he knew that's what it was. "That's right," she said, "when they take out the CNS, the soul comes with it. And the voice will come along. It takes practice, and I only just started day before yesterday. I didn't realize how poorly I'd laugh though. I hadn't tried it till just now."

It was only then he realized: she'd asked about his bandages. She could see as well as hear. The nurse said they had ten minutes, then left them alone. It turned out to be more like fifteen, and they got quite a bit of talking done. The best was, Jael told him she'd rather be a bot than an invalid. "As for a bot agreement bringing bad luck," she finished, "I didn't sign one, and look what happened anyway."

Then the nurse returned and shooed Esau out. He found a place in the woods where he could sit alone and think, and weep some more, and talk to himself. Till after a while he felt pretty good. He even laughed at his own joke: grubbing stumps would be a lot easier, with a wife that was a warbot. She could not only pull up the stump; she could shake the dirt off the roots!

Not that he expected to farm after all this. Not really. He could, but he didn't expect to, even if they lived through this war. But there'd be something to do.

◇

That wasn't the end of Esau's day. He'd gone to the hospital to check on Ensign Hawkins, who turned out to be asleep, sedated, with his broken leg hoisted up. The nurse said he'd been in pretty bad shape from prolonged, untreated shock. But he'd heal all right. It would just take a while.

"How long?" Esau asked.

"His bones should heal fast. He should be ready for rehab in six weeks.

~ 201 ~

"Six weeks! Esau left depressed. He didn't feel up to being platoon leader himself. During raids maybe, but not in the day-to-day activities between times. Or defensive fighting in foxholes, as in the first days, or in the breastworks he'd heard about that morning... He felt sure he didn't know enough to be platoon leader in those circumstances. He hadn't been platoon sergeant long enough. He'd make mistakes.

After supper, Isaiah Vernon looked him up. Isaiah was a staff sergeant now, too. When the bot cases from the Battle of the First Days finished their familiarization training, he'd been given a whole platoon of them, as their sergeant. He'd just hitched a ride north to see a couple of them, in the bot shop for repairs. An entire long company of bots had been in a firefight the evening before—been put down near a Wyzhñyñy field headquarters, moved in on it, and pretty much wiped it out. Then they'd made a fighting withdrawal, and been picked up by APFs that came down on a bald ridgetop.

"And while I was up here," Isaiah said, "I decided to see who was here from 2nd Platoon."

"Did you see Jael?"

"Jael? The hospital called up the names of B Company wounded on their records, and hers wasn't one of them."

"She's in the bot shop," Esau said, wishing a bot face showed expression.

"The bot shop? So she finally decided to sign."

"She didn't. She was unconscious, and I lied to the medic, so he shot her up with Stasis 1. Afterward I was afraid she'd be really mad at me, but it turned out she's not."

Isaiah chuckled. *He does that pretty well,* Esau thought, *and his voice sounds like himself.* He guessed Jael's would too, with practice. It occurred to him how much Isaiah had changed personally; more than his body had got stronger. He wondered how different Jael would be, besides having a bot body. He'd just have to wait and see. And get used to it, he told himself.

Then he realized he still hadn't signed his own bot agreement, so when Isaiah left, Esau went to the hospital and signed one. They stamped out new dog tags for him on the spot, to verify it. *Now,* he thought, *if I get hit bad enough, we can be bots together, her and me.*

Chapter Seventeen
The Battle of Shakti

Admiral Alvaro Soong's 1st Sol Provisional Battle Force had traveled three non-stop months in hyperspace to rendezvous with newly commissioned battle groups in the Dinébikeyah System. The result was a fleet with more than four times the number of manned ships that had fought at Paraíso. The new ships came not only from the Sol System, but from new shipyards in the Indi and Eridani Systems, with colonial crews. So it was renamed the "1st Commonwealth Fleet."

The number of maces, whose performance had been so impressive at Paraíso, was also more than quadrupled. They were quicker and easier to build than manned ships, and being drones, their destruction didn't cost trained crews.

And most of the new ships, manned or drones, had the improved shield generators.

Spanish Soong remained in command. To War House and the public, he was a hero second only to Charley Gordon. Before there was any fleet at all, he'd been judged the best qualified for command, based on temperament, gaming skills, and overall service record. And so far he'd disappointed no one.

While en route to the rendezvous, Soong, via Charley, had been updated on the new fleet units by Admiralty Chief Fedor Tischendorf himself. "And Alvaro," Tischendorf finished, "Axel Tisza is delivering the convoy from the Sol System. He's also commanding one of the new battle groups."

He paused meaningfully. "I've had him in mind as your command backup when he gets there, but I haven't told him yet. I know you two have had—a mixed relationship, so I wanted to run it by you first. What do you think of the idea?"

Think? Or feel? "Admiral, Ax is as able as anyone you could find for the job. Powerful mind. Quick. Aggressive. And basically we saw eye to eye for the most part. Different though we are. As midshipmen we roomed together for four years and never came to blows. Loaned each other money on occasion, drank each other's scotch when one of us could afford it. And on pass in the Springs, we backed each other up in more than one scrap."

Yes, Tischendorf thought, *and you were rivals in almost everything, from the saber team to the classroom. And over Carmen Apraxin, when she came along; that's what spoiled it. Well.* "I didn't bring this up idly," he said. "You two were the chief candidates for command of the Provos, and the difference in your grades and gaming scores was thin. But in your favor. And you had the best command temperament: more objective, and I've never known you to be abrasive."

Soong examined the words and found them true. "Not that gaming scores are so important with Charley Gordon available," he found himself saying.

"True. And there's another point in your favor. You discovered Charley's talent, and had the balls to stick your neck out and make him battle master. I doubt that Ax would have done either of them. I'm not at all sure I would have."

◇

With the specifications in hand on the fleet additions, Charley Gordon plunged into reworking his strategies, tactics, protocols, and fleet organization. At the same time considering possible changes in Wyzhñyñy strategy and tactics. Charley claimed to have a good, if imperfect sense of what those changes would be.

Soong felt uncomfortable with some of Charley's adjustments; they seemed too daring. Nonetheless he accepted Charley's new system *in toto,* showing no misgivings.

He'd always been stoic—his aunts and older cousins had commented on it—and rarely did that stoicism take the form of grim resignation. But now the situation was more urgent than at Paraíso. He'd also be risking much greater resources, and he needed to do even better than before. Because the Wyzhñyñy were getting closer, and time, the Commonwealth's most critical resource, was shrinking.

◇

At the rendezvous, Charley's new battlecomp package was

uploaded to the entire fleet. The battle groups remained the basic tactical units, but in the enlarged fleet, a new hierarchical level was added—the battle wing—to facilitate heavier concentrations of firepower. Instead of five battle groups, there were now four battle wings of five groups each, and part of a fifth. When Vice Admiral Carmen Apraxin-DaCosta's Liberation Task Force arrived, it would complete the fifth wing, with Apraxin in command. She'd brought two savants with her, and one was transferred to Soong on board the *Altai,* freeing Charley Gordon to function solely as battle master.

The maces were not organized into wings and groups. They would operate as coordinated triads, grouped into second-order triads—threes of threes. So far as Soong was aware, the concept was entirely new, and the enthusiastic Charley had big plans for them.

Large and technically upgraded though it was, Soong's fleet was still far smaller than the Wyzhñyñy battle fleet, which seemed to constitute about half the armada. But if Charley's assumptions didn't backfire, it seemed realistic to Soong that he could strike, maintain contact long enough to do serious damage, and get away without critical injury.

And possibly, hopefully, slow the invader; make him wary. Buy time to build enough more ships…and come up with new, hopefully decisive weapons.

◇

Three days after Soong's Provos had gathered with the reinforcements from the core worlds, Apraxin's New Jerusalem Liberation Force arrived, to begin at once the task of resupply and external maintenance. On the "evening" of the same day, immediately after supper, electronic bosuns' pipes shrilled aboard every manned vessel in the entire fleet, and shipsvoice ordered all hands to mustering stations in ten minutes. This was followed as before by the skirls of "Dilly Doo" and other Scottish martial music.

As at Paraíso, it was the admiral who spoke first. His real pep talk would come weeks in the future, not long before battle. But meanwhile, before the weeks of simdrills in hyperspace, a few words from the Old Man should help prepare them—provide context and perspective—and a sense of team, of family.

And the new people needed to meet Charley.

"…We are now the 1st Commonwealth Fleet," Soong said. "Commos for short. With the arrival of you newcomers, we are a much more powerful fleet than when we bushwhacked the Wyzhñyñy at Paraíso. A fleet with a toughness and assurance derived from a core of units with successful battle experience, at the Shakti and New Jerusalem Systems. *And* a fleet with the best battle master in the galaxy—Charley Gordon.

"You old hands know Charley's work. You know I don't exaggerate the advantages he gives us. When I've finished my own short spiel, Charley will speak to you himself. And during the next day or two you'll witness his ability personally, on cubes of the Battle of Paraíso.

"Still, some of you may remain skeptical. Few of you wargamed till you entered the service, and you may not yet appreciate what Charley does, or what it takes. But we'll all be simdrilling his updated battlecomp programs all the way to Shakti. Perhaps even to Ivar Aasen. And if you're not convinced by then, you will be when you've experienced the cauldron."

He paused. "For those who don't know, a cauldron is a large iron kettle used in ancient times to boil things. You won't be *in* the cauldron; that's reserved for the Wyzhñyñy. Your job will be to help stoke the fire without falling in it."

Another pause. "Meanwhile we all have things to do before we generate hyperspace again, so I'll let you hear Charley Gordon now. Welcome to the family."

◇

Charley gave basically the same introductory talk he'd given in the Paraíso System, though he used a new example. It had much the same effect on the newcomers.

◇

Minutes later, on a secure channel, Soong accepted a call from Vice Admiral Carmen Apraxin-DaCosta. "Hello, Admiral," he said. Presumably his wariness didn't show on the screen, but it seemed to him she'd know. "What can I do for you?"

"Not a thing, Admiral. May I call you Alvaro?"

"You may call me Al if you'd like." She still looked great. No longer young—forty-two? forty-four?—but great. She made him conscious of his thickened waist. She probably still practiced aikido.

Her laugh was not as light as it had been, but it seemed genuine. "I'll settle for Alvaro," she told him. "You're my commander now, and two grades above me. Is Charley Gordon as good as he sounds?"

"Every bit as good."

"I didn't know savants could be so...intelligent, in the usual sense. Or is articulate the word?"

"I don't know if 'the usual sense' applies to Charley. He's...superman in a box. But easy to work with. Likeable."

"Hmm. Maybe I'll have a chance to talk with him sometime."

For several seconds they sat without talking, looking at one another on their screens. "I'll bet," Soong said at last, "you had something on your mind when you called."

"Yes I did. I do. It's grown out of the life reviews some of us are guilty of in times like these." She paused, hesitated. "Not so many years ago you asked me to marry you. With good reason to expect a yes. But I had an opportunity to make a four-year patrol with B Squadron—as you had earlier, you'll recall. And I chose it over marriage."

Yes you did, he thought. She'd been given command of a frigate, the largest class of warship the Admiralty boasted then. With Axel Tisza as senior captain—commodore—in charge of the squadron. He had no doubt Tisza and she had enjoyed each other's company on the occasional layovers.

"It was a great opportunity," he finished.

She looked at him mildly, but he had no doubt she saw through him.

"In a year this war will be over," she said. "One way or another. Then, assuming I'm still alive, I expect to leave the service. What about you?"

"I—hadn't thought about it." For a moment the realization

surprised him, but it made sense. The prospect of surviving the war wasn't something he wanted to distract himself with. The odds seemed too poor.

"I can understand that," she said, and paused for a moment. "All I really called about was to invite you to ask me again when this is over."

He nodded slowly. "Thanks, Carmen. I'm surprised, and more than anything else, complimented. It's the nicest thing anyone ever said to me."

"Good. Now all we have to do is win the war." She paused. "We both have things to do. I'd better let us get at them."

Soong nodded. "Right. And Carmen, thank you *very* much for calling. I probably won't return this personal call till afterward."

They disconnected then, Soong wondering what he'd meant by "afterward." It had just popped out. He might survive the upcoming battle, but the war? He hadn't felt—and wouldn't feel—any concern at all about dying. His great fear was of losing, and associated with that, he feared that Charley Gordon might die. *That,* he told himself, would be a tragedy.

But if he did survive, and if Carmen did...

He resolved to lose weight.

◇

The admiral seated himself in the chair indicated by Ophelia Kennah. It was always that chair, an AG chair set at 0.7 gee, large enough to accommodate his burly body comfortably. In front of him, the large wall-window was set to a sky view within Terra's atmosphere. Judging from the elevation of Crux, it might be from somewhere near Rio de Janeiro, where Charley had lived most of his life.

Beside Soong's chair stood a small stand with several "non-fattening" hors d'oeuvres. No more goose-liver paste. Knowingly or not, Kennah was cooperating with his efforts to lose weight. Had she read his mind? With her that wasn't inconceivable, but more probably the command officers' chef had talked to her. He sampled one, washed it down with carbonated punch, then swiveled his seat slightly to face the life-support module and its occupant. "Good morning, Charley," the admiral said.

A tiny light-play danced briefly over Charley's sensorium, perhaps equivalent to an embodied human switching off a music or video cube, and swiveling his seat to face a visitor. "Ah, Admiral!" Charley said. "Since I completed our new battlecomp package, we seldom meet. What may I do for you?"

"I've called twice lately," Soong answered. "Each time, Kennah told me you were studying." Actually she'd said he was "studying deeply," whatever that meant. "And that unless it was urgent, she'd rather not waken you. But today when I called, she said you were listening to music, and suggested it was a good time to visit." He lifted an eyebrow. "And by now, of course, I'm curious about your studies."

"Ah." Charley paused as if considering how to put it. "I have been exploring another facet of my potentials, one I dabbled in occasionally when I was younger, without realizing I was merely dabbling. Actually I was being appropriately cautious. But now Ophelia acts as my security officer, an anchor to prevent my being…swept away. And though some risk remained, it seemed something I needed to do at this time. You see."

Risk? There was a pause of several seconds. He'd been jarred by Charley taking a needless risk, when his ability to function at a high level was so vitally important. "No Charley," he said softly, "I don't see. You'll have to enlighten me."

Charley did, and he didn't. "I have," he said, "been visiting the Wyzhñyñy grand admiral. At the…soul level you might say. It is not a matter of telepathy, but of…call it integration. At the level of souls, that is. Something the grand admiral is not aware of at the physical or personality level. Though his essence is."

Soong stared. Uncertainties stirred in his belly like a nest of snakes wakening from hibernation. "Do you know his thoughts?" he asked.

"His thoughts belong to his personality, not his essence. My level of merging is not so strong that I sense them explicitly. But in a general sense I am aware of his fears, his hopes, his desires. Call it empathy in the fullest sense. The admiral is, of course, a product of his people—his culture and class—and I now understand him, and them, much more deeply than before. In fact, through him I have attained a degree of empathy with them as well."

Charley's answer did not assure the admiral. "Well then—" Soong found himself reluctant to ask the question, but reluctance seldom ruled him in matters of duty. "Can you influence him?"

"I have, Admiral, I have. Not to do some particular act, or assume some particular point of view. At the essence level, that is impossible. But he is influenced by the contact, and to an extent enabled by it."

"Enabled." Soong spoke the word cautiously. "Will he be more dangerous then?"

"Not dangerous. But he may break free of old acculturation and self-protective mechanisms. And do things he previously could not."

Soong looked troubled. After a moment Charley added, "Perhaps more to the point, I have a better sense of our joint vectors."

"Ah!" With relief. "So what you've done is beneficial to our cause. Our defense."

"Definitely, Admiral; definitely beneficial. This will be a costly battle, as you well know, but the vectors appear…not unpropitious."

Not unpropitious. From Charley, Soong would have preferred something more positive. "Good," he replied. "We need all the advantages we can have."

For a minute or so then, they spoke of trivia, until Soong was walking to the door. Then Charley added: "And Alvaro. Do not worry if I seem changed. During my studies, I *have* changed. For the better. I discovered and dropped certain features of my personality that I am better off without."

◇

As the admiral walked back to his quarters, his discomfort persisted. And not just because of possible troubles growing out of Charley's "integration" with the Wyzhñyñy admiral. If it was real. Soong wondered if Charley might be less than sane, perhaps deluded by some experience in trance.

Meanwhile he realized what the change had been in Charley's personality. Previously it had included a subtle sense of ingratiation that Soong assumed grew out of living under constant threats since infancy. Threats of equipment failure, a moment's carelessness by a caregiver…even gossip or rumor. Being bottled, Charley's very existence had been illegal. And if the Institute had been shut down, what would have become of him? His only defense had lain in being liked and thought harmless. Yet today that ingratiation had been entirely absent. Remarkable, after so many years of conditioning by fear.

He'd talk about it with Kennah someday, he decided.

Meanwhile there was one thing he did not doubt: Without Charley Gordon, the coming battle could not end well.

<>

Admiral Axel Tisza had spoken with Soong previously since his arrival, their exchanges strictly business. Before supper, he called again.

"I was impressed with your battle master," said the Ax. "God! A damned tragedy he hasn't been cloned. One damned salvo of torpedos and he could be—gone! There might never be another like him."

The comment annoyed Soong. Cloning humans had become common in the 21st century, and again in the 23rd. More than enough to establish that much of what made a human valuable—beyond athletics and potential intelligence—the members of a clone were more or less different. Sometimes very different.

"Cloned?" he said. "You don't know what sort of body he had, or what he went through while he wore it."

Tisza examined his old roommate, and nodded. "I suppose. My savant reminds me of a frog. But he's worth his weight in anything you'd care to name, even if he's not a Charley Gordon." He shrugged. "Did Fedor appoint me your backup? Or did you?"

"Fedor. Conditionally."

"What condition?"

"That I agreed." *What the hell good is a conversation like this?* Soong thought. He was too old now to play power games.

"If he'd given you your choice, who would you have selected?"

"You. We were always neck and neck. You were always more hair-triggered than I was, and more abrasive when you felt the urge." *Or charming if you wanted to be.* He wished he had some of Tisza's charm. "But if the *Altai* gets cooked, or blown apart, and there's no more Charley Gordon and no more Alvaro Soong, this fleet might still have a chance, with you in command."

Tisza nodded slowly, thoughtful now. "I'd thought you might have chosen Carmen. She's had battle experience."

"I probably would have, if you were still at a desk in Kunming." He paused. "Ax, I've got some things to take care of before we generate hyperspace. Is there anything else we need to talk about?"

He'd put just a little emphasis on *need.*

"No there isn't." It was Tisza's turn to pause. "Thanks, Spanish. But I do want to say I think Fedor appointed the right fleet admiral when he gave you the job. And it's assuring to know you approved me as your backup. Fedor thinks a lot of you. And while you may not know it, I do too. Always did. Ever since we were plebes."

And with that he disconnected, leaving Soong staring at his screen, wondering if he'd been petty.

◇

Tisza too sat with his eyes on the now-blue screen. *Alvaro should have transferred his flag to one of the new battleships, with their two-layered shields,* he thought. For the sake of Charley Gordon, if nothing else. But it was late for that. And it might affect morale poorly, to trade the more vulnerable *Altai,* with its single-layer shield, for one of the better-protected new ships.

◇

The Commo fleet didn't get to the Aasen System. The armada had reached Maitreya's World earlier than expected, and might arrive at Aasen before the Commos were ready. Which would put the fleet at a needless and severe disadvantage. En route in hyperspace, simdrills would groove them all on Charley's revised program. But officers, crews, and Charley himself needed to follow the simdrills with adequate steel drills. So the Commos emerged in the fringe of the Shakti System. And there they waited, drilling until the Commos were fully confident of their skills, and even their fleet admiral was reasonably satisfied with their performance.

If his Commos had half—even a third of the Wyzhñyñy firepower, Soong thought, it seemed to him they'd win. Unfortunately they had nowhere near that. But then, he reminded himself, they didn't need to *win,* if they did well enough, then escaped with losses that weren't too severe.

◇

When the klaxons sounded, and shipsvoice called "Battle stations! Battle stations! Battle stations!" the tension generated was more anticipation than fear. Alvaro Soong had already suppressed his misgivings, and his fleet was as ready as it could be. The Tao would favor him or not.

◇

Aboard the *Meadowlands,* the alarm was a six-second blast of raucous horns, scant seconds after emergence. This time the grand admiral was on the bridge, not in bed. A human fleet lay in the same octant of the local system as his own, but an hour's warp jump in-system. An hour.

This time, he told himself, the humans would not strike him by surprise. His warfleet had reformed its formations only 11.38 hyperspace hours outsystem; they could be tightened quickly. "Shipsmind," he said calmly, "order all battle wings to generate warpspace on my count. We will move outsystem far enough to satisfy the parameters of Plan 1.3, then initiate Phase A. One minute and counting: ninety... eighty...."

On zero his warfleet winked out of F-space.

◇

Charley Gordon was on the bridge, his cart secured at the battle master's station. Alvaro Soong sat on his command seat, his hands resting loosely on its command board. For the moment his curved display screen was unsegmented, and inactive except for small analog and digital system displays.

Charley had predicted the Wyzhñyñy would generate warpspace, move farther outsystem, and set ambushes before emerging. In warpspace, ambushes usually weren't very practical, but facing Wyzhñyñy numbers, the risk was substantial. So the Commos would stay put. He predicted the Wyzhñyñy would then make a warp jump back insystem, and attack simultaneously from multiple surrounding points. He intended to meet them aggressively. His cool confidence had infected all the bridge watch, including his admiral, whose stoicism just now approached tranquility.

They waited, Charley in a trancelike calm, poised, alert, perfectly ready; a state in which durations registered with no sense of waiting. On his orders, shipsmind provided music chosen to calm without dulling. It began with Gustav Holst's *Planets Suite,* thence to Colin Jokisaari's *Uusisuomi Spring,* and others. After a while, a messman brought a lunch cart, and the bridge watch ate at their stations. All but Charley, who never ate and didn't seem to miss it.

Soong wondered how someone could get over wanting to eat. He'd always assumed it was hardwired.

◇

Grand Admiral Quanshûk had emerged in his new, more distant location. Time passed, enough that electromagnetic evidence, poking along at 186,000 miles per second, had informed the human fleet where he now was. Then more time, enough to tell Quanshûk that the humans would not be baited. They were leaving the offensive to him. Clearly this human fleet had a different commander than he'd dueled with before.

"Very well," he muttered. "We'll give them more than they'll like." He spoke his next order with a feeling approaching confidence.

◇

It was late in the following watch, midway through Aleksandr *Borodin's In the Steppes of Central Asia,* that klaxons clamored aboard the *Altai,* cutting off the music. Shipsvoice's strident "Battle Stations! Battle Stations!" was redundant. Officers and ranks were already there. Charley Gordon's Situation One was unfolding.

Twelve mighty wings of Wyzhñyñy warcraft had emerged on the fringe of Soong's fleet. Beyond them, on a larger perimeter, were twenty-four more. Outsystem a hundred million miles, the armada's transports and support craft had entered the relative security of warpspace.

The Wyzhñyñy wings were differently constituted than the Commo wings, but comparable in power, and there were far more of them. They began their attack at once, accelerating in gravdrive, generating shields as they came. The Commo wings in turn started toward the Wyzhñyñy. The maces led, accelerating much faster than humans or Wyzhñyñy could survive. In brief seconds they reached the maximum speed at which they could carry out the intended evasion maneuvers. Then, by triplicate triads—threes of threes—they directed coordinated beam fire at selected Wyzhñyñy battleships. While following evasion courses designed to confound target locks.

<>

Quanshûk stared, chagrined. He'd learned before, the hard way, that certain human cruisers—presumably robots—could maneuver at high speeds. But he'd overlooked the acceleration potentials that implied. Nor had they previously shown him coordinated maneuvers on so large a scale.

His own ships responded promptly with both warbeams and torpedoes, the action swift and violent, with too many craft over too large a volume of space for organics to follow the action. But the battlecomps on both sides took it all in, reacting with a quickness far beyond human or Wyzhñyñy. Shields shimmered beneath the onslaught of warbeams, flared and collapsed from multiple torpedo strikes. Hulls incandesced, exploded.

<>

Then the surviving maces were through the Wyzhñyñy formations. The Commo battle groups followed, their battleships wielding heavy beamguns. Firing torpedoes required complex shield topologies that made them more susceptible to destruction, so it was their corvette and cruiser outriders that wielded torpedoes. The smaller ships' safety lay partly in numbers, and partly in the Wyzhñyñy tactic of focusing on human battleships.

Concentrating on battleships was a sound strategy for both sides. The Commos needed to destroy as many Wyzhñyñy as possible, which meant maintaining fighting contact as long as they could—before the Wyzhñyñy could gang up on them. Inevitably they did gang up on some of them, of course. The trick then became to disrupt the Wyzhñyñy teamwork by throwing in maces. But meanwhile Commo ships were lost.

<>

With the Wyzhñyñy concentrating on the manned wings, the maces dropped their shields, generated warpspace, and disappeared. Their battlecomps had their orders and knew the drill. So far their losses had been modest, and they'd disordered the Wyzhñyñy formations, disrupting their larger-scale coordination before the Commo battle groups struck. More ships died then, mostly Wyzhñyñy, while the Wyzhñyñy battle groups coordinated their fire as best they could.

From the bridge of the battleship *Pyrénées*, Axel Tisza saw the *Altai* caught in a crossfire from three Wyzhñyñy battleships, her shield shimmering strongly with intercepted energy; her shield generator would soon overload. With a quick touch he turned two war beams on one of the attackers; another touch simultaneously ordered torpedoes engaged. Automatically his shield reconfigured, the torpedoes fixing on targets, and launching. A moment later a salvo struck the *Pyrénées,* and her outer shield layer collapsed. On the bridge, the lights flickered. Systems display windows showed generator status red and pulsing. Damage Control cut off the war beam, lessening the stress on the matric tap, in order to regenerate the shield layer. But there was too little time; another salvo struck, and almost simultaneously another. The lights flared and died, returning almost instantly as the emergency backup system responded. Klaxons clamored briefly before two more salvos struck, and the *Pyrénées* died. Axel Tisza hadn't even had time to see if he'd succeeded in saving the *Altai* and Charley Gordon.

Soong had. The two battle groups had been keeping pace. He saw the torpedos flash against the *Pyrénées'* shield, which seemed to expand, then disappear, the instant almost too brief to register. Jabbing he locked a monitor on her. Almost simultaneously, another window showed one of the *Altai*'s three attackers lose her own over-stressed shield, and her beam, as Tisza's first salvo struck; her generator, if not her matric tap, had blown. A second lost her shield a moment later, to torpedos from the *Altai*'s cruiser escorts. The third, seeing the *Pyrénées* shieldless, turned its beams on her. Sprays of molten hull metal scintillated where the beams had locked. Then the final blow struck—two salvos, from two Wyzhñyñy cruisers—and the *Pyrénées* ripped apart.

For perhaps two seconds Soong stared, then he snapped out of it. He'd seen—at the Academy they'd all seen—just such episodes in virtuality many times, preparing for a moment like this. Which helped. But seeing it in reality, and knowing who commanded, the moment stabbed him deeply.

<><

The Commo battle wings passed through the enemy ring, many of the Commo battleships with Wyzhñyñy target locks still attached. Then the maces returned. In self-defense the Wyzhñyñy turned their guns and torpedos on them; the Commo wings dropped shields, and escaped, most of them, into warpspace before the outer ring of Wyzhñyñy could engage them.

This time the maces continued outward, engaging the outer Wyzhñyñy ring, striking selected wings and ignoring others. And scarcely had they passed through the outer ring when the Commo battle groups reappeared in F-space at a distance, reforming formations for their next assault—in which they would change tactics on the Wyzhñyñy, keep them guessing and off balance.

<><

When the confusion had peaked again, the human formations, superbly synchronized, disappeared into strange-space.

Quanshûk stared after them. The bridge of the *Meadowlands* stank with musk and sweat. Almost at once, status reports began to scroll. Watching them, Quanshûk's guts shriveled.

After several minutes it seemed apparent the humans would not return. But the grand admiral did not at once leave the bridge. It would amount to abandoning the watch in a time of trauma. Besides, who could be sure? The humans might suddenly reappear.

◇

This time, when the battle was over, Charley Gordon wasn't jubilant. Instead he "sagged" in sudden exhaustion. With the Commo escape into warp space—that's what it had been, an escape—the battle master's bridge orderly wheeled him to his quarters, where Ophelia Kennah took charge. Ophelia: Charley's nurse, confidante, and best friend.

◇

Alvaro Soong wasn't jubilant either, nor about to take his fleet back into that maelstrom. Reports were incomplete, of course. A host of data had been recorded by the *Altai*'s sensors, and more had been forwarded automatically in real time from his hundreds of other ships. All to be processed—compiled, analyzed and summarized. Only shipsmind could manage it, organizing and prioritizing, then scrolling at a rate his staff could deal with.

But what he did know was, he'd lost about a third of his battleships and personnel, including the *Pyrénées* and Axel Tisza. The *Altai* herself had twice been in serious trouble, and been bailed out.

Inevitably his maces had taken the heaviest losses. About half were gone, despite their evasiveness and layered shields. They'd fought the most, and where the risks were greatest. Without them, Charley could not have maintained battle contact with the Wyzhñyñy for nearly as long, nor done nearly the damage.

In numbers, Wyzhñyñy losses had been much greater, especially of crews. But again, in terms of percentages, Soong's Commos had gotten the worst of it. As expected.

Nonetheless, given the relative numbers and firepower, Charley had performed another miracle. Soong wondered what the Wyzhñyñy commander made of it. Was he shocked? Enraged? Dismayed? Or possibly pleased?

After ordering hot tea and honey for the bridge watch, he went to his channeling savant, to send a preliminary report to War House. A full debrief could wait. He'd emerge in F-space in the cometary cloud; F-space was a necessary intermediate between strange-spaces. Then, after pulsing updated orders to his fleet, he'd generate hyperspace, and debrief to Kunming. And tomorrow—next shipsday—they'd re-emerge for a fleet review and memorial service.

<><

Finally Soong retired to his stateroom. He'd just closed the door, the lock engaging behind him, when it hit—the nervous exhaustion, the loss, the shock—all at once. He sank shaking onto a chair, put his face in his hands, and for the first time since he'd learned of his mother's death, he wept. *All those men. All those men.*

It lasted perhaps thirty seconds. After another minute he stripped and showered, then poured himself a brandy, read for a few minutes from Innocent XV's *Soul and Body,* and went to bed. Where his last thought was of Ax. *I wish,* he told himself, *there'd been time to get drunk together again, after so many years.* Then he fixed his attention on his old roommate and rival, and sent a thought. "Maybe next time," he murmured aloud. The prayer of a skeptic. He wondered if there was anyone, or anything, "out there" to hear it.

Chapter Eighteen
Envoy

The grand admiral had recovered somewhat. The master gender, after all, were genetically warriors, who'd received cardinal nurture from birth to weaning, affecting the postnatal growth of the endocrine system, while setting up gender-unique memes.

He'd retired to his quarters before ordering his XO and chief scholar to meet there with him. This had given him time for a drink; an empty glass was the evidence. After pouring drinks for Tualurog and Qonits, he refilled his own. Masters typically held their liquor well, an interaction of the warrior gene and cardinal nurture.

Unfortunately for Qonits, liquor combined with the sage gene brought impulsiveness and poor judgement. Thus Qonits hadn't drunk alcohol since the evening he'd almost gotten himself expelled from the university. A disgrace for which, in his clan, atonement would have provided only limited rehabilitation.

"Well, Admiral," Quanshûk said to Tualurog, "it didn't work as we'd hoped."

The XO scowled sourly. He hated to be wrong, and hated more to have it known. "Their AI technology was better than we'd realized," he answered.

Quanshûk wasn't about to let him off the hook. "Enumerate for me, please, the things that went wrong."

Grimly, Tualurog listed them. There weren't so many, but they'd been costly. Qonits, who was less than fond of the XO, nonetheless sympathized—until Tualurog glanced at him and added: "Your chief scholar served you poorly."

"As did Operations and Planning," Quanshûk replied. "Surprises are to be expected when dealing with alien life forms. And unfortunately, these humans are remarkably clever, as well as technically advanced."

He paused, smelling his XO's upset. "Meanwhile my thanks, Admiral. You summarized the difficulties nicely. You may leave now. Please prepare a detailed review for me, with your recommendations." *For all the good they'll do. I have dug us a very deep hole.*

The two friends watched the XO leave, closing the door behind himself with icy control. "He is a surly fellow," Quanshûk said tiredly. "But competent."

Also jealous, spiteful, and self-justifying, Qonits added silently. Aloud he said, "All his life he's resented his clan's loss of status."

Quanshûk ignored the comment. "What do you think of our situation? Knowing what you know now."

"We are in serious trouble."

"Elaborate, Chief Scholar."

You already know my views, Qonits thought. *They are much the same as yours.* "Your lordship, easy gains enticed us down a flowered path, never imagining it led to such—unprecedented danger."

The admiral's close-cropped claws drummed on his small bar. "Self-evident, Chief Scholar. But what might I do now to—extricate us from that danger?"

Qonits met his gaze. It was not a time for easing into things, he decided. "Lord Admiral, I suggest we look at the possibility of negotiations with the humans. We have a working knowledge of the language, and a decent translation program. And a fleet powerful enough to provide leverage. We hold many of..."

Quanshûk raised a heavy hand, stilling him. "How can you say our translation program is decent? For me it is a confusion generator."

The grand admiral was avoiding the issue, but to Qonits his reply was encouraging; the idea had not been slapped down. "It is neither perfect nor complete," Qonits answered carefully, "but it has become quite functional."

The grand admiral's jaw jutted in thought. His gaze was on his richly patterned carpet, no doubt without seeing it. "As for negotiation," he said, "it has no precedent; the fleet would never accept it. To propose it would court rebellion. A coup."

Again Qonits answered carefully. "It might accept it, your lordship. One wonders sometimes if the human empire might not extend forever. Already the problems it presents seem overwhelming. We all go to bed worried, those of us who admit what we see."

But there were also those, Qonits reminded himself, who would roar with indignation at such a proposal, Tualurog the loudest. And might undertake rebellion; might even succeed in it. He thought of asking which was worse: the risk of a coup, or destruction by the humans. But all he could bring himself to say was, "It is Krûts who is master of this ship. Tualurog can order him only in your name, as your proxy, and Krûts doesn't like him. Many don't; he is abrasive. And I have seen the worry in Krûts's eyes. After today's battle, I believe many—possibly even enough—would support you."

He paused. "And there *are* precedents of a sort. Tribes negotiate with tribes, clans with clans, merchants with merchants. There are many examples of successful negotiations between groups unfriendly, even hostile to each other. It's a matter of incentive. And our prisoners have shown themselves logical and reasonable. They have deported themselves well." *A sample of two. Who knows what their rulers are like?* "I would be honored to serve as your negotiator."

Quanshûk did not raise his eyes, but his voice, when he replied, was contemplative. "Even aside from your proficiency with human speech," he said, "you are the only one I would consider sending."

Qonits peered carefully at him. The admiral had neglected his drink; now he downed it, poured himself another—and suddenly his chief scholar hardly dared breathe.

"If such a thing were to be done," Quanshûk continued slowly, "I would begin it covertly, then announce it after you were beyond recall, in hyperspace. To speak earlier would surely invite a coup, and our detention. At best.

"Meanwhile I will make a production of crushing the humans in this system. To strengthen both my image and fleet morale."

He said "I will," Qonits realized, and felt the resolve growing in his admiral's mind.

"I will hold the mother and child hostage to ensure the reliability of the father," Quanshûk went on, and a rare glint of humor shone in his eyes. "Do you suppose he'll suddenly know how to find his way to their crown world after all?"

Qonits answered gravely. "If necessary, we will stop at some human-inhabited world, for guidance."

◇

The next shipsday, Quanshûk sent scouts insystem, while the armada lay in the near fringe. The most recently found human worlds tended to have extensive settled areas, more and larger towns, and relatively advanced industrial development. *And* much evacuation. On this one, the scouting report suggested an initial population in the hundreds of millions, judging by the extent and nature of settlement. How many had been evacuated was unclear, but at the edge of forest areas were thousands of abandoned vehicles. There was also evidence of many fugitive camps among the trees.

Quanshûk ordered all his bombards there, with three of his fleet's ground support wings assigned to follow up. Their job was to destroy the towns, the factories—everything that supported the human population there except for a few convenient reservoirs—then scathe the fugitives.

When the job was done, he would send down two tribes. The extensive farmlands would support a score of tribes, and there'd be more fugitives than usual to hunt down, but two tribes would have to do.

◇

It was late shipsnight, and the corridors were dim and quiet. The bombards had started insystem to Shakti a few hours earlier. Now a crewman guided an AG sled down a portside corridor, followed by a larger Wyzhñyñy wearing a lieutenant commander's insignia. From that and his color, he was obviously of the master gender. His head was bandaged, presumably injured during the battle, probably when a torpedo salvo had jolted the *Meadowlands* severely.

~ 224 ~

The AG sled's cargo was covered by a tarp.

Shortly they stopped at the entrance to a scout hanger. The crewman opened it but remained in the corridor. It was the bandaged officer who guided the sled inside. Then the crewman closed the hatch and returned quietly down the corridor.

While shipsmind dogged the hatch firmly shut, the officer unloaded the sled by himself. It wasn't much work, and there was no injury beneath the bandage. Besides, the largest item unloaded itself.

Chapter Nineteen
Hearing Board

Within the Wyzhñyñy Admiralty, it had been customary, over the centuries, to convene a fitness board following a major command failure. Often these cleared the accused of malfeasance, but sometimes they uncovered previously unrecognized malfeasance, and found other, contributive or ameliorative factors. Sometimes procedural changes were recommended.

But never before had so drastic a failure been addressed.

On the stand, Grand Admiral Quanshûk wore his finest red velvet military vest, with every Imperial decoration he owned. Most prestigious were the High Emperor's Medal of Service, the Medal of Military Accomplishment, and two Outstanding Cadet Medals. None were for valor in combat; there had been no combat for more than three centuries. Nor the rare Kôchasska, which protected the bearer from legal actions of any sort, civil or military. None of those had been awarded for nearly two millennia.

The presiding officer was Captain Krûts. As the ship's captain it was his job. The inquisitor was Rear Admiral Tualurog. The fitness board consisted of six admirals, senior wing commanders. There were also the grand admiral's counselor, and several officers of the court. The witnesses numbered eleven, including senior and junior officers, enlisted personnel, and two humans. The remaining seats were occupied by other senior officers, as mandatory spectators.

Just now, Tualurog was walking back and forth in front of the grand admiral, trying to upset him. It wasn't working. Instead of following the inquisitor's pacing, Quanshûk gazed calmly at the fitness board.

"Tell me, Grand Admiral," Tualurog said, "how many ships did you lose in the recent confrontation with the humans?"

"Objection, Lord President!" Quanshûk's counsel was a commander, a member of Quanshûk's own clan. "The inquisitor is implying that the grand admiral was responsible for the losses. Responsibility is for the hearing to decide."

"Sustained. Rephrase your question in a neutral manner, Inquisitor."

"Of course, Your Honor. I apologize to the court. He looked around. "Grand Admiral Quanshûk, how many ships were lost in the recent battle with the humans?"

"You know the number as well as I do, Lord Tualurog."

"I am asking *you,* Lord Admiral."

Quanshûk listed them by classes.

"Wouldn't you say that is a shockingly large number?"

"I would use the term sobering, Lord Tualurog."

"You weren't shocked by it?"

"Your Honor!" counsel cried.

"Inquisitor, restrict your questions to matters of evidence."

"I stand admonished, Your Honor. Grand Admiral Quanshûk, who was responsible for the decisions made in this war?"

"They have been my decisions."

"And the battle strategies?"

"In conjunction with shipsmind, I was."

"'In conjunction with shipsmind.' But shipsmind is an artificial intelligence. Are artificial intelligences responsible, legally or otherwise, for decisions?"

"Artificial intelligences bear no responsibility for anything, Inquisitor. They are a tool. As you well know."

Tualurog looked at Krûts, expecting him to admonish Quanshûk for his added comment. Krûts, however, gazed coldly back at him, saying nothing. *I will remember that, Captain,* Tualurog thought, *when I rule the armada.*

"A tool indeed, Grand Admiral," Tualurog said, "a tool indeed. And what do you propose we do next, to destroy these humans?"

"Objection, Your Honor!"

"Sustained. Admiral Tualurog, I am aware that you have never before acted as inquisitor. But let me make this clear: If you do not restrict your questions to inquisitorial protocol, I will have to replace you. Understood?"

Tualurog avoided eye contact with Krûts. He could easily blow up at the miserable gut picker, and ruin this whole case. "Indeed, Your Honor. I appreciate your forbearance." He delivered the line smoothly. "Let me try to rephrase my question, because... Your Honor, it opens up another, very important part of the investigation."

He looked again at Quanshûk. Having put it as he had, Krûts was obliged to give him greater leeway in questioning, at least so long as he was making apparent progress. "Grand Admiral," Tualurog said, "please give this hearing your best estimate of the volume of space occupied by the human empire when we first encountered it."

Quanshûk knew exactly what Tualurog was getting at. His answer was an estimate made by shipsmind on the day before, expressed as a probability range.

"And what percentage of that space have we swept?"

Quanshûk's estimate was relatively precise, but it was the sheer vastness of the first answer that made the spectators' hearts sink. They'd all known of course, in a general sense, but to have it laid before them like this...

Tualurog looked knowingly at the board, then back at Quanshûk. "And how many planets have we colonized here?"

"Forty-seven."

"Forty-seven. With how many tribes?"

"Fifty-six."

"How many tribes do we have left?"

"Sixty-four."

Quanshûk's counsel had been tapping notes on his neckpad. In his own questioning, he would have the grand admiral explain his decisions. They were convincing enough. Even compelling.

"Sixty-four tribes left," Tualurog echoed, making the number sound every bit as bad as it was. "And our warfleet now numbers?"

"Two thousand, seven hundred and twelve fighting ships. The reduction has been due largely to leaving defense forces in the colonized systems, but losses to enemy action have also been substantial."

Tualurog looked meaningfully at the hearing board, then turned to Krûts. "Your honor, I would like to leave that train of questioning for now, and open a new train, which I am confident will change the complexion of this hearing. I respectfully request your indulgence."

Krûts eyed him mistrustingly. "Proceed, Inquisitor."

Tualurog drew nearer to Quanshûk now, and his tone became almost confidential. "I have not seen your chief scholar for several days. Is he ill?"

"Your Honor!" counsel complained. "I seriously object!"

"Denied for now. Proceed, Inquisitor. But this had better lead somewhere."

"It will, Your Honor. I have witnesses. Lord Admiral, your answer please."

Quanshûk had known this was coming since he'd seen the two humans in the witness section. And there was no way to explain it except with the truth. It seemed to him he'd botched the whole affair—everything since they'd arrived in this galaxy— and there was no way in the universe to fix it. He would tell it as he knew it, and take whatever came.

"Lord Inquisitor," he said, "Chief Scholar Qonits is not ill, so far as I know. I have sent him on a mission."

"Sent him?"

"In a long-range scout."

If the courtroom had been quiet before, it was now quiet cubed. "With the human known as David?" Tualurog asked.

"With the human known as David."

Now Tualurog feigned reluctance. He'd guessed the answer as soon as Qonits' absence had taken his attention. With that, uncovering witnesses had been easy. Then he'd requested a fitness board, proposing himself as inquisitor.

"And what, Grand Admiral, is that mission?" he asked slowly.

"I greatly underestimated the size of the human empire, Lord Inquisitor. As a result we are dangerously overextended, especially given the potency of the enemy fleets. However, our limited knowledge of humans suggests that while fierce, they are a life form that can be—negotiated with."

A buzz filled the chamber. Krûts hammered it into silence.

"Proceed, Grand Admiral," he said.

"Of course, Captain. The mission, Lord Inquisitor, is to negotiate peace with the humans."

This time, instead of a buzz, there was an indignant hubbub. Krûts banged his gavel till the chamber stilled. "Lord Inquisitor, Lord Counselor, members of the fitness board," he said, "this hearing has grown to encompass far more than envisioned. I hereby adjourn the fitness hearing, and recommend that we deal first with this new development."

He scanned the gathering. "All spectators will leave the chamber until further notice. Security will escort the witnesses to the waiting room, except for the two humans, who will be taken to their quarters. Guards will remain with the humans to prevent suicide. Officers of the court, clear the chamber."

◇

When spectators and witnesses had gone, the hearing board declared itself an emergency board, and elected Rear Admiral Tualurog as its chairman. Then work began on what to do about the predicament they were in.

Quanshûk, as a witness now, pointed out that no known empire except their own had exceeded twenty-eight habitable worlds. And their own had long since ceased to be an empire in its original sense. The second swarm had extended it to twenty-two worlds, and strained the power of the government to govern. The third swarm had set out with the understanding that it would form a sister empire, with loyalty to the same traditions, the Wyzhñyñy species, and the high emperor—the ruler of the parent empire. But the sister empire would rule itself.

Two millennia and six swarms had spread the Wyzhñyñy widely, but even so, the "Wyzhñyñy Empire" occupied an expanse only a small fraction as large as the human empire.

During the day's meeting, no consensus developed regarding the nature of the human empire. The remarkable lack of high technology on any of the worlds so far conquered seemed to rule out a group of sibling empires. And the long interval without military resistance, and the considerable gap between fleet encounters, suggested the human core worlds were not well prepared for invasion.

But there was consensus on a new strategy, and it did not involve anything so outrageous as negotiation. Speed was the key, and further colonization would be postponed. Strike for the imperial core. When a star was found within detection range in hyperspace, the armada would emerge promptly, and determine from the electronic signature whether the system held a core world. A *core* world. If not, they'd generate hyperspace at once and speed onward. In that way they'd advance far more rapidly.

If they encountered a human fleet waiting in other than a core world system, they would bypass it, generate hyperspace and speed on. The first priority was to destroy the core worlds, and particularly the crown world.

When finally they fought, it would be with the human's main fleet, and the battle would decide once and for all which life form would survive. If they won, and they must, then scouting forces would be sent to search out the remaining core worlds. The fleet could then be sent to destroy their technical infrastructures. The following mop-up might take generations, but bit by bit they would exterminate the human life form.

Rear Admiral Tualurog was elected grand admiral by acclaim. Quanshûk was stripped of rank and privileges, and sentenced to death by suffocation, for treason. Tualurog's first act as grand admiral would be to question the human known as "Yukiko"—a parent fixated in female phase—and learn, if possible, the location of the crown world.

Then he intended to kill both humans. Evil was evil. It was probably contact with the prisoners that had corrupted Qonits, and through Qonits, Quanshûk. He would take no chances.

Chapter Twenty
Strange Message

"Blessed Buddha!" Foster Peixoto barely breathed the oath, while Chang Lung-Chi watched and listened silently. The screen showed only Ramesh lying in trance, but the words!

For many months, Annika Pedersen had channeled faithfully. And presumably accurately, Terran as Terran, and Wyzhñyñyç as Wyzhñyñyç. All seemingly without knowing what she did, or that she did anything at all. David MacDonald and Yukiko Gavaldon always spoke in Terran, except for a few, infrequent Wyzhñyñyç interjections. While Qonits' words... Seemingly they'd been channeled as faithfully as Ramesh's vocal apparatus allowed, whether slurred Terran from Qonits' lipless mouth, or Wyzhñyñyç muttered to his throat mike or spoken to his guards.

But now Annika and Yukiko were clearly in very different surroundings. David was either absent or silent, while Yukiko murmured only occasional soothing words to the savant. Everything else was in an incomprehensible mixture of Terran and Wyzhñyñyç, in Wyzhñyñy voices that differed in pitch, tone, and personality.

But the numerous intermixed Terran words included the labial phonemes, all properly sounded! A Wyzhñyñy could not have pronounced them that way. It was as if Annika was mentally translating from Wyzhñyñyç into Terran, live, so far as her mental database allowed. And what she could not translate, sent in the original Wyzhñyñyç! At least that's how it struck the president, and the prime minister agreed.

The proceedings seemed to be a legal hearing of some kind.

Peixoto and Chang were listening for the second time. When the chamber was cleared again by the—judge?—and Yukiko and Annika had been sent to their cell, Peixoto turned off the recorder/player. "This is incredible!" he said. "Unimaginable!" Then switched on his desk comm. "Gisella, connect me with the university. This is urgent!"

◇

A page interrupted Professor Pelle Clough in class, with a murmured, "The president and prime minister want to speak with you at once." Puzzled and only half believing, the professor took the call. It was brief, but extremely exciting. After dismissing his students, he was picked up on the roof by a security floater, and taken to the Palace of Worlds.

Linguistics was a modest department in the Institute of Antiquities, but within his specialty, Charles Clough was prominent worldwide. He taught and had written fascinating books on the history and evolution of languages, was reputedly expert in a dozen, and competent in perhaps a dozen more. Which implied a rare, intuitive sense of language.

He had, of course, never heard Wyzhñyñyç. But he and the two leaders played and replayed the cube, and with the help of the PM's artificial intelligence, wrung as much understanding as they could from it. They quickly agreed it was a courtroom proceeding, and Peixoto was a lawyer with courtroom experience. Before they were done, they'd gotten the sense of it. It seemed that Grand Admiral Quanshûk was being tried for malfeasance, or treason, or both.

And what seemed almost certain—he'd sent an envoy, Chief Scholar Qonits, as a negotiator to the Commonwealth, apparently with David MacDonald as an aide. The thought first dumbfounded, then excited the two statesmen.

They'd hardly finished—Clough hadn't left yet—when they were interrupted by Burhan Gokhale with another recorded channeling. This one was ugly, shocking, and very short. An apparent question was barked, repeatedly. Seemingly in Terran, but unintelligible, as if by someone who'd never tried to speak it before. Perhaps getting the words from the Wyzhñyñy's shipsmind via an ear button.

Clearly Yukiko understood it. She cried out as if in pain. "I don't know! God help me I don't!… Please don't hurt her! She's harmless! She can't…"

Abruptly the recording ended, leaving the eavesdroppers

with no doubt at all. Annika was dead, and Yukiko either was or soon would be.

<>

Ramesh had been deeply disturbed by what he'd channeled, though as always he remembered none of it. Afterward he sat at his piano and played somber music somberly, until Burhan initiated a shallow trance—the attendant called them "healing reveries"—and put him to bed.

Then Burhan went to the prime minister's apartment, where the two leaders sat waiting.

"How," Peixoto asked, "could Annika have translated like that?"

"Sir, how do savants do any of what they do? We only know *what,* not how. But Annika was present at all the language lessons. She heard everything any of the others heard. And it all registered, perfectly and permanently. Somewhere in her mind it all registered.

"And how did she communicate to us over all those months? Instantly, in real time, from how many light years away? She simply did it, in the same way little Esko Rautasjaure can look at a star chart and tell you the travel time to anyplace you'd care to go. Or not go, including a supernova in Andromeda."

Listening, Chang marveled at this young man—no savant and with only an ordinary education. But his intelligence was obvious, and his humanity beautiful. The president was glad to belong to the same species.

Then Burhan Gokhale said something else. "Sirs, Charley Gordon may have useful comments on the courtroom material."

<>

A savant in trance cannot ask or answer questions. He can only channel. Thus Charley heard the cube of Annika's courtroom account via Ramesh, through Admiral Soong's new savant. When it was over, the prime minister added: "We cannot expect anything further from Annika, and we very much want some idea of what to expect. Can you help us?"

"Sir," Charley said, "this brings two vectors to mind. I'd felt them both, but they were too vague to articulate. This clarifies them. I feel quite confident of them now. The Wyzhñyñy armada will postpone further colonization, and advance much more rapidly. Expect them among the core worlds in weeks instead of months, to destroy cities, industries, the entire infrastructure. And our fleet if they can pin it down. They particularly want to raze Terra. After that they will have all the time they need to root out the colonies. Decades. Centuries if necessary.

"Also, the Wyzhñyñy envoy will arrive at the Sol System somewhat sooner than the armada. He will have no diversions, and only astrogational stops. The Admiralty can approximate his arrival time for you, from his departure time from Shakti. Obviously his diplomatic accreditation is no longer in force, but he will have valuable knowledge.

"As for Annika and Yukiko—I agree, they are dead. The Wyzhñyñy commander wanted help in finding Terra, and Yukiko could not or would not help him."

It was the president who asked the final question: "Is there, then, any hope at all?"

"Oh yes, Mr. President, there is hope. But there is not much time."

◇

When they'd finished, Peixoto gave himself a moment to recover, then looked at the president. "Whew! When I asked what to expect, I didn't imagine such detail. Now we have less time than ever." Keying his desk comm, he had his secretary call War House.

Chapter Twenty-One
An Envoy Received

David MacDonald listened to shipsvoice count down to emergence. He remembered Maritimus, and the armada's 16,000 blips, and couldn't imagine the Commonwealth producing a viable defense. Yet twice there'd been battles, and the last one had shaken up not only the flagship, but Qonits as well.

And apparently the admiral. Otherwise why send an envoy to Terra? And on the sneak, as if Quanshûk couldn't rely on his officers. If that was true, how could negotiations possibly succeed? Coup city!

They emerged into deep, star-glittered blackness, one star far brighter than any other, uncomfortable to more than glance at. It had to be Sol; they'd emerged just half a day earlier to orient themselves for this jump.

Shipsvoice spoke while words scuttled across the navscreen, all unintelligible to him. "We are within a million miles of a pod beacon," Qonits said. "A useful locational reference, and a good omen."

Good omen, David echoed mentally. *Wishful thinking.*

Qonits poised a hand above a rocker switch and looked questioningly at him. "Try it," David said. The Wyzhñyñy touched it. A HUD marked with three symbols—a Wyzhñyñy acronym—appeared on the "window." Looking at David, Qonits gestured at the mike. "Speak," he said softly.

David licked his lips. "War House, War House, War House." The words felt strange to him. At one time they'd been a mockery. It was said that in Proto-Terran—essentially Old Anglic—the words had meant a brothel. War House had long been regarded as a perverse waste of time, a place where grown men spent years in a universe of make-believe. How that viewpoint must have changed!

"This is David MacDonald. David MacDonald. Research leader of the Maritimus Project. I am on an alien long-range scout in the vicinity of a pod beacon. On an alien long-range scout in the vicinity of a pod beacon.

"I've been a prisoner on the invader's flagship, apparently for a Terran year or more. I have come here with Lord Qonits of the Wyzhñyñy Empire. Lord Qonits of the Wyzhñyñy Empire. I am his guide and aide. Lord Qonits is the envoy of Grand Admiral Quanshûk, of the Wyzhñyñy armada. The grand admiral has sent him to discuss possible peace terms. Repeat: peace terms." He paused. "We will remain where we are, and await an escort. Repeat: we will remain where we are and await an escort."

He switched off the mike. It would take about six hours for the message to reach Terra, and the government would take—how long? A day? An hour? A minute?—to decide what to make of this, and respond. Or perhaps decide that someone was hoaxing them. Six hours after that would bring the reply. Unless a courier was sent via warpspace, or some system patrol craft intercepted his message and responded sooner.

He turned to Qonits. "Now we wait," he said.

Qonits nodded. They were used to waiting. They'd done long weeks of it. Long but not idle weeks. Most of their waking hours had been spent in the expansion and refinement of Qonits' Terran, until it seemed to David the chief scholar spoke it better than he did. Qonits had remarkable recall, and approximated human phonemes about as well as a Wyzhñyñy ever could, without electronic enhancement. Meanwhile their busyness minimized David's fretting about Yukiko, and Qonits' about what might have happened to Quanshûk when he'd announced what he'd done.

Now, while waiting for an escort, Qonits explained the seven Wyzhñyñy genders, which clarified a lot for the Terran. And David elaborated on Terran and Commonwealth history. After a bit they napped. David's dreams were strange but not troubling. Qonits's were troubling enough for both of them.

◇

The long-range scout remained parked for ten hours, then its two occupants were picked up by a courier. On the trip insystem, both passengers, secured in their seats, slept again as if they'd been sleep deprived. The copilot wakened them when he emerged from warpspace above Kunming. Near enough that Qonits could appreciate the city's layout, but high enough to give it context. Looking southeast across 400 miles of grasslands and forests, they could see the Gulf of Tonkin. Northwestward, the view was dominated by the deep rugged gorges and towering snow-topped ridges and peaks of the Yun Ling Shan. To the east, spreading to the horizon, lay tawny farmland with intermittent woodlands.

To David MacDonald it was unbelievably beautiful. He wished Yukiko were there to see it with him. For Qonits the view was interesting and aesthetic, and for the moment he forgot his mission—its responsibilities and dubious prospects.

The radio snatched their attention. Internal Security had further instructions for the pilot. They didn't want Qonits seen by the public. Not yet. His presence would no doubt would leak, but let it seem only an unlikely rumor.

The city drew nearer, details multiplying, sharpening. Then they were above the Palace of Worlds, lowering quietly, unremarkably to its roofpad. There was no band, or red carpet, and the squad of marines who met them wore dress greens, not ceremonial whites. Looking hard and businesslike, if a bit distracted. They'd never seen a Wyzhñyñy before, of course, nor any sapient alien. To them, Qonits looked bizarre and dangerous.

If anyone imagines these people won't talk about this, David thought, *they're crazy.* It seemed to him he got almost as many looks as Qonits. He wondered if they considered him a hero or a turncoat. *Try victim,* he suggested silently.

The president and prime minister waited in business clothes, without insignia. David had never, of course, seen either of them in person, but they were familiar from newscasts. It was to the much shorter, thicker-bodied human he gave precedence, ad-libbing. "Mr. President, Mr. Prime Minister," he said, "it is my honor to present to you Ambassador Qonits, chief scholar and personal envoy of Grand Admiral Quanshûk, Ruler of the Seventh Swarm."

David turned to Qonits then. "Mr. Ambassador," he said, "it is my honor to introduce to you the honorable Chang Lung-Chi, President of the Commonwealth of Worlds. And the honorable Foster Peixoto, his prime minister."

Qonits was surprised at Foster Peixoto's height, and wondered what gender he might be. Meanwhile he bowed slightly: David had coached him. "I am deeply honored," he said.

"I too am honored, Mr. Ambassador," the prime minister answered. It was the president's reply that surprised both Qonits and David: "It is good you come here," he said—in understandable Wyzhñyñyç! It suggested to them that somehow, somewhere, the government had had contact with other Wyzhñyñy. Actually, the recorded language lessons (even as one-sided as most had been), the limited exchanges between Qonits and his bodyguards, and Annika's mixed channeling of the fitness hearing had been enough for the government's powerful artificial intelligence to create a very partial and provisional translation program. And Chang Lung-Chi had taken the opportunity to learn this simple (and ungrammatical) phrase as a courtesy.

Chang and Peixoto, of course, knew what Qonits did not— that the armada was under a new regime, one not interested in negotiating. But Qonits could be a valuable information source, and at any rate, for the president, decency was natural. And judging from the hearing, Qonits was cut off forever from his own people.

<>

No time had been scheduled for resting or getting acquainted. The two human leaders felt strongly pressed by the oncoming armada. Thus, shortly after their introduction, Qonits and David were led through a private corridor to a sitting room in the president's wing. A luncheon had been set for four, and a seat hurriedly improvised for Qonits. He declined to use it, explaining that "persons with four legs commonly stand to eat."

Like bears, the Wyzhñyñy were omnivores despite their fighting teeth. For them, most human foods were digestible and nourishing. Most of them. But Qonits was uneasy. Like humans, the Wyzhñyñy had made a science of adapting to exotic worlds. They'd long since learned that if a planet fell within otherwise habitable parameters, they could usually eat many of its plants and most of its higher animals. Eat them safely and beneficially. But there were exceptions. So on a new world they ate rations they'd brought with them, while technicians analyzed and tested a broad spectrum of plants and animals for safety, digestibility and nutrient values. Without that sort of database, this meal involved a modest risk for the chief scholar.

When they'd finished dessert—*vaclava,* which Qonits found delicious—Foster Peixoto led them to a small conference room. Almost immediately, five humans from War House and the Commonwealth Ministry were ushered in, and the prime minister introduced them to Qonits. "Mr. Ambassador," he said, "we greatly appreciate your courage in coming here. And the courage Grand Admiral Quanshûk displayed in sending you. And finally, the desire for peace shown by you both.

"Before we discuss your mission further, however, there are things you need to know. Please interrupt if I say things you disagree with, or do not understand. Meanwhile I suggest you be seated." He gestured at a large cushion beside the conference table, and Qonits sat down on it like a huge ungainly dog.

"Since you left your flagship," Peixoto went on, "there have been very important developments you need to know about. They are described in a cube I'll play in just a moment." He looked at David. "Is he familiar with what I mean by cube?"

"Yes sir. They have quite similar technology. And sir, we have cubes sent by Grand Admiral Quanshûk, with a player designed to play them. One of them contains the Terran/ Wyzhñyñyç translation program. Another has a Wyzhñyñyç/ Terran program based on it, which hasn't been tested. The third is a message to the president and yourself, recorded by the grand admiral, and translated by his shipsmind. If you'd take time to hear it…"

The prime minister cut him short. "Thank you, Mr. MacDonald. For now we'll proceed as I'd planned, and hear the grand admiral's message later." He looked at Qonits. "The reason will become clear." He glanced at the others around the table. "Now if you will put your attention on the wall screen, please."

The humans swiveled their chairs—Qonits already nearly faced it—and Peixoto touched his key pad. A freeze frame appeared on the screen, showing a dark-complected youth lying on a couch, seemingly asleep. "Mr. Ambassador," Peixoto said, "this young man is my savant communicator. When I run the recording, you will hear him speak. In several voices. He is analogous to a radio, but channels over interstellar distances" —he paused meaningfully— "over interstellar distances with no elapsed time. None. And what he will say is a duplication of conversations *on board your flagship.* Do you understand so far?"

Qonits nodded uncertainly. *Interstellar distances? No elapsed time?* The words seemed clear enough, but impossible.

"Good," Peixoto said, and pressed another key. Ramesh's mouth moved, and words came from the speaker—the fitness board proceedings, as hybridized and channeled by Annika Pedersen. None of the listeners spoke. David MacDonald's jaw went slack. he understood almost none of the Wyzhñyñyç, but the rest...

Initially Qonits stiffened, but as the hearing progressed, he wilted. When the replay was over, it was the president who spoke, his voice soft. "Mr. Ambassador," he said, "we realize what a shock this has been to you. You have my profound sympathy."

Again the chief scholar gave the Wyzhñyñy equivalent of a nod, saying nothing. Except for the first few seconds, he'd had little difficulty with its hybridized content. The Wyzhñyñyç diction, and the sense of speaker identity, had been reproduced surprisingly well.

When it was over, he simply sat, and after a long moment spoke, aware that the humans had been waiting.

"Is there more? There must be more."

Chang nodded. "Yes. We have no record of the later proceedings, but we do have a recording of something else that seems important." He paused, turning. "Those of you from War House and Cee Ministry, please go to the waiting room. What follows is personal. I'll call you back shortly."

David watched frowning as they left. What was this about? Qonits waited numbly. When they were alone with the president and prime minister, Chang nodded, and Peixoto played the next section, the one in which Yukiko was questioned. It left little doubt: Annika, and almost surely Yukiko, were dead. David MacDonald was pale and stony as marble.

"David, we are terribly sorry," Chang said quietly. Peixoto said nothing at all; didn't trust his control. David's nod was wooden. *I should have known it would come to that,* he thought. *It was inevitable. All of it. This mission was a charade, by an admiral trying to convince himself, and two fools who wanted to believe.*

After half a minute, the president spoke again. "I will call the others back in now. There are questions that must be looked at." The people from War House and the Commonwealth Ministry had heard the entire cube before. He'd sent them out as a courtesy to David, in case he broke down.

They did not question Qonits at length, but they did play Quanshûk's cube. Then they reviewed possibilities they'd discussed before, and the conclusions they'd drawn, asking Qonits for clarifications, and his opinions. The chief scholar's comments were brief but informative.

Peixoto's closing comment was to Qonits: "Mr. Ambassador, your grand admiral was correct in believing we prefer negotiation to war. We do not wish to destroy your people, nor be destroyed by them. When your fleet has been smashed, perhaps the survivors will agree to terms. Then you will have a major role in this."

Peixoto didn't actually lie, but he didn't imagine that terms could be agreed on, even assuming that Soong's Commos won the battle to come. For he knew things that Qonits still did not. The armada had stopped very briefly in the fringes of two more inhabited systems, departing quickly without attacking, leaving only their emergence signatures. Clearly, Charley had been right: they'd decided to postpone further conquests, and were inbound with the intention of forcing a showdown, a final battle. Given their new rate of progress, they'd reach the Eridani System in about three weeks. The Eridani System had a home-grown population of nearly two billion, a bevy of universities, burgeoning industries—and millions of colonial evacuees, armed and more or less trained.

Soong and his Commos would be there, waiting with reinforcements, and Charley Gordon was refining a strategy and tactics to include the new spook drones, whose functions were deception and confusion.

With the new weapons and Charley Gordon, there was still a chance. The Admiralty thought so and Soong thought so. The *Altai*'s shipsmind rated it one in four, and War House's AI agreed. Charley Gordon rated it even. "Wait and see," he'd said. "If we survive the first phase, we will beat them."

Peixoto had never known Charley Gordon to fool himself, but in this situation he might. *Because this will be the final battle,* Peixoto told himself, *with everything at stake. And it is on Charley's shoulders. The pressure will not break him, but it might bend his judgement.*

Chang, on the other hand, believed the Tao wanted humanity to survive, and therefore that it would. And of course if all else failed, there was project Noah.

<>

David and Qonits sat in the palace guest suite they shared, neither speaking at first. Finally David suggested they have something to drink, something alcoholic, and diagrammed the ethanol molecule, elaborating. Qonits nodded. Ethanol was the active ingredient in most Wyzhñyñy liquors. Then David asked their marine orderly to send for dark rum.

The orderly, who wore a stunner and a lance corporal's stripe, seemed a competent young man. Qonits assumed the stunner was a weapon, and the marine as much guard as orderly, but the chief scholar did not feel threatened. And rightly. The lance corporal had been warned that a stunner was lethal to Wyzhñyñy. He was there to *defend* his charges, and forbidden to use it on the ambassador under any circumstances, however desperate.

Another lance corporal delivered the bottle. Each "guest" took a drink; both marines declined. David took his straight. Qonits sipped his with water, but drank nonetheless.

"So it will only be a few weeks," David said. "Who do you suppose will win?"

"The grand admiral feared that you would, eventually," Qonits answered. "Your resources are enormous."

"But your fleet is enormous," David replied, "and we have not been a warlike species for a very long time."

"Perhaps not. But your battlecomps have proven much better than ours, and you have robot cruisers that can maneuver—" he failed to come up with the word 'evasively,' so he zigzagged a hand. "And obtaining target locks requires milliseconds—not an easy matter when a target moves erratically at such speeds." He paused, then added: "Also your shields are stronger."

David still had trouble imagining an effective Commonwealth fleet. Certainly not one so quickly constructed and trained. He peered thoughtfully at Qonits, who sipped his rum again.

"We lost many more fighting ships than you did," Qonits continued. "And a majority of our ships are not fighting ships."

It occurred to David that the chief scholar would be keeping those things to himself, if he thought there was any chance at all of meaningful negotiation. And the prime minister had told Qonits about the savants, which he wouldn't have done if he expected to negotiate.

"Many are colony ships, supply ships, factory ships," Qonits went on. "It is necessary that our colonies set up manufacturing industries, with different tribes having different industries.

"And therein lies a greater problem." He paused again to sip. "Agricultural tribes are landed first, to establish food production and a planetary data base. And when shipsmind decides we have occupied as large a sector of space as we can administer, the tribes not yet landed are assigned by shipsmind to worlds already occupied. On the basis of planetary environments, tribal affinities, and an integrated, practical industrial program.

"Usually there is no technologically potent empire to destroy. And when there has been, it has never been too large to swallow. Until now."

He took another swallow himself, then fixed his bleak gaze on David again. "We never imagined an empire so large as yours. Not a hundredth as large. We were already badly over-extended when we fought the first human fleet. We would not have enough tribes. And our industries would be so widely dispersed, they would not constitute a viable system."

"Then why…"

Qonits fist slammed the table top, making David jump. "Because we dared not stop! Not within the bounds of a technologically advanced empire! We would have been mortally exposed!"

He paused, staring ruefully at his fist. "I am sorry, David. I should not have committed violence, even against a table. The scholar gender does not tolerate ethanol well. And you are my friend. My only friend in this galaxy."

"In this galaxy," David echoed. "You've said that before, and I've assumed it was a figure of speech. Don't tell me the Wyzhñyñy are from another galaxy."

"We are." Qonits began to rock, forward and back. "We are," he repeated. Then he finished his drink and sat quietly.

Contemplating only the All-Soul knows what, David thought. "But surely you hadn't filled up your own galaxy. And how could you have gotten here from so far away?"

He'd never before heard Qonits laugh, but it seemed to him that's what this sound was. Not an amused laugh; probably ironic. The chief scholar refilled his glass himself, and drank. "We do not know," he said, then briefly described the experience. "Nor do we know which other one we came from. Not that it makes any difference. The nearest would be too far."

◇

Briefly they sipped without speaking. Then David, groping for a change of subject, asked what Qonits' home world was like. They spent the next hour exchanging reminiscences of childhood and youth. And drinking. Finally Qonits slumped onto his side and closed his eyes.

"You're drunk, old buddy," David said. And laughed. "And so am I. How about that! We need to get ol' Pollywog or whatever his name is to get drunk with the president. What *is* his name? Pollywog."

Qonits eyes opened. He giggled. *That's what it is,* David thought. *Giggling.* "I don' remember," Qonits said. "Tooley Rooley." He frowned, trying to get it right. "Toolarog. Thass it."

His eyes closed again. David wobbled to his bed and flopped down on it. It promptly began to rotate on its axis. He knew it was the alcohol, not the bed, but nonetheless tried physically to hold it still, until the sensation stopped. Then he nested his cheek in his pillow. "David," he mumbled, "you juss did something no human ever did before. You know that? You got drunk with an alien."

It was the last thing he thought before sleeping.

<>

Marine Lance Corporal Artemis Shaughnessy looked at the two sleepers. What a story to tell his children and grandchildren, when he had some. Surely the security restrictions would be off by then.

It seemed to him he knew more about the aliens now than even the president did.

<>

He didn't, of course. The suite was bugged, and the two leaders had all of it on cube. Including David waking later from a dream of Yukiko, to soak his pillow with tears.

It was the last time he would grieve for her. It was done.

Chapter Twenty-Two
The Battle of Epsilon Eridani

Abruptly, Alvaro Soong's command screen registered 221 radio sources, twittering code. He'd been expecting them: a corvette herding 220 spook drones, newly arrived in the Eridani System from Sol. They'd emerged sufficiently nearby that their emergence waves preceded their electromagnetic signature by only a few seconds. The corvette's captain, a lieutenant, had done an excellent job of delivering his herd.

A similar herd had arrived from the Indi System four days earlier and six days late, badly scattered, sixteen spooks short—and on the wrong side of the system. Far enough that the guide ship's signal lag was more then thirteen hours! What a mess. Gathering the spooks had been slow and frustrating, and the fifty-seven hours wasted would be time lost later from steel drills. As for the sixteen spooks lost in hyperspace—an admiral hates losing even unmanned ships.

The Indi guide ship had been a long-range scout, and her commander a mere ensign! Policy required a board of review, which took less than four hours to absolve the young officer of malfeasance. He'd had only introductory training in hyperspace radio—not nearly enough to reliably monitor and control the drones in hyperspace. As for gathering them for the closing jump—that accounted for most of the six-day delay.

The review board concluded he'd done well to lose so few.

Soong savanted a strongly worded message to War House, criticizing Indi Command for appointing someone so unqualified. It was Admiralty Chief Fedor Tischendorf himself who replied, very mildly. Ensign Fahzi had been at the head of his class when Indi Command had pulled him out of training, bestowed a premature commission, *and with Kunming's blessing* had given him the job. On Indi Prime, everyone of certified competence— short of Command and training staff—had already been sent with the 1st Indi Battle Wing. All they had left were midshipmen.

"Consider yourself well served, Alvaro," Tischendorf had

finished. "Ensign Fahzi was the best available, and whatever spooks arrived are ships you wouldn't otherwise have. If he'd lost half of them, you'd still be better off than if they hadn't been sent. And if they hadn't been sent, they'd be meaningless. Because if you don't severely blunt the Wyzhñyñy advance at Eridani—and I stress *severely*—we're lost. All of us.

Soong had listened with chagrin. He'd popped his cork—rare for him—and the indignation that sprayed out had turned to rue. He didn't counter that Indi Command should have held back a qualified officer from the 1st Indi Battle Wing, then transferred him back to it on arrival. Fahzi *had* done the job. And historically, war was notorious for erroneous planning assumptions, pressure situations, decisions made under severe stress, and the need to use unqualified personnel. In fact, Soong told himself, a perspective review of this war would probably discover fewer and less critical foul-ups than in most historical wars. Because regardless of its other shortages, War House was rich in resourceful ingenuity. Not to mention long centuries of contingency planning and simulation testing.

And no one in War House had joined the military for prestige or benefits.

◇

Now Soong's fleet was fully gathered. Since Shakti, it hadn't grown much in manned fighting ships: his losses had been made up, but he had only a single new battle wing. War House had decided to concentrate on drone production; he had nearly twice as many maces as before.

And now spooks, drones of quite another type. With the 220 from Sol, he totaled 404. Named "Ball Spooks" (for a fabled 21st-century gamer and writer), they carried opaque-image generators which could disguise them as battleships, maces or cruisers. Spooks had long been part of science-fiction gaming, and a War House budget proposal for their development had been rejected by the government centuries earlier. Then the Wyzhñyñy had come, and industrial and research resources became the limiting factors, with maces and improved shield generators the Admiralty's top development priorities.

And properly so. Maces could kill enemy warships, layered shields could save ships and lives, and definitive research and development had already been done on them. But there was a role for sacrificial lambs—spook ships—that looked enough like lions to fool the enemy and occupy his efforts. So a project was also begun, small and exploratory at first, then more intensive.

When a spook-field generator had been successfully demonstrated, production was begun. Because spooks could be produced quickly in quantities. Prospector hulls would serve, and could be mass-produced cheaply.

Prospector hulls had limited capacity, of course. And while spooks needed no crew facilities, but they required lots of hardware, particularly generators of several kinds. Spook-field generators not only required hull space, they made serious energy demands, because ordinary holos were not enough. And of course there could be no skimping on strange-space generators; without them they couldn't travel. But limits could be set for other equipment. A spook without an energy shield would not fool enemy sensors, but their shield generators could be single-layer models, and needn't produce modified topologies.

As for "weapons"... Wyzhñyñy shipsminds would be dealing with great volumes of urgent sensory intake, thus spook "warbeams" needed only to fluoresce a battleship's shield convincingly. They required far less hull space, and drew far less power than a cruiser's guns, for example. And they carried no torpedos at all.

<>

Soong had gotten the necessary performance and operating specs in advance, and Charley Gordon had considered them in reprogramming the battlecomps. The Wyzhñyñy would face a whole new set of Commonwealth Fleet tactics; the Commos had been simdrilling them for days. Now the *Altai*'s shipsmind uploaded them to the newly arrived spooks from the Sol System.

Extrapolating, shipsmind had provided a probabilistic window of Wyzhñyñy arrival. It left only four days for steel drills, then Soong would have to order ready formations, and wait. Wait for the final and decisive fight. If they lost, snooze ships on Terra, Indi Prime, Lüneburger's World and Masada, there to load liberation forces, would instead embark women, children, and chosen specialists. None of whom knew yet the great and terrible secret. While cargo ships—so-called colony resettlement ships—loaded selected colonization equipment. They would rendezvous, then seek a new home, half a dozen hyperspace years distant.

But only a tiny fraction of one percent of humankind could be taken. Thus the iron-bound secrecy. The plan was too terrible to become known.

As for the rest of humankind—their future depended on the Battle of Eridani. If it was lost, they were lost. There'd be no opportunity, nor any meaningful force, to make a stand elsewhere.

<>

In reviewing simdrills and coordinating steel drills, Alvaro Soong had occasionally spoken by radio with all his wing commanders. And on his secure, private channel, had twice spoken privately with Carmen Apraxin-DaCosta. Neither had mentioned marriage. This was neither the time nor place to discuss it.

<>

Less than four seconds after his armada emerged, the raucous blare of an alarm horn resounded through the Wyzhñyñy flagship. Grand Admiral Tualurog tensed. It was what he'd been hoping for, and he reacted with a mixture of eagerness and anxiety. His command screen showed several sources of technically produced radiation. The main source, very powerful, was the system's second planet, and there were numerous others farther outsystem—within an asteroid zone, and in the vicinity of a jovian giant. Their strength and distribution was far larger than in any system encountered since they'd left the Empire. Clearly a core-world system—but hardly the crown system. The radio output wasn't that intense.

Also insystem, in the near fringe, was a source array that could only be a space fleet larger than any the armada had encountered before. Though still much smaller than his own.

So. Not the Commonwealth's main fleet then. It was simply there to bleed him. That was the human strategy; had been all along.

That moment was pivotal, and even Charley had not foreseen it. For a moment, Tualurog considered generating hyperspace again and speeding onward. Find the human crown system, where their main fleet would be waiting. Defeat it and behead the enemy. But he rejected the idea almost at once. Because the fleet here would undoubtedly pursue him, and with his power advantage, it was better to deal with it now, by itself, rather than later, while engaged with their main fleet.

He voiced an order to shipsmind, and the armada, not greatly dispersed during the approach jump, began forming battle formations.

◇

Alvaro Soong examined the pattern of emergence loci. A few yards away, Charley Gordon sat relaxed at his battle master's station, absorbing the displays on his screen, and no doubt much that was not on the screen. Calmly he began to give orders to shipsmind, the code words measured. Later they'd flow from him quick as pulses from a blaster. And this time he would not wait for the Wyzhñyñy to start the fight.

◇

The first strike was by an entire echelon of maces, doing something no one had imagined before: instead of emerging stationary from warpspace, they emerged with momentum—surged forth. There were no organisms aboard to be crushed by inertia, and shipsmind, on Charley's order, had computed an entry velocity the sturdy maces could withstand. At the instant of emergence they began accelerating, generating shields, and achieving target locks for war beams and torpedos.

The Wyzhñyñy had generated shields in advance, but still the concentration of fire wrought havoc, and within seconds the maces were deep inside the Wyzhñyñy formations. Nor did they pause. A second echelon followed, at the same unexpected speed. And a third. Meanwhile a human battle wing emerged a little distance out, stationary, then accelerated toward the enemy, firing both torpedo salvos and war beams, concentrating on individual targets.

The maces had charged all the way through the Wyzhñyñy battle fleet with modest losses, and dropped their shields on the run, the survivors winking into warpspace. And in warpspace, maneuvered promptly into a reverse vector, to emerge again on the fly, ripping through the same formations they'd already savaged.

By then the first-arrived human battle wing had closed with the Wyzhñyñy, the two sides fighting in a close-range slugging match. And of course the other wings replicated that behavior elsewhere within the Wyzhñyñy battle fleet. In those formations they attacked, less than one Wyzhñyñy battleship in three was targeted, but of those targeted, most died. A few survived derelict, their matric taps blown, maintaining life support systems on backups if at all. The human battle groups ignored them, concentrating on ships still dangerous.

This drew the Wyzhñyñy reserves, of course. It was their kind of fighting. Their mistake, foreseen by Charley Gordon, was to move cautiously. They'd been fooled too often. Thus the maces reached the dueling field ahead of many of them, sucker-punching and killing Wyzhñyñy duelists, winking back into warpspace, then charging out again toward the oncoming Wyzhñyñy intervention. And when the maces reemerged, Soong's battle groups used the opportunity to take refuge in warpspace themselves.

They did not stay there long. Warpspace was suitable for covert maneuvering, but poorly suited for actual fighting.

◇

So far, Charley Gordon had not committed his spooks. He knew the circumstances he wanted them for, and it wasn't time yet.

◇

The fighting continued, the Commos repeating the same tactics. Charley would change them when opportunities or difficulties required. In the vicinity of the *Altai*, the Wyzhñyñy had killed nearly a dozen human battleships, and twice as many lesser warships. And that was only one segment of the scene. Comparable scenarios played throughout the battle zone. Wyzhñyñy losses were gruesome. The *Meadowlands'* bridge reeked with anxiety. Tualurog had chewed his cheeks bloody, and his eyes bulged wide and wild. *This cannot be allowed! Those cursed robots! Sixty-two tribes depend on us!* Torpedos struck her shield, and the *Meadowlands* jarred. Her lights dimmed, then brightened again. The bridge screens, however, did not blink; shipsminds were powerfully buffered. Damage alarms jangled and systems checks ran. Her shield recovered, and her war beam generator rebooted.

Meanwhile another human battle wing re-emerged in the vicinity. Tualurog decided, and barked a command to shipsmind, which passed it on. "All battle groups! All battle groups! This is your grand admiral! Your grand admiral! Do not allow the humans to run away! Choose a target, lock on and close! Attack, pursue and kill! Attack, pursue and kill! Do not be distracted! Do not disengage for any reason! Do not let them generate strange-space again!"

The order sounded on every Wyzhñyñy bridge, in every compartment, down every corridor. And whispered in Charley Gordon's mind in the form of an intuition: it was time to call in the spooks. On Charley's order, couriers generated warpspace and radioed the waiting spook groups. Which emerged at the edge of action, and received explicit orders via the *Altai*'s shipsmind. Then they winked into warpspace again, to emerge at rendezvous coordinates with battle groups and mace triads.

Meanwhile the battle wings fought in slow motion, to permit maneuver. The maces, with their heavy shields, repeatedly disrupted Wyzhñyñy contingents attempting to gang up on Commo battleships. Among the Commo battle groups, patterns of mutual support fluctuated with the need, their fire coordination adjusting constantly to threat and opportunity. And always the key was teamwork.

Most often the spooks mimicked battleships. And because they were less responsive than manned ships, they attracted much more than their share of Wyzhñyñy fire.

Mostly the Commos had the advantage of two-layered shields, but not the veteran *Altai*. She took a heavy torpedo salvo, the energy overload collapsing her shield. Her escort cruisers saved her, two of them deliberately intercepting war beams, breaking their target locks. "Generate warpspace!" Soong snapped, and after a long moment the *Altai* disappeared, her battlecomp automatically steering an avoidance course "on the other side," against the high probability that more torpedos had been launched at her. They would follow, but the transition would break their target locks, letting them pass into hyperspace limbo.

Soong exhaled through rounded lips, half whistling. He had, he realized, very nearly lost both his ship and Charley Gordon.

"Admiral," Charley told him, "the battle vectors have evolved almost ideally. I expect your Commos will get by without us while Engineering repairs our shield generator."

Then he ordered the navcomp to take them to a location in the F-space potentiality, one from which they could emerge outside the battle zone. Meanwhile Soong watched the array of screens, which for the moment showed only systems rundowns.

<>

Engineering required little more than five minutes to replace the *Altai*'s matrix tap and breakers. Then she returned to F-space, somewhat removed from the fighting and unnoticed by the enemy. The battle had continued relentlessly. Few of the human ships with single-layer shields still lived, but many with two-layered shields fought on. This time Soong held the *Altai* clear of the fighting, and Charley began to issue directions to the fleet's battlecomps. Even during the *Altai*'s absence, his battle programs had been decisive. Some of his simdrills and steel drills had assumed the loss of the *Altai* and her battle master.

Most of the spooks had died, but they'd played a crucial role. Meanwhile the Wyzhñyñy could not waltz with the maces, which repeatedly disrupted Wyzhñyñy formations and fire coordination. The *Meadowlands* had been destroyed, and no one had taken command. Tualurog's "attack, pursue and kill" order had hampered teamwork, dispersed formations, and seriously reduced responses to opportunity and threat.   Increasingly fragmented, his warfleet simply followed his final order, until teamwork had almost totally unraveled.

Now Charley's main attention was on directing disengaged Commo units to strategic locations. Finally a critical point was reached at which the Wyzhñyñy reactions became effectively suicidal, and their warships were overwhelmed.

The battle was over.

<>

Soong remained on the bridge while the names of surviving ships scrolled. He had to know. When the list was complete, the *Uinta* was not on it. Even then he stayed, while shipsmind extracted and scrolled the identities of Commo ships destroyed.

Finally the *Uinta*'s name appeared. She'd been ruptured and melted down.

When the rundown was complete, he left the bridge, the victor of the most important battle in human history. His back was straight, his head high, and his eyes dry. When he reached his stateroom, he drank himself to sleep.

Chapter Twenty-Three
Proposal

Morning sunlight slanted through ten-foot windows, causing the polished table and walls to glow a deep golden mahogany. A product of more than expensive veneer and thorough polishing. There were also the window fields. It had been years since David MacDonald had been exposed to advertising, but he recalled the trade name: Rich Light. *Because you have to be rich to own them,* he thought wryly. The light itself was free though: sunlight. But altered to order. The window fields controlled the intensity and wavelengths transmitted.

A gavel tapped lightly. The president had gotten to his feet. "We have asked you here," he said, "to help us through a dilemma. A situation much preferable to yesterday's, but... We have a choice to make that on the one hand threatens humanity with centuries of trouble and grief, and on the other, a burden of guilt very difficult to bear. We need a third alternative, one that avoids both.

"Under our Emergency War Powers, the prime minister and I have the authority to make that choice ourselves, and in fact there is no time for parliamentary debate and clearance. So we especially want and need your counsel now."

Chang Lung-Chi scanned the assemblage: Admiral Fedor Tischendorf, Admiralty Chief; Dr. Arthur Shin, Minister of War; Melani Honghi, Commonwealth Minister; Dorje Lodro Tulku, Chaplain of the Office of the President; and Ambassador Qonits. With their principal aides, including David MacDonald.

Just now it was Qonits at whom Chang looked. "Mr. Ambassador, last night a great battle was fought in the Eridani System," he said. "A decisive battle. Analysis of battle recordings indicates that none of your warfleet survived, or even undertook to escape. They fought till the last was destroyed."

The words stunned Qonits; it was Quanshûk's vision realized.

"But that was the warfleet," Chang went on. "Your

armada's noncombat ships—estimated at more than three thousand—still sit parked in warpspace, neither fleeing nor able to defend themselves. Experience suggests they even lack force shields. And we have the task of deciding how to deal with them."

He sipped honeyed tea, allowing Qonits a moment before he continued. "How many of your people do they carry? Ten million? Call it ten million in stasis. And their crews number what? Another quarter million? Along with the colonists you've set down, they are all the Wyzhñyñy that exist in this galaxy."

His gaze was on the mahogany table now, but his attention was on his thoughts. "Do we destroy them? If not, what *do* we do with them? A month ago, when the question was rhetorical, I would have said destroy them. Said it regretfully. But alive in this galaxy—certainly in this sector of it—they pose a threat to the human species. Already they've murdered perhaps a hundred million of us. Given another week or two, they'd have killed more than a billion on Eridani Prime. A billion! Why should we feel compassion for them?"

Why indeed? thought Qonits.

"The answer," Chang said, "is that you are a sapient species. And in our various philosophies, almost without exception, the destruction of a sapient life form is a grave—a major crime. Thus to exterminate your people is almost too ugly to contemplate, although they—you—intended to exterminate us."

Again he scanned his audience. "I will ask all of you to comment, but first I would like to hear Ambassador Qonits' thoughts. If you will, sir."

There was a long silence—twenty seconds at least—then Qonits swayed his head, a negative. "There is nothing I can say now. Perhaps after others have spoken."

David MacDonald exhaled softly. *Having Qonits here makes it harder to say 'kill them.'* He wondered at his own calm, his objectivity. Yukiko was lost to him, at least until he died himself. Probably, he thought, it was Tualurog who'd killed her. Tualurog himself was surely dead, and while that didn't lessen the loss, it had quenched the thirst for vengeance.

Chang's gaze moved to Admiral Tischendorf. "What do you have to say, Admiral?"

Frowning, Tischendorf pursed his broad mouth. "To stand off and fire torpedos at unarmed ships...? If I order it, our people will do it. And for the life of me, I can't see any way around it. But doing it will...leave a scar on everyone's soul, even beyond this lifetime. As you said, we would carry it forever.

"On the other hand, if we start firing, I suspect that those not in the first target set will generate hyperspeed and leave. Then we'll have the long job of hunting them down; a long, unpleasant, unpromising job."

He sat back, finished.

"Dr. Shin," Chang said, "what do you have to say?"

"At this point, Mr. President, I can only echo Admiral Tischendorf. Perhaps next round." Shin knew Chang's style. The rounds of comments or questions would continue until he'd heard all he felt was needed.

"Ah. Ms Honghi?"

"Mr. President, my concern is for the evacuees, and freeing their worlds of Wyzhñyñy occupation so they can go home again. Those who want to. Considering all the relatives and friends who died, and the farms and towns destroyed, many may not want to."

The president nodded gravely. "I'm sure that's true." His gaze paused on Qonits, then moved to Dorje Lodro. "Your Wisdom," he said, "what guidance do you have for us?"

"Guidance?" Her tone was mild. "You and the prime minister are quite able to make your decision on this without my input.... But since you ask, consider. The Wyzhñyñy are dangerous only if armed. Presumably they have weapons and munitions aboard their troopships and ordnance ships. If you can collect those, and launch them by gravdrive into the sun, the Wyzhñyñy are no longer dangerous."

You hope! David thought.

"Of course, if you spare them, you must decide what to do with them. They cannot go home. And if you do not spare them…" She paused. "As has been said: they are ensouled. You will bear great karma." She looked at Qonits. "Ambassador, within the Commonwealth boundaries, has your armada colonized planets which had no human occupants?"

Qonits looked at her with the first glimmer of hope. "Three that I know of," he said.

"Ah." She turned to Chang. "If all the Wyzhñyñy in the armada were landed on one of them—perhaps the most favorable, or that nearest Terra—they would be relatively easy to monitor and police. Then the Wyzhñyñy colonists on other planets could be offered transportation to that world."

She bowed slightly. "I have said enough."

Chang nodded, then looked at Qonits again. "Mr. Ambassador, you were sent to negotiate with us. Could you speak *for* us? Talk your people into surrendering, and settling on a world of their own? We of course would dictate the terms, but if those terms are not punitive…" He paused, waiting.

Dorje Lodro's words had revived Qonits. "I can try," he said quietly, "but I cannot guarantee success. It depends on who has taken command of the colonization fleet, if anyone has.

"The colonization fleet has no admiral of its own. It was commanded by the grand admiral—Lord Quanshûk and then Lord Tualurog. Each of the colony tribes had a commanding general and a governor, both of the master gender—but…"

Foster Peixoto raised a hand and interrupted. "What do you mean by master gender?"

"Let me first finish answering the earlier question. Those generals should all be in stasis, and at any rate are unqualified to command a ship, let alone a fleet. It is unlikely they've been revived, but the possibility is worrisome: We could find ourselves dealing with a commander strong in pride but weak in understanding.

"Whomever I must negotiate with will probably, hopefully, be a warrior, not a master, and normally my status is superior to a warrior's. But they will distrust me. And with Lord Quanshûk dead, my status is…" He groped for the word ambiguous, and settled for "unclear."

"On the other hand their situation is desperate, and I expect they will listen." He puffed a Wyzhñyñy sigh before finishing. "There is little more I can say about the prospects, until I know more about the terms you have in mind."

He gestured a shrug. "And now, Mr. Prime Minister, I shall explain the genders for you. It is important that you know; they are central to understanding us."

There are, he told them, four genetic genders and three nurture-actuated, "exalted" genders. One of the exalted genders—"matrons"—develops functional breasts, and if assigned a newborn, nurture it. As a result, this "nurtured" infant develops distinctive anatomical, morphological and mental traits. That is, it becomes "exalted." With nurture, a genetic warrior becomes a master; a genetic artisan becomes a scholar; and a genetic nanny becomes a matron. Each quite distinct from the unnurtured phenotype.

Frowning, Chang said: "We were told by—another source that both sexes nurse the young."

"That requires clarification. We have only one parent gender. Each adult of the parent gender alternates between male and female sexual phases, and only the parent who carried the child nurses it. But the non-sexual nanny gender, which is larger, will also nurse any unweaned young in its care."

"You told us the matron gender nurses selected young."

"In a sense. But what the matrons produce is not what you might call 'milk.' They provide something quite different, and in smaller quantities."

"Seven genders," Tischendorf mused. "What percentage are warriors?"

David had asked the same question while they'd waited aboard the scout, to be picked up, so Qonits recognized Tischendorf's problem. "About twelve percent," Qonits said, "but the parent gender, and the nannies and artisans are also trained to fight. Masters, as exalted warriors, are physically the largest and most powerful, and well able to fight. But they are seldom called upon to physically participate in combat. Their command powers, and sense of responsibility, are too valuable."

The admiral regarded the information thoughtfully. "And only the parent gender has sexual intercourse?"

"Only the parent gender is appropriately equipped and hormonally inclined."

"What is the difference between a warrior and a—parent in uniform? On the battlefield that is?"

"Warriors are larger and stronger, and have more appropriate reactions. In fact, they are bolder and more aggressive in all matters, and in war, more ready to put their lives in danger. In peacetime, warriors both accept and seek responsibility more than any other gender excepting masters. In the military, the great majority of commissioned officers are warriors, but they do not attain the higher ranks. All elite units are made up of warriors."\

Tischendorf nodded thoughtfully. "So then, all— citizens?—are trained as soldiers?"

"All but matrons. Matrons have seriously limited intelligence. Also they are very precious to the species, unique and uncommon. All the exalted genders are; nurturing a newborn for exalted status commonly results in the infant's death. We have a saying, half serious: 'Death by deranged morphogenesis is God's way of helping us appreciate the occasional success.'"

David wondered how such an odd system had ever evolved. And Qonits had mentioned God. Had he said it to mislead them, or was the proverb genuine?

"That is why," Qonits continued, "the exalted genders are exposed to actual combat no more than necessary. But matrons are especially precious. A warrior is most fierce when protecting a matron."

He bowed then, and the president reclaimed the floor. "Tell us about scholars, Mr. Ambassador."

"Ah, scholars. I have slighted my own kind, have I not. Scholars are exalted artisans. The artisan genotype in general absorbs information more easily than other genotypes. And artisans tend to apply information in practical ways. Scholars excel artisans in their affinity for information, but are less focused on its practical applications. Also we look more deeply, and analyze with greater facility."

He displayed what David knew was a grimace. "Unfortunately those strengths are not always accompanied by wisdom. They can give rise to overconfidence and vanity." He paused. "And it is a scholar weakness to become so engrossed in some area of interest—learning your language, for example— that we lose track of relative importances."

Chang regarded Qonits for a long moment. "Thank you, Mr. Ambassador," he said. "You've been very enlightening."

◇

Chang led his de facto council through two additional rounds before he and his prime minister thanked and dismissed them. The last thing he said was that he would consult next with Charley Gordon, then perhaps talk further with them.

Leaving the council room, David felt relief at the direction the meeting had taken. For despite the death of Yukiko, he did not want the Wyzhñyñy eradicated. Qonits, who had become his friend, was a Wyzhñyñy. Also he remembered the pastry chef on the *Meadowlands,* who out of goodness of heart had been friendly to him and Yukiko and Annika. And who now was dead.

◇

After lunch in their suite, Qonits napped, while David sat in one of the small roof gardens and read the Kunming *Daily Reporter* in detail. Later, Qonits also came up, accompanied by Lance Corporal Shaughnessy, who removed himself a dozen yards, as if to give them privacy. Nonetheless, David supposed the marine was bugged—surely something was—and that everything they might say would be recorded.

"Tell me about Wyzhñyñy history," he said to Qonits. "Not the details, but the broad features."

"The broad features? That is feasible, yes. I will begin at the beginning." Qonits also believed they were being recorded, and that David was leading him. Nonetheless he talked frankly, almost till supper.

◇

Via Ramesh, the president and prime minister tried to

consult with Charley Gordon after lunch. Admiral Soong, however, asked that they postpone it a couple of hours. Charley was still sleeping off the nervous exhaustion of the long battle. And the colonization fleet showed no sign of leaving. There was constant warp radio traffic between Wyzhñyñy ships, but while no one on the *Altai* had any idea of what was being discussed, it sound desultory, rather than intense.

Chang and Peixoto gave him half an hour, then eavesdropped on the ambassador and David MacDonald, gaining useful insights.

Forty minutes later they called the *Altai* again, and counseled with Charley, and Alvaro Soong. When the armada had arrived in the system, Charley told them, the colonization fleet had obviously been ordered to park where they were, and wait. But they wouldn't wait forever. Their commanders were surely aware that their warfleet had been destroyed. His impression was, they'd been discussing the dangers of fleeing— of being dispersed and isolated, with the separate units lacking adequate technical-industrial equipment for long-range survival. Along with the probability that many would be torpedoed when they booted their drives. They were aware that a human fleet was standing by, also in warpspace, with target locks on Wyzhñyñy ships. And that survivors would almost certainly be hunted by the humans.

But they wouldn't wait forever. Unless something intervened soon, they'd leave, unless a peace proposal changed their minds.

An hour's discussion resulted in a plan. Half an hour later, Qonits, using a bottled savant in Cee Ministry, sent the basic features of an offer via Charley himself, who forwarded it using the Wyzhñyñy command frequency. The vocators of the bottled savants provided a much better approximation of Qonits' Wyzhñyñyç speech than any human vocal apparatus could.

The Wyzhñyñy commanders could expect an "imperial" ambassador in two Wyzhñyñy shipsweeks, to confer with them directly. Qonits would leave in a cruiser the next day, with David as his companion.

Chapter Twenty-Four
Unfinished Business

Months had passed since the Wyzhñyñy offensive on New Jerusalem had been broken. The Burger engineers had worked diligently, transforming the army's base from a tent camp to prefabs, electrified for heat and light. The battalion officer's dayroom had a wooden frame and a subfloor of newly-sawn planks, provided by the Burgers' portable sawmill. Walls, ceiling, roof, and the floor itself were sheets of Plastosil brought from Pastor Lüneburger's World with the army. The New Jerusalem Liberation Corps was ready for winter.

Which would soon be upon them. It was early ElevenMonth by the Jerrie calendar—dark, cold and wet—when Ensign Esau Wesley came in after supper. He'd brought his platoon back from patrol an hour and a half earlier, had cleaned up and eaten, then come to the dayroom to read. He'd never been much for loafing, and over the months had read and reread the books Captain Zenawi had loaned him. He found them engrossing, full of facts and ideas—even wisdom—useful to a leader.

And that's what he'd become. The previous SevenMonth he'd been officially posted as acting platoon leader. He'd never known or wondered why. In the army, orders came from on high—the company commander, Regiment, Division, War House—and you went along with them.

He knew very well, of course, how he'd become *unofficial* acting platoon leader. Ensign Berg had been killed on the Tank Park Raid, then Ensign Hawkins had broken his leg on the Artillery Base Jump. But taking over in an emergency was one thing. Having the post on the company Table of Organization was something else.

<>

There was a story behind it. It had been SevenMonth. The entire corps had taken a lot of casualties, and the regimental commander, Colonel Leclerc, had called in his company commanders to work on reorganizing the regiment. They'd begun right after breakfast, and had pretty much wrapped it before lunch. Some companies had been deactivated—combined with other companies, or their personnel distributed within the regiment as replacements.

Division wanted airborne-qualified personnel kept in airborne-qualified platoons; something Leclerc would have done in any case. "Zenawi," he said, "your 2nd Platoon has the most distinguished record in the regiment. With another very fine commander. But according to Major Hatta, Hawkins won't be out of the hospital for eight weeks at the soonest. Add three weeks or more for rehab…" He shrugged. "And Hatta strongly recommends that Hawkins not jump again—not in this gravity.

"Fortunately Ensign Hussain is available. From 3rd Regiment; a good man. His platoon covered Demolitions while they'd wrecked the Wyz howitzers, and taken a lot of casualties. Including Major Chou, which left Hussain the senior officer, in charge of the rear guard action and evacuating the casualties. Then the Wyz elite hit. Hairy business, and he handled it well, all of it.

"I'm assigning him to you, to lead 2nd Platoon B."

Captain Kemau Zenawi Singh chewed a lip. "Colonel," Zenawi said, "2nd Platoon has a platoon sergeant who acted as platoon leader throughout the Artillery Base Raid. I'd hoped to see him get the job."

Leclerc frowned. "Esau Wesley? I reviewed his commendations last night, before okaying his promotion to sergeant 1st class. A remarkable young warrior. But he doesn't have anything like the training and the leadership experience Hussain has. Are you sure you don't prefer him because he's B Company, and you're loyal to your own people?"

Zenawi set his jaw. "That's part of it, sir. But on the other hand, I'm an old friend of Hussain. We were in the same cadet squad at the Academy. Went into Tehran together a few times, to sample the ethnic eating places.

"The thing is, young Wesley's a sort of icon in B Company, though I doubt he knows it. He's better than his official record, sir. For one thing he's got natural presence. Charisma. Berg,

Hawkins, Captain Mulvaney, all made a project out of him early on, at Stenders, because of his leadership qualities. And he never disappointed them.

"On the Tank Park Raid, he took out the southwest tower by himself, with cover by a couple of blastermen. Then, at the Pecan Orchard, he led a stealth team into the middle of the Wyzhñyñy camp and stole their headquarters, a floater—took it from under their noses—which was vital to our success there. And..."

Leclerc interrupted. "Kemau," he said patiently, "I know those things. But his reputation stems from his individual exploits. Leadership's another matter."

"But not unrelated, colonel. In that disorganized melee at the Tank Park, before he took out the southwest tower, he functioned effectively as a leader. He and his squad were one of two sent into an utterly chaotic melee to support 3rd Platoon when it was getting swamped. And it was Wesley that Mulvaney turned to to get the flak towers handled. And on the Artillery Base jump, Esau directed Hawkins' Platoon at the same time he..."

Leclerc cut him off. "All right. So he's a natural warrior and a promising leader. Hussain's another natural warrior, *and* a trained and proven leader. Where's Wesley's advantage?"

"You already identified it, sir." Zenawi showed no sign of backing off. "You wanted to keep units intact so far as possible; 'for morale and unity,' you said. Wesley's been 2nd Platoon from the beginning, and he's a legend in B Company. In Airborne A Temp for that matter. He's got a reputation: they believe he can do anything, even salvage bad situations. He's smart, tough, fearless... *and lucky!* The men talk about it. The men of B Company, especially 2nd Platoon, would feel slighted, insulted, if he got passed over now."

Zenawi's expression was intense, his white eyes hard in his black face. "Hussain is a good man and he *is* a proven officer. In time, 2nd Platoon would forget their resentment, and like him. But it wouldn't be the same, and it would take awhile." He paused, and put his hand on his chest. "Speaking respectfully, sir, their company commander wants Esau, and so does his company!"

Leclerc pursed his lips, then grunted. "All right, you've made your case, Kemau. I'll post Wesley as commander of 2nd Platoon B Company. But I want you to work with him. Help him with whatever he's short on. Give him some reading: *The Infantry Platoon Leader; Working with Men*; and that old 20th Century classic, Nye's *The Challenge of Command.* And if he's willing, Gopal Singh's *The Wise Leader.* Then quiz him."

Zenawi relaxed. "Thank you, sir, I will. And sir, if you were the CO of B Company, I believe you'd have made the same request I did."

Leclerc stifled a smile. *You got the old man to back down, didn't you, he thought. And now you're rubbing a little oil on. Well, it's healthy to back down now and then, when the case is good enough. But pick your spots carefully, Kemau.*

◇

That had been high summer. Now they were at winter's doorstep. Esau was rereading *The Infantry Platoon Leader* when Jael came in. For months they'd been in different units, quartered in different hutments, living different lives. He hadn't seen her for weeks; didn't often think about her anymore. So far as he knew, they were still married, but it felt remote.

"Hi, Esau," she said, walking over to him.

He lay down his book and stood up. "Howdy, Jael," he answered smiling. "It's been awhile."

Her voice sounded enough like her old voice now, Esau couldn't hear the difference. Normally, when a person signed a bot agreement, there were questions, the volunteer's answers were recorded, and they were asked to read selected lines. Then, if they were bottled, they were given a cube of the recording, to help them learn their old voice again. Jael had learned without a cube, fitting her new voice to her personality, and to the "voice print" in her speech center.

"How're you liking your new servo?" Esau asked. Lamely, it seemed to her, as if he had trouble finding something to say. It was the same model as her old one, which had been damaged by

~ 268 ~

a heavy slammer bolt two weeks earlier, on night reconnaissance deep inside Wyz Country. It had torn up her left knee.

"It's better than the old one," she answered. "It doesn't overheat." She paused to laugh. "The techs say that's because they've got them figured out. I told them it's the weather. Have you seen any action lately?"

He shook his head. "I've heard some a time or two, off in the distance a ways. Maybe things'll heat up when we get snow." He chuckled at the incongruity of terms. "Snow can come any time now, and Captain Zenawi said the last supply run brought down skis. If it gets belly deep, like sometimes, we ought to get around on foot better than the Wyz do."

"You folks still cutting timber every third week?"

He shook his head. "Haven't for...it'll be four weeks on Sixday. Things are getting dull around here." He half grinned. "Now if they'd let me start making a farm..." It had already occurred to him he didn't want to farm anymore, but the old thought patterns were still there, semi-active.

"If things keep going like they are," she said, "us and the Wyz might get so used to each other, we'll just say to Tophet with the war. You farm east of the river and we'll farm west of it." She didn't really want to farm anymore, either. Or live on New Jerusalem, where most women of child-bearing age didn't live to see their thirtieth birthday (about thirty-nine Terran years). But she'd never thought of it as a cruel world. Most folks had been happy enough. And she'd accepted it—until she'd shared reminiscences with Terran women among the bots. Heard about their seventy-year-old grandmothers, even ninety-year-old great grandmothers!

She'd wondered how long she'd live as a bot. A long time maybe. There were two schools of thought on that in the bot camp. The first was, your CNS would finally wear out. And the second—you'd live till you died of boredom. To her, the first seemed most likely.

Esau sat without saying anything, so she asked: "What're you reading?"

He held the book up—a regular paper book—showing her

the cover. *"The Infantry Platoon Leader,"* he said. "This is the severalth time I've read it. Seems like there's stuff in it that wasn't there before. Like someone come in while I slept, and added new stuff to it. I've been reading others, too. Read three by Gopal Singh! Quite a lot different than the testaments, but I suspect Elder Hofer wouldn't fuss too bad. Some of it—a lot of it—he'd probably like.

"What you said about us and the Wyz getting used to each other... Nearly nine hundred years ago—when folks still fought each other some—Gopal Singh wrote that humankind was learning little by little to live in peace. And afterward, for a long time, folks did live in peace. Wouldn't be fighting today if the Wyz hadn't come along."

Jael nodded. "To start farming here again, the womenfolk would have to come back. And might be lots of them wouldn't want to."

"Yeah."

There was silence for several long seconds before he added, "I sure do miss...some of the things you and me used to do together."

"Me too. But not as much as you do, I don't suppose. I don't have the juices I used to. I'd settle for being able to cuddle and nuzzle. But I'm afraid cuddling wouldn't do much for either of us anymore. The way I am now."

Esau rocked a little on his unmoving chair, before saying: "Sometimes I've wondered if we oughtn't have chosen a labor battalion, instead of the army. Then, when it was over, we could have been—still really married. Had those children we never got."

He looked and felt absolutely bleak now. *Not healed,* he thought. *Not healed. Just scabbed over.*

Reaching, Jael touched his arm as gently as if she were still flesh and blood. "Esau dear, don't regret. We always did the best we could, and had lots of good times. Back on the farm, and on Lüneburger's World, and even here in the war.

"And there are other girls besides me. Organic girls, flesh and blood. Indi girls in tanks and floaters, Burger girls wiring and carpentering. Terran nurses at the hospital."

The door opened and two Sikh's came in. Then Jael said she needed to go. "Even bots need their sleep," she told him, and left.

◇

Her walk back to the bot hutment was five minutes of depression. That first time Esau had come to see her, at the bot shop, he'd been so sweet, and she'd been so happy to see him. It had seemed to her they'd get used to one another again, and if they lived, make a life together.

You were dreaming, Jael, she told herself. *The old Jael was killed at the Pecan Orchard. Now you've got a new life, and it's the one you've got to live, because you can't get the old one back.*

◇

On the following Sixday, at evening muster, the troops were told that General Pak would speak to them at 1900 hours. There'd been no rumor of any plans, and the army had gotten used to relative peace and quiet. Something was bound to happen sooner or later, of course. They knew that. The Wyz were still there, and had to be rooted out.

With more time to reflect on matters, the Jerrie troops had come to realize how little New Jerusalem felt like home anymore. Too changed. Nearly every one of them had wondered if he could even find where he'd lived, so thoroughly had the Wyzhñyñy changed the face of the settled land. As if they'd deliberately undertaken to eradicate all signs of the humans who'd lived there before them.

Now it seemed as if they were going to be given another job to do. And at seven o'clock, they were in their mess halls, expecting to hear their general outline an offensive. The screen was rolled out; its power light glittering green. Captain Zenawi gave the order "at ease men," and the picture popped on, showing General Pak seated at his desk.

"Men and women of the New Jerusalem Liberation Corps, I have important news for you. And a confession. Eight days ago, I was informed that the 1st Commonwealth Fleet had destroyed

~ 271 ~

the Wyzhñyñy fleet in battle." He paused. There wasn't a sound in B Company's mess hall. "The Wyzhñyñy warships fought till none were left." Again he paused. "My confession is that I kept the news from you until I knew what this meant to us out here.

"Their warfleet fought to the death, but that doesn't mean the Wyzhñyñy here will. Because the Wyzhñyñy's *non-fighting* ships surrendered. More than three thousand of them are parked in the fringe of the Eridani System, defenseless. Snooze ships, supply ships, factory ships—all of them. And they've signed a treaty of peace with the Commonwealth. They've turned over all their ordnance, and our fleet is in the process of sending it plunging into the sun.

"The Wyzhñyñy have colonies on forty-seven Commonealth worlds, and the peace treaty agrees that those colonies are also to surrender. The question now is, will the colonies believe and accept that? Let's hope they do. If they don't, Commodore Kereenyaga is to send down both his Dragons to wreck the Wyzhñyñy caves here. Then any survivors will get another chance to surrender. If they still don't, the war will not be over for us; we'll have to dig them out. But our enemy will be fewer, his firepower greatly reduced, and we'll have the support of the Marine wolf packs. And winter will arrive any time now.

"For those of you who care to, I suggest you now pray silently with me that they do surrender. For our sake and for theirs."

◇

After the prayer, the general announced a party at 2100 hours, to be held in all the army's mess halls. He'd heard of the Jerrie penchant for bachelor folk dancing, and the Indis and Burgers would have their own ideas about partying. He knew that Burger cooks had been fermenting mash, and distilling and stashing liquor.

1st Battalion folded and stacked most of their tables, converting mess halls into dance halls. Other tables were placed strategically along the sides, and loaded with sandwiches, cookies, and urns of hot chocolate—something the Jerries had learned about in the army. At 2050, the company was already gathering. Two accordions, two fiddles and a harmonica had arrived, but so far not Captain Zenawi, with his bass guitar. Lieutenant Hawkins, now B Company's XO, was setting up his keyboard.

A bot ducked in. Not surprisingly; seven bots treated B Company as their other family. This bot was Jael; Esau and no doubt others knew her by the necklace of dried, orange-painted bank beans she'd put on. And who else would bring two female organics with her? They paused just inside the door, then Jael's eyes found Esau, and all three women started toward him.

Esau met them halfway, stopping before Jael. "Will you dance with me, ma'am?" he asked. From her elevation, he looked more dutiful than eager.

"I'd love to," she said. "I do believe you're the best looking man here. But first I'd like to introduce my friends. This is Sergeant Ruta Mossland, Headquarters Company, 1st Indi Armored. And this is Ensign Björg Aribau, 12th General Hospital. Björg was born on Terra, but grew up on Indi Prime. She was Ensign Hawkins' nurse, and she wanted to meet the man who saved his life."

Blushing, Esau bowed and shook each young woman's hand in turn. Then Ensign Hawkins called out above the crowd buzz.

"Captain Zenawi will be here in a few minutes. He says don't wait." He gestured at the other musicians. "We've only played together a few times, so I don't know very much of the music they'll do. They'll start off, and I'll join in when I can. Consider the party officially started!"

A caller named the dance, and pairs of laughing soldiers walked to the middle of the floor. All were men, except for Jael and the two women she'd brought. Ruta and Björg had accepted eager partners.

When they'd formed lines, the caller and the music began. The dance was energetic, and the two women were totally unfamiliar with it. Do-si-do meant absolutely nothing to them. But the confusions created were treated as fun, not problems, and before the number ended, everyone was laughing and sweating.

Almost everyone. Esau had discovered how awkward it was, dancing with someone twenty inches taller and twice his mass. So before the next number began, they left the dance floor and went to one of the benches.

"Seems like we don't dance as well as we used to," Esau commented.

"It does, doesn't it. But we can still laugh together. And you can dance with Ruta and Björg. Actually I brought them for you."

The statement didn't surprise Esau. "I wish you wouldn't have," he said.

She nodded. "I thought you'd feel like that."

"Why then?" His voice was pained. "Why did you?"

"Honey, because I love you. And I want you to get used to touching other women. Organic women. I'm not trying to matchmake, although they're both heavy-worlders, and very nice people. And pretty, don't you think?"

"Not as pretty as you."

"Why Esau, what a nice thing to say! This model 7C warbot servo does look quite nice, and maybe in peace-time they'll let me polish it. But I never thought of it as pretty."

Esau had no reply. After a moment, Jael stood. "Let's go outside," she said quietly.

He didn't meet her gaze. Together they walked out into the now-freezing evening. "Esau," she said softly, gently, "please don't pout. It hurts me, especially when I'm trying hard to do what's right."

She stood with her hands on his thick shoulders, her *large* hands, larger than any organic human's, and crushingly strong. "This is a *party,* honey. It looks like the war may really be over, and the killing and dying done with. What I'd like best to do is sneak off with you somewhere—a water-heater room would be fine. But I can't...do..." Her voice broke unexpectedly, hitting him like a heavy punch in the chest, in the heart. "I can't do... the things we used to any longer." She recovered herself quickly though. "I just can't *be*...your wife, your lover, any longer. No matter how much I'd like to. And I want you to find someone who can." Her fingers had tightened, and realizing it, she let her hands fall. Crouching, she peered earnestly, urgently into his eyes. "Do you see, honey?"

With that she broke entirely, sobbing and shaking despite having no tear glands. Esau watched silently dismayed, spilling enough tears of his own to do for both of them. She even managed a hiccup! Finding her hand, he led her farther from the mess hall, to the shelter of a large tree, where they embraced, metal against flesh. Without warning his control melted, grief surging out, grief he hadn't known was still there. Surged violently enough, bitterly enough, it snapped Jael out of her own grief. "It's all right," she murmured, a large hand patting him gently. "It's all right."

Half a minute sufficed him; then they separated. He discovered he didn't have a handkerchief, so he pulled out a shirttail, mopped his cheeks, then blew his juicy nose with his fingers, and wiped them on his pants, behind the thighs.

"There," he said, and surprised her with a shaky laugh. "I believe that's it. Sorry I was so messy. I still forget to carry a handkerchief sometimes." He smiled ruefully. "What d'you want to do?"

"We need to get an annulment. Not a divorce, an annulment. They're different. I talked to Sergeant Major Rinaldi and she checked with the chaplain." Jael paused. "But honey, I want you to dance with those girls that came with me. I know them both. They're really nice. And if either of them makes a play for you—I'd feel so..." For a moment it seemed she might break again, but she rallied. "I'd feel so pleased if you'd go along with it."

Esau met her gaze. It was...metallic. There was a soul there, and goodness, and love, but the eyes weren't really eyes. He nodded. "I'll dance with them if you'll dance with Isaiah. He just now went in. I think it was him."

Now it was her turn to stand silent a moment. "All right," she said, "I will. But I need to tell you, dancing won't be the same wearing—this." She gestured at her body. "Not even with someone else my size. Now let's go back."

◇

Esau danced with both women, several times during the next hour, but it was Ensign Aribau who made a pass at him. Ensign Gaughan, Esau's hut-mate, saw them leave the mess hall, and told himself to stay away from the hut till the party was over.

Meanwhile, dancing with Isaiah was more enjoyable than Jael had expected. Moving her body—gracefully!—in time with the quick and lively music, was enjoyable by itself. Enough that she didn't notice Esau leave with Björg. When she realized they were gone, she felt warmly fond of them both. It was a milestone for them.

Epilogue

Soldiers has been the story of a war, and of two sapient life forms. And with the Treaty of Eridani Prime, the war and the story were over—officially, and pretty much in fact. But whether Human or Wyzhñyñy, those who'd survived had futures, reset by the war itself, and by the treaty.

The war had never been named, officially or otherwise. It was just "the war." There was no other. There hadn't been since that earlier turning point, that long-ago fraternal conflict known as "the Troubles." In his speech announcing the peace agreement, President Chang asked that it not be referred to as "the Wyzhñyñy War." The surviving Wyzhñyñy would become part of the Commonwealth, and their integration would not be eased by naming the war after them. Describe it as it was, he said, but call it simply "the Invasion."

A millennium earlier he'd never have gotten away with a suggestion like that. But now, near the end of the third millennium, his request was very largely complied with. Gradually over the centuries, humankind had become increasingly civilized, with a civility pretty much beyond political correctness. A consensus civility. Without it, civilization and quite possibly humankind would not have survived in the Sol System long enough to meet the Wyzhñyñy. There was still significant and occasionally noisy social discord, but all in all, people were remarkably and comfortably civil.

Even on the hundreds of colony worlds settled by reclusive ethnic groups, and religious, political, and philosophical sects, civility tended to be the rule—at least as long as they were let be, to live as they pleased.

Among the people of the forty-four human worlds conquered and depopulated by the Wyzhñyñy, cultural disruption had been extreme. But the people lacked the passion, the zeal of their expatriate forebears. Many of the evacuees harbored bitterness or grief, but few felt seriously gnawed upon for revenge.

And most did go home, arriving to find it unrecognizable.

With core world help, they rebuilt farms, villages, and towns, but it would never be the same. The genie didn't fit in the bottle anymore. Their cultural realities had been irreparably changed by the war and their brief exiles.

◇

On Terra, a number of antiwar activists had already been tried for terrorism. A remarkable phenomenon: antiwar terrorists! And among the Terran public, zeal had become more distasteful than ever.

The Justice Ministry had aimed at penalties befitting the crimes. Thus **Günther Genovesi** and **Kuei-Fei Wu,** who'd conceived and planned the Night of Blood and Fire, were sentenced to visit every Wyzhñyñy-conquered world, and listen to the tales of non-evacuees who'd survived in hiding. Both were reprieved before completing the tour. President Chavez (Chang Lung-Chi had retired) felt that five years had been enough. The two spent the rest of their lives in tolerably comfortable exile, under house arrest on a colony world outside the invasion corridor.

Paddy Davies, Jaromir Horvath, and several other Peace Front kingpins had been sentenced to accompany the Terran 6th Infantry Division to New Miocene. It proved to be a Wyzhñyñy hold-out world. Thus they experienced battle, loading wounded and dead onto grav sleds. Davies himself was mortally wounded, trying to help a wounded Wyzhñyñy. Always an idealist, he'd signed the agreement, and awoke as a medic-bot. Back on Terra, Horvath became a sort of hermit, more misanthropic than ever.

Fritjof Ignatiev's role, on the other hand, had been little more than inspirational orator. And after the Night of Blood and Fire, he'd voluntarily come forward to work with the government in its terrorist roundup. Thus his sentence had been only thirty days on a work gang. But in his youth he'd been an emergency medical technician, and prevailed on the judge to send him to New Miocene with the others, as a battlefield medic. There he was wounded, and cited for bravery.

After his return, Ignatiev dictated his memoir of the Peace Front and his service on New Miocene. He'd always had an excellent memory, and his recounting fitted the known facts. It would become a useful source for historians of the war.

◇

The New Jerusalem Liberation Corps saw no further combat. Commodore Kereenyaga's flagship had parked 300 miles above New Jerusalem, and broadcast the peace treaty through Gosthodar Jilchûk's command channel. It was received in every Wyzhñyñy unit headquarters on the planet. The cube had been recorded by a savant bot—Melody Boo'tsa, whom Admiral Apraxin had left with the commodore when she'd departed for Dinébikeyah. Thus Qonits's cultivated Wyzhñyñyç was well reproduced and easily understood.

But still detectably foreign, so Jilchûk rejected it. Two days later, a Dragon parked above the limestone ridge in whose extensive caverns Jilchûk's headquarters was hidden. Along with what remained of his elite force, and other important units of his army, notably his two remaining tank companies. The earlier surveillance buoys had located the entrances and exits, and the Dragon thoroughly smashed them. It also pounded the ridge in general, and parts of the caverns collapsed. Elsewhere the Dragons hit the caverns sheltering most of the rest of the army. Little remained on the surface but patrols.

In the caverns, casualties had been moderate, and their geogravitic power converters continued to provide light, heat, and interior air circulation. But the air-intake and waste-air expulsion systems had been destroyed. Jilchûk reconsidered his refusal, and sent engineers to work their way through a collapse hole, to radio his acceptance to both the humans and his command.

This presented the Burger engineers with a new highly urgent project: to hastily set up secure, reasonably livable POW stockades—tent camps. One for the Wyzhñyñy officers, another for the elite companies, and several others for everyone else. Meanwhile many kilotons of key Wyzhñyñy military material were collected, and lightered into near-space. There they were magnetically bundled, and the bundles sent on trajectories that would plunge them into New Jerusalem's sun.

◇

Four other Wyzhñyñy-occupied worlds had been invaded by liberation forces. Major fleet detachments were dispatched to visit the rest. The size of the forces tended to convince the local gosthodars. Those who were adamant had their colonies visited by Dragons and wolf packs. In several cases where a gosthodar still refused, coups or mutinies resulted in a more rational leader. On six planets that still held out, colonies of *Apis mellifera scutella* were widely introduced during the current or next growing season, and the colonies recontacted a few months later.

Only two had eventually to be liberated "the hard way," several years later. *After* being liberated from the African bees by the introduction of enhanced strains of American and European foulbrood. Then regiments were landed—with Wyzhñyñy interpretors!—to root out the remaining holdouts. Most of whom surrendered more or less readily.

◇

Qonits Zu-Kitku was appointed advisor to the president and prime minister. Later, in a sort of reverse appointment, the prime minister named him Wyzhñyñy Ambassador to the Commonwealth.

In time, Qonits would also oversee the establishment of the Wyzhñyñy and human youth exchange programs, a School of Wyzhñyñy Studies at Kunming University, and a Department of Humanity at the Institute of Knowledge, on Wyzhuursôk, the world on which the Wyzhñyñy survivors were settled.

Twenty-three Terran years after the treaty was signed, Qonits died in his apartment on the Kunming University campus, of cardiac arrest.

◇

David MacDonald worked with Qonits throughout the ambassador's career. After Qonits' death, he served for two years as advisor to the Wyzhñyñy's new ambassador. He then retired to the new, Commonwealth-sponsored colony on Maritimus, referring to himself as "the ambassador to the dolphin republic." The dolphins were amused.

◇

At the end of hostilities on New Jerusalem, **Jael Wesley** and **Isaiah Vernon** returned to Terra. By that time they'd become close friends, and married in Kunming—a union necessarily platonic. Meanwhile, rapid progress was being made on pseudo-organic civilian servos for ex-warbots. These were made as humanlike as feasible, and the couple was transferred to customized android servos. A meaningful sexual relationship resulted, between these two who'd already developed a very considerate and affectionate relationship.

A few years after leaving military service, they joined the Gopal Singh Order of Compassion, and were trained to help the mentally afflicted. This period of relatively normal life, however, was rather short. Among ex-warbots, the peripheral nerves controlling the limbs began to deteriorate ten to twenty years after first installation. Use of the limbs was then lost within weeks or months. The only treatment was to rebottle the CNS for installation into a sensorially-equipped life-support system like those designed for savant bots. In any case, senile dementia set in, mainly at age sixty to seventy Terran. Persons inhabiting such life-support systems generally arranged for life support to be discontinued at some predefined point in their deterioration.

Jael and Isaiah died within seven weeks of each other.

◇

Esau Wesley and Björg Aribau returned to Terra with the 1st New Jerusalem Division, and were married at Björg's family home in Tarragona, in the Catalunya Prefecture. Both converted to Sikhism (the Gopal Singh Dispensation), and remained in the military. They volunteered to serve in a New Jerusalem Battalion assigned as the low-profile embassy garrison on Wyzhuursôk (*Wyzh*: root of Wyzhñyñy; *uur*: the seventh [swarm]; sôk: world).

After ten years they returned again to Terra, where they wrote a joint account of the war on New Jerusalem, from a soldier's and a nurse's point of view. Its substantial success encouraged another book, of their years on Wyzhuursôk. The experience there had been enriched by a powerful hypno-tutorial of the Wyzhñyñy language and culture. And by considerable involvement in Wyzhñyñy life, aided by friendship with several Wyzhñyñy of varied genders and status. The book's best-seller performance surprised them.

The marriage produced two sons and a daughter. One son was named Arjan, the other Isaiah. The daughter was named Jael. The family visited the senior Jael and Isaiah several times after returning from Wyzhuursôk.

Retiring from the military, Esau and Björg lived on Eridani Prime, to enjoy the 0.87 gee gravity. There they bought and resided on a small frontier "hobby farm," which Esau worked himself. They died in their nineties of natural causes.

<>

The pirate ship *Minerva,* with **Drago Draveç** and his crew, showed up haggard and hungry in the Hart's Desire System. This was two days before, and most of a hyperspace year away from, the battle of Shakti. Draveç helped set up the planet's own "Project Noah," and a few weeks later married **Ambassador Annalis Khai.** After the peace, he managed a marginally legal import-export office for Harlan Cheregian, but seldom traveled off-world.

He is credited with having introduced war-gaming to Hart's Desire.

<>

After the war, Male Infant Doe 731 had his name legally changed to **Charley Gordon.** Charley chose to continue his "life in a box." He and Ophelia Kennah left government service on substantial pensions, fortified by a very generous annuity to Charley, voted by parliament, no less. Meanwhile, **Alvaro Soong** retired from the Admiralty and married Ophelia. Charley "gave away" the bride. For several years the three shared a comfortable condominium, in an affluent retirement community in the mountains of the Chiapas Prefecture, in the Central American Autonomy.

During those years (with travel breaks to attend live concerts all over Terra), Charley's major activity was research on a unified field theory that accommodated psionics. His mathematics was largely incomprehensible, however, except to a relative but influential few. Far better known was the music he composed in odd moments. Strange, mostly beautiful music—some for instruments, some for voices, some for both, it was found therapeutic for many persons, with physical as well as mental conditions. (For still others it was becoming psychologically addictive.)

Charley's research period led into what came to be known as "Charley Gordon's meditation phase," ending with three years spent mostly in silence, beneath a lovely canopy in a chán (zen) monastery garden near Kunming. There he was tended by monks, and visited by pilgrims not only from all over Terra, but from other worlds, including exchange youths, diplomats and merchants, from Wyzhuursôk, where his music had birthed a cult.

Afterward Charley remained at the monastery, but treated himself to a well-accessorized artificial intelligence, and spent a year secluded with his new "toy." After programming it to suit his needs, he composed a musical work which he titled "Opus Number Six: *Logos for the Emotionally Centered.*" It was premiered by the Melbourne Symphony Orchestra, to a first-year video/holo audience estimated at 2.7 billion, and a live audience of 11,736. In a post-performance interview, Charley described it as an improved form of his unified field theory.

Following a brief period of CNS deterioration, Charley Gordon died at age 67, one of the best-known and most beloved persons in human history.

Ophelia Kennah, then 84 years old, dictated her best-selling *Memories of Charley,* and died shortly afterward.

The End

Books Published by Sky Warrior Books

Purchase them through online resellers and better independent bookstores everywhere. Visit us at www.skywarriorbooks.com **for news and upcoming books and promotions.**

Alma Alexander

2012: Midnight at Spanish Gardens (E-book, Trade Paperback)

Embers of Heaven (E-book, Trade Paperback)

S. A. Bolich

Firedancer (E-book, Trade Paperback)

Seaborn (E-book)

Windrider (E-book, Trade Paperback)

M. H. Bonham

Daemons and Shadows (E-book)

Prophecy of Swords (E-book)

Runestone of Teiwas (E-book)

Samurai Son (E-book)

Serpent Singer and Other Stories (E-book)

John Dalmas

The Signature of God Part 1 (E-book)

The Signature of God Part 2(E-book)

Soldiers! Part 1(E-book, Trade Paperback)

Soldiers! Part 2 (E-book, Trade Paperback)

The Second Coming (E-book, Trade Paperback)

Deby Fredericks

Seven Exalted Orders (E-book)

Carol Hightshoe (Editor)

Zombiefied: An Anthology of All Things Zombie (E-book)

Gary Jonas

Acheron Highway (E-book)

Modern Sorcery (E-book, Trade Paperback)

One-Way Ticket to Midnight (E-book)

Quick Shots (E-book, Trade Paperback)

Frog and Esther Jones

Grace Under Fire (E-book)

Michael J. Parry

The Oaks Grove (E-book)

The Spiral Tattoo (E-book)

Phyllis Irene Radford

> Healing Waves: A Charity Anthology for Japan (Editor) (E-book)

> Gears and Levers 1: A Steampunk Anthology (Editor) (E-book, Trade Paperback)

> Gears and Levers 2: A Steampunk Anthology (Editor) (E-book, Trade Paperback)

> Lacing Up Murder, A Whistling River Mystery (E-book)

> So You Want to Commit Novel (E-book, Trade Paperback)

Dusty Rainbolt (Editor)

> The Mystical Cat (E-book)

Deborah J. Ross (Editor)

> The Feathered Edge (E-book, Trade Paperback)

Laura J. Underwood

> Ard Magister (Book One of Ard Magister) (E-book)

> Dragon's Tongue (Book One of the Demon-Bound) (E-book)

> The Hounds of Ardagh (E-book)

www.ingramcontent.com/pod-product-compliance
Lightning Source LLC
Chambersburg PA
CBHW020605260626
47157CB00003B/876

* 9 7 8 0 6 9 2 2 0 6 4 4 7 *